Jason and the Draconauts

Paul D. Smith

Jason and the Draconauts is a work of fiction. Names, characters, places, and incidents either are the product of the author's imagination or are used fictitiously. Any resemblance to actual persons, living or dead, events or locales, is entirely coincidental.

Copyright © 2013 **Smittyworks Productions**
Second Edition
All rights reserved.
ISBN: 0615866247
ISBN 13: 978-0615866246
Library of Congress Control Number: 2013914886

Cover art by Sierra Reep

Author photo by Andrew Shipman

This book is dedicated to my wife, Margaret, and my two boys, Zachary and Samuel.

A man couldn't ask for a better family.

Acknowledgements:

This book wouldn't be possible without the support of the eighty-plus backers who supported the Kickstarter project, including: Joanna Balcom, The Beckwith Family, Jerry and Miranda Bennett, Bill Bitner, The Daniels Clan, Marilyn Debole, Pat Dunning, Nancy Bennett Fulton, Mr. and Mrs. Frank Hays IV, Jason and Sarah Hill, The Howell Family, Lisa Kowalewski, D. Toby Lyon, Philip M. Rogers II, Margaret L. Smith, Dixon and Mary Lou Smith

In Memory Of:

Grant McKenzie
Margaret B. Lyon

Chapter 1

"DAAAAAAAAD!?!"
Jason waited then took a deeper breath.
"DAAAAAAAAAAAAAD!"
     He listened and heard a muffled grunt come from the direction of his father's room on the second floor of the old homestead. If he used his imagination, it sounded like "what?"
        "I gotta head into town to work," he shouted. "I won't see you for, what, two days?"
A second grunt came. Jason shook his head and muttered, "Yeah, whatever" to himself as he opened the old screen door into the early June sunshine.
     Jason Hewes was wearing his usual attire: faded blue jeans, a t-shirt bearing the logo of a computer component manufacturer, his custom-printed Chuck Taylor sneakers, and an old red and black flannel shirt with the sleeves pushed up. At this time of year in Montana, the weather was getting warmer, but the old flannel shirt was a great substitute for a jacket as he was riding his Vespa into work. His brown hair was slightly neater than his tousled look; he usually ran a comb through it before work.
     At fifteen, Jason was lucky to have even found a job in a town the size of Malta, especially one he enjoyed. It didn't pay much, but even a janitorial job at the Great Plains Dinosaur Museum in Malta was, to him, a cool position to have. But what he thought was cool most kids his age thought was geeky. Jason didn't play football. Or baseball. Or soccer. Or even run track. He wasn't the president of any student associations, nor did he belong to any civic clubs. He was just Jason. Straight-B student. Computer nerd. Janitor.
     He and his dad lived on an old farmstead. Back when farmers could make a decent living on their own, the land was a producer of wheat and corn, supplying quite a large area in northern Montana. But as difficult times hit and small farms lost business to larger, corporate-owned farms, the previous owner shut down the business and sold the land to Jason's family. So now they had a whole lot of land and a whole lot of stuff on the land doing

nothing. The barn was in disrepair, a couple of old tractors and combines were being slowly overtaken by the tall grasses, and nary a corn stalk or wheat sheaf was in sight. But at least the house was still livable.

He walked across the dirt driveway to his old Vespa. When his dad was first hired by the Montana Dinosaur Trail, he bought the maroon motorized scooter for Jason. Dad knew he was going to be away for days at a time, and Jason would need a way to travel the ten miles into town, so the Vespa was the answer. At the time, Jason thought there was no way he would be allowed to ride the thing. But Malta was small, and the sheriff knew the family's situation, so he gave Jason and his dad a break and let him ride the little vehicle back and forth.

He got ready to put on his helmet as he reached the scooter and paused to look around the homestead. It was a beautiful day, and he was again reminded of why Montana was known as "Big Sky" country. It was a little deceiving because in certain parts of the state there were hills and even mountains, especially to the west. But there in northern Montana, there was just flat land and sky as far as you could see. As Jason had once heard someone say, "There's nothing but miles and miles of miles and miles." But on a day like this, he kind of enjoyed living there.

Until the tomato hit him in the head.

His head jerked to one side, reacting to the blow of the rogue fruit. He whipped his head around and saw the old white Chevy pickup barreling down Highway 2. He hated the pickup, or, more precisely, he hated the thug driving the pickup. Stan Whitman, senior at Malta High School, neighbor three miles down the road, and bane of his existence was in the driver seat with two more of his thugs-in-training occupying the passenger places in the rusting jalopy. Stan had been bullying Jason for years now, but it became really annoying after the accident. Stan had given Jason a few weeks off after the car wreck, but Jason had only been back at school for a few days when Stan decided vacation time was over and hid a dried cow pie in his locker. Jason had hoped that as Stan matured with age, he would grow out of this bullying. Five years ago, Stan was an overweight, smelly, foul-mouthed bully. Now, he was a tall, well-muscled, foul-mouthed bully. When he thought about it, Jason was actually surprised Stan achieved a mastery of the finer things in life like speaking English and using utensils and that he actually made it to his senior year of high school. He was convinced Stan's life motto would be: "Tenth grade was the best four years of my life!"

As Jason was wiping the mushy tomato innards from his cheek, he could still hear the laughter of the bullies as they sped away from Malta and into the Montana countryside. A few choice insults ran through his mind as he pulled the helmet on and straddled his Vespa, which he called Bob, an affectionate and somewhat accurate abbreviation for "bucket of bolts." He pressed the ignition button; Bob's little engine whined to life, and a small puff of smoke came from the exhaust. It was the vehicle's way of burping a hello to Jason, but the smoke eventually subsided as the engine warmed up. He couldn't help but laugh at himself; he could build a working computer from scratch, create a successful website, and even write applications for open-source wireless device platforms, but he couldn't fix the engine of his little motor scooter. He kept reminding himself to stop by the service station on his way into town, but he usually didn't have the money to actually repair Bob. Most of his earnings went into his technology purchases. Between the job at the museum and the computer repair work he did on the side, he had been able to buy himself a laptop and a smart phone, both of which were fastened securely in the padded backpack strapped over his shoulders.

Within a few moments, Jason was speeding down US Highway 2 on his way into Malta. He was glad he wore his flannel shirt; it kept him warm while he was riding. It usually took him fifteen to twenty minutes to get into town on Bob, so Jason settled in and watched the world go by, looking for any changes in the Montana landscape that would break the monotony of his commute. On a normal day, he would have been disappointed— but today wasn't a normal day.

He could see some crows and turkey vultures circling in the sky up ahead, and he strained his eyes to try to make out what they had found. The Montana landscape relied on scavengers to clean up any road kill or leftovers from predators. Jason guessed it was a deer, but as he got closer, a large black heap was visible just off the road. Jason said out loud, to no one in particular, "What the—" as he pulled Bob to the side of the road to investigate. Jason had a habit of talking to himself, even while driving his Vespa into town. When you spent so much time alone, as he did, the sound of a voice—even if it is your own—can be comforting.

Jason walked into the field and approached the black mass, noticing two horns projecting off the sides of what would be a head. He immediately knew what the creature was. Bison were still wild in some parts of Montana, but he wasn't aware of any herds of these cattle relatives wandering in this part of the state. Much bigger than normal cows, these large, black-furred plains-grazers were making a comeback in recent decades. Many wildlife conservationists were pleased that one could now see large herds of bison grazing the plains states again, as you could over a hundred years ago.

"What could bring down something that big?" Jason asked out loud. As he knew there were no bison in the Malta area, he also knew there were no predators to bison in the region either. Coyote were too small to hunt a creature that could get up to two thousand pounds, and wolves and mountain lions hadn't been seen near Malta for many years.

"Poor thing must've been sick," he mused to himself, but as he got close enough to make out details of the fallen beast, his brow furrowed. Half of the bison was gone, torn away in predator-like fashion, but this was done all in one bite. Or at least that is how it appeared. There wasn't much of a smell to the creature, so it must have died fairly recently, but how did it get there, and where was the thing that killed it? He tried to imagine scenarios, but all his mind could conjure were images of various monsters from the many computer games that he played. Jason was amused at the thought of a huge mountain giant coming down out of the Rockies and deciding to take a chunk out of a lost bison for an afternoon snack, like you would on piece of beef jerky while on a road trip. But nothing that actually made sense came.

"No way," he said. "Nothing is big enough to do that." He wondered what to do. There was no way he was moving the thing, and he figured the sheriff wouldn't believe a computer geek's description of the condition of a wildlife anomaly. He looked at the scavenger birds circling overhead and concluded the corpse wouldn't be there too much longer. So he grabbed the smart phone out of his backpack, snapped a few pictures of the grisly sight, got back on Bob, and continued his commute into town.

He was mulling over his find, and, before he realized where he was, he was passing a familiar sign:

Welcome to Malta
A Premiere Sight on the Montana Dinosaur Trail

No matter how many times Jason saw that sign, it always made him smile. He loved dinosaurs when he was little, so it was a dream come true for him when his dad, an archaeologist, got a job with the Montana Archaeological Society as the lead researcher for the Montana Dinosaur Trail. One of Big Sky country's claims to fame was the large number of dinosaur fossils that had been found across the state. In response, a string of museums were opened all along northern Montana featuring the many fossils and dinosaur skeletons that had been found. This "path" of museums was named the Montana Dinosaur Trail.

Jason, with the help of his dad, managed to get a job at Malta's stop on the trail: the Great Plains Dinosaur Museum and Field Station. It was a janitorial job, but Jason also helped maintain their website in his free time. The job wasn't glamorous, but he did get to spend time with Giffen (Montana's first stegosaurus skeleton), Ralph (a long-neck sauropod), and Leonardo (a rare mummified dinosaur). The museum was like a second home to Jason, and he often found himself there even when he wasn't working. After a stop at the Dairy Queen down the road to say hi to his best friend and get a chocolate shake, Jason parked Bob next to the museum and went inside.

The Great Plains Dinosaur Museum and Field Station wasn't an awfully big place. It had the room to house several dinosaur skeletons but lacked the elegance of a museum in a big city. The central hall contained five large fossils, and spread throughout the rest of the building were other smaller fossils, including rare marine invertebrates and prehistoric plants and fish. The museum also hosted children's programs, birthday parties (which usually involved Jason wearing a large dinosaur costume to provide additional entertainment), and dinosaur dig activities. However, there were no visitors today as he entered the side entrance. The director was out on errands, and Julia was tidying up the gift counter.

Ahh, Julia. She graduated from the high school last year but stayed in town to help out her dad at home and work at the museum. She was the quintessential girl next door, even though she lived about twenty miles from Jason. She wore cowboy boots, faded jeans, and usually some sort of patterned-print, button-down shirt. Her blond hair was always pulled back into a ponytail, and she wore little to no make-up. And, in Jason's opinion, she didn't need any. There was a natural beauty to Juila that was only accentuated by her temperament; Julia was always sweet, never flustered, smart as a whip, and savvy as mountain lion. She treated Jason like a younger brother, but, to him, she was more. Not that he would ever tell her that; it was an impossibility.

"Hey, you," her voice lilted as he came in the door. Jason sighed at the sound.

"Hi, Julia," he managed to say without his voice cracking. "Slow day today?"

Julia nodded and shrugged her shoulders. "Yeah, just thought I'd do some tidying up. Susan left some directions for you by the mop bucket. You're slipping a little bit, Jace. Something bothering you lately?"

Susan was the museum's director. She would leave him notes every now and then pointing out if he was getting sloppy in his cleaning duties. He answered Julia.

"Nah…Dad's been on the road a lot, and Stan has been particularly horrid of late. Just a little distracted, I guess."

Julia commiserated with Jason for a few minutes, but then he settled in and got to work. Jason paid extra attention to his duties; he hated it when Susan had to write him a note. He was only fifteen, but he took his job seriously and cared about the museum. It was around noon when he heard the door open, and a familiar figure entered.

George Jaworski, Dairy Queen employee and best friend of Jason Hewes, arrived carrying a DQ paper bag, obviously weighted down with something inside. George was an awkward teenager; he was overweight, had a moderately bad case of acne, and didn't always take care of his hygiene that well. He was sixteen, and the Dairy Queen was his first real job. George wore his DQ uniform with pride, right down to his hair tucked neatly under the baseball cap.

Julia smiled. "Hiya, George."

George answered, his voice quivering, "Hi, Julia."

She smiled and shook her head as she shouted, "You got a visitor, Jason!"

Jason was already walking to the door. "Thanks, I see him, Julia."

Julia disappeared into the backroom and George continued to gaze at the door through which she exited. Jason rolled his eyes.

"George, you're pathetic. Could you be any more obvious?"

"Come on, Jace," George replied. "*You* like her, too."

"I don't drop thirty IQ points whenever I'm around her."

"Someday, my friend, someday she will be my bride," George joked with a playful pride in his voice.

Jason laughed as he pointed at the bag. "Whatcha got there?"

He handed it to Jason. "Comfort food, minus the tomato. You had enough of those this morning, from what you told me."

Jason said flatly, "You're a funny man. You should go on tour." He took out the cheeseburger and fries and nodded a thanks to his friend.

"What're you doing tonight?" George asked.

"Ahhh, not much. Dad is on the road again, so I think I'm just gonna stay home. I wanna finish up the Steveson's PC anyway; they've been waiting for a week now."

George nodded. "Okay, man. We were gonna stream a movie or something tonight, so you're welcome to hang."

"Thanks, but I think I'll pass."

"Jace, it's not good to be alone so much. Come over tonight. Mom'll make us dinner."

Jason answered playfully, "What, and pass up another opportunity to have frozen leftovers? Perish the thought!" He got serious. "You know it's always a downer for me the first night Dad is gone. I'll be fine…really. I have work to do, so it's all good."

George relented and clapped Jason on the shoulder as he left to go back to the Dairy Queen. Jason spent the rest of his day cleaning the museum. He made sure he hit all the major areas at least twice over to get Susan off his back. The museum closed at seven on Saturdays, and the sun was sinking to the horizon, so he jumped on Bob and sped off toward home. He watched for the bison carcass as he rode by and could tell it was still there, but the scavengers had been hard at work on it throughout the day. By the next day, the remains would probably be gone.

Nighttime arrived, and Jason had finished off some defrosted lasagna and began to work on the Stevensons' computer. His computer-repair skills brought in the money he needed to purchase his various gadgets, but one can only replace so many hard drives or motherboards before one gets really tired of fixing computers. He had passed that point well before he even started working that night. So he did everything he could to distract himself: put on the TV, made himself a milkshake to sip, even thought of clever ways to get back at Stan Whitman. His schemes involved mild electric shocks, exploding cell phones, or even sabotage to his white pickup. But Jason knew he didn't have it in him to attempt revenge; it just wasn't a part of who he was. Too much had happened to him and his family to get caught up in silly stuff like that.

It was getting late. Ten o'clock ticked by on the old kitchen wall clock, and Jason packed up his tools for the night. A storm was brewing outside, and the flashes of lightning weren't too far ahead of the thunderclaps. He pulled out his smart phone and checked his weather app.

"Weird," he said aloud. "No storms called for tonight. Weatherman needs to go back to school." He laughed at himself. "Right after I go to not-talking-to-yourself school."

The storm intensified quickly. The winds howled, and Jason began to run around the house, shutting windows against the rain. Just as he got to the last window, something odd happened. He heard a loud thunderclap followed by a flash of lightning. Jason knew enough about weather to know that thunder always comes after the lightning, not before. It was a simple way one could measure how far away a storm was. The closer the thunder was to the lightning, the closer the center of the storm. But what he had just heard was impossible.

Then came the sound.

It was like nothing he had ever heard before, and it made his heart leap into his throat. The roar of a lion combined with the cry of an eagle and amplified to the volume of a jet engine would have come close to matching what Jason heard but with an indescribable, other-worldly quality. He jumped at the sound and then half crouched to the floor in fear. Then came another lightning flash, then the sound again, then a thunderclap. What was that? What was out there in the darkness? He grabbed the large flashlight in the kitchen drawer and ran out onto the wrap-around porch. The wind blew the rain nearly sideways, and it pelted him as he shone the light out over their property, straining to make out any sort of shape. The rain drops appeared as tiny streaks of white as they passed through the beam of the flashlight, but he couldn't make anything out.

As he was about to give up, the ground quivered, accompanied by a very loud thump, and Jason's anxiety reached a new level. It felt as if something very heavy had landed on the earth. Jason's breathing became more rapid as he whipped around in circles, pointing the flashlight into the darkness but not finding anything. His anxiety turned to fear as he shouted, "Who's out there?" But the storm was too loud, and his voice didn't carry far.

In a split second, his fear became panic as a sound came back to him through the stormy night: the sound of the doors to the old barn creaking open and then closing again.

"It's just the wind, Jason…just the wind. Wait and listen—it'll happen again," he tried reassuring himself. But as he listened, straining his sense of hearing against the cacophony of the storm, the sound did not come again. Someone, or something, had opened the large doors of the barn and had gone inside, closing the doors afterward.

In his heightened sense of alarm, he said, "At least they were polite enough to shut the doors. Gotta keep the rain out…it's only neighborly."

Jason sprinted into the house and grabbed the largest kitchen knife he could find. Then he took a second in his other hand. Then he put a meat mallet in his back pocket. And then, for some reason, he grabbed a carrot peeler, just for good measure. He ran back to the front of the house and burst out of the screen door into the yard as he shone the flashlight ahead of him and mumbled, "Stupid, stupid, stupid" all the way to the barn.

But in the short run to the old barn, the rain stopped. It was enough of a dramatic contrast that it made Jason pause in mid-run. He looked curiously into the sky and saw the clouds dissipating as stars became visible again. Had Jason been in any other state but sheer terror, he would have asked himself questions about the phenomenon, out loud, and probably made fun of weather forecasters again. But all he could do was keep going to the barn.

Arriving at the barn's large doors, Jason swallowed hard, insulted his own common sense one more time, and then slowly pulled them open.

He saw nothing…mostly because it was night, and he hadn't bothered flicking on the light switch yet. Jason always wondered why the previous owners had run power out to the red wooden structure. But he decided not to complain about it that night, and he groped along the wall until he found the switch and flicked the lights on.

And there it was.

Judging by its size, he could tell this was what had impacted the earth and had caused the tremor that he'd felt back at the house. It was over thirty feet long and resembled—Jason couldn't believe he was thinking this—a dinosaur.

It had a long neck attached to a muscular body and narrowed to a very long tail. Its body was covered in scales that were colored shades of brown and gray. Spines ran along the length of its neck and the length of its tail as well, and each of its four legs ended in a three-toed foot, with each toe ending in a long, curved claw. Its head was oddly shaped; a large curved plate extended back from the creature's eyes on either side, arcing upward into two points and vaguely resembling a plowshare. It had a short snout tapering off to a rounded tip, with two nostrils on the top just short of the tip.

But what made Jason realize that this was no dinosaur were the massive wings sprouting from either side of the creature. The wings were batlike, and Jason estimated the wingspan was close to sixty feet. Wings like those were not vestigial, like those of an ostrich or emu; this creature was made for flight. He noticed the membrane of one wing seemed damaged, burned away to form a hole with seared edges. He followed the lines of the wings back to the body and could see the creature's chest expanding and contracting slowly and rhythmically. It was breathing; it was alive. Unconscious but alive.

Jason finally took notice of his own body; his breathing was shallow and rapid. He whispered to himself, "Get a grip, Hewes. You've played enough fantasy games to know what this is, as unbelievable as it seems. This is a dragon."

Chapter 2

Jason paced back and forth, keeping his eyes on the dragon the whole time. He alternated between raking his fingers through his hair and wringing his hands.

"How can this be real?" he exclaimed to himself. "I mean, honestly, dragons don't exist. I gotta be dreaming, or banged my head, or I'm all hopped up on Mountain Dew, or something. Maybe I've been alone too long. Yeah, that's gotta be it, like that guy in that movie *Castaway.* He was alone for years and started talking to a volleyball or a soccer ball or something. This is probably the same thing, right?"

Jason tentatively reached out with his leg and pushed the tip of the dragon's tail with his foot. It was extremely solid and heavy but did move slightly as he pushed. A deep, rumbling moan came from within the beast as it stirred in its sleep. Jason practically jumped out of his Chuck Taylors as he leapt as far back as he could.

"Ooookay. Okay! There's a dragon, a dragon, in the barn. There is a real dragon in my barn. Not a cow or a horse; that would be normal. No, the Hewes keep dragons in their barn! Yeah, makes sense…I'm freakin' out here!"

He walked a couple of laps around the dragon, taking extra care to not touch it for fear of…he didn't know what would happen if he touched it, so he made sure he didn't come into contact with it at all. There were times he would start to put a plan into motion. But each time he would come to the same conclusion: he really had no idea what to do.

"I don't know…I don't know…I don't know… There is a *huge* stinkin' dragon in my barn, and I don't know what I'm going to do with it!"

"I object to the term 'stinking,'" the dragon stated without warning.

"GYAAAAHGGH!" Jason shrieked as he stumbled backward, tripping over a hay bale and landing flat on his back. He scrambled to his feet and fumbled for the two kitchen knives he brought with him. Jason watched as the dragon groaned in pain and pushed itself slowly up on its front legs until it was resting on its elbows. Jason noted how its front legs were quite similar in structure to human arms.

It opened its eyes and looked at Jason. They were a yellow-green color with no discernable iris but a vertical pupil, similar to a cat's. The dragon had amazing facial muscles, and it made human-like expressions. It winced in pain as it tried to get comfortable in its current position.

It turned its head to face Jason, and the boy instinctively reacted by holding the two knives in front of him. The dragon raised an eye ridge in surprise. Jason watched as it reached its great foreleg out and grasped a pitchfork. It jammed the pitchfork into its own neck and then pulled the tool away; the three tines had bent at awkward angles after impacting the dragon's hide.

Jason's eyes widened in horror. He dropped the knives and raised the meat mallet against the creature. The dragon's shoulders slumped as it looked around the barn. Spying an old blacksmith's anvil, it took it in its claw, dug the talons of the other front claw into the anvil and then tore the object in half. Jason muffled a cry of terror and did the only other thing he could think of; he brandished the carrot peeler. The dragon sat up in surprise and raised its eye ridges. It then narrowed its eyes and said, "I have no idea what that is."

Jason became calm for a moment. "Yeah, it's a… just a last-minute thought—" but quickly reverted to panic and stammered, "I…I don't know what you are and how you got here. Well, I'm pretty sure I know what you are…and now that I think about it, I can guess how you got here."

The dragon rolled its eyes and interrupted, "Thus far, you have shrieked, stammered, and been unable to complete a coherent sentence. Are you able to carry on an intelligent conversation, or do you have impaired faculties?"

"I—" Jason straightened up. "Are you getting snarky with me?"

The dragon thought for a moment. "I am not sure of the meaning of 'snarky,' but I am purposefully demeaning you if you need me to be that specific. Tell me, what is your name, Little Knight?"

"I'm not a knight. But my name is, umm, Jason Hewes."

"Ah. So, Umm Jason Hewes, where am I?"

Jason shook his head. "No, no, it's just Jason. My name is Jason Hewes."

The dragon tilted his head questioningly. "Then why did you say 'umm Jason'? I concluded it must be a very odd title."

Jason finally lost his composure. "Why? *Why*! Because you're a big, giant *dragon*! And you're here, in my barn, *talking* to me. And I'm all alone, and you can't be hurt by a pitchfork, and you're snarky but don't know what a carrot peeler is, and I want my daaaaaaaaad!"

Looking very uncomfortable and holding up a claw, palm facing outward, the dragon said, "Very well, very well, I can see you are in a state of distress. What is it humans say?" It made a sound akin to clearing its throat. "There, there, Little Knight, do not be afraid…all will be well."

Jason wiped a tear away and sniffled, oddly calm, "That was awful."

The dragon huffed, "Well, as you might guess, comforting human children is not really my forte."

Jason took a deep breath and slumped his shoulders. "Are you gonna breathe fire on me now?"

"Wha…why on earth would I do that?"

"Be…because you're a dragon. That's what you do, right?"

"We most certainly do not. And, besides, not all dragons breathe fire."

"Oh." Jason genuinely sounded surprised. "So, umm, do you have a name?"

"Yes," replied the creature.

They stared blankly at each other for a few moments. Jason broke the silence. "Aaaaand would you care to tell me your name?"

"I am contemplating it."

Jason mumbled, "Oh, for the love of…*why* would you hesitate to tell me your name?"

"Dragons are not accustomed to arbitrarily revealing our names to any—"

Jason burst out, "Just tell me your name!"

"Fine!" snapped the dragon. "I am Petros," he said with a very regal tone.

"Oh, okay. Petros. That's a—" Jason noticed the dragon grimacing in pain again. "Are you okay?"

Petros shook his head. "I am not sure what 'okay' means, but I am still feeling the effects of my earlier battle."

"Battle?" Jason asked. "What battle? Is that how you got the hole in your wing?"

This time Petros nodded. "I can only surmise that I was spotted last night whilst I hunted. I was not aware I was in the territory of another of my kind, but tonight I was attacked by a Storm dragon."

"Storm dragon?" Jason asked.

"Yes. It was a younger dragon than I, but their species is more powerful than mine. I may have been a match for it if we fought on the ground, but in the air it was a far superior combatant, and I was overpowered."

"What species are you?"

"I am a Stone dragon, one of the Earth Dragons. The storm was an Air Dragon; they are excellent flyers and dominate when airborne."

Jason was about to ask another question when he saw Petros's forelegs begin to tremble. He said, "Look, just lie back down and rest. My dad is out of town for two days, so you can stay here and recover, or rest, or whatever it is dragons do."

The dragon nodded. "Yes, rest would be prudent. I can enter a sleep that will accelerate my healing, but I will be defenseless during that time. My kind calls it the Drake sleep."

Jason cocked his head quizzically. "Really?"

Petros looked at him as he lay back down. "Yes, it is a skill we developed a long time ago through magical—"

Jason interrupted. "No, no, you name your sleep?" Petros looked confused, but Jason went on. "I mean why don't you just call it 'sleep' or 'rest' or something? It just sounds goofy when you name your nap time."

Petros inhaled deeply. "I do not know the meaning of 'goofy,' but I would assume it is derogatory. Just let me sleep, and I will debate the 'goofiness' of the things I say at another time."

Jason asked, "Speaking of the things you say, how are you even understanding me? Don't you speak, like, Dragonish or Dragonese or something? How do you even know English?"

Petros gave an exasperated sigh. "We speak whatever language we need to speak at any time. It is part of being a dragon; our minds instantly translate more primitive languages like yours. Now may I?" He gestured to the area on which he was lying.

Jason replied, "Right, right, sorry. Drake sleep first, trade insults later. Do you want me to turn the lights off?" But Petros was already asleep. Jason could hear Petros breathing peacefully in the dim light of the barn. He was oddly comforted by the sound, which accentuated the feeling of his rapidly beating heart. He actually felt his heart rate slowing as the dragon drifted off into his Drake sleep. Quietly, Jason opened the door of the barn, switched off the light, closed the door, and tiptoed into the night.

Jason's head was spinning as he crossed the yard back to the house. The last several minutes had probably been the most bizarre of his life, but there was a strange feeling of exhilaration in his chest. He remembered that feeling; it was the same as when he would talk about or play with dinosaurs. His dad had let him watch *Jurassic Park* on DVD for the first time five or six years before, and he had the same emotional response then as well. This dragon, Petros, was the ultimate childhood fantasy quite literally come to life. Jason had just stood face to face with something most people encounter only in their imaginations…or perhaps a good Xbox game. He walked back into the kitchen and leaned on the cooking island. The fear left him, and the biggest of smiles stretched across his face. He ran his fingers through his hair again and said, "There is an actual dragon sleeping in my barn!" He pulled out his phone to call George but then saw the time. It was eleven o'clock; knowing George, he was fast asleep by then. Jason figured he had better get some sleep, too, especially if he was going to wake up before Petros did. But after completing his nighttime routine, he lay in the darkness, looking up at the ceiling; his imagination refused to let him drift off easily. Images of dragons, knights, castles, maidens in distress, and magical spells all swirled through his mind. Finally, after two hours of tossing and turning, Jason fell asleep.

***

Jason awoke, very uncharacteristically, at sunrise. Normally, the snooze button on his alarm clock would get a thorough workout every morning. In the past few years, he had to replace it twice due to the beating that particular button got on a day-to-day basis. But the presence of a dragon in the barn was enough to motivate Jason to get out of bed on time. He got dressed in record time, swung the screen door to the porch open, and was down the steps, speed-walking to the old red storage building.

He took a deep breath as he got to the door and then quietly opened it. The sun was streaming through the windows near the roof, casting an orange-hued light across the rusting old tools and hay bales. A couple of mice scattered for cover as the early morning light streamed through the open door. Jason heard Petros's breathing before he stuck his head around the door and saw the sleeping dragon. He quietly padded over to the injured wing until he could see the wound. The hole in the membrane was nearly closed now, and the charred tissue was taking on a healthier, pink color, but there was more healing that needed to be done.

Jason exited the barn, quietly closed the door, and broke into a full-out run toward Bob. "So if he was injured in a battle, that means there is a *second* dragon around here somewhere. In two days, I go from dragons being imaginary to having too many of them to know what to do with." He arrived at Bob, pulled his helmet on, and started the scooter. A puff of smoke later, Jason was riding into town. The commute seemed much shorter that day as his mind reviewed the previous night's events over and over. In no time, he sped past the museum and the Dairy Queen and turned right onto George's street. A few blocks later, he pulled up to the curb in front of George's house. Shutting off the engine, Jason sat in the quiet silence of the morning. It was still early. He wasn't sure if anyone was awake in the house or on the whole block. He took in a couple deep breaths of the morning air, slowing his heart and collecting his thoughts.

He hadn't even taken the time to consider if telling George about Petros was a good idea; he just knew he needed to talk to someone about it. George was always his go-to guy when he needed to talk, but this… Was this something George could even handle? As he considered the possibilities, his phone chimed. He had a new text message from George. Jason surmised he must have just woken up and seen Jason through his bedroom window. In a couple of minutes, George was walking down the driveway. He wore an old blue and green plaid robe, his bedhead was out of control, and his yawn was lowering the air pressure of the entire street.

Jason smiled. "You're up early."

George rubbed the sleep out of his eyes. "It's Sunday…church."

"Ah," replied Jason.

George stared at Jason for a few moments, waiting for an explanation, but Jason just stared at Bob's gas cap. George sighed, looked up to the treetops for a few moments, and then tried to make eye contact with Jason. "Why are you here, dude?"

Jason shrugged. "Couldn't sleep."

George countered, "So getting on your scooter and driving over here at seven in the morning was the best solution you could come up with?"

Jason shrugged again, never looking up from the gas cap. "No."

George impatiently moved some dirt around on the sidewalk with his slippered toe before he said firmly, "What is going on?"

In those short moments, Jason debated if he should tell George about Petros. He weighed the two options in his head; if he told George, he would have someone on his side who could help him figure out what to do with the "mythical" beast snoozing in his old barn. But he wasn't sure how Petros would react to a random Dairy Queen employee showing up to gawk at him, so not telling George was on the table as well. Still, Jason had no idea what to do, and any sort of help—even "George help"—would be appreciated.

Jason's head finally snapped up, and he met George's gaze. His eyes were set, firm, almost desperate. He needed to get this off of his chest. After all he and his dad had been through in the past few years, Jason learned how to handle stress and difficult situations. But this…he couldn't keep this in.

Steeling himself, he said, "We need to talk."

Chapter 3

"Okay, so talk," George said, slightly impatient.

Jason looked around the street. "Well, not here."

George shook his head. "Okay, okay, let's go in and have some breakfast."

"No," Jason said curtly. "I…we have to talk in private. Can we go to my house?"

George looked frustrated. "Jace, it's seven in the morning. I have to go to church with my family, and, besides, do you expect me to ride to your house on the back of your Vespa?"

Jason looked down at Bob's speedometer. "No. Don't you have your permit?"

"Jace, I can't drive without an adult in the car. What am I going to tell my mom when I ask to borrow the keys?"

Jason answered reluctantly, "I know. You're right. It's just," he looked up at George, "I'm not sure what to do."

George's expression softened. "Look, I'll ask my mom if they can drop me off at your place after church, and we can talk then. I'll text you when the service is over. That okay?"

Jason half smiled. "Yeah, that'll be great." He started up Bob, waved at George, and drove off into town. He made his way over to the Bestway to pick up some groceries for breakfast. He had learned how to make a mean bacon and cheese omelet and needed another bottle of Mountain Dew to wash it down. He was disappointed he wasn't able to talk to George, but he also knew just showing up at George's this early in the morning wasn't the best of plans.

The Bestway opened at seven, and it was seven-ten when he arrived. The parking lot was almost deserted, with the exception of one of the largest horses he had ever seen hitched in front of the store. It wasn't a draft horse, but it was close to the size of one—nearly seven feet tall at the withers. This was…what kind of horse was this? It wasn't a breed he was familiar with, and he didn't think mixed breeds got this large. Its color was unusual as well: a mottled gray, but with another color in there; it looked blue, but he knew that couldn't be right.

He got off of the scooter and made his way toward the main entrance, never taking his eyes off the horse. Its mane and tail were a very dark color; when the early morning sun hit the hair, the color appeared as a bluish-black, but there were highlights, a yellow color. He shook his head at the sight of the unusual but magnificent animal and then ran into someone.

Jason bounced off the person coming out of the door and stumbled backward. He caught his balance and began to apologize before he even saw who it was. He looked up and saw with whom he'd collided.

"Oh! Julia, sorry, I wasn't paying attention."

"Jason," she replied. "What are you doing out so early?"

"Just need a couple of things for breakfast," he answered.

She paused and looked into his eyes for a moment. She was wearing a suede jacket over a white t-shirt, blue jeans, and riding boots. Jason melted under her gaze. "Your dad out of town again?"

He nodded. "He comes back tomorrow."

She gently rested her hand on his shoulder. "You take care, okay. It's got to be tough being home alone."

"Used to it," he said with a half smile and shrug of his shoulders. She patted his shoulder and walked toward the parking lot. He watched her approach the large horse and stroke its snout as she unhitched the great animal, gathered the reins, and mounted. She looked so small perched on its massive form, but she took control of the animal, turned it about, and began trotting toward the eastern side of town.

A bag full of groceries later, Jason was back on Bob and speeding toward home. The image of the horse stuck in his mind, and he pondered not only why Julia needed a horse that huge but where she got it. No one was really sure what Julia's home situation was like, but Jason had heard her dad was ill with some debilitating disease. He was a farmer and had recently bought into the industry of growing corn for the production of ethanol, a potential substitute for gasoline. But as his illness took over his body, they were forced to abandon their business, and Julia became her dad's primary caregiver. Julia's mom died when she was very young, so it was just she and her dad for as long as anyone in Malta remembered. And now that he was sick, Julia felt she owed it to her dad to stay in town and take care of him. Jason wished there was a way he could help, not just because he had a crush on her, but because he knew what it was like to not have your mom around. He felt sadness come over him as he remembered, so he quickly pushed the thoughts aside and refocused on the visitor sleeping in his barn.

Jason arrived back at the homestead around eight o'clock in the morning. He parked Bob in his usual place and went inside to make himself breakfast. Within a short time, his bacon and cheese omelet was on his plate with a large glass of Mountain Dew next to it.

"Breakfast of champions," he commented to himself as he dug in. He snapped his fingers as he recalled he had forgotten an important part of his Sunday breakfast. A quick trip to the pantry yielded a package of blueberry toaster pastries. Jason surfed the net on his laptop as he finished his small banquet and was soon walking out to the barn.

He quietly pushed the door open and entered. Petros began to stir at Jason's entrance, and his deep voice said, "Mmm, greetings, Little Knight."

Jason half smiled. "Mornin'."

Petros lifted his head. "How long have I been asleep?"

Jason shook his head. "Not long. Most of the night and part of the morning."

Petros stretched his long neck and turned his head toward the injured wing. He inspected the wounded area and saw that the hole had closed. "That should do for flight," he said.

"You need to be somewhere?" asked Jason.

"I assumed that my stay was limited to the length of time your father is away."

Jason shrugged. "If he doesn't know you're here, you can stay as long as you want."

Petros looked surprised. "I would think your father would notice my presence almost immediately."

"Dad? No, when Dad isn't out in the field, he's at home studying fossils or mapping out dig sites or something like that. He's usually sleeping, eating, or has his nose in a book."

"Sounds like the hallmarks of a very dedicated worker. What is your father's vocation?"

"He's an archaeologist."

Petros looked quizzical. "I am unfamiliar with that term."

Jason answered, "How do I describe this? Archaeologists dig up either the remains of stuff that has been dead longer than anyone cares to imagine, or stuff that belonged to the stuff that died, and study it."

The dragon looked quite confused. "They are grave robbers?"

"Ha! No, they are scientists."

"Science? I understand now. Science is the pursuit of those who cannot master the finer points of magic. Many who fancy themselves magicians but cannot actually use magic eventually become 'scientists.' I can see why you seem upset at the talk of his vocation. It must be very embarrassing to have a relative with such limited mental capacity."

Jason was taken aback. "What? No, that isn't it at all. My dad is really smart; he just seems to prefer spending time with his fossils than with his son."

Petros looked curious. "Do I detect a reproach?"

Jason looked down at the barn floor. "No, just a regret, I guess. Sometimes he's away for days at a time. It starts to feel like we're roommates instead of father and son." Jason watched a stray cat that had taken up residence in the barn chase a mouse across the floor. He had no idea how the cat always got into the barn, but it did keep the mouse population under control. He crouched down and made kissing noises at the feline, but it paused, arched its back, and hissed at him.

Petros said, "Allow me." He lowered his great head and stared at the cat. The cat flattened its back and looked quizzically at Petros. The dragon kept its eyes fixed on the small creature, and it slowly crept its way toward the massive form in front of it. Jason watched in fascination as the cat approached Petros and came nose to nose with him. Then he saw something he couldn't believe; the cat began to purr and rub its face against the huge, scaly snout of the dragon.

Petros smiled and lifted his head, and the cat trotted off happily into the hay bales and disappeared. Jason stood, slackjawed. "What was *that*?"

The dragon looked pleased with himself. "It is something about my kind that even we do not understand, but we have an ability to communicate with cats."

"You mean you were like talking to it in your head?"

"No, it is more of an impression or a feeling. I conjured the feeling that it was my friend, focused that feeling at the cat, and it responded in kind."

"Oooookay. I don't get that at all. Anything else about you dragon types that I should know?"

Petros sat up proudly. "Little Knight, humans have been trying to understand the unfathomable depths of dragonkind for centuries, to no avail." He looked down at the teenager, who was very unimpressed.

"Try me," Jason said flatly.

Petros regarded Jason for a moment then smirked. "Well played, Little Knight. Perhaps I will honor you with insight into the workings of dragonkind. But first I need to stretch my legs, so to speak.

"Umm…yeah," Jason replied. "You mean like take a walk or something?"

Petros looked confused. "Yes, is that an unusual request?"

Jason answered, "Under normal circumstances, no. But, you being, you know—"

"A dragon?" Petros interrupted.

Jason cleared his throat. "Ahem, yes, a dragon. Look, I'm not trying to be rude, but as there are no dragons anymore, seeing someone like you taking a casual stroll down Highway 2 would be, well, earth-shattering for pretty much anyone."

"Anymore?" Petros asked. "*When*, precisely, am I?"

Jason said, "It's two thousand eleven, the twenty-first century."

Petros' eyes widened and darted back and forth in their sockets. He inhaled deeply. "It would seem you have a great deal to tell me as well."

Jason nodded his head. "I guess we could walk out into the fields behind the barn where the crops used to grow. It's away from the road, and there's a forest beyond that, so I think we would have enough cover."

The door to the barn creaked open, and Jason stuck his head out, surveying the surroundings. The driveway was clear, and he couldn't hear anyone coming down the highway in either direction. Above Jason's head, Petros's head appeared, followed by his long, serpentine neck. The dragon double-checked the areas Jason had just surveyed. He looked down at Jason; Jason looked up at him. They nodded to each other, and then Jason flung open both of the barn doors. They began running to the field behind the barn. As Jason full-out sprinted, he noticed the cat-like movements of Petros as the dragon ran; each hind foot landed in the exact spot of the previous forefoot, and his tail was raised and curved inward. He thought that, perhaps, there was something to that dragon/cat connection.

Petros ran next to Jason until the boy stopped, bent over, rested his hands on his bent knees, and gasped for breath. The dragon crouched low and looked behind them then nodded approvingly.

"I would surmise we are far enough away," he said.

All Jason could do was nod between gasps. Petros crawled next to Jason as the teen struggled to catch his breath and eventually said, "It is a shame that your endurance is not up to a relatively short sprint. Do they not encourage exercise for children in the twenty-first century?"

Jason scowled at the dragon. "You…gasp…sound just like…gasp…my PE teacher."

Petros furrowed his brow. "I am unfamiliar with PE. Is it some new combat technique?"

Jason answered through his battle for his breath. "PE. Physical education. Gym class. They make you exercise in the middle of the school day. You spend the rest of the day not only tired but smelling from the sweat as well."

Petros's neck raised to its full height in surprise. "They have to *teach* you to exercise? What is wrong with the children in this time? Little Knight, you should have been able to make that sprint and then been ready to wrestle me to the ground afterward. Pitiful."

"Hey, I'm a techie, okay? I work at a museum; I fix computers. I don't, you know, throw field goals or kick homeruns or anything like that. So gimme a break."

Petros responded. "First, I have no idea as to the meaning of anything you just said. Second, it is inexcusable that a child of…how old are you?"

Jason answered tersely, "Fifteen."

Petros continued, "Thank you…that a child of fifteen years old cannot run from here to there without it bringing him nearly to death's door!"

"Yeah, well, how old are you?"

Petros looked at Jason. "I beg your pardon?"

"How old are you? Since we're so focused on our ages, I want to know how old you are. I hear dragons can live a really long time, but for you to be here…now…you must be the oldest dragon ever."

Petros looked very concerned. "The most ancient dragon I have heard of was approximately eight hundred years old. I am nowhere near that age…or at least until just a few moments ago, I was nowhere near that age."

Jason asked, "What do you mean?"

"It means I have over seven hundred years of lost time."

Jason looked bewildered. "How is that possible?"

Petros shook his head. "I have no idea, but it sounds like there are a great many mysteries to unravel in our time together."

They passed the treeline and entered the woods. The trees were a mix of hemlock and lodgepole pine and were spread apart, leaving enough room for a creature the size of Petros to maneuver. It was quiet, and the pair could hear the twittering of birds as they walked in silence for several moments. They both felt the calm of the glade of trees, and it served to relax them after their run from the old farm.

"May I make a personal inquiry, Little Knight?" Petros said, breaking the silence.

"Sure," Jason replied.

"You speak of your father but not of your mother. Why?"

He took a deep breath. "She died a few years ago. My older brother too. Car wreck."

Petros listened intently. "A car is a conveyance of some sort?" Jason nodded without speaking, so Petros continued, "I offer you my deepest condolences."

"Thanks," Jason answered. "I don't talk about it much. Still kind of a sensitive topic."

"Understood," answered the dragon.

"How about you? You really have seven hundred years of time you don't remember?"

Petros nodded his head. "I have very rich memories of my time, my day-to-day activities and so forth." Jason watched the dragon close his eyes in thought yet somehow manage to avoid the trees while he walked. "I remember…strife…conflict…a red wing. There was war…dragons fighting. I can't see it. Feathers? Birds?" He opened his eyes. "And then I awoke in a cave. I was in the mountain range to the west of here."

"How long ago was that, you know, when you woke up?"

Petros pursed his lips. "The days blended together for a while. Less than a fortnight, to be sure. All I could do for many days was find food and then return to sleep; I was very weak, and the nutrition and the rest strengthened me. But I dared not use the Drake sleep; I had no idea what threats were around me, and I couldn't leave myself that vulnerable."

"What have you been eating?" Jason asked.

Petros shrugged his great shoulder blades. "The indigenous species here: cattle, deer, the large, black cattle-like creatures…"

Jason smiled as he interrupted, "Bison. Now it makes sense; I think I found an unfinished meal of yours on the way into town."

Petros thought. "Ahh, yes. That was very disappointing; it was the day I was forced to switch to night hunting. I found my prey but caught the scent of another dragon, most likely the Storm dragon. A battle in the daylight was not something I felt was prudent at the time, so I had to drop my meal and flee."

"Okay, so I need to ask this then." Jason refocused his line of questioning. "You're a Stone dragon, and the dragon you fought was a Storm dragon. How many different kinds of dragons are there?"

"Not many," Petros answered casually. "There are four species, and then we know of three subspecies in each of the four, so only twelve."

Jason stopped dead in his tracks and paused for a moment. "Twelve?"

Petros looked around, not realizing Jason had fallen behind. "What is wrong?"

Jason was stunned. "I assume there are lots of each of these twelve different kinds of dragons."

Petros answered, "Of course."

"So there is the potential that we, humans in two thousand eleven, could be dealing with hundreds of dragons?"

Petros thought for a moment. "Yes, at least. Is that a problem?"

<u>**Chapter 4**</u>

"Whoa."

Jason was stunned at the thought of hundreds of dragons now living in 2011. Of course, there was no proof that there actually were any besides Petros and the unnamed Storm dragon that battled him, but the very thought was enough to stop Jason in his tracks.

Petros questioned, "This idea concerns you?"

Jason began walking in circles. He often did this when he was deep in thought. "It's just that dragons are, well, considered to be mythical in this century. No one believes that you're real, so when an actual dragon comes swooping out of the mountains followed by a couple hundred of his friends, I can't see the world reacting well to that."

Petros looked confused. "How so?"

The teen continued his circular pacing. "Look, we're pretty, I don't know...skeptical, literal, paranoid of things we don't understand. I mean it was only a few decades ago when people would hunt sharks because they thought they were ruthless killing machines. I mean now we understand them better, and it's not like that anymore, but—"

The dragon interrupted. "But you fear something similar would happen to my kind."

"Well..." Jason hesitated. "Yes, I do. There'll be some who'll want to make peace or be friends or even admit you to the United Nations or something, but the majority will be scared and paranoid. I mean, well, look at you."

Petros began to examine his own body as Jason said, "No, Petros, it's just a figure of speech."

Petros's voice was irritated. "Then why did you say it?"

Jason was waving his hands. "I didn't mean literally."

"You humans seem to have a great many of these figures of speech in your language."

Jason was flustered, "I don't know, we just say stuff like that."

"And why are you walking in circles?"

Jason was taken aback. "Huh?"

"You have been walking in circles since I mentioned there may be more than two dragons in this time."

"I do that when I'm trying to think."

Petros shook his head. "You look like a confused predator circling a field mouse."

"Stop!" Jason shouted. Petros was staring at Jason, almost examining him. He lowered his great head and came face to face with Jason.

"Now I understand. It is not just that I am a dragon. It is because I am intelligent, quick-witted, and, quite possibly, superior to humans. You are not afraid of my size; you are afraid of my capability. Humans cannot bear the thought of some other living thing that would dare to share, or even exceed, your famed level of intelligence." He pulled his great neck up to its full height, his face looking disappointed. "Nothing has changed in seven hundred years. Your kind is still petty and jealous."

Jason didn't know how to respond. He said, "Look, if it helps, I'm not afraid of you. I mean I'm highly agitated and intimidated by your size…and your teeth…the claws are, you know, kinda scary, too, and your—"

Petros interrupted, "Point taken. Go on."

"But I like that you can talk, that you can carry on an intelligent conversation with me. Dad is gone so much, and school can be so boring; I don't have anyone I can talk to like this."

"Surely you have friends?"

"Yeah, but, I mean George is great, he's my best friend and all… Oh, man, George!" Jason had lost all track of time and remembered George was going to text him. Out in the woods, the chances of getting a signal on his cell were fleeting at best. He whipped out the phone and checked the time. "Phew, church isn't over yet."

Petros was intrigued at the sight of the phone. "What is *that*?" He lowered his huge head again and looked directly over Jason's shoulder. To Petros, the phone was smaller than a postage stamp, so he strained his eyes to look at the tiny screen.

Jason said, "It's a phone."

"Little Knight, Jason, what year am I from again?" he asked sarcastically.

Jason shook his head. "Right, sorry…umm, it's a device we use to communicate with each other. When you get one of these, you are assigned a unique series of numbers that goes with the phone. So when someone else has a phone and knows my set of numbers, they only have to enter my numbers on this keypad here. Then my phone will produce a sound indicating the other person is trying to communicate with me, and I press a button, and we can talk to each other through the phones."

Petros regarded the device. "It sounds like a fairly complex magical spell."

Jason smiled. "No, it's science."

Petros looked dubious. "I highly doubt that."

Jason turned to face Petros. "See? That's part of the problem. You dragons just don't fit in with two thousand eleven. So much has happened, especially with technology and science." Jason sank into thought and began walking in circles again.

Petros sat up straight. "Are you circling another rodent?"

Jason pinched his fingers together at the dragon. "Zip it. What we need to do is find a way for you fit in, to bring you up to speed on what is happening right now. There are seven hundred years of history that've come and gone while you were out of commission. A lot has happened, and it may help you to understand *when* you are by knowing what you have missed."

One corner of the dragon's mouth turned down. "Did you just tell me to 'zip it'?"

Jason was completely distracted by his musings. "Look, I think that's it!" He stopped pacing and met Petros's eyes. "We can't deny the fact that you are in the twenty-first century. You're here; it's done. But we *can* get you caught up; we can prepare you for life in the twenty-first century. Just think about it; we get you all, you know, whatever, then we look for other dragons, and you can act as sort of an educator, an ambassador, and help your entire kind get more prepared for reintroduction into the world."

Petros looked skeptical. "And how do we accomplish this?"

Jason inhaled as if to answer but stopped. He slumped and said, "I don't know."

"Perhaps I can use this phone to communicate with those who can give me information. I would assume that if the conversation is strictly auditory then I could literally speak to anyone without them knowing I was a dragon. Fetch me a phone in my size, and I will begin post haste. I will also need a list of these unique numbers to all of the renowned scholars and philosophers in this century." Petros looked down at Jason, who was looking back up at him.

Jason shook his head, a wry smile on his lips. "Yeah…it's not that easy."

Petros pursed his lips in frustration. "I was correct. Your 'science' is not all that you proclaim it to be."

Jason began walking again, and Petros followed. Jason went on, "What I need to do is get you on the 'net." He looked at Petros. "Can you read?"

Petros scowled at the insult. "If I could breathe fire, I would incinerate you where you stand."

Jason held up his hands. "Okay, okay, you can read. Don't be so sensitive. I need a really big monitor and some voice recognition software, neither of which I have enough money to buy. I could use the flat panel in the house, but my dad would notice it was missing if I moved it out to the barn."

"This would be a scintillating conversation if I was aware of the meanings of 'monitor,' 'software,' and 'flat panel.' Although I could translate the latter by the literal definition of the words, I would not be so foolish to assume the words are being used in context of their actual definitions."

Jason smirked. "You just hate it when you don't know what I'm talking about, don't you?"

"It is irksome, yes."

He grinned widely at the dragon. "I kinda like it."

Jason and Petros continued the conversation about life in the twenty-first century during the remainder of their walk. Jason mostly told the dragon about his life, school, work, and home. By the time there were leaving the forest and heading back into the field behind the barn, Jason was discussing Julia, George, and Stan Whitman.

"So this Stan," Petros asked, "enjoys putting others into difficult and humiliating circumstances all for his own amusement?"

Jason shook his head. "C'mon…are you telling me that there was no such thing as a bully seven hundred years ago?"

Petros shook his head. "Dragons do not 'bully.' It must be a character flaw unique to humans, but, no, we do not engage in such behaviors."

Jason stopped walking and with a wistful expression asked, "Really?"

A look came over Petros's face that, to Jason, seemed like it might be compassion. "Really. It is a very dishonorable thing to do."

Jason tried to process the idea of bullying being nonexistent. He sighed. "That sounds…nice."

As they crossed into the field, they heard Jason's phone chirp. Looking at the touch screen, Jason said, "Uh-oh, it's George."

Petros inquired, "Is there a problem?"

"Well, I went to see George this morning because I needed to talk. But it wasn't a good time, so he said his parents would drop him off here after church, and we could talk then."

Petros looked suspicious. "And what did you need to discuss with him?"

Jason paused. "What do you think?"

Petros nodded. "I can understand that you needed to strategize about what to do with the dragon in your barn."

Jason spoke quickly. "You gotta understand. I just couldn't keep this in. I do that too much without Dad around. I needed help, and he's my best friend—"

Petros interrupted, "Little knight, I understand. Truly, I do. So what is the course of action now?"

Jason was flustered. "I don't know. This walk has…I dunno…made me feel more comfortable, but he's my best friend. What do you think about my introducing you to George?"

"I cannot see the harm in it. How do you predict he will react?"

Jason laughed. "He'll freak out." Then he thought of something. "But it may solve a problem of ours too. Let me fill you in."

***

Jason returned George's text and helped Petros sneak back into the barn. He instructed the dragon.

"Okay, I don't know how I'm gonna do this, but I'll bring him in and then you be...be..."

Petros cocked is head. "Be what?"

Jason made circling motions with his hands. "I don't know...charming?"

The dragon's lip curled slightly. "Charming?"

"Yeah, charming or something. What do you dragons do when you want to win the approval of a human?"

"We rid ourselves of the need to win the approval of humans—that is what we do."

Jason glowered. "That doesn't help. I just don't know what to tell you to do if he wigs out."

Petros's head slumped and shook. "Another figure of speech."

"Sorry." Jason corrected, "If he...umm...loses his composure. That's it."

The dragon nodded understandingly. "Let me handle that."

Jason nodded then did a double take. "Okay, wait...that doesn't mean you're gonna eat him or anything?"

Petros pointed a clawed toe at the barn door. "Get out!"

Jason half ran out the door while the dragon huffed in indignation. A short time later, a dark blue Ford Explorer pulled up to his driveway, and George got out of the backseat. As he closed the door, he shouted to the driver, "I'll call when I'm ready!" and shut the door. The SUV drove off, and Jason came down the driveway to meet George.

"They mad?" Jason asked.

George nodded. "Sunday dinner with the family always follows church, so I'm bucking tradition for you."

Jason replied, "You're very noble. Hey, I heard your dad say he was going to upgrade from the forty-seven-inch flat panel you have at home. What are you going to do with the old TV?"

George stopped dead in his tracks. "That is what all this fuss was about? A TV!"

Jason was confused. "Huh? Wha— No, that isn't what this is about. Well, when I think about it, it's a little related but definitely not the topic that—"

George interrupted. "Tell me!"

He took a deep breath. "Okay. Last night, a drifter of sorts wandered into our barn." George looked a little worried, but Jason went on. "The thing is he isn't normal. He needs my help, and I really want to give him a hand, but if, you know, people find out about him, it could be very bad."

George asked tentatively, "Is he dangerous?"

"No!" Jason paused. "Well, he can be perceived as such."

George blurted, "Jason, he's got a gun?"

Jason turned to face his friend and put his hands on George's shoulders. "No, George, you need to listen. When you get to know him, you realize he is not dangerous. He's intimidating, but you gotta promise me not to blow a gasket."

George was genuinely frightened; his voice wavered. "Why would I blow a gasket?"

Jason looked down his nose at George. "George, remember when we ran into that hog-nosed snake out in the field?"

George exclaimed, "It was huge!"

Jason countered, "It was less than three feet long, and it wasn't poisonous, and we were outdoors in a field. It's not like we were cornered."

George sheepishly said, "It *looked* dangerous."

Jason said, "You blew a gasket."

George admitted, "I don't like snakes."

He gripped George's shoulders more tightly. "What's in the barn is bigger than that snake."

George took a deep breath. "I'll try not to wig out."

Jason put his arm around his friend and walked with him to the barn. Jason took the handle of the door, gave George one more reassuring look, and pulled the door open. Petros was already sitting, facing the door, looking as friendly as he could. He sat back on his haunches with his head tilted to one side, much like a cat would as it waited for its owner to come home. The dragon did his best to smile.

George's eyes went as wide as his eyelids would open; his jaw dropped so far his uvula was clearly visible. A look of absolute terror came over his face.

Jason tried to head off the storm of George's panic. "George, this is my friend Petros. He is a Stone—"

George began to stammer.

"D..ddd....drr...drrrrrrrrrr....ragggg...."

"Dragon," Petros's deep voice boomed.

"AAAAAAAAAAIIIIIIIIGGGGGGGGHHHHHHHH!" George began to scream without abandon, yet he didn't move from the spot where he was standing. Petros actually startled at the scream, and Jason winced but stayed calm; he expected this from George.

Jason looked at Petros and shouted, matter of factly, "He's wigging out!"

Petros's cheeks puffed slightly as he blew a stream of tiny glowing cubes of energy at George. Each cube was less than half the size of a six-sided die, and the jet of bizarre force washed over George. Petros held the stream for less than a second and then stopped blowing. The energy immediately dissipated, and George's face was still contorted in terror, but he was completely still and silent. His skin had taken a slightly gray pallor, but his clothing was unaffected.

Jason walked a lap around his friend, astounded by the turn of events. "Wha...what did you do?"

Petros looked very proud of himself. "All is well; I petrified him."

Chapter 5

"You did *what*?" Jason shouted, grabbing his head with his hands.

George was perfectly still. His face was still contorted in the scream of panic that he unleashed when he saw Petros but was completely devoid of sound. Jason walked a circle around him and then whipped around to face Petros.

"You killed him!" he exclaimed.

Petros was offended. "I did nothing of the sort. What kind of monster do you think I am?" Jason opened his mouth to answer, but Petros cut him off by pointing a clawed toe at him. "Do not answer that!"

Jason shook his head furiously. "Then what did you do to him?"

Petros explained, "All dragons have a breath weapon. Each one is a different breath weapon, but we all have them regardless. A Stone dragon, such as myself, breathes a petrifying energy. A being that is fully exposed will indeed be turned to stone. However, I can vary the exposure to simply paralyze and neutralize a target for a short time. This is what I have done to George; the magic of my breath weapon has simply immobilized him for probably fifteen to twenty minutes."

Jason's eyes squinted as he looked at George. He tentatively reached out a finger and pushed it into George's cheek. The skin was colder and more rigid than normal, but when he put his fingers over George's carotid artery, he could feel his friend's pulse. He relaxed some, having proof that George was still alive. "This only works on living things?"

"I could transmute inanimate objects to stone if I can completely envelop them in my breath."

Jason was fascinated by now. "What about something big like—"

Petros interrupted, "Like another dragon?"

Jason nodded. "Well, yeah."

"It would take a very prolonged exposure to truly petrify another of my kind. In combat, I can create a numbing effect or paralyze part of another dragon's body."

Jason looked confused. "Doesn't sound as good as breathing fire."

Petros furrowed his brow. "A Flame dragon needs to expand its chest or contract its throat muscles or open its jaw to breathe fire. If I paralyzed any of those areas of its body, it would render its breath weapon unusable."

"Flame dragon?" Jason asked.

"Another type of dragon, yes. It is one of the Fire Dragons."

"Cool," he commented. "Now, what are we going to do with George? Like, does he even know what is going on now?"

Petros answered, "No. His mind is paralyzed as well."

Jason countered, "Well, not paralyzed. His autonomic brain functions are working; otherwise he wouldn't be breathing."

"I suppose your 'science' told you that is how things work," Petros said sarcastically.

Jason rolled his eyes. "We have got to get you caught up with the twenty-first century. But we need to figure out what to do with George first." He looked around the barn. In the corner, two walls were built out to form a small room for tack, tools, and other farm-related objects. Jason said, "Let's move him into the tack room. When he wakes up, I can get him calmed down before he comes back out to see you."

Petros said, "Why do you not just move him back into your house?"

Jason stated, "Look at me. He's easily got forty pounds on me; there is no way I could move him."

"I will move him," the dragon said.

Jason gave Petros a critical look. "You're gonna carry him from here to the house in broad daylight?"

Petros paused. "Very well. The tack room will have to do."

Petros cradled George gently in his large claw and moved him to the tack room, where Jason took over. He grunted and groaned as he moved his paralyzed friend into the small room.

Jason got his friend settled and impatiently waited for the effects of the dragon's breath weapon to wear off. Fifteen minutes later, Jason watched in amazement as the gray faded from George's face, and the natural pink color of his skin returned. George's eyes blinked first, and then his mouth closed. He proceeded to smack his lips and tongue repeatedly; his mouth had dried out from having been open for such a long time.

George looked around. "Where am I?"

Jason answered, "You're still in the barn; we're in the tack room."

George looked confused. "Why am I still—" Realization came over his face, and he reverted to near panic immediately. "There's a dragon in your barn!"

Once again, Jason rested his hands on his friend's shoulders. "George, I know. He's good; he's a friend. Look at me…" Jason took a step back. "See? No wounds, burns, nothing like that. I was with him last night and all morning. We even took a walk. He won't hurt you."

"*But he's a dragon! How* is he a dragon? How is there even a *dragon*?"

Jason held up his hands soothingly. "Don't wig out again, okay? This is a 'no wigging' zone."

George took several deep breaths. "Right, no wigging, got it."

Jason explained, "We don't know how he got here, but I want to help him figure stuff out. How about you?"

George swallowed hard and whimpered, "Will he eat me?"

Jason raked his hands through his hair. "No, George, he won't eat you. Let's go talk to him, okay?"

George nodded, but as Jason put his arm around him to lead him into barn, George wouldn't move. Jason pulled a little harder, but George was set firm in his fright. Jason looked at his friend in frustration; his eyes were fixed on the door and terrified of what was beyond it. His body was completely unwilling to leave the tack room. Jason looked around and spied an old riding crop hanging on the wall. He took it and gave George a little swat on the behind. George jumped at the sting of the mini-whip. "Hey! What's up with that?"

"Move it, Captain Courageous."

Jason was the first to enter the main area of the barn and saw Petros seated patiently, trying to look as unassuming as a thirty-foot-long dragon could look. George peeked his head around the doorjamb, saw Petros, and an almost inaudible squeal of fear began at the back of his throat. Jason grabbed George's arm and gave him a sharp tug, pulling his friend forcibly to a position next to him. Jason tugged a little too hard, and George stumbled into him. They both fought for their balance for a moment but quickly righted themselves, Jason looking put out at the indignity and George still looking terrified.

There was an awkward silence as Jason and Petros exchanged glances, and George fought to restrain his screams of terror. He was still making a quiet squealing sound as he fought back his fright.

"So," Jason broke the silence, "this is good."

Petros quickly added, "Yes. Agreed. It is good. Very, uh, good."

George was trying, unsuccessfully, not to quiver.

Jason said, "George may be able to help us with the plan we discussed, Petros."

Petros nodded in affirmation. "Yes. You shared that with me, Little Knight. I would obviously be grateful for whatever help George could offer."

George swallowed hard and stammered, "Hhh…how did I get in the tack room?"

"What?" Jason asked.

He repeated, "How did I get in the tack room?"

"Ah," Petros said, "I simply—" Petros noticed Jason shaking his head emphatically from side to side. Petros changed his story. "I simply noticed you must have, uhh, lost consciousness from your fright." Jason was now nodding in the affirmative, so Petros continued. "Yes, that is precisely what occurred. In your state of alarm, you lost consciousness. We, uh, moved you to a more private location."

George looked to Jason, who said, "Yes, that is exactly what happened. The whole fright/moved you thing."

Petros and Jason waited a few moments, hoping George would buy their story. George finally responded, "Oh, um, okay. That was kind of you, I guess."

Jason and the dragon breathed a quiet sigh of relief as Jason said, "So, George, we could really use your help." Jason looked to Petros for support.

Petros saw the look and said, "Oh, yes. I need help that only you can provide. Definitely." He looked back to Jason, who motioned with his hands for Petros to keep talking. Petros didn't take the cue.

Jason asked leadingly, "And why do you need George's help?"

Petros echoed tentatively, "Why do I need George's help?"

Jason said, "Yes, tell him."

"Why *do* I need George's help?" Petros said through gritted teeth.

George kept turning his head from Jason to Petros and back, as if he were watching a tennis match.

Jason rolled his eyes. "It's like this; we want to be able to get Petros on the Internet and—"

George interrupted, "The dragon wants to surf the Internet?"

Petros answered, "Not particularly, no."

Jason countered Petros, "Yes. You do. Now, what we need—"

Petros interrupted, "I prefer being read to, but if there are no servants around then I prefer using books and scrolls."

George asked, "Who reads scrolls anymore?"

"Listen!" Jason shouted and then paused for a moment. "The dragon," he glared at Petros, "needs to get caught up with seven hundred years of history. The best way to do that is on the 'net."

Petros looked at George. "Is that true?"

George nodded reluctantly as Jason continued. "But because of his size, he can't use a computer. I was wondering if there was a way we could get our hands on the flat panel your dad is getting rid of and use that as his monitor."

Petros snorted. "Would one of you do me the courtesy of explaining what a 'flat panel' is?"

Jason held up his smart phone. "A screen like this for viewing information, only a lot bigger."

George swallowed hard, afraid of the dragon's reaction. "Sss..sorry, but my dad already promised it to my uncle. Pleasedon'teatmebecauseit'snotmyfault."

Petros shook his head. "Young George, I am not going to eat you. If I were going to eat anyone, it would be Jason here. He is certainly more exasperating, and I would enjoy the silence."

"Hey!" Jason shouted, and George actually laughed.

Petros smiled. "There, much better. Since this flattened panel is not available, are there any other options?"

George said, "Jace, doesn't your dad have that LCD projector?"

Jason nodded. "Forgot about that. It would work, and I don't think he'd notice if it went missing for a little while."

George asked, "But how would we get the 'net out here in the barn?"

Jason began walking in a circle. George looked to Petros. "He's thinking."

Petros nodded. "Yes, I am aware. He looks slightly ridiculous."

Jason kept circling, "I have the spool of cat-five ethernet cable that dad let me buy last year. There is about two hundred and fifty feet of it left, which should reach out here. Pop a couple of ends on it, and we should be good. The problem is finding a way for Petros to navigate the 'net; he sure can't use a keyboard."

George nodded. "Voice recognition?"

Petros grumbled, "I am glad I am a part of this conversation."

Jason ignored the dragon. "I don't have any software, but I suppose we can use the program built into the operating system. It's not that great, but I guess we can make it work." He turned to Petros. "Do you think you can enunciate well enough?"

Petros glowered at Jason and, with perfect diction, said, "You are a very annoying child."

George snickered again, and Jason said, "That'll do. Let's get to work."

Over the next couple of hours, Jason and George managed to run a length of ethernet cable from the farmhouse out to the barn and set up a makeshift learning library for Petros. A sheet was hung from the rafters for a screen, and the projector shone the display from the laptop on the screen. Jason attached a microphone from an old PA system his dad had used to the laptop to accept voice commands and rigged the mic up in front of the dragon.

Jason turned to George. "I think that's as good as it's gonna get. We're pretty limited on what we could've used."

George shrugged his shoulders. "It'll work. It's not supposed to look pretty."

Petros asked, "So I speak into the small wand, and this laptop device will respond to my commands?"

Jason was fiddling with the voice recognition software. "That's what we're hoping."

For the next hour, Jason worked with his laptop and Petros, getting the program to appropriately recognize Petros's voice and understand his vocal inflections. He noted how he only needed to tell the dragon something once, and Petros would remember it. Jason was becoming more and more convinced that the mind of a dragon was far more advanced than that of a human.

It was midafternoon by the time Jason was comfortable saying to Petros, "Well, I think you're ready to start exploring cyberspace. You've gone to a few search engines on your own, and it's just up to you now to study what you want."

Petros was intrigued and nodded. "I must admit, Little Knight, this is a fascinating way of obtaining information. I would like time to explore this 'Internet.'"

Jason replied, "Okay, I need to do a little cleaning up in the house, and George needs to head home, so I'll just leave you to guide yourself."

"Very well," Petros answered, and Jason and George left the barn. George made a call home to get a ride back to his house.

He said to Jason, "Well, dude, I have to give you credit."

"For what?" Jason answered.

"Because you have given me a reason to say something I never thought I would say."

"Oh, yeah, what?" Jason asked.

George smiled. "Good luck with the giant dragon surfing the Internet in your barn."

Chapter 6

The rest of the day passed slowly after George went home. Jason wanted to leave Petros alone to study, and he really needed to do a little house cleaning in preparation for his dad's return the next day. Jason was never really sure exactly when his dad would get home; it could be first thing in the morning or after dark. But he had a sink full of dishes, and various things were askew from the search for materials to make a learning lab for Petros.

The sun had started to set, and Jason flopped on the couch for a few minutes to rest his eyes. The next thing he knew, he awoke at a half hour to midnight. He rubbed his eyes. "Must've been more worn out than I thought." He walked over to the window and could still see the glow of the projector leaking between the old wooden planks. Jason pulled on his sneakers and, still half asleep, plodded out to the barn.

He opened one of the doors to find Petros wide-eyed and staring at a website outlining American history. He turned his head to Jason.

"Greetings. It is late. Should you not be asleep?"

Jason rubbed the back of his head. "I could ask you the same thing."

Petros shook his head. "I can go days without sleep."

"How about food?" Jason asked. "I haven't seen you eat since you got here."

Without looking away from the screen, Petros said, "A few deer wandered into your field approximately one hour ago. I consumed them."

Jason wrinkled his nose at the thought. "Did anyone see you?"

Petros waved a foreleg at Jason. "Of course not. Little Knight, I am amazed at how the world has changed. The Internet would be the dream of scholars and historians from my time."

Jason walked next to Petros to get a better look at the screen. "Yeah, well, you can't believe everything you read."

Petros nodded. "Yes, I concur, but if you visit enough websites on the same topic, you can extrapolate that which is truthful from that which is opinion or conjecture."

Jason smiled and shook his head. "It's so weird to hear you talk about websites like that. How many have you visited?"

Petros thought for a moment. "Mmm…several."

"Can you be more specific?"

Not missing a beat, Petros answered, "Just under nine hundred."

"What? How is that possible?" Jason exclaimed.

Petros made a motion similar to shrugging shoulders. "I need not spend much time at every site I visit. If I read something, I remember it. Just like if I see something, I can remember that too."

Jason paused in amazement then asked, "Are you telling me you have an eidetic memory?"

Petros looked confused. He turned to the microphone and said, "Access Google dot com. Search 'eidetic memory.' Select top result." The definition of the term came up on the screen, and, after reading it, Petros said, "Hmm, interesting. It would appear that I, and all dragons, have eidetic memory or photographic memory, per se. I just thought that was normal, but apparently it is something special."

Jason was astounded. "So anything you see, read, or hear you can remember after only experiencing it once?"

"Yes, of course," the dragon answered. "Why is that so odd to you?"

"Because it's—" Jason chuckled. "You know what; I guess I'm not surprised by that at all."

Petros nodded. "Very well then. Little Knight, you must realize this will lead me to only one conclusion."

"What's that?"

He turned to face Jason. "That I am going to want to leave this barn. That I will want to explore, learn your culture, and find others of my kind."

Jason sighed deeply. "I know, I know. I wish I knew how to make that work. I just know that the world will not react kindly to you showing up on its doorstep. I wish there were a way." He squeezed the bridge of his nose. "I can't think right now."

Petros acknowledged, "You are tired. We will discuss this in the morning."

Jason shook his head while saying, "It'll have to wait until the afternoon. Now that school's out for the summer, I have a shift at the museum a few mornings a week. But I'll stop in when I wake up, and we can make a plan for the day."

"Very good," Petros said. "Sleep well, Jason."

"You too," Jason replied.

Petros smiled. "I plan to study all night. I want to have visited two thousand websites by sunrise."

Jason left the barn, smiling in wonderment at the dragon.

***

Morning came all too quickly for Jason. He made up for the previous morning and gave his snooze button quite the workout before he got out of bed. A quick shower and an even quicker breakfast later, he was walking out to the barn. After pulling on his helmet and starting up Bob the Vespa, he had to dodge another assault of tomatoes from Stan Whitman, who was brazenly parked at the end of his driveway as opposed to waiting in ambush somewhere along the highway. Bob sacrificially took one of the flying fruits, but the rest were narrowly avoided by some rather fancy skidding on Jason's part. The rest of the trip into town was, fortunately, uneventful.

There was a little more activity at the museum that day, as Julia was working and Susan was shuffling through papers in her office. After a few hours, Jason heard the door open, and a familiar face walked in. Timothy Hewes, Jason's father, came through the doors wearing khaki cargo-style shorts, laced-up work boots with thick white socks, and a short-sleeved cotton shirt. He wore wire-rimmed glasses, and his salt-and-pepper hair was just as tousled as Jason's was. Jason smiled at his dad and gave him a welcoming hug.

"Welcome back," he said to his dad.

Timothy smiled. "Thanks, son. How've things been?"

The events of the last two days raced back through Jason's head. "Meh, you know…the usual."

Susan Elwick heard Mr. Hewes's voice and came out of the office to greet him. She was in her late forties, heavyset, with long, straight hair almost completely gray. She wore an oversized t-shirt bearing the logo of the museum and a pair of jeans with the cuffs rolled up to her calves.

"Well, how is our resident archeologist today?" she asked Mr. Hewes, somewhat starry-eyed at seeing the scientist in her museum.

"I had a very good trip, and I have some great news. This year, the annual convention and picnic for the staff of the Montana Dinosaur Trail is being hosted in Malta! Isn't that fantastic?"

Susan's face lit up in response to news, but Jason's countenance dropped. The annual convention and picnic was usually less on the convention and more on the picnic. Since the Montana Dinosaur Trail was spread across the state, the powers that be provided a time every year for all of the museum employees and their families to gather and celebrate the vision for preserving the archaeological and paleontological history of Montana. It sounded very noble on paper, but for someone Jason's age it was nothing more than a bunch of strangers getting together, eating barbecued chicken, and talking about fossils. Jason loved dinosaurs, but even for him it was a bit much.

Trying to sound interested, Jason asked, "Hey, that's…that's really something. When's it happening?"

His dad answered, "We only have two weeks to get ready."

Jason looked suspicious. "We as in the general 'we' of Malta, right?"

His father answered excitedly, "Yes and no. Since we have an old farmstead, we have plenty of land to host all of those people, so the event will actually be on our property. Exciting, isn't it?"

Jason struggled very hard to make the panic on his face look like excitement. But all he could picture was some seven-year-old from Fort Peck wandering into the barn and coming face to face with an Internet-surfing dragon. He struggled to process the information as Susan and his dad went into her office to start making arrangements for the event.

Jason was lost in his thoughts when he felt a hand on his shoulder. He jumped before he realized it was Julia. She asked, "You look pale. Are you all right?"

He didn't know how to answer. "I, uh, haven't been sleeping since dad's been gone. I guess it's catching up with me."

She nodded. "Look, they'll be in there for a while. You know Susan; she has that little crush on your dad, and I'm sure they have a lot to do to plan this picnic. Why don't you go home? I'll make up an excuse for you."

Jason couldn't even process the concept of Susan liking his dad. He knew it was the truth, but the thought was borderline repulsive to him. Susan was his boss, and when his dad wasn't around, she wasn't all that pleasant of a person. But she was committed to the Montana Dinosaur Trail, and she viewed his dad as a rock star of sorts.

But Jason had a bigger problem. He had to figure out what to do with Petros. He didn't want the dragon to leave, but at the same time he had no idea how to hide the dragon either. He had to get home and let Petros know what was going on. He turned to Julia. "You know, that's a good idea. You sure it's not a problem?"

She shook her head. "Nah. I can get Susan to believe anything I tell her. You go feel better."

Jason packed up his belongings and walked out to Bob. He thought about his dad worrying that he went home sick, but a little pang of sadness entered his heart. He loved his dad; he was a good father and a good man. He just wasn't all that good at being nurturing. His mom really was the caretaker in the family, and now that she was gone, his dad hadn't really figured out how to pick up that slack. Sure, when Jason was sick he would suggest what medicine to take or what to do to rest or take care of himself, but that special touch wasn't there. It was like he was getting a treatment plan from a doctor as opposed to some TLC from a parent. But that was how dad was: really good at the intellectual part of life, but not emotionally deep.

Jason pushed the speed limit of Bob all the way home. The little scooter skidded as he turned into the gravel driveway, and Jason set his backpack on the edge of the porch as he sprinted to the barn. He knocked twice and yanked open the doors.

Petros was lying down, his head resting in his claws as he leaned on his front elbows. Playing on the screen was a movie called *Reign of Fire*, a movie about dragons awaking in modern times and decimating the world. Petros's expression was one of amazement, like a child experiencing his first movie on the big screen of a theater. He turned to Jason, eyes wide.

"Streaming movies are *amazing*!"

Jason was dumbfounded. "What are you doing?"

"I am watching streaming movies! Are you aware of how many movies have been made about dragons? They are complete rubbish from an accuracy point of view, of course, but this form of entertainment is brilliant. How are you not watching movies all the time?"

"I…uh…but…" Jason was at a loss for words. "Look, Petros, we have a problem."

A look of concern came over the dragon's face. He paused the movie. "What is it?"

Jason went on to explain the situation with the picnic and the crowd of visitors that would be at the farm in two weeks. Petros listened intently as Jason concluded, "I don't want you to leave, but we have to figure something out."

Petros nodded thoughtfully. "I could always begin my quest for others of my kind when the visitors arrive, so that would address the issue of my presence on the farm. But it only underscores the bigger problem we need to solve."

Jason asked, "Which is?"

"We cannot hide in barns or caves for the rest of our existence. We need to get out into society, which means if the humans of two thousand eleven will truly have a difficult time accepting us then we need to find a better way to disguise my kind." The dragon set his jaw as he thought. "If only we had a mage."

Jason tilted his head. "A what?"

"A mage—sorcerer, magic user, wise man, magi, warlock. Do you not read the fantasy novels of your time?"

Jason sighed. "I know what a mage is. I just don't think they exist anymore."

Petros countered, "Little Knight, users of magic existed hundreds even thousands of years before my time. Ancient Egypt, Persia, Babylon all had weavers of magic of some fashion. Why would you think they would cease to exist just because the era of the dragons has passed?"

Jason was stumped. "Well, umm, because no one hears of them anymore."

"Impeccable logic, Little Knight. In this age of extreme skepticism, any mages worth their weight would be in disguise, in hiding. They would still practice their arts but in secret. The problem is how to find one."

Jason held up an index finger and then ran to his laptop. He unplugged the projector and sat cross-legged on the barn floor. Setting the laptop on his legs, he started typing while he spoke. "So, tell me, what would a mage be like? What would their interests be, no matter what century they live in?"

Petros rubbed his claw over his jaw in thought as he responded, "Mages are studiers, avid readers. They are interested in history, always trying to learn secrets of the past. Since various baubles and items are often crucial to their spell making, they are always obtaining ingredients, charms, talismans, or whatever word you wish to use. Mages are very intelligent but prefer keeping to themselves; they are introverts. But somehow they manage to maintain a living as well. They cannot support their studies without money to purchase what they need, but they will also resort to bartering. Sometimes, mages have followers—not apprentices, per se; there has to be some innate talent in one who can wield magic. But they would be…what is the word I have seen on the Internet? Oh, yes, they would have 'fans.'"

Jason typed madly as Petros spoke. When the dragon finished his description, Jason lifted his head. His eyes were wide with amazement.

"I…I think I found something!"

Chapter 7

Jason's eyes were transfixed on the computer monitor as Petros looked confused.

"How did you find something?" the dragon asked.

Jason rested his chin in one hand as he studied the computer. "So I went onto Facebook, which is a social networking site, and started searching the different groups."

Petros said, "I have not gotten to 'social networking' in my studies yet."

Jason nodded. "It's a way for people to connect over the Internet. Basically, you create a mini webpage for yourself on this bigger website. You can connect your page with the pages of friends or people with similar interests. But you can also join groups. So if there are a lot of people who like dragons, you can join a group of other dragon lovers and talk about dragons and what you like about dragons."

"That sounds like a very beneficial group to belong to." Petros said, one side of his mouth turned up in a smile.

Jason deadpanned, "Yeah, I'll get right on that. Anyway, I started plugging in and comparing various groups on Facebook: book groups, collectors, online auctions and traders, small business owners, introverts. After some cross referencing, I actually have a list of names of people who are interested in all the different things you described to me."

Petros paused. "Are you saying there are mages on Facebook?"

Jason answered, "Well, it kinda makes sense. If they are part of modern society then the Internet is a fantastic way of studying, bartering, finding fans, all that stuff. It would be of great use to them. I even plugged in groups of people interested in magic and got quite a few results. I have a list of profiles here that may be actual magic users. I'm kind of in disbelief myself."

Petros asked, "Where would we find one of these people?"

"Here's the kicker: there's a name that comes up in Billings."

"How far is Billings?"

Jason thought for a moment. "It's about a four-hour drive."

Petros nodded. "How long of a flight would it be?"

Jason looked up at Petros. "What're you proposing?"

"I am proposing that I fly you to this Billings, and you go to this potential mage. You confront this person; what is his name?"

Jason looked at the computer screen. "Umm, Norman."

Petros paused. "Norman the Mage?"

Jason shrugged. "I just read it; I didn't make it up."

"Very well. You go confront Norman the Mage to find out if he can help us."

Jason looked concerned. "But what if he isn't a mage?"

"What?" asked the dragon.

Jason went on. "I can't very well just walk into his shop or whatever and say, 'Hey, you…you're a mage, right? Me and my dragon need your help.'"

"My dragon and I," Petros said.

"What?"

Petros corrected, "The proper grammar would be 'my dragon and I.'"

Jason glared at Petros. "My point is I can't just go in there and confront him. You dragons are smart and all, but subtlety seems to be in short supply."

Petros waved a dismissive claw. "Subtlety is a waste of time. Say what you have to say and be over with it."

Jason countered, "But what if what you have to say is flat-out wrong."

Petros answered, "Then don't be wrong."

He rolled his eyes. "Whatever. Look, we need a plan. Whether he is a mage or not, I can't just march in there and say, 'There's this dragon I know that could use a hand.' If he's not a mage, he'll think I'm nuts, and if he is a mage, what reason would he have to believe me?"

Petros acknowledged, "True. What is your suggestion?"

Jason thought. "Is there something I could give him or show him that he would recognize as coming from an actual dragon?"

"Dragon scales were coveted items in my time. For spell ingredients to armor pieces, humans were always trying to get their hands on our scales. We could show him one of my scales; if Norman is a true mage, he will know what it is almost immediately."

Jason nodded. "Okay, that might work. Now I need to figure out how do get to Billings."

Petros said matter-of-factly, "I will fly you there, of course."

Jason explained, "Yeah, but I gotta get dad to let me go. I can't just disappear for a day without him knowing. I suppose I could wait until he goes out of town again, but I never know when that'll be. It would be risky gambling on that."

"Do we have a choice?" Petros asked.

"Not really," Jason admitted. "And the challenge will be for me to get back."

Petros was surprised by the statement. He said, "I will fly you back."

Jason interrupted, "Look, you'll be four hours out of Malta already. It would be great time to start on your quest for more dragons. I could probably take a bus back, but I'll have to scrounge the money for a bus ticket. I can take it out of my savings; it shouldn't be too bad."

Petros looked dubious. "I am uncomfortable with that plan."

Jason replied, "I think it's the best we've got. But that brings up a lot more questions; for starters, what do we do if Norman really is a mage and recognizes your scale? And what do you do if you find more dragons?"

Petros said, "You simply tell the mage that we need his help in disguising the dragon you know. He should be thrilled to even be involved in aiding one of my kind. As for the other plan, I was going to return here with my kin."

Jason's eyes widened. "Where are we going to hide more dragons?"

"I do not know," Petros said resignedly.

Jason started to speak, but he turned his head toward the faint sound of a vehicle coming up the highway. "That's Dad. I recognize the sound of the hole in his muffler. I have to run inside, but I'll come back out when I can. You're going to need to lie low and keep the projector off; Dad may see."

Petros acknowledged, "Understood. Now go."

Jason sprinted inside, flew up the stairs to his room, kicked off his sneakers, and, with a leap, landed on his bed. He whipped the sheet half over his body and lay as still as he could. He could hear the door to his dad's truck shut, and, within a minute, the front door opened. Jason strained his ears to hear his dad shuffling around downstairs then the stairs started to creak as he tried to quietly ascend them. Jason heard a faint knock on his door.

He tried to sound sleepy. "Come on in."

The door opened slowly. "You okay, son? Julia said you were sick."

"Mmm," Jason replied. "Just tired. I didn't sleep well while you were gone."

Dad entered the room, sat on the edge of Jason's bed, and said, "I'm sorry, Jason. Really."

He nodded. "I know, I know. But you gotta know it just gets lonely here, especially at night."

Timothy shook his head. "Son, you know they add fifteen percent to my salary if I am willing to travel."

"Dad, I know. Really, I understand," Jason said. "It still doesn't make it any less lonely."

His dad replied, "No, I get it. That's why I'm sorry."

Jason detected a tone in that last statement. "Sorry for what, Dad?"

Timothy took a deep breath. "That I have to leave again in two days."

Jason let his frustration show. "Oh, come on! Do they ever let you stay in town?"

His dad held up his hands. "It's a three-day trip to Bozeman. I have to meet with the board and then the picnic planning committee. After the picnic, I think I will be home for a couple of weeks. I'll get a break soon. I promise."

Jason flopped down in his bed and rolled over with his back to his dad. "Yeah, yeah, yeah." He didn't say anything more. His father sat on the bed for a few more moments in silence then got up and left the room. The trip to Bozeman solved the problem of Jason and Petros going to Billings, but he secretly felt a pang in his heart, a hope that his dad would have stayed home and their plan would have been foiled. He was tired of all the traveling, the nights at home alone, fending off Stan on his own. It was getting very, very old. As he lay in his bed, lost in thought, he wiped a tear from the corner of his eye.

***

Jason came downstairs close to dinnertime. As he got to the bottom of the stairs, he saw his dad working on his laptop at the kitchen table.

"Feeling better?"

Jason rubbed his hair. "Yeah, sleep helped." He paused. "Sorry I got upset."

"You're entitled," Dad replied. "I'm not the fifteen-year-old being left alone for days at a time." Jason heard a surprising sincerity in his dad's voice.

Jason said, "Dad, look, sorry I lost it. I just get frustrated, you know?"

His father nodded in agreement as he was drawn back into the work on his laptop. Jason waited a few moments until he knew his dad was completely distracted before he surreptitiously made for the barn. Opening the door as little as possible, he slid in the opening to find a sleeping Petros.

"Hey, Petros," he hissed. The dragon's eyes snapped open, and they focused on Jason. He didn't lift his head as he spoke.

"Are you alone?"

Jason thought the question was silly. "Of course I'm alone. I wouldn't lead my dad in here."

Petros sat up. "After the George incident, I wasn't too sure."

"I'll always ask you first, all right?"

"Very well." Petros nodded. "Any new news?"

"Yeah, Dad's heading out of town again in two days. We can start making plans." Jason's face was downcast as he made the announcement.

Petros regarded him curiously. "You look troubled."

Jason whipped around to face the dragon. "Troubled? You bet I'm troubled! My dad spends more time on the road with his job than he does here with me. I gotta make my own meals, get myself to work or school, deal with bullies by myself, all the things a dad should be helping his kid with. But, nooo, not the Hewes family. No, in the Hewes family, fifteen-year-olds have to raise themselves!" He flopped down in the hay and buried his face in the palms of his hands.

Petros sighed deeply. He walked over to Jason and sat on his massive haunches. He curled his tail around Jason's form with the tip resting against the teen's criss-crossed legs. He paused a few moments before he spoke.

"Jason, I do not know the full history of your family, but you have lost your mother and an older brother, and those are tremendous losses. Your father and you are left in a very adverse circumstance, and although it seems to have been some time since the tragedy, circumstances such as this take a very long time to resolve. I would surmise your father is doing the best he knows how to do, as are you. And for the moment, it is acceptable—not ideal, not optimal but acceptable. And sometimes that is all you can do."

Through his covered face, Jason sobbed, "Yeah, well, the 'best' pretty much stinks."

Petros drew Jason a little closer with his tail. "True, but I have lived a long time, Little Knight. The years have taught me that sometimes situations change given time. Give yourself and your father time; the situation will change, most likely for the better."

Jason lifted his head. His cheeks were moist with tears, and his eyes were red and puffy. "You really believe that, don't you?" The dragon nodded, a sympathetic smile on his face. Jason stood up and wiped his face dry with his sleeve as he went on. "Well, at least we have the chance to get into Billings now."

Petros said, "Yes, I've been giving the situation some thought. Hypothetically, I find more of my kin, and we decide to stay united. Whether it is here or some other remote location, I highly doubt there is any place that can secretly house multiple dragons for any length of time."

Jason was uncertain as to where Petros was going. "Ooookay?"

The dragon went on. "What if we were able to match dragons with humans as you and I inadvertently have? It would be easier to remain hidden if we were spread out, and it would provide an envoy or advocate of sorts to teach the dragon about this new world, just like you have done for me."

"You mean you want to pair dragons with teenagers?"

Petros was insulted. "Well, when you say it that way, it sounds preposterous."

Jason tried covering. "No, I don't mean it like that. I'm just saying that finding someone who is accepting and accommodating like I've been to you isn't easy. You could easily end up with someone who will react like George did."

Petros countered, "Yes, but George adjusted quickly. And I seem to recall you were not the model of a level head when we first met; you armed yourself with kitchen utensils. I believe you attempted to hold me at bay with a carrot peeler."

Jason chuckled. "Okay, point taken. What are you suggesting?"

Petros said, "There is a large gathering of people and their children coming to your farm in several days, is there not? Perhaps there will be candidates within the crowd."

"Whoa," Jason reacted. "I hadn't thought of that. I guess it would be good to have us all from the same area; it would make communication easier. But how do I pick people? I can't just go up to a random teenager and ask, 'Hey, do you like pets? I've got a cute little dragon that's looking for someone to love him.'"

Petros shook his head. "Do your ridiculous examples have no bounds?"

Jason smiled. "Isn't it great? They just come to me! It's a gift; I have to share it."

Petros ignored him. "I need to think about a selection process, but aside from that detail, what do you think?"

The teen replied, "Hey, I'm having a hard time managing just one dragon. Any help I can get would be great."

For the next two days and in secret, Jason and Petros planned their trip to Billings and Petros's subsequent quest. Jason snuck out to the barn as much as he could when his dad was distracted or involved in his work, and Petros spent quite some time exploring the geography and topography of the western United States, trying to target areas where he would be most likely to find a dragon.

In the meantime, Jason had been rifling through the tack room, finding an old saddle and trying to jury-rig it to fit the huge dragon. He devised an elaborate system of bungee cords to accomplish the task, but after Petros suggested that Jason find a way to secure himself to the saddle, Jason dejectedly had to go back to the drawing board.

The two had decided the trip would take place very early in the morning the day after Jason's dad left for his trip. They had considered flying down the night Timothy left, but an overnight stay was not feasible. But Jason figured he could go and be back the same day without anyone really taking notice. He had the day off from work, so he was actually free for an entire twenty-four hours.

The morning of the flight came. Jason's dad had departed the previous evening, and Jason was disgusted when the alarm went off at 3:30 a.m. He more or less fell out of bed and crawled to the shower. Jason didn't remember turning on the water, but he knew he had cleaned himself when he detected the dampness of his hair while he filled his thirty-two-ounce travel mug full of

Mountain Dew. The adrenaline started to pump through his body as he marched out to the barn, caffeinated beverage in hand and backpack slung over his shoulder. He was very excited at the thought of flying on the back of a dragon over the Montana countryside. He still couldn't believe everything that had happened to him over the past several days: a highly intelligent, immensely powerful, and slightly sarcastic dragon was taking up residence with him, and they were now about to embark on their first actual quest. All he needed was a suit of armor and a British accent, and his life could be a fantasy movie.

He reached out, pulled open the door of the barn, and said quite proudly, "Let's do this!"

Chapter 8

Typically, the last thing Jason expected to see when he opened the doors to the barn on the old farmstead was a living, breathing dragon having taken up residence. After the last several days, this was a normal sight for Jason upon entering the dilapidated storage building. On the morning he and Petros were to leave for Billings under the cover of dark, predawn skies, Jason saw something else completely unexpected when he opened the barn.

Petros was wide awake, lying on the dusty floor, and the stray cat that often frequented the barn was completed splayed over Petros's snout, rubbing its face over the dragon and purring so loudly that Jason could hear it as he entered. Jason knew this cat; it was ill-tempered, tortured the prey it caught, and didn't like any human being that it encountered. He couldn't believe what he saw.

"What is going on here?" he asked, bewildered.

Petros answered, "I am refining my detection system for finding companions for my dragon kin." The cat was now rubbing itself on the large plates sweeping behind the dragon's head.

Jason noticed he hadn't let go of the barn door. "I'm sorry. I must have opened the door to someone else's life."

Petros looked reproachfully at the teen. "Stand still and watch." He closed his eyes, and the cat suddenly turned its head to Jason. It tilted its head a few times, and then with a pleasant-sounding trill, it leaped off Petros and padded across the barn floor to Jason. It looked at the shocked boy for another moment and proceeded to rub itself against his legs, twisting between them and trying to get itself as close to Jason as possible.

Jason stood stiffly. "Is...is it going to consume my soul?"

Petros huffed. "Do not be ridiculous. I have told you about our empathic relationships with felines, correct? Well, cats are often excellent judges of character. I have communicated my feelings about you to this cat, so now this cat knows what to sense in humans it can trust. When all of the people from the museum get here in several days, the cat will be friendly to only those that it feels are similar in temperament to you. These select few will be our ambassadors."

Jason blinked. "So let me get this straight; you are leaving the future of human-dragon relations and the ultimate integration of dragons into modern society to a cat?"

Petros answered, "You say that as if it were outrageous."

Jason shouted, "It is outrageous!"

Petros countered, "Do not be so narrow-minded. What is your idea then, Little Knight?"

Jason stammered, "I…we need…you can't—"

Petros was staring across the barn at Jason, his eye ridges raised and waiting for an answer. Jason finally said, "Yeah, I've got nothing. Fine, we'll let the stray kitty decide who gets to be friends with all of the other dragons."

Petros smiled. "I would surmise you never thought that would be a sentence you would say in your lifetime."

Jason laughed. "You have no idea. Now, can we get on with this?"

Jason retrieved the saddle from the tack room and slung it over the base of Petros's neck. He used the bungee cords to secure the makeshift seat to the dragon, looping them around the base of the neck as well as behind the front legs and then back to the saddle. After a few minutes of fiddling with the cords, Jason swallowed hard and proclaimed, "I think I'm ready."

Petros answered, "Then let us proceed."

The dragon pushed the barn doors open with his snout and carefully stuck his head into the predawn air. The sky was still dark, and not a thing could be seen anywhere around the farm. Petros walked into the open field; Jason could feel the alternating motion of the shoulder blades beneath the dragon's hide as he strode majestically into the field. In the short walk to the old corn field, he marveled at the thought of the Montana computer geek about to take flight on a real-life dragon. His "How I Spent My Summer Vacation" essay this year was going to be a doozy.

Petros stopped silently. Jason could feel the dragon's great lungs expand as he took in the fresh air, reveling at being out of the barn and ready to fly again. The great wings unfolded. Their length was astounding, stretching nearly thirty feet in each direction. Jason felt his heart racing as the wings reached up to the starry sky. Petros crouched; his muscles tightened. Then, all at once, with a great jump and a powerful beat of his wings, they were airborne. Jason's breath was taken away as the wings beat a second time, then a third, then a fourth. After five wing beats, they were well into the sky; Jason's house, barn, and two fields were far below and behind them. Tears were flowing from Jason's eyes, both from the rush of wind and from the sheer exhilaration of flying. All Jason could manage was, "W..wha…WAHOOOOOOOOO!"

Petros put some more distance behind them before he fully extended his wings, rode the wind for a few moments then gracefully banked to the south and began the flight to Billings.

After a few minutes, Jason sat up in his saddle and stretched his arms out to either side of him, feeling the wind flow over his body. He closed his eyes and simply let his body experience the feel of flight without the "noise" of his sight. A combination of elation and serenity washed over him; he couldn't explain it, but he was both peaceful and excited at the same time. Petros glanced back at the teen and saw him relishing the experience of the flight. The dragon felt immense satisfaction at lifting the boy's spirits.

After ten minutes, Jason finally settled in to the flight and raised his voice above the wind to Petros. "I couldn't help but notice…you've told me there are Earth Dragons, Air Dragons, and Fire Dragons. Are there Water Dragons?"

Petros answered, "Yes, yes, there are. What led you to that conclusion?"

Jason smiled. "It makes sense; those are the four elements of the ancient world." He noticed some clouds gathering. "It's what everyone from your time thought were the basic building blocks of the world."

Petros noticed the gathering clouds as well. A faint rumble of thunder sounded in the distance as he said, "Yes, I saw your periodic table of elements on the Internet. It is very complicated; I am not sure how we would have named ourselves if we had to choose from that."

"Earth, air, fire, and water are much simpler. I can't remember the periodic table to save my life," Jason said. A clap of thunder was followed by a flash of lightning, and he felt his stomach sink. "Petros, did you—"

The dragon interrupted. "Yes, I saw it." Jason realized his friend was no longer smiling, and then the sound came again. It was the same horrible and unidentifiable sound he'd heard the night he and Petros first met.

"Petros!" Jason shouted.

He yelled back, "It is a dragon call; the Storm dragon has returned!" Petros began to look in all directions around them, and Jason joined his friend in trying to locate the second creature. Over his left shoulder, Jason saw an ominous black shape zooming in and out of the clouds.

"There!" he screamed, pointing in the direction of the silhouette. Just then a lightning bolt arced from the direction of the Storm dragon and barely missed Petros, sizzling through the air just beneath them.

Petros shouted, "It is trying to keep us in the air, where we are an easy target. We need to be on the ground now! Hang on!"

Jason lay as flat as he could against Petros, grasping desperately at one of the spines protruding from Petros's neck. The dragon rolled to his right, pointed his head toward the earth, folded his wings against his body, and began a power dive straight down. The G-forces from the dive kept Jason pinned to the dragon's hide, nearly crushing him. He tried to scream, but he couldn't get enough air in his lungs to do so. The hair on the back of his neck stood on end as two more lightning bolts lanced by them, but Petros weaved back and forth, dodging the attacks from the Storm dragon. Jason felt as if the dive would never end. Then all at once Petros's wings snapped open, caught the air and pulled them out of their descent. They thumped onto the Montana countryside as Petros looked desperately to draw a bead on their opponent. There was another flash of lightning, and then both saw the massive shape of the Storm dragon in the air turning ominously toward them.

Petros shouted, "Hold fast, Little Knight!" as he turned to face the Storm dragon. Jason watched as Petros sunk his claws into the earth, and eerie veins of white light began to flow up his legs, following the path of the blood vessels hidden beneath the tough scales. Petros's wings stretched out behind him as the veins of light wound their way through his chest, over his shoulders, and into the very membranes of his wings. His chest expanded as he drew himself up to his full height, his muscles rippling beneath his skin. The Storm dragon was nearly upon them when Petros threw his wings forward like a protective shield in front of his body, the veins of light now completely interwoven through the wings.

Another lightning bolt shot from the storm dragon and impacted Petros's wings. The electricity lit up the area and deflected off of the wings into a myriad of tiny bolts that struck the earth and scorched the soil everywhere they touched. The dragon kept pouring the energy down at them while Petros held fast, his wings somehow rejecting the power and keeping them safe. All at once, the electricity stopped, and Petros threw his wings back to see the Storm dragon almost on top of them. The light faded from his body, but his chest was still expanded as he pointed his neck and unleashed a powerful jet of glowing orange cubes from his mouth. The breath weapon connected with the Storm dragon's wing, paralyzing it and making the dragon career out of control. As it passed them, Petros spun with surprising deftness on his forelegs and angled the front of his body downward, swinging his tail into the air and battering their passing foe. The dragon was knocked out of the sky and crashed to the earth, rolling over and over several times before it righted itself. It was some distance away, but Jason and Petros could still see its silhouette against the night sky; it was facing them defiantly.

Petros shouted, "Cousin! Why do you attack us?"

A voice came back over the wind. It was loud but with a breathy quality that made it sound like it was one with the very air: "Thou dost threaten to expose our kind! The humans are a danger to us; they will verily be our undoing."

Jason lamented, "Oooooh, no; he's talking in old English. That can't be good."

Petros ignored Jason and responded to the Storm dragon, "They are paranoid and suspicious, but they can be good. They can be allies. We cannot survive in this time without them!"

"Alas," the Storm dragon countered, "thou hast been corrupted already!"

Petros pleaded, "No, cousin, no! I am going to find more of our kin. Let me bring them back; I will show you how dragons and humans can live in peace, how we can benefit each other."

There was a pause that was uncomfortably long for Jason. The voice came back, "I grant thee a boon at this time, cousin, but be thou warned; shouldst thou expose us to any further danger, I will not stay my hand at our next encounter."

Jason guessed the dragon had regained feeling in its wing, for the creature took back to the skies. As it flew in front of the moon, Jason saw for just a moment an odd shape on the dragon's back, as if it, too, had a rider. He started to say, "Petros, did you see—"

Petros interrupted, "We need to get back on course." The dragon was visibly shaken and weary. It took him several flaps of his wings to get airborne again, and he didn't feel as steady as he did when they first took off from Malta. For the next two and a half hours, they flew in silence; Petros was obviously shaken by the encounter, and Jason did not want to distract him from focusing on the flight.

Eventually, Jason saw the glow of the city lights ahead and looked for a suitable place to land. The sun was rising, and it was a perfect time to get out of the skies and maintain their cover. Jason and Petros had studied Billings before their trip and knew that six different mountain ranges could be viewed from Billings, and to the north of the city a ridge of long cliffs called the Rimrocks, or the Rims, ran right into the northern neighborhoods. The Rims could climb as high as five hundred feet, and although it would be quite the climb down to the city, Jason felt this was the best place to land. He gave Petros a few hard slaps on his scales and pointed to an area in the Rims. Petros nodded and descended to the high shelf, landing less steadily than their earlier landing.

Jason clambered off the saddle and landed a little unceremoniously on the dusty earth. Petros was hanging his head and breathing heavily. Jason wasted no time in asking, "What happened back there?"

Petros regarded the teenager. "It wasn't the flight or the battle itself; what I did to protect us from the lightning was taxing."

"The thing you did with the glowing veins and all?"

Petros nodded. "Have you noticed both times the Storm dragon has been active that an actual storm surrounds it?" Jason nodded, and Petros continued. "We all have a connection to the element we are named after: fire, earth, air, or water. We can draw on the power of the elements, either directly or indirectly. For example, when the Storm dragon feels aggression, the atmosphere itself is stirred, and the weather is affected. That is an indirect influence. What I did was a direct channeling of the element I am tied to. It can produce a very powerful result, but my strength is all but depleted afterward."

Jason asked, "What did you do exactly?"

"I drew on earth itself to exponentially harden my skin, protecting us from the lightning. It worked, but I will not be able to do that again for quite some time."

Jason didn't understand. "Yeah, but the other dragon…he was channeling the storm and all and throwing lightning bolts right and left."

Petros shook his head. "No, Little Knight. That was its breath weapon."

Jason's eyes widened. "The thing breathes lightning bolts?"

Petros nodded solemnly. "That is just one reason they are so dangerous."

Jason was speechless. Petros reached around toward the tip of his tail and pinched a small scale between two of his claws. With a sharp pull and a slight wince of pain, he pulled the scale free and handed it to Jason. In the boy's hand, the scale was two inches in diameter and was as hard as a piece of granite. The side that had been connected to Petros's tail, however, was softer—not quite as soft as human skin, more like the texture of a callous. Jason shoved it into his pocket.

Petros said, "Now go find this Norman. Follow the plan and get back to Malta tonight. I will rendezvous back there with you in several days."

Jason nodded and looked at his weary friend. "Are you going to be okay?"

Petros smiled a weary smile. "Nothing a little rest will not fix. I will find a secluded area here in these hills and Drake sleep during the daylight hours. I will be fine by this evening."

Jason was anxious about leaving Petros. "I…look, don't—"

Petros interrupted, "Follow the plan. Do not take any unnecessary chances. If something goes wrong, head for the most populated area and get lost in the crowd. Find your way home from there, understand?"

Jason nodded. Petros took several steps backward. After several laborious flaps of his wings, he began to achieve lift. Jason shielded his eyes from all of the dust the dragon kicked up, but he was able to watch Petros take a low and erratic flight path into the Rims and disappear over a hilltop. He was worried; Petros seemed so weak, and now he was venturing out into the world on his own. Several deep, cleansing breaths later, Jason turned toward Billings and began a careful climb down from the Rims toward the city below.

Chapter 9

"Yeah, it was tough, but I got down okay with only a few scrapes. What? No, George, look, I'm gonna be okay. I just gotta find this guy and…huh? No, I don't know what I'm gonna do if he recognizes it."

Jason let the bathroom door of the McDonald's on Grand Avenue shut behind him as he sat down at a table. He held his cell phone awkwardly between his shoulder and his ear as he wiped the extra water from his hands on his jeans. He realized he had forgotten to tell George anything about his quest for the mage called Norman, so he called and brought his friend up to speed.

"I know, I know, I should have told you ahead of time. George, we were so caught up in the plans… What? Well, to be honest, yeah, you do have a hard time keeping things to yourself. I didn't want anyone knowing I went to Billings for the day, especially Dad. Well, I know you wouldn't have told him directly, but you know how fast news travels in Malta. Look, George, this guy's shop opens soon, and I gotta figure out how to get there, okay? Yes…yes, Mother, I'll call you later. Bye."

Jason rolled his eyes as he ended the call and put the smart phone back in its holster. He booted up his laptop, connected to the wi-fi, and searched Google Maps for a place called Norm's Random Stuff. He found the entry on Billings's Chamber of Commerce website, complete with the address and description of the store:

Looking for that oddity for a unique gift? Can't find the collectible that no one else but you is collecting? Want to surprise someone with that thing they have always wanted but never knew they wanted it? Come to Norm's Random Stuff. We feature the most eclectic assortment of hobbies, crafts, collectibles, and even antiques. Take some time and browse our inventory—we guarantee you'll find something you want. And if you can't find it, our capable staff will search eBay tirelessly until they can find what you need.

"Hmm," Jason said to himself. "Sounds like my kinda place, even if I wasn't looking for a mage." Jason frowned when he saw the location of the store. It was in midtown, the most densely populated portion of Billings. Jason's family hadn't always lived in Malta. His dad had done most of his studies and field work in Colorado, near some much bigger, metropolitan areas. Jason was six when his dad was hired as the director of the Great Plains Dinosaur Museum and Field Station, so the family moved to Malta and settled down. Since then, despite his penchant for technology, Jason had become a small-town kid, and life in a big city was nothing he was comfortable with. Being on his own in Billings, even if only for a day, heightened his anxiety and made him quite uncomfortable, but he screwed up his courage and found the correct bus route to Norm's Random Stuff.

Jason was fairly proud of himself for not only finding a bus stop but actually paying attention to make sure he boarded the correct transport. The trip to the store was uneventful, and he kept the GPS on his phone displayed the whole time so he knew when to get off the bus. His stop came up, and he hopped off onto the sidewalk. A few doors down the street he saw a nondescript sign hanging from the side of a building reading "Norm's Random Stuff." It looked as if it were handpainted, but as he got closer, he realized it was designed that way. Norm apparently wanted an eclectic look to his store, and the sign lent itself to that exact look: one of purposeful disorganization.

The store itself occupied the first floor of a multistory building. It was an older structure, built from brick, that had seen the wear and tear of years. Some of the bricks were crumbling at the edges and had lost their original color to become a dull grayish red. The storefront consisted of a glass door with one large window to the right. An old plant hung in the window, its leaves a mix of bright green and pale yellow, showing it got just enough water to keep it alive but not thriving. A very old window treatment framed the poor plant, seemingly made of a heavy velour material with an elaborate and somewhat tacky flower pattern. Displayed in the window was an unusual collection of objects: a small crystal ball, a few books of poetry held up by kitten bookends, a scented candle, a stuffed and mounted prairie dog, and a digital clock shaped like Darth Vader. The "open" sign hung crookedly in the door, and Jason reluctantly pushed it open.

The opening door disturbed a small set of wind chimes hung over the frame, indicating a customer had arrived, and Jason was hit with the smell of some sort of incense. He wasn't sure, but it may have been a mix of jasmine and lavender. Norm's Random Stuff had to be one of the most unusual places of business Jason had ever seen. The walls were covered with a wood paneling, and the floor was mostly hidden beneath overlapping area rugs, all in Oriental patterns. At the top of the walls, old wooden shields were hung around the entire store, each painted differently with its own unique "crest." One was a black castle on a yellow field, another was a red bat-like wing surrounded by a circle with a line through it on a white field, and yet another was a yellow lion chasing a deer on a blue field. A chandelier made of moose antlers hung from the ceiling, providing illumination to the store, and in one corner two overstuffed leather chairs sat facing a small flat-panel television that was displaying cable news networks.

Norm seemed to have crammed as many shelves as he could into the area; the aisles were narrow and treacherous as objects too large for their shelves frequently stuck out. The items on the shelves seemed to be perfectly described by the store's name: random stuff. Jason saw that essential oils were neatly organized next to the baseball cards, and a little farther down the collections of Dutch poetry were carefully surrounded by the hard-to-find DC Direct action figures. On one wall, Jason saw broad swords and curved daggers arranged artfully next to framed scripture verses, and wall shelves holding scented candles had been mounted above sci-fi-themed USB thumb drives. The only things that stood out to Jason even more than the stuff that Norm sold were the number of shoppers. The place wasn't packed by any stretch of the imagination, but there was at least one person in every narrow aisle looking at something and examining the price.

It didn't take long for Jason to get absorbed in the multitude of objects displayed in the store. Norm was either the most disorganized shop owner in Billings, or he was a genius. Every time Jason saw an item on a shelf that disinterested him, he only needed to walk a few more steps before he found himself reaching for an item to both examine it and also to check the price. He didn't think that anyone would purposely arrange the shelves this way, but maybe this Norm had some unique marketing talent. Jason was so taken in by the inventory of Norm's Random Stuff that nearly an hour went by before he remembered why he was there. He began to scan the store for employees.

It only took him a few moments to locate the cash register and spy a man behind the counter talking to a couple of patrons, the first in a sport shirt and tie and the other in a tye-dye shirt and wearing Birkenstocks. Jason guessed the man behind the counter was in his midforties. He was thin, almost gaunt, and had shoulder-length brown hair, graying at the temples. He wore a faded, oversized denim shirt over a gray t-shirt and camouflage cargo pants. His face was unshaven, and his wire-rimmed glasses rested on the top of his head, nearly obscured by his hair. Jason assumed this was Norm, but he didn't look how Jason thought a mage should look. He wasn't exceptionally old, nor did he have very long fingernails, nor did he wear long robes; mages always wore robes. Jason eased up to the counter, which was above a glass display case. The case housed jar after jar of dried plants, flowers, and spices, many with names he didn't recognize. Jason eavesdropped a little.

"Look, man, I'm not sure I can find jewelry like that. At least not on eBay," the man who might be Norm said.

Shirt-and-tie man responded, "It would be just the perfect engagement ring. She is nuts for things from that era. Tell him, Dave."

Birkenstock Dave said, "My sister has loved that stuff since she was a kid. Isn't there another option?"

The man who might be Norm replied, "Look, I can keep searching, but you are approaching black-market type stuff here, man. I like to keep unusual stuff in my store, but I don't want any trouble. Some of my best customers are cops, and I want to keep them that way—customers, not law enforcement."

Shirt-and-tie man looked at Birkenstock Dave, who shrugged his shoulders in resignation. Shirt-and-tie said, "I understand. Look, you have my cell number if anything comes up."

The man who might be Norm answered, "Yeah, of course. Sorry I can't be more help, man." He watched the two leave the store and shook his head in frustration. The odd proprietor then noticed Jason and started talking to him. "Gotta run an honest business nowadays, you know."

Jason looked to either side of him and saw no one. "Me?" he said, wondering if the comment was directed at him.

"No one else around you, kid. You think I'm crazy or something, talking to nobody?"

Jason answered, "No, I'm just not used to strangers striking up conversations with me."

"Well, I'm Norm. There, not a stranger anymore," he said as he arranged some of the pamphlets on the counter. Jason smiled back, and Norm said, "Can't say I recognize you; ever been here before?"

Jason shook his head. "No, it's my first time. Just visiting from Malta for the day."

Norm looked curious. "Malta? Malta…Malta…Malta…" He was rifling through the papers as he repeated the word over and over. He produced a copy of the pamphlet about the Montana Dinosaur Trail. "Oh, yeah, you're one of those towns with the dinosaur places."

Jason nodded. "You got it."

Norm asked, "Do those places ever get rid of the bones from old fossils when they bring in new ones? I bet I could get a good price for real dinosaur bones."

"Ummm, no, I'm pretty sure they keep them in their collections."

Norm shrugged. "Pity, I could put those to good use." Norm went over to the electronic cash register and started keying in some information, but a look of consternation quickly came over his face. He started banging the keys harder and then slapped the side of the machine.

Norm lamented, "Bah! Electronic piece of garbage! I should go back to just using a cash box and written ledger. These things never work."

Jason walked over and looked at the back of the machine. "You have a frayed wire here. It's bent at too much of an angle, and the wire is finally breaking. Here; skooch it forward a few inches." He took the backpack off his shoulder, reached into one of the pockets, and produced a roll of electrical tape. Jason tore a piece off, straightened the wire, and gently rolled the piece around the old cable. "Okay, that'll only last you a few days. You have to replace the cable, but that should hold you until you get a new one."

Norm pulled his glasses down over his eyes and inspected the work. "Not bad, kid. It's not that I don't like electronics—just look at some of the stuff I've got around the store. I just hate it when they don't work."

Jason smiled. "I hear that." He paused for a few moments. "Hey, I was wondering if you could take a look at something for me. I found it the other day, and I can't figure out what it is." He reached into his pocket and pulled out the scale.

Norm answered, "Sure. Whaddaya got there, kid?"

Jason handed it to Norm, who moved the glasses to the end of his nose and examined the item. Norm's brows furrowed as he looked back at Jason and then back to the scale. He carefully felt the weight and then stared squeezing it with his fingers. When he got to the softer, callous-like part, his face became very serious.

"Everybody out! Store is closed!" he shouted as he came out from behind the counter and began to hurry people out the door. There were lots of protests, but Norm never gave a reason as he kicked his customers out. Jason began to panic at Norm's reaction, but Norm clearly wanted Jason alone and was prepared to risk his profits for the day to accomplish this. When all of the customers were gone, Norm locked the door, pulled a shade down over the store window, and spun on his heels to face Jason.

"Where did you get this?" he asked sternly.

Jason stammered, "I, uh, I told you, I…um…found it."

Norm shouted, "You're lying!"

Jason was startled but answered, "Look, I don't want any trouble."

Norm ignored Jason. "How did you find me?"

Jason stammered, "I...I don't..."

"How did you find me!" Norm bellowed. He was only a few inches from Jason now.

Jason was feeling the same palpitations in his chest that he got when Stan was bullying him. Jason remembered all of the things he had learned in school about confronting bullies, and, realizing this was no Stan, he decided to call Norm's bluff. "It's not like you're subtle or anything. You put yourself and all of your interests on Facebook and leave your profile open to the public. You may as well just paint on your sign what you really are." Jason was terrified at what Norm would say or do. If Norm was truly a mage, Jason's new life as a newt or a toad might be just about to begin.

Norm thought for a few seconds. "I told you I hate technology. Sure, my cousin says I should be on that Facebook but now look at where it got me!" He held the scale back up. "But you didn't answer my question, kid. Where...did...you...get...this?"

Jason decided to stick to his story. "I don't know what it is."

Norm became infuriated. "Liar! This is a dragon scale, and it is fresh! So you are either a time traveler who just arrived from the past, or you have been in the company of a dragon."

Jason threw up his hands. "You got me, okay? You got me." He sighed deeply. "I'm a time traveler from the twenty-eighth century. This backpack I wear is my time machine, and I jump from era to era finding mages and doing my best to get them to yell at me. The cat's out of the bag." Norm growled at Jason, and he held up his hands in defense, chuckling slightly. "Okay, okay, okay...yes, I got it from a dragon."

The anger on Norm's face changed to wonderment as he walked back behind his counter and pulled out a magnifying glass. He held it between his eye and the scale and began to examine it. "It's...amazing. It feels like rock, but the soft tissue gives it away as organic."

Jason nodded. "You should see what it was attached to."
Norm looked up at Jason. "Color?"
Jason answered, "Gray and brown."
"Flight-capable?"
Jason replied, "He's got nearly a sixty-foot wingspan."
Norm inhaled sharply and covered his mouth, his eyes
wide. He moved his hand from his lips. "Breath weapon?"
"Petrification."
Norm began to pace back and forth behind his counter,
almost giddy. "You know they all just mysteriously disappeared
about seven hundred years ago. You read about everyone wanting
to fight one, and then they are just gone. The record goes silent.
Oh, we used to be able to craft such amazing spells with dragon
scales, but we've been handicapped for seven centuries now." He
held up the scale. "Do you know what this means?"
Jason answered, "It means that you *are* a mage, and you
may be able to help us."
Norm regarded Jason very cautiously. "Okay, kiddo. You
got me. Yeah, I'm a mage. There aren't very many of us left in the
world. I'm part of a long line of practitioners of magic, and we
don't like people—especially teenagers—poking around in our
business. I have several spells I'm thinking of right now that could
remedy your knowledge of my situation, but since you have
someone I would like to meet, I think we can do some business.
Now, what sort of help do you need?"
Jason explained their situation to Norm, and he listened
attentively. Norm finally said, "I guess I'm not sure what you need.
You want this Petros to be able to interact in society today?"
Jason nodded. "Yeah, I don't know what that would look
like; that's why I need you. But I want to be able to go out into the
world with Petros, and potentially other dragons, and show them
how the twenty-first century works."
Norm began to pace back and forth behind the counter.
"I'm not sure; there are options—invisibility, shape changing,
mind melding—but it's gonna be tough. I can do magic on
humans, kid, but I have no idea how it will affect dragons. Magic
is part of their biology, part of their being. People have to learn to

use magic; for a dragon, it just flows in their veins. Makes for an entirely different situation when you are casting a spell *on* them. Why are you so eager to help them?"

Jason pondered the question. "I was terrified of him when I first saw him, like he was going to kill me on the spot. But then he spoke, and I listened, and we talked and stuff. He's noble, you know? He's so *not* human, but at the same time he has more humanity than a lot of people I know. I've never felt a connection to anyone like that, even my da... Look, I just feel like they need to survive, that they can make us better. We've made such a mess of this planet; maybe some real nobility could turn things around. I don't know...I'm not making any sense; I just know that I have to help him."

Norm didn't respond for a few seconds. "Well, look, kid, I don't get it, but if you are giving me a chance to meet a dragon, or even more than one, then I'm in."

Jason narrowed his eyes. "Yeah, okay, you know a real dragon scale when you see one, but I haven't actually seen you do any magic yet. How do I know you aren't—"

Norm interrupted, "A fraud?"

Jason said, "Well, yeah. That's it exactly."

Norm snapped his fingers, and the lights dimmed in the store. He began to wave his hands gently in front of his body, and a breeze began to blow in the building. It made Norm's hair wild, and all color in his eyes faded to an eerie white. Then, all at once, Norm thrust his hands into the air, and every shelf in the store burst into flame. Jason jumped and braced himself against the counter. He could feel the heat from the fire, but nothing was being consumed. Norm slowly swiveled his wrists back and forth, and, with the movements, the fire oscillated in color from orange through the entire color spectrum. Then with a thrust of his hands back down to his sides, the fire disappeared, the wind ceased, and the lights came back up. Norm's eyes returned to their normal state, and he combed his hair back with his fingers.

"Whoa" was all Jason could manage.

The air still faintly smelled of ozone as Norm said, "Does that put your doubts to rest?" Jason nodded rapidly as Norm went on. "So where do we go from here?"

Jason and Norm decided to exchange contact information and that Norm would do some research on using magic on dragons. Jason agreed to contact Norm after the Dinosaur Trail's picnic; hopefully by then he would have more teenagers and more dragons to get involved. Jason left the store and quickly yanked out his phone to call George and update him on the situation.

***

Norm stood on the other side of the closed door, leaning against it. The shades were still drawn. He stared at the floor, lost in thought; this turn of events was completely unexpected. He started to reluctantly walk to the back of the store where, next to the restroom, there was an old metal door labeled "office." He took out his keys and unlocked the door. Inside, the office was lit with a buzzing fluorescent light fixture. A metal desk was off center in the room, and it, along with two metal filing cabinets, was piled with papers. Norm plopped down in the chair behind the desk and took a business card out of the center drawer. He contemplated the number on the back of the card, his stomach uneasy from the knowledge of what would be set into motion if he called it. He opened the lower left drawer of the desk, a deep drawer with an old, heavy rotary phone in it. Norm sat the phone on the desk and, after a deep sigh, dialed the number on the card.

A voice answered on the other end. Norm said, "Yeah, I was told to call this number…"

***

Petros soared low to the ground and passed over the area known as Neah Bay in Washington State. It was the community nearest to Cape Flattery, the northwesternmost point of the United States. He flew over the formation in the rocky coastline known as the Hole-in-the-Wall and landed on the grassy plateau overlooking the Pacific Ocean. Just off the jagged coast was Tatoosh Island, a small bit of land surrounded by an equally jagged shoreline. In that shoreline was what appeared to be a cave. It looked perfect to Petros.

He examined the area for signs and was not disappointed. Bones from consumed prey were neatly stacked just outside the cave entrance, which had apparently been widened and scraped clear of any moss, barnacles, or anything else that would make the opening look sloppy. Petros flew to the flat top of the island and positioned himself over the cave entrance. He took a deep breath and let out a loud cry. Petros waited a few moments and then heard a deep voice come from within the cave: "Who dares to disturb me?"

Petros smiled.

Chapter 10

The bus ride back to Malta was uneventful. Jason was the only one on the bus as they approached the town borders, and the driver offered to take him right back to his home. Jason gratefully accepted the offer and was back to his house by 9:00 p.m.

He dumped his backpack inside and began to make for the barn when he realized he was alone. Petros was off finding other dragons, and Jason realized how quickly he had gotten used to the visitor in the barn. Amid his musings, he also realized how tired he was; he was up at three-thirty that morning. He made the decision to turn in early with the hope of being awake and alert for work

The next few days were, in Jason's mind, boring. Dad was gone, work was work, and there was no dragon to go home to and teach about life in the twenty-first century. Jason hung out at the Dairy Queen waiting for George's shifts to end, put in a little extra time at the museum, or did whatever he could to fill the hours. It wasn't until his dad came home that the pace of life picked up a little.

Timothy Hewes arrived at home from his latest work in the field with an exceptionally large to-do list to get ready for their visitors. When Jason saw the list, he realized how lackadaisical he and his dad had become about upkeep of the house and the farm in general. Cleaning, household repairs, lawn care, mulching, painting, and much more were the order every day for the next week and a half until the guests arrived.

"And just wait until the tents and the barbecue pit arrive!" Dad said excitedly.

"Tents? Barbecue pit?" Jason asked tentatively.

"Well, sure," Dad answered. "People need to sit under something while they eat. And how else could we cook fifty chickens?"

Jason was taken aback. "Who's cooking fifty chickens? Not me. I can make an omelet, and that's about it."

Dad smiled and reassured Jason there would be help for the day of the picnic, but it was up to the two of them to cross off the items on the to-do list. Dad handed Jason a bottle of Windex and some rubber gloves and told him to get to work on the windows while he went into town to pick up some gardening supplies. Jason let out a sigh of resignation and began to clean.

***

Petros and his new companion soared over the Cascade Mountains in Oregon. The weather was miserable; a heavy, steady rain spattered on their scales, and thunder often interrupted their conversation. The wind blew fiercely, but the two dragons were strong and held their own as they flew.

Petros asked, "Are you sure there is another of us so close to your cave? It would seem likely that we would be more spread out."

The other dragon answered, "I caught the scent a few days ago when I was surveying the countryside, but I did not want to risk being seen by the humans. As much as I wanted to locate him or her, I knew the prudent thing would be to come back another day."

Petros nodded. He remembered that Water Dragons were smarter, more cunning, and more sensible than any other dragons, and his new companion was no exception. She would prove to be a valuable resource.

Petros asked, "Does it always rain so much here?"

She replied, "I do not know, but between the mountains and the weather, this is an ideal habitat for an Air Dragon to take up residence. The weather and the terrain are ideal. Perhaps we should try calling out, as you did when you searched for me."

Petros said, "Agreed."

They banked gracefully in formation and circled to a landing on a nearby peak. The clouds floated by just above their heads as they surveyed the small mountain range. Petros nodded to his companion, and together they took in deep breaths and simultaneously let out long dragon calls. The sound bounced off the mountains and quickly faded into the rainstorm. They waited for several moments before Petros suggested, "Perhaps we should move on."

The female was looking over her shoulder as she was about to agree when she said, "There!"

Petros looked to see a large shape taking flight from a mountain in the distance. It rose up, paused in midflight, and then headed directly toward them. Petros smiled as he quickly came to the realization that this was no bird.

***

The old homestead began to look more presentable as the week wore on. George often found himself recruited by his best friend to help with the chores both in and around the Hewes home.

As they were mulching around the hedges on the side of the house, George asked, "Why am I helping you again?"

Jason looked around before he answered, "Because I'm your bestest friend in the whole wide world, and because I'm letting you hang out with a real dragon."

George frowned playfully. "'Bestest' isn't a word, genius, and I don't see any dragon around here. And since we're on the subject, why am I not in consideration for being one of these dragon ambassadors you are trying to recruit?"

Jason held up his hands. "Hey, it's not up to me. You gotta ask the cat." Jason was pointing to the stray cat that was over by the barn, licking one of its back legs.

George was thoroughly confused. "I…what?"

"If the cat likes you then you're in," Jason explained as he spread the brown mulch.

"You're kidding," George said flatly.

Jason shrugged. "I wish I were. This is Petros's plan, not mine. Go give it a shot."

George stood up and put his hands on his waist. "Jace, that cat hates everyone."

Jason hung his head, sighed deeply then stood up and walked over to the cat, saying, "Kitty, kitty, kitty" in a high voice. The cat stopped licking itself, looked at Jason for a moment then flopped on the ground and exposed its belly to Jason. He stooped down, rubbed the feline's stomach several times then walked back to George and continued mulching.

George was flabbergasted and couldn't find the words to respond. He tentatively began to walk over to the cat, saying, "Kitty...kitty...kitty," much more slowly and hesitantly. As it did with Jason, the cat stopped licking itself and looked at George. George continued to approach and bent down holding his hand out to the cat. Without warning, the cat hissed angrily and violently swiped its claws at George's outstretched hand. George shrieked and jerked his hand back, but not before the animal drew blood. George muttered under his breath as he walked back to Jason, who was doing everything he could to stay focused on the mulching and not burst out laughing. George scowled and thrust his hand out for Jason to see. As casually as he could, Jason looked down his nose at the bleeding claw marks and said, "Hmm. Guess no dragon for you, Georgie."

George huffed off and went inside to clean the wounds as Jason exploded into laughter.

***

It took several days for Petros and the two other dragons to reach the Mojave Desert. They had stopped at every stretch of terrain that seemed likely to attract a dragon. But their multiple searches came up empty. They knew the exploration of a desert region would be difficult; only Fire Dragons would be comfortable in this kind of punishing heat. But they had to try.

The Mojave Desert is the location of the hottest place on earth: Death Valley. Temperatures in Death Valley have been known to reach over 130 degrees, and it is the lowest elevation in North America, over 280 feet below sea level. The three dragons soared over the desolation, their wings stretched out widely as they rode the rising heat currents from the desert floor. While Petros and the Water Dragon maintained a straight, solid vector, the Air Dragon literally flew circles around them. It couldn't help itself; of all the dragon species, the Air Dragons were the most agile and most suited for flight. Their unique wing configuration allowed them to dominate all of the other species in aerobatics. Given the choice of flying or walking, even short distances, an Air Dragon always chose to fly.

Petros felt Death Valley itself was a dead end, so they began expanding their search outward in concentric circles looking for any sign of a dragon. The Water Dragon spotted something and signaled the other members of the trio to follow her. They descended and landed in a ghost town near the rim of Death Valley. It was abandoned many decades ago and devoid of life yet oddly preserved by the hot, dry desert air.

The three dragons set down in front of a stable/blacksmith shop. The large building drew the interest of the Water Dragon; all random debris and brush and been cleared from around it, despite the fact that all the other structures were cluttered with the detritus of the desert. Being naturally fastidious creatures, dragons always kept their lairs neat and tidy, and if a cave, abandoned castle, or forest glade had been carefully cleared and organized, it was always a sure sign that a dragon lived there.

The trio sat back on their haunches as they examined the building. The Water Dragon said, "The building is large enough. And it is most certainly hot enough."

Petros responded, "I agree. Shall we call out?"

The Air Dragon replied, "Allow me." It began to inhale deeply and expand its chest, readying to unleash its breath weapon instead of a dragon's roar.

"No!" Petros scolded. "Look how old that structure is; you will blow it off its foundation!" He let out a cry into the blowing wind and waited for a response. There was nothing at first, but the three began to feel the temperature around them rise. It grew hotter and hotter until the air was shimmering wildly as the temperature skyrocketed. Soon, they noticed the wood of the building beginning to smolder and smoke. Eventually, a section of a wall spontaneously burst into flame, and, within a few moments, the old smithy was a raging inferno. The three backed up from the intense heat, and it took only five minutes for the timbers to start collapsing and falling to the ground. Ultimately, the entire structure collapsed in a shower of sparks and smoke, and a massive form could be seen rising in the blazing ruins. Two enormous wings unfolded, and the trio knew they had just become a quartet.

The Air Dragon said, "Well, they certainly have a flair for the dramatic, don't they?"

***

Jason, George, and Mr. Hewes stood at the end of the driveway looking over the Hewes property. All of the shrubs were neatly trimmed, the lawn was mowed and "weed-whacked," and the house had been pressure washed. A large white tent had been erected in front of the barn, and next to the tent a barbecue was set up. A master griller and Dinosaur Trail employee from Chinook was at the barbecue, getting it up to temperature and seasoning the chickens. Mr. Hewes stood between George and Jason, an arm around each of the boys as they surveyed their handiwork. Jason felt odd; he and his dad had let the farmstead fall into disrepair after his mom and brother had died. But the last two weeks were a sort of catharsis for him; it felt as if they finally acknowledged it was time to clean up the mess their life had become after the tragedy and get living again. There were none of the flowering plants that his mother had been so fond of, nor were things in the house as quaintly decorated, but this was a definite start.

Jason said, "It looks…good, Dad."

Mr. Hewes replied, "The help you boys have provided has been invaluable. George, I can't thank you enough."

"Not a problem, Mr. H," George said.

Mr. Hewes reached into his pocket and pulled out a twenty-dollar bill. He placed it in George's hand and said, "It's not much, but you deserve something for your efforts."

Jason objected. "Hey! I would appreciate not much for my efforts too."

Mr. Hewes smiled. "The satisfaction of a job well done is your payment. And you can't attach a dollar value to that."

Jason frowned as George laughed. They surveyed their handiwork for several more moments. Susan and Julia were busy under the tent, setting up tables and warming trays to keep the food hot. Julia's remarkable horse was hitched up next to the barn, munching happily on the tall grass and pausing every so often to look around. A contingent from Havre was placing the folding chairs around the dining tables, setting up a volleyball net, and inflating a portable bounce house. The Dinosaur Trail had even paid for the rental of a sno-cone machine and cotton candy maker, which George and Jason had been trained to operate. Mr. Hewes gave them each one more pat on the shoulder as he left them and went to assist with the set-up.

Jason looked around. "Do you see the cat?"

George scowled. "No, thank goodness."

"I have a bad feeling about this," Jason said.

"Why?"

Jason answered, "The picnic hasn't even started yet, and I'm already bored silly. Why on earth would teenagers from all over Montana even want to come to a farm in the middle of nowhere and eat chicken with a bunch of archaeologists?"

As they stood at the end of the driveway, they noticed a line of cars coming from the west. The cars slowed as they reached the Hewes driveway marked by a dinosaur-shaped placard. It bore the logo of the Montana Dinosaur Trail, and a few helium balloons were attached to the top. They turned into the driveway and parked on the large area of lawn next to the house and in front of the tent. Two of the stops along the Dinosaur Trail had apparently caravanned to Malta, and they exited their cars and greeted Susan and Mr. Hewes with hearty smiles and handshakes.

Jason gave a deep sigh. "Well, here we go…it's showtime."

***

Four dragons flew in a diamond formation high in the sky: an Earth Dragon at the point, a Water and an Air Dragon on each flank, and a Fire Dragon bringing up the rear. Though they could not see it, far below they passed a large sign reading, "Welcome to Montana."

Chapter 11

"Enjoy your cotton candy."

Jason tried as hard as he could to smile as he handed over the sugary treat to a pair of eight-year-old girls. His hands were coated with bright blue strands of sticky confectionary, mostly due to how distracted he was looking for the cat. An hour had gone by since he started handing out the cotton candy, and he hadn't seen it at all.

He was surprised at the number of kids his age attending the picnic this year; probably at least a half dozen. Most of them kept to themselves, looking as reluctant as he was about having to be there. A tall African-American boy was throwing a football to some of the younger children, three others were huddled in corners texting away on their phones, and one girl, dressed in black, sat under a tree reading a book.

George was having a great time. His job at the Dairy Queen taught him the fine art of being "customer friendly." Whoever came to him for a sno-cone was greeted with a smile, pleasant conversation, and a cheerful "enjoy the picnic" as they walked away. His fingers were discolored from the syrup he used to flavor the shaved ice, but George didn't seem to mind in the least.

The two boys were back to back under the tent at their various stations. During a break in the crowd, George turned to Jason.

"See? It isn't bad. Kind of fun, ya know?"

Jason frowned. "Haven't had this much fun since my last trip to the dentist."

George gave a disapproving sigh as he saw Julia and Susan approaching them.

"How is it going, boys?" Susan asked. She saw Jason's hands all covered with cotton candy and said, "Well, well, Jason. Looks like you clean the museum almost as well as you make cotton candy."

Julia put her hands on her hips. "Susan, ease up. Can you make them any better?"

She replied, "I don't intend to find out; that's why we have these two doing the dirty work."

Jason's dad appeared from outside the tent. "How's everything going here, guys?"

Susan was suddenly all smiles. "They're doing a great job, Tim. A credit to the picnic team."

Jason made eye contact with Julia, and they both rolled their eyes at Susan's two-faced reply. Julia said, "Mr. Hewes, you think these guys could use a break?"

Mr. Hewes answered, "Of course. They should get a chance to enjoy the picnic too."

Julia said, "Would you like Susan and me to take over? I can make a mean sno-cone."

He replied, "That would be wonderful. I hope you don't mind, Susan."

Susan stammered, "I...oh, well, I...no, that would be great. Of course."

Mr. Hewes gave them a clap on the shoulder as he walked away. Jason and George couldn't get out from behind the tables fast enough as Susan looked disgustedly at the cotton candy machine. As they hurried away, Jason turned to Julia, and as dramatically as he could, he mouthed "thank you" to her. She winked at him as they ran into the house to wash their hands.

They consumed some barbecued chicken as Jason lamented, "What're we gonna do? We gotta find that cat."

George spoke with his mouth full. "And then what? You gonna start throwing it at random kids, hoping it'll point to a few and give you the paws-up sign?" George tried to make a "thumbs up" gesture without using his thumb.

Jason was about to say something mean to George when two little boys, no older than six, came to one of the women at another table in the tent. One of the boys was crying, "Mommy! The kitty scratched me!"

Jason's eyes lit up at the news that first blood had been drawn. He turned to the woman. "Ma'am, you can take him inside the house. There is a sink in the kitchen where he can wash up and band-aids in the cabinet to the right of the fridge." He looked to the boy. "Where did you see the mean kitty, buddy?"

The boy said through his tears, "It was with the girl reading under the tree."

Jason was curious. "What do you mean 'with' her?"

His bottom lip was still quivering. "It was lying on her lap, and she was pettin' it. We thought it was nice, but it is a mean kitty."

The mother thanked Jason as she hurried her son inside. He said, "Did you hear that? The cat scratched the kid, but it's sitting on the girls lap. Great news!"

George replied, "Yeah, I'm sure the little kid's heart is all a-twitter now that the cat has mangled him."

Jason looked sternly at George. "You know what I mean. C'mon, we need to meet that girl."

George put his hand on Jason's shoulder. "Wait, what if she's cute?"

Jason replied, "Huh?"

George clarified, "I don't want to meet a cute girl and sound all nervous or something."

"George, you're kidding me; we're having this conversation now?"

George countered, "Hey, I'm sixteen. I don't wanna go to the prom alone or anything. Mom keeps asking me when I'm gonna meet someone nice and—"

Jason interrupted. "George! Dude, you...are...killing...me! Can we talk about your social life when I'm not preoccupied with preserving the future of dragonkind?"

George nodded in agreement as they hurried out from the tent and began to search for the girl under the tree. They rounded the corner of the house and saw a figure reclining under a tree next to one of the fields. He nudged George in the arm with his elbow, and they began to stroll to her.

She was wearing all black; her combat-style boots came up over her calves and were tightly laced. Her denim pants and black t-shirt, emblazoned with several skull logos, clung to her thin frame. Her jet-black hair was parted to one side and fell down past her shoulders. She wore heavy black eyeliner and makeup that gave her skin a pale look and was reading paperback horror novel. She glanced quickly at the two boys as she saw them approaching but returned to her book.

Jason carefully phrased his greeting. "Umm, hi."

She waited a few uncomfortable moments before answering, "Hi." Her voice had a gravely quality to it.

Jason took a deep breath. "Look, sorry to bug you and all, but I'm looking for this cat that hangs out around here. It scratched this little kid, and we don't want it hurting anyone else."

Without looking up from her book, she asked, "What does it look like?"

Jason said, "Kind of scraggly, tiger pattern to its fur, usually hissing or trying to steal your mortal soul."

She didn't smile at his joke. "There was a cat like that here, except for the hissing part. Seemed perfectly friendly to me. He kinda deserved it, you know."

Jason asked, "Who deserved what?"

"The kid. He rubbed the cat's fur the wrong way and pulled at its whiskers. I wanted to scratch him too."

Jason smiled. "Unfortunately, that cat hates everyone. I'm Jason, by the way."

She still didn't make eye contact with them. "Well, it didn't hate me. I'm Tiffany Baumann."

Jason tried to be as casual as he could, but his heart was beating wildly in his chest. "Nice to meet you." He felt George nudge him and added, "This is George."

Tiffany actually looked up from her book. "He doesn't say much, does he?"

Jason answered, "Only when ordering a meal." This earned him a punch in the arm from George as Tiffany half smiled. Jason continued trying to break the ice. "Your parents drag you here?"

She nodded and asked, "You?"

"Worse," Jason answered. "I live here. This is my family's home and farm. Where are you from?"

She answered, "We live in Jordan. You ever been there?"

Jason shook his head. "Sorry, no."

Tiffany replied, "Don't apologize. You think Malta is small; you should see Jordan."

Jason nodded. "Got it. Sorry to hear that."

She continued reading her book as Jason looked to George for guidance. George held up his hands, and Jason frowned in frustration. Finally he said, "Hey, did you get anything to eat yet? The barbecue isn't bad."

Tiffany closed her book and smelled the air, inhaling the scent of the cooking meat. She acknowledged, "I supposed I should eat something. It'll make my parents happy." She stood up. "Lead on."

Jason tried to engage in small talk, but Tiffany only replied with one-word answers as they approached the food tent. Their attention was abruptly drawn to the direction where the tall boy was throwing a football with some of the younger children. One child was shrieking and running toward a group of adults, and the tall teenager started walking toward Jason, George, and Tiffany. He had something furry under his arm. The three altered their path to go and meet the boy. He was easily six feet tall and had very broad shoulders. His football jersey was of no team Jason recognized, but the guy was obviously athletic. His hair was closely cropped in a fade style cut, and, as he approached, Jason noticed that the fuzzy thing under his arm was the stray cat. It looked very content being where it was, which immediately drew Jason's attention.

The teen pointed to the cat under his arm and said, "This yours?" His voice was rich and deep.

Jason answered, "It lives here, but it's actually a stray. What happened?"

"The thing couldn't seem to get close enough to me, but when the kids wanted to pet it, it hissed at them and all that."

Jason nodded. "That's pretty much what it does. I'm Jason, Jason Hewes, by the way."

He smiled. "Marcus Wellton." He put the cat down, and it wound its way through his, Jason's and Tiffany's legs before it gave George a hiss and scampered off. Marcus was slightly taken aback as he said to George, "Cats not like you, man?"

"Just that one," George answered.

Tiffany said, "So, he does talk."

George blushed as Jason said, "We were just going to eat. Care to join us?"

Marcus nodded. "'M always hungry. Lead the way."

Despite the fact they had just eaten, Jason and George each took another helping of food and sat down at a table. Tiffany joined them with one chicken leg on a Styrofoam plate, a spoonful of potato salad, and a roll. In contrast, Marcus returned with two half chickens, a mound of macaroni salad, three rolls, a bowl of fruit, and a large cup of lemonade.

"Where you from, Marcus?" Jason asked.

"Bozeman," he replied through his food-filled mouth.

Jason was surprised. "Wow, that was quite the drive to get here then."

Marcus answered, "Mom's got an aunt that lives in Fort Peck. We don't see her often, so we decided to make a trip of it. Got family all over Montana, so when school's out, we do a lot of traveling."

Jason replied, "It's just the opposite for me; it's just me and my dad."

Tiffany was picking at her potato salad and added, "My foster parents both work for the Dinosaur Trail, so I have twice the dinosaur intensity at my house."

Marcus smiled. "I was all into dinosaurs when I was a kid—had all the toys, books, t-shirts, and stuff. When I finally saw *Jurassic Park*, it was the greatest thing ever."

Jason laughed. "Me too. I used to play like I was friends with dinosaurs, or they would respond to my commands and stuff."

Marcus laughed, agreeing with everything Jason said. Tiffany spoke up. "Can't believe I'm sitting here talking about dinosaurs."

Jason furrowed his brow. "What do you mean?"

She continued, "Never thought I would actually find people here to talk to, much less those my own age. It's not as bad as I thought it would be, and, believe me, I see the dark side in everything."

Jason asked, "But it's still a little bad?"

"It's a picnic with a bunch of museum people and archaeologists. We're all pretty much at the wrong end of the 'cool' spectrum, don't you think?"

They all paused for a moment and then burst out laughing, even the very stoic-looking Tiffany. An overhanging corner of the tent flipped back, and immediately Marcus and George, who were sitting facing that particular corner, diverted their attention to the person entering the tent. She wore a spaghetti-strap, flower-printed dress and flip-flops adorned with rhinestones. Her beautiful black hair was pulled back into a ponytail, which only enhanced her mocha brown skin and almond-shaped eyes. She wore makeup on her cheeks and eyelids but only in subtle amounts to accentuate her features. She was a lovely sixteen-year-old girl, and judging by how Marcus's and George's eyes were transfixed on her, they believed so as well.

Tiffany and Jason turned to see what the other two boys were staring at. As soon as Tiffany saw her, she turned back to her plate with a scowl on her face and mumbled, "Party's over; prom queen's here."

The girl spoke. "I heard laughing, and I needed to be with people exuding a positive aura."

Marcus answered, "We've got lots of positive aura; have a seat. What's your name?"

"Kinaari Landau," she answered. "Ugh, can this be any more boring?"

Tiffany mumbled, "I think it just got more boring."

Not hearing her, Kinaari went on. "I just can't listen to my dad talk about fossils anymore."

Jason nodded. "We can all relate, except George here. He's not involved with the trail; he's just eye candy."

Tiffany and Marcus laughed, while George gave an exasperated sigh. Jason went on. "I'm Jason; this is Marcus and Tiffany. Kinaari…that sounds Indian."

She nodded. "My mother is from New Delhi, and my father is from Duluth. They met in college and eventually settled in Glendive. So here I am."

Marcus smiled a wide smile. "And we're glad you're here."

George squeaked, "Yeah." He was mortified at how his voice cracked even during a one-syllable word. Tiffany rolled her eyes.

Kinaari asked, "So how are you all tolerating this dreary picnic at this rundown old farm?"

Jason spoke up, "Well, I'm tolerating it because I live here."

Kinaari asked, "In Malta?"

Jason countered, with anger in his voice, "No, at this rundown old farm."

Kinaari blushed and dropped her eyes. Tiffany smiled and said, "Awkwaaaaard."

Jason was about to give the attractive girl a piece of his mind when she shrieked and jumped off of the picnic bench. She squealed, "Something brushed past my leg!"

Tiffany said dryly, "Maybe it's your manners."

Before Kinaari could answer, they heard a feline trill, and the haggard cat appeared from under the picnic table and tried rubbing against the girl from Glendive. She nervously switched her balance back and forth on each leg as she said, "Ooooh, no, no, no…cat, no…I'm allergic to you, and I forgot my Claritin. Shoo! Shoo, kitty, shoo! Jason, can you help me, please?"

Jason sighed deeply and shook his head at the irony of the cat's choice. "It's not my cat; it's a stray. Wait, I know…George, go try to pet the cat."

George slumped his shoulders. "Jace…"

Kinaari batted her eyelashes at George. "Please, George? I don't want to break out in hives."

Tiffany murmured, "Yes, that would be a shame."

George got up from the table and went to pet the cat. As soon as the cat saw him, it hissed and bolted out of the tent.

Jason smiled and gestured toward George. "See? Instant cat repellant. Works with high school girls too."

George protested, "Hey!" as Marcus laughed and said to Jason, "You're funny, Hewes. You and George here known each other long?"

Jason answered, "We've been friends since elementary school. In fact, George is my best friend."

"*Was!*" George huffed.

Kinaari came to George's rescue. "Well thank you, George, you're very sweet." George blushed and looked down at his plate. Tiffany rolled her eyes again.

Marcus looked at Kinaari. "So, we were just talking about our parents and the Dinosaur Trail and how we loved dinosaurs when we were kids. How about you?"

She nodded. "Well, my father wanted me to be his archaeology sidekick, but my mother was much more into girly things. So she let me have dinosaur stuff, but only if it was sweet or looked cute or something like that."

Tiffany growled, "Because that's how dinosaurs really were."

Kinaari closed her eyes and folded her arms matter-of-factly. "It was a compromise. That is what good couples do."

Jason asked, "Ever wish you could see them or meet one?"

Kinaari looked genuinely baffled. "M...my parents?"

Jason couldn't believe her response. "Umm, no, dinosaurs."

Kinaari got a playful smile on her face as she leaned in to the group. "Well, my mother bought me a tea set when I was young and set it up in my room. And sometimes I would put my stuffed animals around the table, but I was really pretending they were dinosaurs. Like tea with a T-rex."

They all stared back at her, the absurdity of the story leaving them with confused looks on their faces. Jason finally said, "Let me ask you all this. What if aiiiiaaRRGGH!"

He looked down, and the cat was stretching its body on his leg, digging its front claws into his calf. Jason was about to kick the cat when it bolted out of the tent, turned to Jason, and gave him an intent look. He got up and went to the cat, who casually looked up to the sky. Jason looked and saw a few birds, but then much higher he saw four very unusual shapes flying in a diamond formation. They headed toward the forest glade where he and Petros walked over two weeks ago. The other four teens joined him and looked up toward the sky as Marcus asked, "What's the matter? Something wrong?"

Jason looked to George, who looked back at him. George quickly figured out what the cat was trying to tell him and was looking to his friend for their next move. Jason said, "Eh, this cat is always freaking me out. I wish it would move on to some other farm. You know how cats are; they give you that look like there's an axe murderer in the next room or just randomly charge off for no reason."

Tiffany replied as she bent down and picked up the cat, "That's why I like them."

Jason screwed up his courage. He had to make a plan or he would lose the opportunity. The dragons had returned, and the cat identified the teenagers. He had to get the two groups to meet but figure out how to explain it all to the teens at the same time. They needed to move, but he needed time to think. Finally he said, "This is getting stale. Anyone up for a walk in the woods?"

<u>Chapter 12</u>

Jason put a third sixteen-ounce bottle of spring water in George's hands while he took two more and headed for the door. The day was turning out to be hot and dry, and he'd offered to get everyone something to drink before they embarked on their mini-trek to the woods. However, his goodwill was just a ruse to stall while he came up with a strategy to introduce three teenagers to the dragons.

"Tell me you have a plan," George said nervously.

"Umm, yeah, I have a plan," Jason responded. "I plan to walk to the woods with you, Marcus, Tiffany, and Kinaaari."

"Aaaand?" George said, fishing for a better answer.

"And if we happen to run into anyone we know then that would be, umm, nice."

George stopped in his tracks as Jason took a few more steps. Jason asked with false curiosity, "What?"

"That's it?" George bellowed. "How do you know they aren't going to respond like I did or worse? And I still don't know how I got into the tack room!"

Jason growled back at George through his gritted teeth as they continued walking outside, "I don't know what I am going to do! I'm just gonna have to wing it and hope for the best. It's not like I've done this before, George, have you?" George sheepishly shook his head, and Jason went on. "Then cut me some slack and work with me."

They rounded the corner of the house as George couldn't help but lament, "How can I work with you when there is no plan?"

Jason tried to look composed but fumed, "I don't know. George, stop being so…Georgish, okay? We're gonna have to wing this, and I can't deal with three new friends, four dragons, and your free-floating anxiety at the same time. I need to you be responsible Dairy Queen Employee George and not Wigging Out at Harmless Snakes George."

George took a deep breath and nodded. "I can be that George."

"Good," Jason replied as they approached the three teens, "'cause it's showtime."

Marcus said, "Hey, thanks for the water, men."

"No problem," Jason answered. "Let me just check in with my dad, and we'll be on our way."

The five were soon strolling casually through the fields and headed for the treeline as the conversation continued on random topics. Soon, however, Marcus commented, "Hewes, I gotta tell you that I'm impressed."

"With what?" Jason asked.

"Kids our age seem to try to do everything they can to distance themselves from their parents, but your checking in with your dad and all before we walk off is, I don't know, pretty cool."

Tiffany jumped on the topic. "Yeah, I would have just walked off. My foster parents can figure it out for themselves."

Jason shrugged. "I don't know. Since my mom and my brother died, I feel like I just owe it to him to be a little more responsible. He'll say I'm taking their deaths worse than him, and I say he's taking it worse than me. I think the reality is we're both equally affected in different ways, and I want to try to make it easier, you know?"

Kinaari said, "Oh, Jason, I'm so sorry. I didn't know they died. That is so sad."

Jason looked at the girl, thinking she was being falsely genuine, but he saw nothing but sincerity in her face. Maybe there was more to her than he thought.

Tiffany asked, "How did they die?"

Jason took a deep breath. "Car accident."

"Sorry," she replied in her gravely voice.

"Thanks," he said. "You said you have foster parents?" She nodded but didn't offer any explanation. They waited for a few uncomfortable moments before they realized she wasn't going to give them anything more. He broke the silence. "So what are you all into?"

Marcus smiled. "You saw it: football. 'M a linebacker on the varsity team."

Jason asked, "What do you do when the season's over?"

Marcus answered, "Got a couple'a gigs goin' on the side. I do some volunteer work at the museum, and I'm involved in an anti-bullying program. Seems that when you got a message about bullying coming from a linebacker, younger kids sit up and listen."

Jason said, "I know an eighteen-year-old I'd like you to meet. He acts like a younger kid. Would that be good enough?"

Marcus got a serious look on his face. "I'd like to meet him."

Kinaari changed the subject to her. "Well, I'm involved in several things in my school. I'm the vice president of my class, I'm a cheerleader, and I'm part of the drama club and the band."

Marcus asked, "What do you play?"

"French horn," she answered. "But I'm also learning to play guitar on the side."

"Guitar, really?" Jason queried.

"Yes," she went on. "I find it a pleasant diversion. Oh, I'm also in the honor society in my school."

Tiffany mumbled to George, "Pretty, talented, and smart. Now I really can't stand her."

Marcus asked, "How about you, Tiff? What do you do?"

She growled, "I read. I listen to music. I like to write poetry. Jason?"

"Huh?" Jason realized it was his turn, "Well, I'm pretty good at earning Bs. I work at the museum, stay home by myself a lot...umm, I fix computers on the side, earn a little cash from that."

Marcus nodded approvingly. "Funny, responsible, and a businessman. How about you, Georgie?"

George was taken aback that he even got a turn. He thought they all forgot he was there. "Ummm," he tried as hard as he could to not let his voice crack, "I, ahem, I work at the Dairy Queen?" George didn't know why he made that sound like a question, but he was completely mortified at himself.

Marcus smiled. "You sure about that, big guy?"

George blushed as he nodded rapidly. They continued walking, and George faded to the back of the group. Marcus noticed and slowed up until he was next to George. He said so only George could hear, "Show a little confidence, man. It'll take you a long way. People, especially female people, like it when you are comfortable in your own skin." George nodded again and gave Marcus a "thank you" smile.

The kids continued to get to know each other and were entering the woods before they knew it. Kinaari gave the occasional shriek or squeal when she had to walk through tall grass or weeds or when any insect bigger than a gnat got too close to her. This caused Tiffany to purposely take paths through the tall grass or weeds, and when an insect landed on her, she just watched it curiously. Jason couldn't help but notice the contrast between the two and wondered how this group was ever going to get along.

They had taken time to compare notes on favorite movies, and Jason and Marcus couldn't help but rank *Jurassic Park* in the top three, which finally gave Jason the courage to ask, "Do you ever wish you could see one, live and up close? A dinosaur, I mean."

Tiffany quickly responded, "It would depend if they were curious about you or just sizing you up as a snack."

Jason chuckled. "True. Well, look, can I be honest with you all?"

Marcus shrugged. "Course. Why not?"

He swallowed hard and gave George his best "here we go" look. "I'm asking because—" But he was cut off by a rather unexpected sound from Kinaari.

"Shhhhhhhhhhhhh!"

They all froze and looked at her attentively. For a fleeting moment Jason wondered why people usually stopped moving when someone says "shh." Kinaari's eyes were wide as she whispered loudly, "There is someone up there! I can hear voices!"

A look of concern came over Marcus's face as he gathered the other four behind him. He took a few steps ahead of Kinaari and listened. He said quietly, "She's right; there is someone up ahead." Kinaari got up very close to Marcus, relying on his bulky form to protect her from whatever was ahead. Tiffany came up next to Marcus; she knew he could protect her, but she also wanted to know who was ahead and wasn't afraid to find out. Most importantly, she wanted to show how she was much braver than Kinaari.

Her gravely voice growled, "Let's go check it out."

She began to take steps forward, and Marcus became alarmed that she was proceeding without him. He quickly gathered her up next to him, and they almost intertwined arms. They got close enough to better hear the voices.

"So you just expect us to wait here in this little glade for this boy of yours to show up?" This first voice was angry, confrontational.

"No," came a second voice. "But if we march out to the farm, we will alarm all of the other humans and compromise our anonymity."

Still a third voice added, "Calor speaks the truth. Hiding like this is unbecoming for us. Besides, if the Storm dragon returned, the four of us should be able to handle it without an issue."

The fourth voice contributed, "Tonare, Petros has explained the situation over and over to us. We need to proceed cautiously, strategically."

"Bah!" the voice of Calor sounded again. "The humans should be revering us, not partnering with us. You and Petros are willing to pander to them, Procella. It is *not* our way!"

Procella replied, "Calor, our way is seven hundred years old. It is no longer relevant; we need to adapt."

Calor growled back, "As long as we are the dominant species on the planet, our way *is* the relevant way."

Tonare chimed in, "I personally would love to see all of their faces if we simply sauntered out of our small dell here and greeted them. They would scatter like dandelion seeds in the wind."

Marcus and Tiffany looked at each other with expressions of consternation. Kinaari caught up with them while Jason and George held tentatively back; they had a very good idea whom the voices belonged to but wanted to pretend as if they didn't. Kinaari shoved Marcus a couple of steps forward and mouthed "say something" to him. Marcus gave her his best have-you-lost-your-mind look before he turned to the trees, screwed up his courage, and shouted, "Who is out there?" He had modulated his voice as deep as it could go.

The voices stopped for a moment. Then one familiar to Jason and George came back, "I could ask you the same question."

Marcus countered, "I asked you first, dude! Sounds like you're planning some serious business in there. All I need to do is call the cops."

There was some inaudible whispering then the voice replied, "No, that is not necessary. We mean no harm. I am here with three of my friends. How many are with you?"

"Five!" Marcus blurted. "So we outnumber you! Ha!"

Another long pause went by before the voice said, "Little Knight, are you out there?"

Tiffany, Marcus, and Kinaari all looked befuddled at each other, but their expressions melted to surprise as Jason stepped forward and sheepishly answered, "Yeah, Petros, I'm here."

Marcus pulled the two girls behind him as he confronted Jason. "What's goin' on here, Hewes?"

Jason shouted to the trees, "Hang on a sec, Petros." He turned to the new teenagers. "Look, I don't know how else to say this, but I, well, we—meaning Petros and I—we need your help."

Marcus folded his arms defiantly. "What's a Petros?"

"He's a friend; I met him a little over two weeks ago. He kind of wandered into my barn, and he needed my help...he didn't remember anything. He was, well, alone, and he was injured, and—"

George interrupted Jason. "Look, guys, we're not trying to fool you or anything like that."

Kinaari looked hurt. "You're in on this too, George?"

His voice cracked. "Yes and no." George bravely cleared his throat and continued, "I wasn't there when Jason met Petros, but I know Jason was terrified to tell me and let me meet him. I didn't know what was going on, and I kind of wigged out when I first met Petros, but after I got over the initial shock, he was kind of cool and unbelievable all at the same time." George shook his head. "I know I'm not making sense, but trust Jason; he's not trying to steer you wrong."

Without warning, George stepped toward the trees. "P...Petros?"

"Is that you, George?" the voice came back.

George nodded. "Yeah, it's me. I think maybe just you should come on over here, and it will explain a lot."

"Very well," Petros responded. George looked to Jason, who nodded a "thanks" back at him but had a very anxious look on his face. This was what Jason feared—that the three new kids would completely reject his plan. But at the same time Jason was feeling an even deeper concern he didn't expect; he liked Marcus, Kinaari, and Tiffany, and he didn't want to lose three potential new friends.

The trees began to sway in the woods, and the sound of branches bending and breaking cut through the relative calm of the forest. Finally, Marcus, Tiffany, and Kinaari all inclined their heads upward as their eyes widened when the massive form of Petros came into view. Jason took a position between Petros and the three stunned teenagers as he said, "Guys, this is Petros. He is a—"

His speech trailed off as Tiffany broke away and slowly walked up to Petros. A look of curiosity came over the dragon's face as the small girl boldly approached him. He smiled at her and gave her an approving nod, and she closed the distance until she was directly under his head. She made eye contact with him, and all fear faded from her face. She spoke, and her voice was soft, smooth, and clear. "He's a dragon."

Petros lowered his head until he was face to face with Tiffany. "That I am, young one. You show no fear; most do not react in such a way when first meeting a dragon."

Tiffany's eyes were wide with a childlike wonder. She lifted a hand and moved it toward Petros's snout but paused just short of touching it. He nodded to her, and she gently laid her hand on his massive muzzle. She inhaled sharply at the exhilaration of touching a dragon as she moved her hand over the smooth, dry scales. Petros smiled widely, letting her maintain contact for several moments, then gently separated and lifted his head back up. Tiffany whipped around to the others; tears were flowing from her eyes, but a smile of joy spread widely across her face.

Kinaari had a much more distressed look on her face. Her hands covered her mouth, and her eyes gave away a very palpable fear. She nearly shrieked, "Tiffany, what are you—"

Tiffany interrupted. "It's…he's…you're amazing." She turned to Jason as she realized she was crying. Wiping the tears away and trying to regain her composure, she asked, "How is this possible?"

Jason began to answer, but Petros said, "What is your name, young one?"

She started at Petros's voice addressing her. "I'm Tiffany."

Petros continued, "Tiffany, the story has too many gaps to provide you a complete answer, but let me tell you what I know." The mighty dragon took several minutes to recount all that had happened to him leading up to that day. "And the other voices you heard were the three dragons I was able to find on my quest. I have brought them back here to provide them with companions similar to what Jason has been to me."

Marcus looked perplexed. "So wait a minute; you orchestrated this whole picnic thing to get us here and offer us up to these dragons?"

Jason answered, "No, Marcus. Seriously, how could I have done that? The picnic's been a tradition for years with the Dinosaur Trail, and I had absolutely no idea who was going to show up this year. It was an opportunity to find people who may be good candidates, but it could've just as easily been a bust. And I'm not offering up anyone—we're actually at your mercy. You can turn and walk away, no questions asked, and we would just have to trust you to not give away our secret."

"I'm in," Tiffany blurted without prompting. "You don't even need to ask; I'm in."

Jason found himself smiling ear to ear. Marcus asked, "Why us? Why did you pick us?" As if on cue, the stray cat trotted out from among the trees. Giving George a cautiously wide berth and hissing at him as it went by, it wound its way against the legs of the other four teens before flopping down in front of Petros, exposing its belly to the dragon. A look of realization came over Marcus's face. "You gotta be kidding me."

Jason held up his hands defensively. "I didn't believe it either, Marcus. That was Petros's doing."

Kinaari looked genuinely confused. "What? What did the dragon do?" Petros very gently nuzzled the cat's stomach with his great snout then explained the relationship of dragons and felines to the three newcomers. Kinaari's look of confusion didn't depart her face. "So the cat picked us?"

Without missing a beat, Tiffany bent over and picked up the purring cat. "Of course, it makes perfect sense." She touched her nose to the cat's.

Petros raised an eye ridge. "You understand the nuances of an empathic relationship."

She shook her head. "No, but I understand cats. I've had them all my life, but we just had to put our last one down a few weeks ago. I think I just found a new one, though." She hugged the stray a little tighter; it looked very content.

Petros smiled again at Tiffany then turned to Marcus and Kinaari. "What of you, young friends? Will you help us?"

Kinaari still maintained her look of terror as Marcus relaxed some. Perhaps Tiffany's unconditional acceptance of Petros put him at ease. Marcus said, "I want to say yes, but I want to see who else is back there in the woods. Hard for me to commit to a team unless I know who I'm playin' with."

"Understandable," Petros stated. "I sense a very noble spirit in you, Marcus. I respect that." Marcus found himself grinning at the compliment as Petros turned his attention to Kinaari. He lowered his head to her level as best as he could. His voice changed; it was quieter, soothing. "M'lady, I still see fear in your eyes. I wish you no harm."

She swallowed hard. "This is the last thing I expected to happen on a picnic. You're really not going to eat me?"

Petros grinned. "Young Jason here asked me that question several times when we first met, and, as you can see, he is still here. While his incessant talking has tempted me to take such a drastic action on several occasions, I am convinced you would never elicit such a response from me."

Kinaari laughed nervously while Jason interjected, "That's still not funny!"

"I will make you an offer; you do not need to answer me but at least come and meet my cousins. If you find yourself unable to help after that then leave with no questions asked and no harm done—just as Jason said." Petros waited for a response, and Marcus and Kinaari nodded in the affirmative. He turned halfway back into the woods and said, "Excellent. If you all would be so kind as to follow me, I would like to introduce you to the three dragons that returned with me from my quest across your great land." He began walking back into the woods, and all five of the teens followed him.

*****

Stan Whitman and one of his Stans-in-training stood in the bed of his white pickup truck, leaning on the roof of the cab. The truck was parked just down the road from the Hewes property, close enough so they could see the festivities of the picnic but far enough that it wouldn't be considered trespassing.

Stan chewed on piece of hay. "Just look at that geek fest."

The thug next to him grunted, "Yeah."

Stan fumed, "Don't know what they're thinkin' swarming all over Malta like that. They should stay where they come from."

An identical grunt: "Yeah."

"What's this town comin' to?" he asked. "Hardworking folk gotta contend with these brainiacs and their science and new ideas and all. This is Montana! Big sky! Old-fashioned! Hardworkin'! We don't need no museums or computer hackers or any of that nonsense!"

"Yeah!"

Stan turned to his lackey. "That all you got to say?"

The brute looked perplexed. "Uhhh…yeah?" Stan spit an annoyed sound through his lips while his associate looked ahead on the road. He pointed a sausage-like finger. "Wuzzat?"

Stan rolled his eyes. "What're you sayin'?"

He slapped Stan on the arm with the back of his hand and pointed again. "Wuzzat?"

Stan looked up the road and saw a motorcycle parked ahead just past the Hewes' driveway. The machine was completely black with no license plate or identification of a make or model. It was shaped like a Japanese-style racing bike, not a cruising model like a Harley Davidson, Indian, or others. The paint was a flat black; little light reflected off the edges and curves. This was a machine modified for stealth.

A rider straddled the bike dressed head to toe in black leather. The jacket was adorned with stainless steel shoulder pads, and a similarly metallic spine guard ran down the back of the coat. The visor of his helmet was lifted up, and he held what looked to be binoculars up to his eyes. He was staring intently at the crowd on the farm, methodically scanning back and forth across the entire area. No discernable features were visible on the rider, save for an odd red insignia patch on his left shoulder. From the distance, Stan couldn't make out what the patch was.

"Hey!" Stan bellowed. "What're you doin'? Your kind ain't welcome in these parts!"

"What kind you talkin' about?" the other thug asked.

Stan growled out of the corner of his mouth, "I don't know! He's a stranger; he needs to leave!" He focused back on the rider. "Go on now! Git!"

The sinister figure lowered the binoculars and closed the visor of the helmet. He turned his helmeted head toward Stan as he flipped the ignition switch on the motorcycle, and it roared to life. With a twist of the throttle, the mysterious rider sped away down Highway 2.

Chapter 13

Petros invited Kinaari to walk next to him, talking quietly to her, pushing large amounts of brush to the side so she could easily pass and other such polite gestures. George's reaction to meeting him was all too clear in his mind, and he wanted to avoid such problems with Kinaari.

They soon came to a clearing. As the last clump of brush and overgrowth was parted, Petros said, "Children, I would like to introduce you to three of my cousins: Calor, Tonare, and Procella." Jason, Kinaari, and the other three couldn't help but react with slack-jawed wonder at the sight of three more living and breathing dragons waiting patiently in the small, treeless space. They were each similar in size to Petros, but their features were very different. One of the dragons, whose scales were a turquoise blue on its back and green on its abdomen, approached them; a welcoming look was spread across its face. Its snout was more tapered than Petros's, and there was a fin-like appendage just behind each side of its jaw. A singular, central horn rose from the top of its head and pointed over the back of its neck. The dragon's wings were folded at its side but not in the same fashion as Petros's. They were not folded neatly against its body but rather collapsed straight back from where they joined its sides. It was as if they were unable to fold.

The dragon kept a nonthreatening distance from Kinaari and lowered its head. "I welcome you here as my cousin Petros does. It is a pleasure to meet you."

One of the other dragons, tan and brown in color, rolled its eyes and huffed as Petros said, "Kinaari, this is Procella. She is a Wave dragon, from the family of Water Dragons."

Procella raised her head. "I know Petros has explained this to Jason and George, but there are four different families of dragons: Earth, Air, Fire, and Water Dragons." Her voice was not as deep as Petros's and had a very smooth and soothing quality to it. All of the teens noticed simultaneously; she spoke with pleasant tones. It was enjoyable to listen to her.

The tan dragon couldn't hold back any longer. "I fail to see the benefits of this arrangement. Clearly we intimidate them, and it seems a few of them have no desire to interact with us!" This dragon was the brightest-colored of the four: tan and beige scales flecked with different shades of brown. Jason was reminded of the desert camouflage fatigues he saw American soldiers wearing during the Iraq war. It had a very pronounced line of tall frills extending up its back and over its forehead. Two long horns swept back from either side of its head and were serrated on the undersides. Its face was a peculiar shape compared to Petros's and Procella's; the snout was much shorter, and its mouth was set higher on its jaw. This dragon seemed slightly larger than Petros, and its features seemed more intimidating, harsh, and menacing.

Petros gave the dragon a reproachful look as he said to their human guests, "Calor here may not possess the tact that my cousin Procella does, but she is the first one you want with you in a battle."

Tiffany broke away from the group again and approached Calor without fear. She regarded the dragon curiously. Her voiced grumbled, "You seem less accommodating than the rest."

Calor snarled, "You seem less fearful than the rest. Be mindful, small one; fear can save your life."

Tiffany countered, "Or ruin it."

Calor narrowed her eyes as she regarded the small, darkly clad girl. The corner of the dragon's mouth curled slightly. "A wise response. You may possess some merit after all."

Petros threw a surprised look at Procella, who was equally taken aback. They listened as Tiffany asked, "What sort of dragon are you?"

Calor sat up proudly. "I am a Heat dragon, of the family of Fire Dragons. What sort of human are you?"

Tiffany searched for words. "I don't know; I'm just me—a kid, and apparently one that isn't afraid of dragons, even those determined to scare people."

Calor nodded at Tiffany. "A curious answer. I may grow to like you."

Tiffany grinned as she replied, "See? You may possess some merit after all."

Petros's eyes went wide with surprise as a smile spread across his face. He looked back to Jason. Jason was slack-jawed and mouthed the word "wow" at the interaction between Tiffany and Calor.

A voice came from the back of the clearing. It wasn't as deep or resounding as the other dragons, and there was an irreverent tone as the last dragon spoke. "As much as this human/dragon peace conference warms the depths of my heart, I think we should just walk out there with no reservations. This cowering in the forest is unbecoming, and I carry little concern for what the humans think. If they accept us, fine. If not, we go our separate ways and let the fates decide what happens next."

"Tonare," Petros began, but his voice trailed off. The Earth Dragon shook his head in frustration as he turned to address his kinsman. Tonare was an Air Dragon, and the shape of his wings set him apart from the other three. They did not fold to the side but were connected by spines along the length of his body from shoulder to the tip of his tail and gradually lessened in size as they progressed down either side of his body. When Tonare flew, his wings formed a distinct "V" shape. Blue scales adorned the entirety of his form with disc-like colorations spaced evenly down his neck, along the base of his wings, and terminating just at the base of his tail. His snout was longer that Petros's, and two large horns protruded from either side of his head. The horns were oddly segmented, as if they were meant to bend.

Tonare cut Petros off. "Petros, I must side with Calor on this topic. I fail to see the value of this pursuit."

Surprisingly, Marcus responded to the Air Dragon, "Hey, I may be just a teenager and all, but sounds like you're the only one with a problem here, blue boy. Your girl over there, the heat one, seems t'be getting along fine with my friend Tiffany."

Tonare rose up to his full height. "What could you hope to know of the workings of a dragon's mind, little boy?"

Marcus actually looked incensed. "Enough to know a bully when I see one. You're getting' all high and mighty with us, like we should be serving you or something. As far as I can see, you're the one who should be asking for our help 'cause you have no idea what the world is like now!"

Tonare took a step toward Marcus as Marcus took several steps to the dragon. Jason muttered to George, "Yep, he's dead."

George asked, "Marcus or the dragon?"

Tonare raised his voice. "Whelp, the last dragon you want to get in a shouting match with is a Thunder dragon."

Marcus was seeing red by then. All reason and fear had taken a flying leap out of the proverbial window, and Marcus was in full confrontation mode. "Yeah? Well, the way I see it, Blues Clues, is that the last kid you wanna mess with is a varsity linebacker from Bozeman!"

To everyone's surprise, Tonare lashed out with one of his front claws, seized the irate Marcus with lightning-like speed, and threw him onto the back of his neck. But Marcus's reaction time was well-honed from his years on the football team. Despite not knowing what was about to happen, he rapidly shimmied up the dragon's neck until he could wrap his arms and legs around enough to get a sure grip. Before anyone else could react to the turn of events, Tonare was in the air, soaring above the trees and away from the farm. Marcus was hanging on for dear life.

From an observer's point of view, a flying Air Dragon was a thing of beauty. Their wings didn't just flap; their entire body undulated in the air as they used every inch of their extended wing structure to move themselves through the skies. There was no need of banking for turns, taking wide arcs to change course, or circling around to reapproach a target. Their bodies were amazingly flexible, and with a twist of a tail, rotation of a muscle group, or arch of the back, Air Dragons could accomplish spectacular feats of aerobatics that no other living creature could. Unfortunately, Marcus did not have the luxury of examining Tonare objectively; his biggest concern at the moment was to not fall off the psycho-dragon's back and get inadvertently skewered onto one of the trees below.

Tonare skimmed the tops of the trees with excessive velocity then made a ninety-degree turn upward and shot straight into the sky. Hitting the apex of his climb, the Thunder dragon leveled off and began a series of barrel rolls with a dizzying speed. Marcus's muscles screamed for relief as he held on for everything he was worth, but letting go was clearly not an option, and he gritted his teeth and squeezed as hard as he could with his arms and legs.

Tonare was annoyed the upstart human was still holding on, and as soon as he cleared the treeline, he dove for the earth again. As he held on, Marcus was able to see the horns on Tonare's head flatten against his body and flex outward again as he performed his maneuvers. They weren't just biological ornamentation; they were actual control surfaces for flight.

Tonare abruptly leveled off again, this time inverted with his ventral armor facing the sky and poor Marcus skimming only a few feet off the ground. Tall brush and small trees lashed over his back as Tonare was literally trying to scrape the linebacker off his neck, but Marcus had now arrived at a state of stubborn survival. He was going to hold on and not die for the sole purpose of showing this dragon what humans could do when they put their minds to it.

Back in the small forest, Jason shouted at Petros, "Someone go after him!"

Calor answered, "No, young one. This is a contest of wills now."

Jason was dumbfounded. "Contest? Your buddy there grabbed Marcus and threw him on his back. Marcus didn't ask for that to happen!"

Procella responded, "Jason, most dragons do not back down from challenges. Marcus did not challenge Tonare to a direct battle, but their verbal exchange amounted to such, especially to an impulsive breed like Air Dragons. Tonare is fairly young as well; he was looking for a fight."

Jason yelled, "Well…I…someone go after them!"

Petros sighed deeply. "Little Knight, that is an Air Dragon; none of the three of us have a chance of catching him. It would be like one of your propeller aircraft chasing a fighter jet." The other two dragons gave Petros a confused look, prompting him to explain, "Flying machines. I learned about them in my studies." He turned back to Jason. "Our only chance is to see this through to its end. It may have an unexpected conclusion that will work in our favor."

Breaking out of his inverted path, Tonare curled his body inward and flew skyward again. He was shocked to see Marcus still gripping on to the back of his neck and actually smiled. He pointed himself back toward the forest but not before executing the hardest and fastest loop-de-loop he could perform, and then a second, and then a third. But the boy held fast, and Tonare was now impressed. He relaxed his flight plan and soared on a straight but much more leisurely path back to their companions. Within minutes, he landed in the clearing, and the rest of the kids ran up to help Marcus off his neck. Petros and Procella glared at Tonare disapprovingly, while Calor waited curiously for what would happen next.

Marcus unceremoniously flopped to the earth as his friends crowded around him to help him to his feet. He started pushing them away, "Get off...get offa me!" His body rejected the concept of standing, but he fought the dizziness and nausea as and he rose to face his challenger again. He wobbled but steeled himself to stop the spinning in his head as he looked Tonare in the eyes.

"That..." he swallowed hard, "that the best you got?"

Tonare paused for several very tension-filled moments then burst out laughing. "Well played, young one, well played indeed!" He pointed a claw at Marcus. "*You* are worthy of being in the company of dragons. Come stand by my side, Sir Marcus; I can see we will have many glorious adventures together."

Marcus smiled then threw up all over the forest floor.

Jason muttered to Petros as he watched poor Marcus lose his lunch. "Is that the unexpected conclusion you mentioned?"

Petros turned up a nostril at the rapidly returning midday meal. "As long as it works in our favor, I suppose."

***

The next hour was spent helping Marcus recover his faculties. Jason told his human and dragon friends alike about his experience with Norm the mage and the possibilities to help them.

Calor frowned. "Feh! Mages cannot be trusted. In our time, you could count on a mage for two things: to search for glory by slaying a dragon and to beg for mercy when facing death at the claws of a dragon. They are opportunistic and cowardly."

Procella had a thoughtful look in her eye. "I am somewhat surprised their order has survived. From what you have told me, Petros, technology has made impressive strides to replace what only magic could do. I can't say I'm completely surprised, but the fact that you found one so easily, Jason, has me a little unsettled."

"How so?" Jason asked.

Procella shook her head. "He is either a very careless mage, or he was deliberate in his carelessness."

Petros stated, "I see your concern, Procella, but I do not see any other option at this point. He is the only one we know that has the skills to help us in our pursuits."

Tiffany interrupted. "Sorry to break up this speculation about the magic guy, but don't we have a bigger problem we need to figure out?"

"What is that?" Procella asked.

Tiffany pointed methodically at Procella, Calor, and Tonare. "The three of you. The picnic will be over soon, and if each of you is supposed to be with one of us then we need to do something before this Norm can help us. I'm pretty sure Jason can't keep four dragons in his barn, and I know I'm not prepared for Calor to come home with me, so what're we gonna do?"

Kinaari shrugged her shoulders. "There is a lot of space in Glendive where I'm sure Procella could hide." But Kinaari caught herself. "I mean assuming you want to, you know, be paired up with me?"

Procella smiled. "It would be my honor, Kinaari."

Marcus shook his head. "That won't work for me. Bozeman's quite the place—nowhere for me to hide a dragon in the middle of a city."

Tiffany added, "I live in a second-floor apartment. I can't even get them to let me have a Chihuahua. I'm pretty sure a dragon is an impossibility."

Jason smirked. "But we did decide that Procella will match up with Kinaari, Calor and Tiffany will be a pair, and Tonare and Marcus will work together—even if they did start out a little shaky. Are we agreed on that?" They all looked nervously at each other then each nodded in agreement with the plan.

Petros said, "Very good. I am glad that is decided. But, children, I would like an opportunity to speak with my kin. I have a proposal, and we need to discuss it on our own."

The teenagers left the dragons alone in the small clearing for several minutes. They were close enough to hear the creatures' voices but not understand what they were saying. The dragons worked to speak quietly, but occasionally a raised voice was heard, usually Calor's, over the rest. Finally, Petros summoned them back.

He said, "We feel the best option is for us to stay here."

Jason looked confused. "Here in Malta?"

Procella answered, "More specifically, here in this glade. Three of us will live here together, with the fourth taking a daily turn in Jason's barn, getting caught up with this twenty-first century on what Petros is calling 'the Internet.'"

Calor snorted his disagreement as Petros added, "I will forego my turn in the barn; I have had enough opportunities to develop a rudimentary knowledge of this time."

"Wait, wait, wait," Jason chimed in. "You three are just gonna switch in and out of my barn? I mean this is really risky. It will work when my dad is out of town, but if he is around, you're going to have to be careful and quiet."

Kinaari actually spoke up. "I'm not sure if I like this. I mean, like, Jason here has had all this time to hang out with Petros and all. Now we are expected to be, like, BFFs with these other dragons, but we're not going to have any chance to get to know them."

"BFF?" Calor muttered to Tonare.

"It must be a human code or something," Tonare muttered back, shrugging his massive shoulders.

Procella responded, "I completely agree with you, Kinaari, but I don't think we have any other option."

Jason opened his mouth to retort, but he knew the dragons were right. He held up his hands in surrender and nodded a reluctant agreement.

Marcus said, "Hey, yo, it's getting late. We need to get back to the picnic before they start looking for us. It sounds like we have a plan, but how we gonna know when this Norm guy is ready to lay down all of his magic whammies on us?"

Jason answered, "Just give me your email or texts or Skype numbers, and I'll get with you when I know something."

Tiffany was shaking her head. "I can't believe I'm saying this, but I have to agree with Kinaari on this one. We come out here, and you introduce us to real, live dragons and tell us to be their ambassadors or whatever and then expect us to leave and act like it never happened."

Jason responded, "Tiff, I know. I agree with you, but I—"

Tiffany interrupted, "Jason, I hear you, and I know there is no way around it. It just stinks." She walked back over to Calor, who, despite her ferocity, had a measure of compassion in her eyes. Tiffany went on, "This is life-changing for me, and you can't expect me to walk away from it and be happy about it."

Jason nodded. "I know; really, I get it. Let me think about this. I dunno...maybe there is something I can work out. Just...just let me think about it."

The frustrated Tiffany began to storm her way back to the edge of the woods. Marcus and Kinaari reluctantly followed her. Jason looked to George, who just shrugged his shoulders in response, and then he turned to Petros. The great dragon said, "Go; we will be fine." Jason frowned, grabbed George by the sleeve, and hurried off after the three.

The walk back to the farm was relatively quiet. Marcus tried to engage with Tiffany, but she wouldn't have any of it. Meanwhile, Jason and George walked farther back as Jason growled at his friend, "You know you could have said something, anything, to help me back there."

George answered, "Oh, I'm sorry. Was I a part of that?"

Jason rolled his eyes. "What're you talking about?"

"You know," George spat back. "I was pretty much just decoration back there. You didn't talk to me…heck, no one talked to me. And now you expect me to fix your problem? Make me part of the conversation then I may be more willing to help."

"Come on, George. Don't to this to me now! You know—"

George interrupted, "No, Jason, no. Don't tell me to 'stop being George' like you always do. You were rude to me, plain and simple. I'm supposed to be your best friend, not your backup friend when no one else is around." George started walking faster, purposely leaving Jason behind. George hurried past Marcus, Tiffany, and Kinaari as well. Kinaari called after George, but he didn't respond. Marcus and Kinaari turned back to Jason, and Marcus held up his hands in a questioning gesture. Jason waved at them to go on without him as he slowed down to a plodding pace and ran his hands through his hair, trying to rub the stress out of his brain.

"Way to go, Hewes," he said to himself. "Way to take a situation that was working itself out and screw it up beyond all recognition."

Chapter 14

Clean-up from the picnic had gone well into the evening, but even
the end of the awkward event was of little comfort to Jason. His
best friend had left in a huff, and Tiffany drove off with her foster
parents without even saying a word to him. She even forgot to take
the barn cat with her. Marcus and Kinaari had convinced their
parents to stay a little later and help with tearing everything down,
which offered some reassurance to Jason that he hadn't managed to
offend every one of his friends.

"Look, Hewes, we'll work this out," Marcus offered. "If
I'm a guessing guy, Tiff seems like the kind who doesn't handle
loss well. Y'know, she's got no parents and all that stuff. You saw
how she reacted to the dragons; she pro'ly woulda dropped
everything she had and stayed with them full time if she could've."

Jason shook his head. "Yeah, I know, but she probably
feels like I set her up for disappointment or something."

Marcus slapped him on the back. "She's a scrapper. She'll
be okay before you know it."

Jason half smiled. "I really ticked off George too."

This time, Kinaari addressed him. "Jason, I think he felt left
out. We all got picked to have a dragon, but George didn't. Does
he get left out a lot?"

"Y'know, Kinaari, you're way more perceptive than I
thought. Yeah, George and I aren't exactly at the top of the
popularity heap or anything. Me, I don't care much about it. I got
enough to worry about than to waste time with who thinks I'm
chill or whatever. But George, he's more sensitive to it. He puts
more value in being accepted than I do."

A look of compassion came over her face. "Oh, I'm really
sorry. I guess I don't know what that is like completely. I mean I
just have a lot of friends, and, oh, that didn't come out right either.
I'm trying to say—"

Jason interrupted, "Kinaari, I get it. I know what you're
getting at. It doesn't bother me, really. Girls like you, well, they

just don't want anything to do with guys like me or George. It's the way things are, and it really eats away at George."

She thought for a moment. "Well, would it help if I called him?"

"What?" Jason asked, taken by surprise.

"I can call him, smooth things over a little. Would that help?

Jason pondered the thought for a few beats. "He would love that. I'm not sure how much it would help with all of his yearning in the long run, but having a hot girl call him would make his day. He may forgive me too."

Kinaari blushed at Jason's use of the word "hot" but then looked over her shoulder toward the crowd. "My parents are waving me down. Time to leave. You'll send me George's number?"

Jason was already composing a text. "Doing it now. Thanks, Kinaari, and stay in touch, okay?"

She nodded as she waved good-bye and jogged to her waiting parents. Marcus and Jason watched her go then Marcus said, "There's more to her than I thought."

Jason smiled. "And to you, man. Bet you never thought when you woke up today that you'd be holding on to the back of a dragon for dear life."

Marcus smirked back. "Dude, most'a what happened today I never thought I'd be doin' when I woke up." He pointed over his shoulder with his thumb, indicating it was time for him to go. "Look, email or Skype me tonight, okay? This isn't gonna get less complicated, so keep us in the loop; let us help. Got it?"

Jason felt a weight lift at Marcus's statement. "Got it. Safe travels." A quick fist bump later, and Marcus was walking to their family van. Jason found himself alone. He sighed deeply as he realized his life had just gotten more complicated, and he couldn't help but wonder if it cost him his best friend. They didn't always see eye to eye, but George was always loyal to Jason, and he reflected that he might have taken advantage of that loyalty far too often. He hoped this day wasn't the proverbial straw that broke the camel's back, but he knew he was going to have to do some serious apologizing. Jason took yet another cleansing breath then turned to join his dad as the clean-up committee was starting the tear-down process.

***

After the cleanup crew and a few random stragglers finally departed, the only evidence left of the picnic was the tire tracks on the lawn. Jason and his father were soon inside, feet up on the coffee table and watching whatever was coming up next on the Discovery Channel.

Timothy exhaled. "Remind me never to volunteer us to do that again."

Jason grinned. "Eh, it could've been worse, I suppose. I didn't have to wear the dinosaur costume."

Jason's dad tousled his hair. "You know how to make cotton candy now, right?"

"The machine does most of the work. I just pour the sugar in."

"Ah," he replied obliquely. "Looks like you made some new friends too."

"Mmm?" Jason tried to sound casual. "Yeah, they were cool. They're from all over the state, though, so it's hard to keep in touch."

"Oh, I don't know…looked like there were a couple of pretty girls there. Seems like you may want to make the effort to keep in touch."

"Daaaad! 'Pretty girls,' really? What're we, in third grade?"

Timothy backed off. "Sorry, son. Your mom was better at talking about this."

Jason felt bad. "No, I'm sorry. Yes, you're right. They were pretty."

His eyebrow raised. "Did you get their phone numbers?"

Jason sighed. "Text numbers. It's texting and Facebook and Skype these days." He paused. "And, yes, I got them."

His dad smiled and playfully slapped him on the arm. "Nice work."

Jason blushed a little, feeling a swell of pride at successfully interacting with two girls but at the same time realizing the conditions by which he met them. Still, all things being equal, he was going to count it as a victory. He saw the time and realized that it might be the perfect opportunity to use some of his newly obtained personal contact information. He gave his dad a slap on the leg and said, "You know what, Dad? I'm gonna use one of those numbers now, if that isn't a problem."

His dad replied, "Go get 'em, kid."

Jason walked out onto the porch and pulled up the Skype app on his phone. His model had a forward-facing camera, so he found Tiffany's contact information and placed the call. Within a few moments, her picture filled the small screen in his hand.

"I didn't expect a call from you so soon," she said to Jason. The usual gravel in her voice was even more pronounced from weariness. It had been a long day.

He cleared his throat. "I wanted to make sure you were okay."

She nodded. "I told you I was. I just wanted some time alone."

He didn't know what to say. "You forgot the cat."

She answered, "Yeah, I realized it halfway home. It's for the better anyway; foster parents would have pitched a fit if I tried to bring another stray into the apartment."

He casually walked the perimeter of the wraparound porch. It was a quiet, cloudless night in the Malta area. Jason could hear the chirping of the crickets during the awkward pause as he tried to think of what to say next. "Look, I'm sorry it all went down the way it did. You realize I didn't know who the cat would pick, or how you would react, or anything. I especially didn't expect you to, you know, take to the dragons like you did."

She smiled shyly. "Yeah, yeah, I kind of didn't expect that either. I don't know; I've read enough books with dragons that I never saw them as frightening or anything. So I just went right up to one, you know?"

"I wish I had reacted like that."

"How so?"

He ran his hand through his dark hair. "Yeah, when I first met Petros, I pulled a knife and then a carrot peeler on him."

"A carrot peeler?"

"Don't ask; it was all I had at the time. I thought he was gonna eat me."

She shook her head at his story, but he could tell she was trying not to laugh. Jason came around the corner of the porch to where he could see the old barn. He could see light spilling through the gaps around the windows and doors, so he assumed Petros was using the Internet again. He said to Tiffany, "Seems that Petros is in the barn. You wanna go say hi?"

Her face lit up; Jason felt his heart uplifted as he began to walk to the barn. As he stepped off the porch, Tiffany noticed the smile fade from his face as his expression changed.

"What is it?" she asked.

Jason paused in midstride and felt his weight shift to his back foot—a defensive posture. "I…I think there is someone sneaking around the barn," he whispered, directing his voice at the small microphone on the phone.

"What? Who is it?"

Jason shook his head. "Look, I don't know, but I have to check it out. Call the others, George included. Tell them what's happening." He set the phone down as Tiffany's cries of protest faded into the night. He slowly padded a wide arc in front of the barn, trying to approach the figure from behind. Jason did the best he could to sneak around the intruder, but he thought the pounding of his heart was sure to give him away. Nightfall had cooled the air significantly, but Jason was breaking out in a sweat from the sheer anxiety of what he was attempting. He couldn't make out who it was; no light was reflecting from the body. Jason assumed the person was dressed in black but then saw the light that was leaking through the spaces in the barn reflect off of some kind of dome over the individual's head.

It's a helmet, Jason thought to himself. Whoever this was had a helmet on and was trying to look through the space between the barn doors. He had to do this carefully; if he was too close to the house, his father was going to hear what he was about to do and come out and find the dragon in the barn, but if he got too close to the barn and the mysterious figure attacked, he had nowhere to retreat. One thing Jason did know for certain: this was probably the stupidest thing he'd ever done. He closed to the distance he judged the best and then said, "Hey! What are you doing on my property?" Jason directed his voice as best he could toward the barn and away from the house.

The individual startled and whipped around. A black motorcycle helmet covered the entire face, and, with a swift and fluid motion, the dark intruder pulled something from a belt and pointed it at Jason.

Instinctively, Jason dove to the ground as two projectiles attached to very thin wires sailed over him, targeting the space where his chest used to be. A voice from the barn that did not belong to Petros bellowed, "Who goes there?" The trespasser jumped even higher at the voice and, spinning deftly on the heel of one foot, sprinted into the darkness. One of the barn doors flew open, and an angry-looking Calor stood at the door, quickly surveying the area and finding Jason lying on the ground, pale with fear.

Jason hissed, "Close the door and get back inside before my father sees you! I'll be right there." To Jason's surprise, Calor complied without an argument. He figured Petros must have coached her on the need for subtlety and stealth. Whatever the figure in black had fired at him, it was dropped as the person fled, and Jason fumbled in the darkness to gather it up. He ran to get his phone, peeked in a window of the house to see his father had fallen asleep on the couch, and, with a deep sigh of relief, went back to the barn.

After closing the door quickly behind him, he explained to Calor what happened.

A look of suspicion came over her face. "What was it trying to do?"

Jason swallowed hard, still breathing heavily from the stress. "It seemed like it was trying to get a look at you."

"What? Why?"

Jason shook his head. "I have no idea. I don't want to think our arrangement has been compromised because I have nowhere else to put you. We need to accelerate our schedule and get Norm up here."

She replied, "Did you battle and vanquish whatever it was?"

Jason answered, "What? No! I didn't want to get myself killed."

Her brow knitted. "Mmm…pity. I would have liked to examine the body. Can you describe it to me?"

He blinked purposefully. "It was black."

She waited a moment for more. "That is all?"

He rolled his eyes. "It's night. The sky is black. There is little light, so everything else is black. I saw a person dressed in black wearing a black helmet. So that's the best I've got for you; it was black. Oh, and it tried to shoot me with this."

He pulled out the object he had tucked into his pocket and quickly realized what it was. A frown came over his face.

Calor asked, "What is it?"

"Pretty sure this is a taser." The dragon looked confused, so he went on. "It's a modern weapon designed to incapacitate instead of kill. It delivers an electric shock and makes the target seize up and fall to the ground."

Calor looked more confused. "What good is a weapon that is not for killing?"

Jason was a little frustrated. "Look, Calor, in a civilized society we invent weapons that can score a victory without killing someone, okay?"

"So you leave the villain alive to commit more crimes in the future?"

"No, it's not like that. Look, can we just focus on the scary guy in black who was trying to catch a glimpse of you?"

She shrugged her shoulders. "Very well. You brought up the topic; no need to become incensed."

Near exasperation, Jason remembered that he had to call Tiffany back. As he readied the call, he remembered Calor had the laptop on and the projector running. "What're you studying? And, for that matter, why are you here? I thought you said you wouldn't need to get on the Internet," he asked.

She answered, "Ah, Petros recommended I view something called a 'streaming movie,' specifically something called *Dragonslayer*. I must admit that it is a fascinating confluence of magic that allows me to view a play in a medium such as this, but the plot of the story itself is highly ridiculous. The dragon alone is anemic and completely unrealistic, like someone tried to put a costume on a lizard and pass it off as one of us."

"It's not magic; it's techno—" But Jason realized the futility of the argument and began placing the video call as he muttered something about getting dragons addicted to bad cinema.

Tiffany's face appeared on the screen. "Don't you ever do that again, Jason! You scared all of us half to death. What happened?"

He brought her up to date on the happenings of the night and asked, "Did you get a hold of George?"

She nodded. "He was actually talking to Kinaari when I called but yes, and he is worried sick. He almost violated his curfew to come check on you. I'm sending him an IM now to let him know you're okay."

Jason felt a weight lift when he heard George was worried. It seemed at least he still had his best friend. Now all he had to do was eat a little crow and make amends. "Thanks, Tiff. Hey, Calor is here in the barn; you wanna talk to her?"

Tiffany's expression brightened, at least as much as a goth teenage girl would let her face brighten. She contained her excitement and grumbled, "Sure, that would be nice."

Calor regarded Jason dubiously as he quickly explained what the device was doing and laid it in her massive claw. Calor squinted to see Tiffany's face, but she quickly engaged in conversation with the girl and hobbled on three legs back to the computer projection on the screen. She began to barrage Tiffany with questions about the computer and about 2011 in general. Jason waited patiently for the call to end, but after twenty minutes of nonstop talking between the two, he realized he wasn't getting

his device back anytime soon. Throwing his hands up in
frustration, Jason exited the barn, checked carefully around for any
more intruders, and then speed-walked back to the house and up to
his room to go to bed.

***

Jason flopped out of bed at around ten o'clock the next
morning and found his dad sitting at the kitchen table, typing away
on his laptop and sipping a cup of tea.

"Mornin'," he said brightly to his son.

"Caffeine," Jason murmured as he opened the fridge, pulled
out a twenty-ounce bottle of Mountain Dew, and took a deep
draught from it before he sat next to his dad.

Without looking away from his computer, his dad said,
"Here, I found this on the porch." He held Jason's smart phone in
his hand. Jason's eyes went wide, both at remembering where he
last saw the phone and with surprise at how it ended up in his dad's
hands.

He swallowed the soda in his mouth slowly as he tried to
formulate a response. "Oh, thanks. I must have left it there. I think
I fell asleep in one of the chairs and never brought it in with me."

"Did you have a nice talk?" his dad inquired pointedly, his
eyebrows oscillating up and down repeatedly.

"Oh, right. We're just friends but, yeah, I guess we had a
nice talk." He tried to indulge his dad's fatherly curiosity but
couldn't figure out how the phone got from Calor's claw to the
wraparound porch. He knew there was only one way to find out.

Jason stood up and half-faked a very cavernous yawn and
scratched his head. "Oy. I gotta wake up; maybe some fresh air
would help."

"Maybe I can meet this friend of yours sometime?"
Timothy asked.

Jason smiled. "Maybe, Dad, maybe. She lives in Jordan, so
it's more of a long-distance thing. I'm gonna go walk before you
start making wedding plans or anything, okay?"

Dad smiled back and nodded then returned to typing at his laptop. Jason slipped his feet into his flip flops and started walking toward the barn. He got there as quickly as he could and slipped inside. Calor had presumably been up all night, for she was still transfixed to the makeshift screen, surfing the Internet.

He held up the phone. "How did this get on my porch?"

Calor looked at him with only half of her attention. "Hmm? Ah, I put it there."

Jason was startled at the pronouncement. "You left the barn in the middle of the night to put this on the porch?"

"No, of course not," she responded under her furrowed brow. "I waited until dawn."

"What! Are you kidding? You came out of the barn in broad daylight to return a phone to my front porch." He pressed the power switch, but the screen stayed blank. "And you ran its battery dry!"

Annoyed, she turned to him. "Do you see where you live? There is no one close to this house who would have a chance of seeing me. You worry far too much, boy."

"Dragons!" Jason bellowed as he stormed out the barn and returned to the house.

After he plugged his phone in to charge, Jason went to his room and powered up the old desktop he had jury-rigged under his desk. His laptop was his primary computer, and his smart phone served as his backup. But now that both of those were otherwise occupied, he had to rely on the beast of a machine under his desk. He powered on the old device and then waited for the laboriously long startup process.

Jason looked around his room and wondered if it was time for a change. His bed was unkempt and jammed into one of the corners. Being a typical teenage boy, Jason had foregone the nuances of a headboard or bedframe and simply slept on a mattress and boxspring on the floor. The walls were covered with old, diamond-patterned wallpaper that had been there since probably the house was built. His dresser and desk were mismatched pieces of furniture, and the drawers of the dresser were all pulled out in various degrees with items of clothing in each drawer not fully within the containment of their depths. The hardwood floor was covered with a random area rug they had found, one that was so faded with age Jason could no longer really label what color to call it. He thought to himself, *It's kind of a brownish purplish gray.*

The computer finally decided to boot up, and Jason went right to the Internet and emailed Norm. He asked the mage how much notice he needed to get to Malta and said he would inform him as soon as he knew his dad was going out of town again. He then emailed his fellow dragon-human explorers, copied them on the message he sent to Norm, added George to the distribution list, and sent the message, telling them to start thinking of excuses for how they were going to get to Malta on such short notice.

Over the next few days, Jason didn't know what to expect every time he went to the barn. Calor was gone the next evening to be replaced by Procella, whom he enjoyed having conversations with as opposed to the much more aggressive and stubborn Heat dragon. Kinaari didn't have any video chat capabilities, but he put her on speakerphone and let her have an extended conversation with Procella. When Calor explored the Internet, she focused on information about the military, tools of warfare, and even modern fighting techniques. In contrast, Procella dug intensively into world history, even more specifically looking at the colonization of the West, the world wars, the American civil war, and studying the different types of government. Procella was smart, possibly even smarter than Petros. Her ability to see and understand the nuances of relationships was uncanny. As she looked at the histories of countries, governments, and even societal conflicts, she was able to grasp the points of view of both sides equally and suggest ways those conflicts could have been resolved. Jason felt she could run for Congress if she wasn't a forty-foot long, giant, winged dragon.

In sharp contrast, Tonare's time in the barn was much more annoying. He wasn't as gruff and aggressive as Calor, nor smart and logical as Procella. The dragon was impulsive and wouldn't pick one topic and study it. His focus went from subject to subject, and it wasn't with the curiosity for learning demonstrated by Petros and Procella and, to a lesser extent, Calor. Tonare felt he needed to criticize what he learned and insert negative commentary on human understanding. Jason knew the dragon was arrogant, but he also swore the creature had ADD. It wasn't until Petros returned to the barn that he helped Jason understand that Tonare was the youngest of the four. Comparatively, Tonare was in his later teen years, and as teenagers often do, he was questioning conventional wisdom and authority and trying to find his own path. "Not unlike you and your friends, Little Knight," Petros commented. As much as Jason hated to admit it, he knew Petros was right.

Jason finally heard back from Norm, who told him to name the time and the place and that he would need GPS coordinates. Jason questioned this. First, Norm didn't seem like the kind who would even use a GPS; he wasn't very fond of technology. Second, he was planning on meeting Norm at the train or bus station in town and escorting him to the site where, well, whatever would happen. After consultation with Petros, they decided they would use the forest glade as the site where Norm would, both proverbially and literally, work his magic. He sat down on his couch to send the others the update when there was a knock on his front door. He opened it.

"Hey," George said, standing just on the other side of the threshold.

"Hey," Jason replied back. "Long time no see."

George nodded. "Yeah, well, you know how it is."

Their nodding heads bobbed up and down for a few beats. Jason finally said, "Look, George—"

George interrupted, "Thanks for having the girls call me. Mom hasn't been this excited in years."

"They wanted to know if you were okay," Jason responded.

"And you?" George asked.

Jason nodded. "I did too. I didn't mean to leave you out."

George looked very vulnerable. "It really hurt, Jace."

Jason sighed. "I know; I screwed up. I was just sending an email to the others now. I finally heard back from Norm."

George's face lit up. "And?"

Jason answered, "We, umm, just need to set a date, I guess."

"You sound less than enthused."

"I'm scared. I hate even going to the doctor. But now I'm gonna let some hippie guy cast a major magical spell on me. What's not to be scared about?"

George regarded his friend. Jason didn't let his guard down that often; after the situation with his mom and brother, he figured a guy like Jason wasn't that easy to get to. This was getting to him. George said, "C'mon. Let's pick out a date. Lemme use your comp in your room, and I'll send the mail, okay? I can help that way, right?"

A look of relief came over Jason's face as he slowly nodded. They went upstairs to his room and tried to convince the old desktop to power up; an email needed to be sent.

Chapter 15

The four teens and the four dragons stared impatiently at each other. Sunset was long since past, and the stars were visible through the gaps in the treetops above the glade's clearing. The teens held flashlights in their hands, providing faint illumination amid the pitch-black trees. Crickets voiced their presence in their typical nocturnal way, and the darkness was occasionally broken by the random green sparks of fireflies.

"Well?" Calor asked impatiently.

Jason looked a little sheepish. "Uh, what do you mean?"

Tiffany responded, "She means that it is ten past midnight, and we're standing out here in the forest waiting for this supposed mage to show up."

Kinaari tried to ask diplomatically, "Jason, are you sure this guy isn't, well—"

Marcus interrupted, "Yankin' your chain, dude?"

Procella jerked her head up curiously. "Yanking your—"

Tiffany answered, "Purposefully deceiving."

Procella tilted her head slightly. "Interesting metaphor."

Petros said, "I believe Jason. If this Norm is not what he advertises himself to be then he is a bigger fool than I thought because he will face the wrath of four grown dragons."

Jason raked his fingers through his hair and smiled gratefully at Petros as he recalled the events from just one week ago: George had become Jason's point for communications with the other three teens and Norm the mage. After the previous day when George had emailed everyone, Jason quickly saw the look of delight come over his best friend's face at feeling involved, and Jason turned those duties over to him. He would even send George on missions into the forest to bring random status updates to the dragons hidden in the woods. The opportunity of spending time alone with the dragons simultaneously brought George to the brink of panic and filled him with delight. He had earned the nickname "Squire George" from Procella. She was keenly perceptive of

George's feelings and place in the group of teens and dubbed him with his own "title" to boost his confidence.

George fully cemented his quasi-administrative role in the group when his managed to get the date of Tim Hewes's next trip out of town without raising suspicion. With George's coordination, they were able to carefully time Mr. Hewes's departure with the arrival of Marcus, Tiffany, and Kinaari, so Dad was well on his way when the other three arrived in town. George had even convinced his parents to let him try his first "solo" drive around town and used it as an opportunity to pick up their three friends and deliver them to Jason's house. Jason was somewhat put off at all of George's duplicitous behavior, and when he finally asked his friend about it, the answer was, "Are you kidding? I feel like I'm on some covert ops team; I'm having a ball!"

***

Midnight was the appointed time for Norm to arrive, and it was quickly approaching.

"Does anyone know what he is really going to do to us?" Marcus asked.

Jason shrugged. "No…he just said he has a way to help us help the dragons integrate into society. We're gonna be…well, I don't really know. Explorers, adventurers, ambassadors—"

George interrupted, "Draconauts! You know like from the Greek stories *Jason and the Argonauts*. Except with dragons instead. Whaddaya think?"

They exchanged oblique glances with each other for several uncomfortable moments before Tiffany said, "It sounds kinda goofy."

George looked crestfallen, but Kinaari said, "It's not that bad, George. Maybe it'll grow on us, y'know?"

Ten minutes after midnight ticked by, and the humans and dragons alike were showing a quickly waning patience.

Jason said, "Look, if you saw the guy, you would know that timeliness probably isn't a concern of his. He's kinda—"

But Jason stopped midsentence as a point of bright red light appeared out of nowhere, bathing the entire clearing in an eerie red glow. The point began to track straight upward to the sky, leaving a trail of light behind it. It stopped about six feet from the ground then moved parallel to the earth for four feet before dropping back down again. A rectangle of glowing crimson now stood, and then the color began to expand inward until the entire shape was filled with shimmering, colored brightness. The intensity of the light grew brighter and brighter and forced all present to shield their eyes until there was a brilliant flash. Inside the rectangle, still outlined in glowing red, was what appeared to be a doorway to a small office.

And then Norm stepped through.

The gaunt man was wearing Bermuda shorts with sandals and thick gray socks. He had on a multicolored, faded poncho made from very rough wool, and his wire-rimmed glasses were seated on his face this time, as opposed to on his head. But his choice of headgear was the oddest of all; he had outfitted himself with a large, fur-lined Russian-style winter hat, complete with earflaps tied over the top.

Without looking to see who was there, he turned back to the magical doorway and produced a chalk eraser from under his poncho. He waved it over the upper corner of the portal, and, with a faint puff of dust, the doorway vanished. Norm replaced the eraser, and, as he slapped his hands clean against each other, he turned and said, "Okay, kid, I'm here. Where are...oh!"

Norm froze in midsentence. His eyes became like saucers, and his jaw hung open. Petros, Calor, Procella, and Tonare had all lowered their heads to examine him closely, and all had expressions of the most serious nature on their faces.

The mage stammered, "G...good Lord, y...you're real."

Calor sneered, "As are you, mage. We have heard much about you, all of which has found you wanting."

Tonare huffed, "You are late; we do not appreciate being kept waiting."

Petros turned his head to Jason and winked. Jason's muscles relaxed, and he fought back a smile. Petros turned back to

Norm. "I find your lack of respect for dragonkind unsettling. It is not wise to keep one dragon waiting, much less a quartet of us who have not eaten in some time."

Norm was terrified; sweat poured from under his gargantuan fuzzy hat.

Procella mused, "Perhaps we should test his mettle. Do you suppose he could withstand one of my shockwaves or your heat breath, Calor?"

The Heat dragon growled, "I would like to see him try."

"Wait, wait, wait!" Norm shouted, his voice cracking in terror. "I didn't, I mean, I'm sorry that I...help me out here, kid!"

The four teens came out from behind the dragons and approached Norm, who immediately got as close to them as he could, looking for some sort of protection. Kinaari turned up her nose. "This is him, the mage?"

Jason answered, "What were you all expecting?" as he laughed on the inside, knowing how un-magelike Norm looked.

Tiffany grumbled, "Shouldn't he have a staff or long robes or something?"

Norm protested, "Hey, I didn't come all the way here for a fashion intervention from a bunch of snot-nosed—"

Calor sneered, "Watch your tongue, little man."

Norm held up his hands in surrender. "Okay, okay, I see the dynamic here...the pecking order, so to speak. Dragons and kids on top, only mage around that can help them on the bottom. Right?"

They exchanged glances with each other, realizing they might have overdone the intimidation. Jason said, "Right, Norm. We hear you. We're all a little tense, y'know?"

Norm straightened up and craned his neck from side to side, trying to stretch out the tension. "So," he began, "we have four kids and four dragons, and you want a way to integrate dragons into society without giving the entire free world a coronary. That about sum it up?" They nodded, and Norm continued, "Right...well...I did, um, some research, and our options are really limited. Then when you add performing magic on a dragon, it gets really messy."

"Why's that?" Marcus asked.

"Like I told the skinny one over there," he pointed to Jason, "dragons are inherently magical creatures. It's part of their DNA and flows in their blood. When you try to superimpose one type of magic on top of another type of magic, you get interference, or resistance, or whatever scientific word you want. So I can cast a spell on you kids and know what is going to happen…but throw our other four guests into the mix, and it gets really tough."

Petros spoke up. "Which is why it is always a challenge for mages to battle dragons; their spells are not as effectual."

Tiffany asked, "So it's like a magic resistance?"

Norm shook his head. "More like an incompatibility. Best I can describe it, kid, is how you can't plug a toaster from the United States in an outlet in England. The voltages aren't the same; you need an adaptor."

Jason asked, "So you had to build an adaptor into your spell and hope that it works?"

Norm regarded Jason. "You're smart, kid. Yep, that's exactly what I had to do."

Tonare still felt like intimidating and lowered his head almost face to face with Norm. "And what it is you intend to do to us, mage?"

Norm swallowed hard. "Look, man, back off a little. I get the whole I'm-bigger-and-badder-than-you thing, okay?" Petros looked hard at Tonare, who looked to Marcus. Marcus gave Tonare the nod to back off, and Tonare pulled his head back.

Marcus approached Norm. "It's like this: we've got no idea what you're gonna do to us, and frankly we're all nervous at best or scared to death at worst."

Norm looked Marcus up and down. "You're a big one, aren't you?"

Marcus folded his arms. "Football does wonders."

Norm turned up his nose. "Sports are a waste of time. I can understand your being scared and all; I'd probably feel that same thing. But remember this was all at your request, okay? Anyway, the best I can describe what I've figured out is called a fugue."

No one responded. All had confused expressions on their faces.

Norm rubbed his hand over his unshaven jaw. "Okay, look, for the sake of our discussion, a fugue is a sort of overwriting of personalities, but in this case it isn't so much of an overwrite as it is a sharing. The spell I'm casting is gonna allow the dragons to see through the eyes of the kids and feel the same emotions as well, so they can experience whatever the kids experience and hopefully learn all the different nuances of this messed-up country of ours."

Jason shook his head. "Hey, spare us the commentary, okay? Is this thing you're gonna do something we can turn on and off? 'Cause I'm not too comfortable knowing that someone—no offense, Petros—is gonna see me, like, you know, in the bathroom or something."

Norm nodded. "Yeah, I thought about that, so that's why we're gonna need a conduit to establish the connection."

"Conduit?" Procella asked.

"Well, yeah, something that will establish and terminate the connection at will."

She continued, "And what sort of 'something' did you have in mind?"

He swallowed, knowing this next point would not go over well. "I, umm, need two scales from each of you?" The dragons, almost as if on cue, opened their mouths to protest, but Norm cut them off. "Yeah, I know, I know that people like me back in your time would come after scales from, uh, 'people' like you for money or profit or whatever. But I need one scale as an anchor that the kids will be keeping on their persons, and the second needs to go into the spell to help resolve the incompatibilities. I'm not keeping any of them."

The dragons exchanged cautious looks with each other before Petros spoke. "Very well. Go on."

Norm's shoulders slumped in relief. "Well, that's about it. I need two scales from each of you, and I need to lay out the spell. After that, it's showtime."

Jason decided to be the one who collected scales from each of the dragons, hoping it would minimize the stress of handing their scales over to a potentially opportunistic mage. Norm instructed the dragons to use their claws and poke a small hole at the back of one of their scales and then gave Jason four lengths of leather cord. The cords were strung through the holes, and the teens each hung the scales from their necks, like a pendant.

While they were accomplishing this task, Norm produced a can of bright orange spray paint from under his poncho and began to spray large shapes over the forest floor. He created a large square, and then from each side he painted a long isosceles triangle, ultimately creating a large, bright orange, four-pointed star on the forest floor. Finally, he connected the tips of each triangle with a large arc, completing a circle around the entire shape with the tip of each triangle touching the circle. Norm then instructed the teenagers to gather wood for a fire in the center of the square. It took them several minutes to find decent wood in the darkness, but soon the makings of an impressive bonfire was gathered. Norm borrowed Jason's flashlight, shone it on the wood, and, with an unintelligible utterance, he sent a pulse along the beam of light and instantly ignited the fire. Everyone present was startled at the unexpected ignition, and he handed the flashlight back to Jason as he smirked. "Heh...never was a Boy Scout."

The newly lit fire cast a soft, amber light on the clearing. Norm and the girls took a few moments to warm themselves by the fire, and Petros summoned Jason and Marcus back to speak with him and the other dragons.

"You are positive you wish to go through with this, Little Knight?" Petros asked.

Procella added, "There is no shame in terminating these activities. The outcomes are uncertain."

Jason answered, "I won't lie that my anxiety level is up to here," he held his hand up to his forehead, "but it's for the best. You can't spend your lives hiding in forests and caves."

Marcus added, "Hewes is right. It doesn't seem like it'll be much of an inconvenience or anything. You'll see through our eyes when you want to, and we take the scale off when we need privacy. S'all good. Let's get this done."

Jason felt his heart swell at Marcus's inspiring confidence and gave a nod of agreement back to his friend. He walked over to the fire and laid a hand on each of the girl's shoulders. They looked up at him with smiles on their faces, and he said, "I think we're just about ready."

Norm blurted, "Good! Let's get this over with."

Jason rolled his eyes. "Dude, I'm giving you access to four magical creatures that, until a couple of weeks ago, you thought didn't exist. You could show a little gratitude."

Norm countered, "Right, creatures that've made every effort to frighten and intimidate me since I got here. Yeah, good times, kid…good times."

Jason thought about continuing the debate but knew that Norm was right to an extent. He was doing all of this without asking for any type of payment, or anything in return for that matter, so they probably shouldn't have been giving him so much grief. Jason changed the subject. "I gotta ask, what's with the hat and poncho?"

Norm shrugged as he began making some final arrangements for the spell. "They're enchanted—tools to aid me with big stuff like this. The hat is a source of focus, and the poncho protects me from any magical feedback."

Kinaari overheard the conversation and innocently asked, "Couldn't you have picked something more, you know, stylish?"

Norm leveled a stare at her. "Like what, princess, a robe or a pointed cap? Or maybe a fedora and a trenchcoat? That would look all 'cool' and everything, right?"

Kinaari shrugged. "Well, yes. Maybe a designer baseball cap and a bomber jacket. I don't know; it's hard to make a hat look really mystical, but—"

Norm interrupted. "Wow, you're naïve, aren't you? It's sarcasm, princess, sarcasm."

She lowered her head. "Don't call me that."

Norm went on. "If you must know, the materials in each of these are ideally suited for the kinds of enchantment I put on them.

I don't give a flip how they look 'cause, like I said, they're tools, not accessories. Maybe if you put down the latest issue of *Cosmopolitan*, you'd understand the world doesn't operate from the Paris runways, Barbie."

Jason felt a flare of anger and stepped between them. "Hey! It was just an innocent question. Back off; you don't have to get all up in her face like that. Just go get ready for the spell. Let's get this over with." He turned to Kinaari; the firelight betrayed the tears welling up in her eyes. "You okay?" he asked.

She dabbed at the corner of her eyes with the cuffs of her shirt sleeves and nodded. "Yes. I'm not like that, you know. Not a princess."

Jason turned one corner of his mouth up in a sympathetic smile. "I know, Kinaari, I know."

Kinaari turned and started walking the perimeter of the bright orange circle. Tiffany went to join her but said to Jason, "Norm's kind of a jerk."

Jason nodded. "Yeah, leave it to me to find the only mage in this part of the country, and it turns out he's got all the tact of a rabid badger."

Tiffany coughed out a laugh. "Rabid badger, I like that." She laid her hand on his shoulder and slowly let it drag off as she walked away.

Norm was giving the circle a final inspection when Procella craned her head down next to him. "I regret our behavior toward you; it was not a becoming way to treat someone who is about to grant such a monumental favor."

Norm nodded. "Yeah, yeah, yeah. We're all just full of manners, aren't we?"

Procella went on. "That being said, I heard how you addressed Kinaari there by the fire."

Norm didn't make eye contact with her. "Kin...oh, Princess Fashion Plate, right. Those kind of kids get on my nerves."

Procella hissed through her teeth quietly but firmly, "Look at me when I am talking to you, little man!" Norm's head whipped around, his eyes wide as Procella went on. "Despite my apology, I strongly suggest you take what I am about to say with every degree of seriousness that it is intended. If I ever…*ever* hear you address that girl in such a fashion again, there will be no force in the world that will stop me from decimating you where you stand without thought or regret. Do I make myself clear?" Norm swallowed hard and nodded vigorously. Procella said, "Good. Now work your magic and be gone. There is no need to draw this out any further."

Norm had the four kids stand inside the square, each facing one of the sides. He then asked the dragons with whom they were to be bonded to sit at the tips of the large triangles so they were facing the teenagers. He laid the extra scales inside the large triangles that formed the four-pointed star. The mage spent a few moments adjusting everyone's precise placement, making everything as symmetrical as he could. He took a few steps backward when he was satisfied with everything then produced what appeared to be a small quilt from under his poncho.

Tiffany said to Marcus, "How is he fitting all of that stuff under his poncho?"

"Shhh!" Marcus hissed. "He's magicating."

The quilt was a patchwork of completely mismatched colors and fabrics; unidentifiable symbols and runes were randomly sewn across the entire surface of the small throw. Norm sat cross-legged on the quilt after he spread it on the ground, closed his eyes, and began to mutter something under his breath.

The onlookers were underwhelmed initially, but they soon noticed a small breeze began to pick up. The wind grew stronger, and as the fire began to falter at the smaller gusts, the orange paint on the ground began to glow an eerie green color. A small pinpoint of white light began to flow in the glowing green lines then another and another until an entire current of pinpricks of light were following the glowing green lines in a frenetic fashion. Soon, blue points of light appeared, then yellow, then violet until the base green of the glowing lines was lost into multicolor streaks of magical energy flowing within the entire shape Norm had painted into the detritus of the forest floor.

The increasing wind was now strong enough to cause Kinaari's and Tiffany's long hair to blow wildly about their heads, and they fought to keep it out of their eyes so they could watch the spell being woven. The dragons watched intently and began to realize Norm was a man of true magical knowledge and actually relaxed as the incantation became more and more complex. Norm's eyes were tightly shut, and his incantation became louder and took on a more fevered pitch as the quilt he sat upon began to quiver beneath him and then, to the surprise of all, levitated off the ground. Norm's concentration seemed unaffected as he focused harder on the spell, the winds converging on him and swirling around the quilt, making his poncho wave furiously.

The points of light flowed with ever-increasing speed through their geometric paths and then began leaping in small arcs off their two-dimensional channels. The teens watched with wonder as the glowing pinpoints jumped completely free on occasion, swirling toward their bodies, and then began orbiting around them and their corresponding dragons. More and more colored motes followed in this fashion until four figure-eight-shaped, flowing currents of countless tiny spheres of blazing magic circulated around the teens and their dragons. The clearing in the forest had become a torrent of magical activity, and the kids struggled to comprehend what was happening. Then the last thing they, or the dragons, wanted to see occurred.

Norm's eyes snapped open, and he said, "Oh…no!"

All at once, the lights flowing on the ground simultaneously exploded in a ninety-degree turn and became cascades of magical power flowing upward in the air, forming scintillating curtains of energy in the shape of the original pattern Norm painted on the ground. The teens and dragons all froze, backs arched, eyes wide and facing skyward. The energy flowing around them increased its speed exponentially until it was impossible to perceive the individual points of light. A second pulse of energy erupted outward, and Norm was thrown off his quilt and rolled to a stop on the ground. He scrambled to his feet and ran toward the curtain of power shouting, "No! I've lost control of the spell!"

Norm's hands began to glow with green energy as he thrust them into the shimmering magical screens and was physically trying to force the power back to the ground but to no avail. "No, no, noooo!" he bellowed as a third, more powerful pulse of eldritch power burst from the entire area, casting Norm fifteen feet backward and shaking all of the trees around the clearing. The flow of power increased; the intensity of the light magnified until all color muted into white. Then, in one final pulse of magical cacophony, everything exploded in a blaze of pure, white, gleaming brilliance.

And then…darkness.

Chapter 16

"Unnnnnggghhh…"

Petros's head pounded, and he could feel his vision spinning even while his eyes were closed. He could tell he was lying down and assumed it was on the forest floor. He fought hard to open his eyes, but his optic nerves protested against the sunlight seeping between his eyelids.

How long have I been unconscious? he thought to himself. *The sun is shining again.*

He forced his eyes open, and after adjusting to the daylight, he found himself lying on his back and staring at the tops of the trees around the clearing. He blinked his eyes several times; the top branches seemed much farther away than he had remembered, and the colors seemed muted or muddy. The word escaped Petros, but his vision was changed somehow. He could only surmise it was a side effect of the spell.

"Hello?" he called out, lying still, his body refusing to move. No answer came, and the pain in his head intensified. Needing to soothe the severe throbbing behind his eyes, he reached up with his hands to…

Hands? Human hands came into his field of vision, and he realized it was his will that moved them. The panic that washed through his body drowned the pain he felt as he sat bolt upright. He examined his body and saw nothing but human anatomy where his powerful dragon form should be. Blue jeans, Chuck Taylor sneakers, red flannel shirt over a t-shirt. This looked like Jason's…

"Oh, no," Petros said audibly as he looked around the clearing. The unconscious bodies of Marcus, Kinaari, and Tiffany were all sprawled on the forest floor, but no signs of the dragons could be seen. Petros felt around Jason's chest and found his own scale still suspended from its leather cord around the boy's neck. He could tell that the other human children still wore their scales as well, but the second scales Norm had laid in the large triangles were nowhere to be seen. In fact, the entire shape Norm had spray painted on the ground was gone; all evidence of the spell had disappeared.

Petros struggled to stand on Jason's legs. It wasn't completely unusual for him to balance on two legs; dragons reared back on their haunches quite often. But a solely bipedal mode of locomotion was foreign to Petros, and he struggled for several minutes to find the appropriate balance before he felt comfortable enough to walk as a human did.

"How these humans get about on these scrawny little toothpicks I'll never know," he said out loud as he practiced and realized for the first time that the voice expressing his thoughts was Jason's, not his own. He shook his head and frowned deeply. "I should have let Tonare eat the mage."

He looked at the other three still unconscious on the leaves and needles of the forest floor and assumed the same fate had befallen them. He walked over to Kinaari, whom he surmised was actually Procella, arguably the smartest of the group. Petros tried two or three times before he successfully crouched down without falling over. He reached out with Jason's hand and shook her shoulder.

"Procella? Procella, you must awaken," he said loudly.

Kinaari stirred and groaned, "Jason? Little Knight, what has happened?"

Petros answered, "You need to open your eyes, cousin, and see what has befallen us."

"Jason, why are you referring to me as—" She paused, and her eyes snapped open, realizing her voice was not her own. Pushing herself to her now-human elbows, she looked over Kinaari's body and then Jason's. Her head dropped and solemnly waved back and forth. "It would appear the spell did not have its intended results."

Petros stood back up and offered Procella his/Jason's hand. She took it, and he clumsily assisted her to Kinaari's feet. She struggled for balance but finally found her footing as he let her stand unassisted. Procella looked at their surroundings with narrowed eyes. "What is wrong with my vision? Everything looks...how do I describe it?"

Petros interrupted. "Yes, colors are muted; we cannot see as far. I can only assume it is the difference in the human eye versus our own. And I find it very unnerving that Jason's voice is expressing my thoughts." He stretched his neck and rubbed his hand over his throat. "This human biology is quite disconcerting."

Procella was examining Kinaari's deep black hair. "I have hair. What does one do with hair?"

Petros answered, "I do not know, but I gather that the female of the species seems more concerned over the organization and general tidiness of their hair than the male does."

She looked at the hair on Jason's head. "Yes, it would appear so. You, umm—" She reached forward and plucked a small leaf out of Jason's/Petros's unkempt coif.

He saw it and said, "Ah, umm, yes, thank you."

Procella cocked her head curiously. "That is odd; your skin appears to be spontaneously changing hue. It is becoming a more pronounced shade of red."

Petros nodded. "Yes, I feel a slight temperature change in my face as well. It coincided with a feeling of embarrassment that you needed to pull a leaf out of my hair. It would seem a human's skin changes when they are embarrassed. It is an unsettling feeling."

They were interrupted as Tiffany/Calor began to stir. She pushed herself up and started at the realization that it was with human hands. She regarded herself then saw Petros and Procella staring at her with looks of understanding and sympathy.

Realization came over her, and the girl's face twisted in a vicious snarl. "I am going to kill that mage."

***

Tonare soon regained consciousness as well, in the body of Marcus, and the four spent the next several minutes working out the basics of human kinesthetics. They agreed that all but their sense of touch was diminished in their human forms, and they felt a substantial degree of fear at being both small and vulnerable.

"And," Tonare emphasized, "we now have to wear clothing!"

Petros stated, "Humans need it both for protection and for modesty. Walking around without clothing is not a socially acceptable practice for humans."

Calor sneered. "I cannot believe this; I feel cold! Tiffany needs to get some flesh on these skinny bones of hers. It is almost unfathomable for a Heat dragon to feel cold."

Procella calmly responded, "You are not a Heat dragon anymore, Calor. At least not for now."

Tonare demanded, "And what is this hollowness in my stomach?"

Petros shook his head. "It is what humans most likely feel when they are hungry."

Procella said, "We should probably return to Jason's home for both food and shelter."

"And then what?" Tonare demanded.

Calor added, "What a humiliation! The only vestiges of our true selves are hanging around our necks on a leather cord! And it would seem our other scales were consumed by the spell."

Petros countered, "It would seem that way."

Calor asked, "You believe the mage scum took them?"

He shrugged. "Based on our current predicament, I can no longer believe anything he said."

Procella purposely changed the topic. "Let us return to the house. We can take shelter and then decide what to do from there."

The walk back to the house was without incident, but the dragons quickly realized they could not cover ground as quickly. From their perspective, each step covered very little distance, and they began taking strides as long as their legs would stretch. They looked ridiculous but felt they were, as Procella described it, maximizing the efficiency of their human forms without running, which they had not yet attempted.

In time, the four were standing on the porch and staring at the door leading into the kitchen. Calor had impatiently taken the lead.

"I am unsure as to how to make the portal open," she admitted after a time of examining the door.

Petros looked over her shoulder. "I believe the polished, metal orb is the mechanism for access."

Calor turned purposefully toward Petros. "Well, I *know* that! I just don't know what to do to it."

Tonare rolled his eyes. "Step aside, step aside," Marcus's deep voice rumbled. "This is technology, remember? It is not handled in traditional fashions. You need to be of a younger generation." He cleared his throat and stared intently at the door. "Open!" he projected to the doorknob.

They waited.

Petros asked, "At what point does your generational youth actually make the door open?"

Tonare was about to object, but Procella let out an exasperated sigh and budged her way to the front. "Wings and scales, did you not learn anything from watching the streaming movies?" She reached out with Kinaari's hand, took the knob firmly, and twisted it. There was a click, and she pushed the door open. "There. See what an educational source streaming movies can be?"

The other three reluctantly shrugged their shoulders in agreement as they entered the kitchen. They stood in the doorway for several moments, taking in the objects around the room. The stove, microwave, refrigerator, dishwasher, and sink were all unfamiliar to them. The only things they actually had any idea how to use were the table and chairs placed in the middle of the large country kitchen. Each took a reluctant place around the table and simply sat, unsure what to do next. Their faces were sullen as their minds struggled to process their unexpected and fateful transformation. Soon, however, Calor held up her arms and looked disgustedly over Tiffany's body.

"Why am I leaking water? First I was cold; now water is oozing from my skin."

Tonare looked very concerned. "Humans leak? I know they bleed in typical fashion, but this is repulsive. Look at her!"

Procella held up her hands. "There is no need to panic; a similar phenomenon occurs to a cold liquid in a glass container; water forms on the outside in a warm environment. Here..." She ran her finger across Calor's forehead and touched the liquid to her tongue. Her face quickly contorted into a grimace. "Ugh. It has a very salty taste."

Tonare, Petros, and even Calor herself were curious, and each took a turn sampling the sweat on Tiffany's body. Petros shook his head. "That is highly unusual. We are nowhere near an ocean, so I do not understand why the water forming on the outside of her body would be salty. Calor, there appears to be a cloth of some sort on that counter there. Perhaps you can use it to absorb this odd leakage while we try to figure out what to do next."

Calor nodded in agreement, and, after fetching the towel, she returned to the table when the "Imperial March" from *Star Wars* began blaring from under the table. The four started at the sound, and their heads whipped back and forth trying to determine its source.

"What is that?" Tonare demanded.

"It is a horrible sound," added Calor. "Perhaps some sort of weapon!"

Procella tried to remain calm and spoke loudly. "Petros, it sounds as if it is coming from your leg."

A look of deep concern came over his face, and he stood up quickly, knocking over his chair. Reaching into Jason's front pocket, he produced a cell phone. He pointed to it emphatically. "It is Jason's phone!"

Procella said, "Yes, I concluded that on my own. Do you know how to operate it?"

He looked at the screen. "Ah, George's name is on it. Perhaps George is attempting to contact Jason."

Tonare shouted, "Well, why would he do that? Does he not know that you now occupy Jason's body?" The other three shot looks at Tonare in response to his less-than-intelligent statement. He conceded, "Ah, no, of course not. Can you not see the stress I am under? I cannot make statements that even make sense anymore!"

Petros said, "Very well, calm down. I have seen Jason do this once or twice. There, you see? There is a square that reads, 'Answer.' If I touch that—" He touched it, and the ringtone stopped. Looks of relief came over all of their faces.

Calor nodded. "Well played, Petros, well played."

They all reveled in the silence but in moments heard a very tiny voice coming from the phone. "Jason? Hello? Jace, hello?"

Petros held the phone to his ear as he saw Jason do on several occasions and heard George's voice coming from the device.

"Jace, you there? Helloooooooo? Jason Hewes, paging Jason Hewes…"

Petros responded awkwardly, "Uh, yes, umm, is this George? George?"

"Jace? You there? It's George."

"Hello? Greetings, George. This is George to whom I am speaking?"

"Jason, what's the matter with you? Yes, it's George."

"Ah, George? This is George. I am speaking to George, correct?"

"Yes! It's George!"

Petros held out the phone and pointed to it, showing the other dragons. "It is George."

Procella replied flatly, "Yes, we gathered."

Petros held the phone back to his ear. "Go ahead and speak, George. I am listening."

"Dude, you're acting like you've never used a phone before. You told me you'd call and tell me what happened with Norm and the spell and all. You and the dragons linked somehow?"

Petros searched for an answer. "You could say that, yes. The spell had, how do I verbalize this? Unexpected results."

George paused for a moment. "Hmm, could you be a little more vague? I almost understood what you were saying."

"I do not know how to respond to that. I cannot see your face. This phone talking is very unnerving."

"Jason, what's wrong with you? What did that spell do? You're talking weird, you're not using contractions…jeepers, you sound like—" George paused. "Oh, no. Am I really talking to Jason?"

Petros paused even longer. "I think it would be prudent if you were to come to the house as quickly as possible."

"On it," George replied, and the phone call ended.

It took George nearly a half hour to convince his parents to let him drive the car and get to Jason's house. He burst in through the front door without knocking and found the four in the kitchen. Procella/Kinaari had the door to the porch open and was crouched next to it, twisting the doorknob back and forth and watching the locking mechanism slide in and out. Calor/Tiffany was seated at the table with three empty twenty-ounce bottles of Mountain Dew lined in front of her. Her pupils were dilated, and she rapidly bounced her right leg up and down while rapping her fingers on the table as fast as she could. Tonare/Marcus was seated at the table as well, but in front of him was an empty jar of mayonnaise, a bottle of chocolate syrup, and an onion with several bites taken out of it. A distressed expression was on his face, and both hands were clutching his stomach. Finally, Petros/Jason was leaning against the counter holding the smart phone in his hand with a look of intense concentration on his face. He was tentatively tapping the touch screen with his fingers when he looked up at a slack-jawed George.

Petros asked, "What is 'Angry Birds'?"

George's worst fears were confirmed. "Oh, dear Lord, you're Petros, aren't you?"

Calor's head whipped around. "ThisbeveragethatJasondrinksisquitedelicious." George's eyes widened as she added, "Yetitleavesmesomewhatagitated."

Procella turned and said, "I find doorknobs fascinating. May I take apart this door to see how it works?"

George tried to shake the confusion out of his head when Tonare added, "I feel a disturbance in my abdomen. Do humans sometimes eject the food they have eaten?" His cheeks puffed out, and he held his hand over his mouth.

George pointed. "Get outside and let what happens happen." Tonare knocked the chair over as he jumped up and ran out to the yard. George ran his hand over his face. "Could someone please tell me what happened?"

Calor said, "Thescummage'sspellwasafailure. MayIhaveanotheroneofthese?"

George shook his head emphatically. "No! No, no, no, you're cut off. Petros, can you help me out here?"

Petros detailed the events of the previous evening as George listened intently. Meanwhile, Procella moved to the refrigerator and was repeatedly opening and closing the door, trying to see if the light stayed on when the door was shut.

George asked, "So where are all of your bodies?"

Petros answered, "We are unsure. We did not see them anywhere on our way back. It could be possible that Norm has taken them, but I do not know how he would have physically moved them back to where he came from."

George asked, "Couldn't he just use the same portal-whatsit that he used to get here?"

Procella responded as she returned to the table, "Very unlikely. Portal magic is much more difficult than one would realize. That is why most portals are only big enough to transport two or three human-sized individuals at a time. Given how Norm could not control his own spell, I highly doubt he had the means to create a portal big enough to accommodate a dragon, much less hold it open long enough to move four."

Tonare plodded back into the kitchen, wiping his mouth with his sleeve. "Human bodies are revolting. How do you even survive on the food you have to eat?"

"Yeah," George answered. "Mayonnaise, onion, and chocolate sauce surprise is not a meal that anyone would recommend you eat. You can't just eat anything in any combination, Tonare."

Tonare looked disgusted. "You humans are so fragile."

George smirked. "We."

Tonare was confused. "Eh?"

George clarified, "We…we humans. You're one of us now, blue boy."

Tonare huffed and flared his nostrils as he folded his arms over his chest and flopped against the wall.

Procella steered herself away from the kitchen appliances, resisting the temptation to experiment with the microwave. "We need a course of action. We obviously cannot remain in this state."

Petros said, "I am open to suggestions. One thing may be to try to locate our bodies; at least we will then know if we will be able to inhabit them again."

George shook his head. "Look, I hate to complicate this, but Marcus, Tiffany, and Kinaari's parents will be expecting them home soon, and Jason's dad will be getting back as well. I'm not sure if we can find your bodies, figure out how to get you switched back, and get you all home in time."

Procella's head dropped. "I had not thought of that."

Petros added, "It is a very complicating factor."

Calor interjected, "I have another complicating factor."

George asked, "What is that?"

Calor said, "I feel an odd pressure in my lower abdomen."

George dismissed it. "You're probably full after three Mountain Dews."

Calor looked confused. "The stomach is here, is it not?" She had a hand resting on her belly. George nodded, and she continued. "The pressure I feel is lower." She moved her hand down to her pelvis.

George's shoulders slumped. "It means you have to go to the bathroom."

Calor's eyebrows raised. "Your bodies have a physiological indication when it is time for you to move to another room?"

Now George looked confused. "What? No, it means you have to relieve yourself. You know…release, um, waste from your body."

Understanding came over Calor's face. "Ah, yes, to the woods then."

George interrupted. "Um, no. We have bathrooms, and toilets, and plumbing for all of that."

Calor shook her head, indicating she did not understand. The other three did the same.

George's head flopped into his hands as he felt the stress mounting over what he was going to have to teach the dragons. This was the absolute last thing he thought he was going to have to do when he woke up that morning. He wanted to be involved in the dragons' lives, but this was not what he signed up for.

Getting up quickly from the table, he said, "Okay, everyone, follow me to the bathroom. You're probably going to want to take notes."

Chapter 17

George sat at the kitchen table, his face covered by his hands. Procella sat with him.

"Squire George, there is no reason to be embarrassed. You provided us with the education we need about human physiology."

George's muffled voice answered, "Under most circumstances, humans don't have to teach others how to use the bathroom until they have their own children. But not for me. I have to teach a group of my own peers the nuances of, well, uuuuugh."

Procella searched for words. "Is your face exhibiting the blushing reaction that Petros did earlier today?"

He turned to her, his face bright red. "I am way beyond blushing, Kinaar...I mean Procella. Ahhh...I'm so confused." He buried his head in his palms again.

"It was very informative. You are a good teacher," she tried to reassure.

"Oh...goody."

She thought again. "Toilet paper is an amazing invention."

George sat bolt upright. "Okay! Can we talk about something else, please?"

She nodded. "Very well."

He asked, "Where are the others?"

"Petros and Calor are watching, what did you call it? Ah, the television. And Tonare is, umm..."

"Where is he?" George asked suspiciously.

"He is using the bathroom."

"Right," George stated and flopped his head back into his hands.

The small bathroom on the first floor of the Hewes homestead barely fit the description in the modern sense. Jason's father had installed it in the space of an old hallway closet shortly after they moved into the house. There was barely enough room for a commode and a tiny sink, and one had to back away from the door and squeeze into the space between the toilet and the wall in order to fully open the door and leave the room. There were lots of jokes from houseguests about the size, or lack thereof, of the facilities, but Timothy's answer was always that with two small children, having a second bathroom was always a good idea.

Tonare had just flushed the toilet and was muttering under his breath, "Human bodies are so revolting" as he turned to wash his hands as George instructed him. There was no mirror over the tiny sink, and Tonare strained to see his reflection in the polished chrome of the sink's fixtures. The curvature of the metal distorted his features, and he grunted in frustration as he turned away to maneuver his body to get the door open. As he exited the room, something nagged him at the back of his mind. He swore that, as he moved away from the sink, his reflection in the metal moved independently of his own movements. He turned to recheck the chrome but then shook the thought out of his head and let logic prevail. He simply grunted, "Pitiful human eyesight" and rejoined his comrades.

Procella saw the disgusted look on Tonare's face as he sat back down and said, "Adjusting to these bodies will take some time."

He growled, "We should devote our energies to reversing this spell rather than adjusting to these pathetic fleshbags."

George lifted his head. "Umm…pathetic fleshbag sitting right here, dude. You can show a little respect, you know."

Tonare waved a dismissive hand. "You do not understand."

George replied, "Look, out of the five of us, you've got the strongest and sturdiest body. If you remember, that body is the one that held on tight to the back of your old body when your old self was trying to shake your new self off your old neck. So show a little gratitude."

Tonare looked to Procella and then back to George. "I did not follow what you just said, but I detect the tone of a rebuke."

George rolled his eyes in exasperation. "I'm just trying to say that you got Marcus: big, strong, good-looking, football player Marcus. Guys like me would give anything to be a guy like him, so just lay off the 'pathetic fleshbag' stuff, okay?"

Procella looked concerned. "We do not understand, Squire George. Dragon bodies are quite different, yet it is never a source of contention among us. Can you tell us why it is so significant for humans?"

George rubbed his hand over his face. "People, teenagers especially, can be petty, you know? There is a tendency to look for something to hold over someone's head and make them feel inferior. Kids like Jason and me, we're just fodder for ridicule. Jason is thin, not especially tall, not into sports, but he's smart. Me, well, look at me. I'm overweight, I work at a Dairy Queen, and girls like Kinaari never give me a second look. Guys like Marcus, well, they usually end up stuffing kids like Jason or me in a locker or something else stupid like that for fun. That's my life. You just try to be the best 'you' you can be, and you get laughed at for it. It gets old really fast, and you get angry and start to die inside. Makes you feel like life's not always worth living."

Procella gave a sideways glace at Tonare, whose expression had softened. He said, "I was unaware humans treat each other like that."

George shrugged. "It's not everybody, and lots of schools are trying to do stuff against bullying. But here in Montana, you know, we're a little more out of the way, and progress is slower. Marcus is different. He's the first football player I've known who stands up for guys like me. I wish—"

Procella said, "Go on."

George took a deep breath. "I wish you could be a little more like him, Tonare."

"But I am not—" Tonare blurted but then saw Procella glancing reproachfully at him. He was silent for a few beats, and a look of shame came over his face. "I did not realize. You have been helpful to us, Squire George, and I thank you. I will take what you said under consideration."

George nodded his thanks, and the tension was broken by the ringing of the doorbell. Procella and Tonare were startled, but George said, "Relax. It's the doorbell."

Procella leaned in closer. "And what does that mean?"

George leaned in as well. "It means someone is on the other side of the door and wants to come in."

"Oh," Procella responded. "I would then go to open the door and greet whoever is on the other side?"

George answered. "It's only neighborly."

She smiled, rose from the table, and headed to the door. The bell rang again. Calor and Petros turned off the television to inquire about the sound. Distracted by his quest for knowledge, Petros passed in front of the television and did not notice his reflection on the screen waving at him, as if it was trying to get his attention. They met Procella as she walked out of the kitchen. She explained, "We seem to have a visitor. I am going to see who it is."

Petros and Calor nodded in approval as Procella walked through the living room to the front door. As she opened it, their looks of curiosity faded to expressions of dread, for at the door stood a tall male, well over six feet, dressed from head to toe in black leather and wearing a similarly black motorcycle helmet over his face. Stainless-steel shoulder pads made the figure's already broad shoulders appear massive, and a red insignia patch was sewn onto the upper arms of the man's jacket. He towered over the form of Kinaari, and his head silently moved downward to meet her gaze. His right arm lifted up, holding a pistol of some sort in his gloved hand. With a squeeze of the trigger, two thin wires lanced from the object and imbedded in Kinaari's shoulder. She began to convulse at their impact, and as the others watched, stunned and unsure how to respond, the girl slumped to the floor motionless.

"Run!" George screeched, but the sound of a human voice growling came from the body of Tiffany as Calor charged at the intruder and, leaping into the air, drove the girl's body into the chest of the black rider. He was unprepared for her assault and staggered backward from the front door before he could compensate for her momentum. He regained his footing, seized the girl as she was trying to bite through his leather jacket, and threw her across the porch. She hit the wood planking with a loud thud and skidded to a stop under the porch swing.

The rider turned to re-enter the house when a silver flash came through the doorway, impacted his helmet, and careened off onto the lawn. The force was enough to drive him back another step, but he stopped just short of tumbling down the porch steps.

The darkly clad trespasser was distracted by whatever hit him, and he turned his helmeted head to see a silver toaster lying on the lawn beyond the porch, a large dent now distorting the once-pristine polished surface.

Tonare used the distraction to charge at the rider and threw his full weight through the air, tackling the villain and bringing their tumbling forms down the stairs and onto the grass. Tonare was careful to keep his opponent's body under his own and protect himself from the bone-jarring roll down the stairs. Tonare was impressed with Marcus's strength and made the decision to use every last ounce of it to fend off this attacker.

Back inside, Petros ran to George, who was in the kitchen, huddled in fear. Petros seized the boy by the shoulders.

"George! Are you hurt?"

George's eyes were wide with terror and wet with tears. He stammered, "Wh…what is—"

Petros set his jaw tightly. "This must be the trespasser Jason saw outside the barn. He must have returned for whatever he came for. You must check on Procella; I need to help the others." With that, Petros sprinted toward the melee and left George alone. Despite his emotional state, George was able to shuffle himself to the fallen Kinaari. As he felt for her pulse, he heard her groan as she began to regain consciousness. He couldn't think of what to do but stay close to her and try to protect her from whatever might come.

Tonare rolled free from grappling with the black rider and crouched in a defensive position, facing the house. He could feel pain in his upper body, and a throbbing pulsed across his scalp. He placed his hand on his head and found a large bump rising; he must have hit the rider's helmet with his head during his attack. Trying to push the distractions away, he watched the rider quickly get back to his feet, seemingly unaffected by Tonare's attack. Tonare knew he couldn't let his foe regain his balance, so he charged again, this time wrapping his arms around the rider's torso, and pushed up and forward with all his might. He landed with his shoulder on the man's sternum, driving all his weight onto the intruder's chest. As they hit the earth, Tonare heard a cracking sound come from beneath the black leather and felt something in his foe's chest buckle. He had no time to revel in the damage he thought he caused, for the rider drove his fist into Tonare's back like a pile driver, making the boy arch skyward from the pain. The second fist impacted Tonare squarely on the jaw and sent him rolling across the grass. Tonare tried to push himself back to his feet and shook his head to clear the stars swimming in front of his eyes. The attacker, whatever it was, was amazingly strong, and Tonare knew he couldn't afford to take another punch like that one.

The dragon-in-a-boy's-body pushed himself back to his feet; he could feel the odd sensation of his face swelling where the punch connected. Tonare watched as the rider once again rose from the ground but this time more slowly, its knees buckling from whatever damage Tonare did. But as his foe reached his full height, Tonare watched him lurch forward as Petros and a recovered Calor wrapped themselves around the rider's legs. Petros shouted, "Hit him high!" and held on for dear life.

With a battle cry, Tonare charged again, this time throwing himself feet first into the air and delivering a two-legged kick to the rider's face. With the other two dragon-teens firmly anchoring their foe's feet to the ground, the black-suited miscreant bent over at the knees and hit the ground hard. Petros and Calor rolled away as the rider lay still on the ground, his legs bent awkwardly at the knees under his large body.

Petros and Calor scrambled to their feet as Tonare rose more slowly, his body aching from the fight. The battle had carried them to the corner of the house, and Tonare stood at the head of the motionless figure, just where the wall turned the corner. The other two stood facing Tonare at their foe's feet.

Petros caught his breath and said, "Well-delivered kick, cousin."

Calor nodded, also breathing heavily. "Yes, that body is well suited for combat."

Tonare was still fighting to catch his breath; sweat was beaded on his brow, and his cheek was quite swollen. "Thank you. He was quite str—"

Tonare's voice cut off rapidly as his eyes went wide, and he started to convulse. He fell to the ground, and Petros and Calor saw two wires running from his shoulder to the taser in the hand of the second black rider standing at the corner of the house. Calor sneered and let out a battle cry as she charged forward with Tiffany's slight body. She threw herself at the new target, but it swung its heavily muscled arm in a backhanded strike and sent Calor sprawling across the lawn. She slid to a stop and was still.

Petros stepped back into a defensive stance, but the rider charged and hit him like a battering ram, throwing him to the ground and landing firmly on top of him. The assailant produced a second taser. Petros got both hands up to intercept the rider's as it descended with the weapon, but he barely slowed it down. Petros couldn't believe he was going to meet defeat trapped in the body of a human, and he gnashed his teeth and pushed as hard as he could against the arm holding the taser. He didn't notice as the cool of the earth beneath him began to grow warmer. The sensation spread into his body, and he felt an odd surge of energy flow from his chest and into his arms. The rider's forward momentum slowed as Petros began to push back the descending weapon. The sensation flowing into his arms strengthened him and enabled him to resist his enemy. Petros let out a cry of rage, and he threw his foe backward and sent him rolling on the ground. He lifted himself up to his elbows again and stared in amazement at his hands, unable to understand what just happened.

His concentration was broken when a vice-like grip in the form of a black-gloved hand closed around his throat and hoisted him off the ground. His feet dangled above the lawn as he gazed into the black, reflective surface of the rider's helmet. He felt pain as his windpipe was constricted, and he clawed desperately at his attacker's arm, trying to get free. His vision began to tunnel as his oxygen was cut off, but then, to the surprise of both Jason and his attacker, a voice came from around the corner of the house.

"Awright, Hewes, I shoulda figured you somehow knew these black motorcycle freaks parkin' their imported, two-wheeled death traps all over Highway Two!"

Stan Whitman came around the corner. He had a head of steam built up and was ready to chew Jason Hewes out, but he stopped dead in his tracks when he saw the dark rider holding Jason by his neck. He went slack-jawed for a moment as Petros reached out for Stan, but nothing but a strained gasp came from his mouth. Stan shouted, "Oh, my G…Hewes! Hey, lettim go!" Stan charged at the intruder, but with nearly imperceptible speed, the rider's other arm darted out, seized Stan's throat, and lifted him off the ground as well. Stan fought to free himself from the cyclist's death grip but to no avail. Petros was now hanging limply from the rider's outstretched arm, and Stan began to panic. He held on to the gloved wrist with one hand while he reached into his pocket with the other and drew out his Leatherman multitool. He managed to unfold it with one hand and flip out the knife. Drawing every ounce of strength he had, Stan jammed the blade into the rider's arm. The hand released him, and Stan fell to the ground in a heap.

Recovering quickly, Stan threw his strongest roundhouse to the midsection of the rider, who flinched at the blow but did not let go of Petros. Stan took a few steps back and then charged at their foe, who adjusted his balance at Stan's approach and was able to skid backward along the ground instead of fall over at the impact. Stan tried frantically to push the rider over, but he was shocked at the figure's strength. He realized that brute force wouldn't gain Petros's release, so he resorted to more precise tactics. Crouching down, Stan delivered a savage kick to the side of the rider's knee. He heard a wet crack, and the joint bent sideways, bringing the tall figure to the ground and simultaneously causing him to release Petros. After the rider fell, Stan kicked his ribcage several times and his head twice before the black-clad villain no longer moved. The large teen ran to the fallen Petros, fell to his knees, and began to shake the unconscious boy.

"Hewes! Aw, c'mon, man, Hewes! Wake up, you skinny freak; don't you die on me!"

Petros suddenly took a gasping breath and began to cough uncontrollably. A look of relief came over Stan's face as he backed up on his knees and waited for the boy to recover.

Petros was finally able to say, "Wh…what was that?"

Stan looked surprised. "You tell me. There were two of them, and they were on your property."

Petros shook his head, still struggling for breath. "I do not know what they were."

Stan replied, "Yeah, well, they wanted to kill you; that's what they were."

Petros made eye contact with the bully. "Thank you, Stan Whitman."

Stan gave him an odd look. "Stan Whitman? Sheesh, you must still be air-deprived to the brain or somethin'. Look, you gonna call the sheriff on this, or should I?"

George appeared in the doorway and answered the question. "Uh, no. We'll call the cops, Stan. It's Jason's property, right?"

Stan started at George's appearance. "Jaworski, you're here too? Where were you when Darth Skywalker here was trying to kill your best buddy?"

George answered, "It's Darth Vader, and I was…in the bathroom."

Stan shook his head. "Nerd. Okay, look. I'm gettin' outta here before someone sees that I saved you and all of your geek friends too. Just tell the sheriff; I don't know who this biker gang is, but they mean serious business."

George shouted as Stan walked away, "Uh, okay, Stan. We will. Thanks for the help!" As Stan walked down the driveway to his truck, George ran down to Petros. "You all right?" he asked.

Petros nodded. "I will recover. What of the others?"

George replied, "They're all still out. We'd better check on them."

Making sure the two riders were still unconscious, they ran to check on Procella, Calor, and Tonare. Tonare was in the worst condition; not only had he taken a beating from the first black rider, but he had also been tasered, which left him bruised and scraped up and also weak in the knees from the shock. Calor had bruises all along her body, but Procella seemed to recover quickly after her experience at the business end of a taser. Petros was developing significant bruising around his neck from his strangulation at the hands of the second rider. He told his companions about the superior strength of the riders and about the brief moment that he was able to resist and push back against his foe's strength.

Procella thought for a moment then said, "That is highly unusual."

"Yeah, but people have been known to have adrenaline surges under conditions of extreme stress. It's a rare but not unheard-of human response," George commented.

Procella responded, "It could be, but I wonder if there is more to it than that."

"What do you mean?" George asked.

Calor interrupted, "We have two unconscious attackers lying on the lawn. Perhaps we should dispense with this oh-so scintillating theorizing and do something with them before they wake up."

They quickly agreed and rushed back to the two fallen opponents, only to find empty clothing lying in the exact positions where they fell. The bodies inside had completely vanished, replaced by a grayish-black ash.

"Well, this is unexpected," Tonare quipped.

Petros said, "That is an understatement."

George was bewildered. "What's going on here?"

Procella rubbed her chin and said, "I have no explanation for this phenomenon. Come…let us get the clothing inside so I can examine it more closely."

They quickly scooped up the leather uniforms and black helmets and rushed inside. George ran out to the road to find the motorcycles that Stan mentioned, but all he found there were two large piles of flakes of rusted metal. Buried under the piles were motorcycle tires, remnants of the black cycles the intruders had ridden to the homestead. George carried one of the tires inside and started to explain his findings to the four as they examined the riders' uniforms. But he noticed their faces were contorted into looks of intent concentration.

"What's wrong?" he asked.

Petros gestured to the logo patch on the sleeves of the jackets. The image was of a red batlike wing on a white field. Surrounding the symbol was a red circle with a single diagonal line through it. He said, "I recognize this symbol."

Procella added, "We all do."

George paused then asked, "Okay, what is it?"

Calor shook her head. "We do not know; that is what is so infuriating."

George was confused. "What does...I don't get it."

Tonare grimaced. "Some infernal magic erased our memories. All that is left is infuriating impressions of the past." He was obviously angry and struck his head, or Marcus's head, several times as he spoke.

George responded, "Okay, okay, no need to beat yourself silly. Let's see if we can get the image into a computer and run a search on it. Maybe something will come up." The four looked to each other and nodded in agreement as George went on. "It's almost lunch time, and I have a suggestion."

Procella said, "What is your suggestion?"

George took a deep breath. "I know we've had one heckuva morning, but I think you could all, you know, get yourselves cleaned up, and I'll take you to the Dairy Queen for some lunch. You can see a little of society, learn how to interact, and get some lunch at the same time. You're human now; why not jump right in and start learning how to be one?"

Calor looked confused. "I must ask who this queen is and why you have such a monarch presiding over the issuance of cows? Will she take our unannounced foray into her kingdom peaceably? And does she serve lunch to all of her visitors?"

George shook his head. "Wow, literal much? No, it's the name of a restaur...a pub, a tavern. Get it?"

Calor nodded her acknowledgement. "Ah. You should have explained it that way to being with."

George fumed for a moment then directed them to the different bathrooms in the house to cleanse their various wounds as much as they could and get ready to go. He ended up in the kitchen with Procella as the rest were getting cleaned up. He said, "You know, I don't even know what to call the four of you anymore."

She looked curious. "What do you mean, Squire?"

He smiled at the nickname. "Well, you aren't really humans, but I'll never say that to Tonare because it's fun to aggravate him. But, at the same time, you definitely don't have dragon bodies anymore either, so you're not dragons."

"Interesting. What would you call us?"

George paused. "I came up with a name before, but I got shot down."

"What was the name?"

"Draconauts."

She thought for a second. "It has an adventurous sound to it. I like it. I will inform the others, and henceforth that is what you will call us."

George's smile extended from ear to ear.

Petros entered the bathroom off of the upstairs hallway. He closed the bathroom door behind him and turned the water on. He looked up into the large mirror and examined the bruising around Jason's neck. As he looked at Jason's reflection, it suddenly contorted in a surprised grimace and shouted back at him, "What did you do to my neck?"

Petros was startled and went wide-eyed. "I do not...what is happening?"

The reflection said, "Dude, how did you get bruises all over my neck? And didn't you see when I was waving to you in the TV reflection?"

Petros's eyes narrowed as he examined the reflection. "Little Knight?"

Jason's reflection nodded. "Yeah, it's me. Norm's spell really messed things up."

Petros asked, "You can actually see me? Do you see me as a dragon or as a human?"

Jason turned his mouth to one side. "Sorry, but you look just like me."

"And where are you standing right now?"

Jason looked around the room. "It's like a TV channel was changed. I remember the spell, then I was seeing you through the reflection of the downstairs television, then suddenly I'm here in the bathroom looking at you in the mirror."

"Can you leave the bathroom?"

Jason looked down at his feet. "Umm, that would be no. Seems I can't move unless you move. Looks like this is the only way we will be able to communicate."

Petros craned his neck around and around, amazed that the reflection that was now Jason moved independently. "Astounding! I had better inform the others."

Jason said, "Yeah, good idea. They're not gonna believe this."

Petros turned to leave but said, "Wait here; do not go anywhere."

Jason glared back at him, and Petros smiled and ran out of the bathroom.

Chapter 18

Within minutes, the four Draconauts were in the upstairs bathroom of the Hewes homestead, examining themselves in the mirror. Their reflections were staring back at them and not only moving independently but actually carrying on conversations with their physical bodies on the other side of the reflective glass.

"This is highly peculiar," Procella stated.

"This is freakin' me out," Marcus proclaimed as he gingerly touched the large bruise on the side of his face. "And what did you do to me, dude? You gettin' in fights or something?"

Tonare related the incident with the black riders. Tiffany responded, "I didn't realize my body could fight like that."

Calor stiffened up proudly. "This body may be small, young one, but it is fierce, I tell you, fierce!" Tiffany smiled and blushed.

Procella asked, "So can you all see each other in...wherever you are?"

They looked back and forth at each other, and Jason answered, "Yep, it's like we're standing all in the same room. We can move our heads and faces, but otherwise we are just fixed in place, unless, of course, you move. Then our bodies move."

Kinaari looked very concerned. "I don't like this at all. I want my body back. I want to be in the real world again." A tear formed at the corner of her eye and ran down her cheek. Procella felt the wetness move down her face as well. She reached up and wiped the tear, causing Kinaari to move and wipe the tear away. "Thank you," Kinaari sniffled.

"Fascinating," Procella marveled.

Meanwhile, George leaned against the wall in the hallway, watching the four talk to themselves in the mirror. As he listened to the conversations, he noticed something about himself. His heart was beating fairly normally, he wasn't sweating, and the urge to run screaming into the horizon was practically nonexistent. He couldn't understand what was happening to him; was he getting bolder...braver? Or was he finally becoming desensitized to all of the weirdness going on around him? George didn't know the answer, but all he could think was that this was how it felt to keep your cool. George gave a deep sigh, reveling in the feeling but fearing it wasn't going to last long.

Jason asked, "Hey, is George still there?"

George heard him and called from the hallway, "I'm here."

Jason's face lit up. "Come in the bathroom, man! I wanna see what happens when a non-dragon-kid-whatever comes into the mirror."

George paused. "Are you sure that's a good idea?" He felt the anxiety building but said, "You know what? Never mind. I'm coming in."

The four Draconauts shifted as far over as they could as George crammed himself into the bathroom. His reflection came into view at the same time. Jason and the other reflections looked at the reflection of George, and Tiffany grumbled, "Okay, that's just weird."

George looked worried. "What? What's weird?"

She looked more intently at the reflection of George. "It's like you're in the room with us, but you're just standing there staring at the glass." She reached out and touched the George-reflection's cheek. Real George started and shouted, "Gah! I can feel that! That is so bizarre!"

Procella and Kinaari rubbed their chins. Kinaari looked concerned. "Why am I doing this?" she shrieked.

Tiffany rolled her eyes as Procella said, "It seems like the spell has created a pocket reality where your consciousnesses are trapped. It would seem the only way you can interact with the real world or each other is through a mirror."

"Yeah, but why a mirror?" Jason asked.

Procella shook her head. "I do not know. Magic can be so unpredictable."

Petros pursed his lips. "Too many questions, not enough answers. I feel responsible for all of this. I brought you to Montana, my cousins. And children, I advocated for the plan with the mage. This predicament is of my doing."

Procella shook her head. "Do not be ridiculous, Petros. We all thought it was a good idea. The duplicitous nature of the mage was our undoing. I'm sure he tainted the spell."

Marcus shook his head. "I don't know; I saw the look on the skinny dude's face toward the end there. That was panic; I don't think he planned for the spell to go like that."

Jason nodded. "Yeah, I gotta agree. Norm is odd, but he doesn't seem malicious or anything."

Calor shook her head. "I cannot agree with you. You do not know mages like my kind knows mages."

Tonare interjected as he looked down at his midsection, "Why does it feel like there is something moving in my stomach?"

George nodded. "It means you're hungry. I think we should do the whole Dairy Queen thing."

Jason looked dubious. "What Dairy Queen thing?" George explained the plan to him, and he reacted, "What? That's a terrible idea, George!"

George put his hands on his hips. "Why?"

Jason looked around. "I…it's just…how are they…we…I just don't think it is a good idea."

Petros responded, "Little Knight, the purpose of this plan was to allow us to interact with the world as it is now. Why would we not want to go and do exactly that?"

Jason mumbled, "Because it's just not…man! How can I argue with my own face? Go…I guess."

Kinaari interrupted, a distressed look on her face. "Wait, what will happen to us when you leave the room? I can't be trapped in a mirror!"

Tiffany mumbled, "I don't know why it's such a big deal; you probably spend half of the day looking in a mirror anyway."

Procella responded, "Nothing will happen to you. The next thing you will remember is when I look in a mirror again. As Jason has stated, it is like 'changing a channel.'"

Kinaari whimpered, "But I'm afraid! What if we're trapped here forever?" Tears flowed down her face.

Petros reassured her, "Kinaari, I will not rest until we find a way to undo this spell."

She shook her head as Jason said, "Okay, we can't stop you from going. Just, you know, be careful."

After explaining the fine art of opening a car door and fastening seatbelts, George was driving the four Draconauts into Malta. Procella and Calor looked between the driver's and passengers' seats, watching attentively, taking notes, and making comments about how George was operating the vehicle. Tonare watched the countryside go by, making inquiries into the top speed of the car and its maneuvering capabilities. Petros was fascinated by the radio and was testing all of the knobs and buttons to see what the result was as he manipulated them. It wasn't long before George regretted his decision to drive the four into town. He tried to block out the cacophony of questions, comments, and changing radio stations, but when they started playing with the power locks and windows, he turned around and shouted, "That is enough! If you don't stop messing around, so help me, I will pull this car over! Then, ooooh, then you'll all have something to complain about!"

The all fell into an uncomfortable silence. It was a few moments later when Calor sheepishly raised her hand. "George?"

"Yes?" he replied tersely.

"I, umm, I have to use the bathroom."

They pulled into the Dairy Queen parking lot, and George jumped out of the car and slammed the door shut behind him. In the few moments it took the other four to get out, he fumed but composed himself before giving them instructions.

"Okay, listen, let me do the talking. It'll be—"

Calor interrupted, "Why?"

George was taken aback. "Why what?"

Calor said, "Why should you do all of the talking?"

George paused. "Because I know how to talk to these people."

Procella joined in. "How are we going to learn how to talk to people if you do not let us talk to people?"

George replied, "Well, because they're gonna realize there is something different—"

Petros jumped in, "It does seem logical to let us interact, George. We are not stupid, just inexperienced."

George nodded, knowing he'd lost the argument. "Fine, here's what we're gonna do. We go in and find a table where we can sit. Calor, I'll show you where the bathroom is. I'll give you the lowdown on how to order, give you some money, and we go from there. Sound like a plan?"

A nod of agreement from the group sent them inside the restaurant, and George directed Calor to the bathroom and reminded her to use the one marked for women. They found a booth in the dining area and seated themselves. A few moments later, they saw Calor running toward them, a look of great concern on her face.

She reached the booth and leaned in low, trying to be discreet. "The mage is here!"

George was taken by surprise. "Wha...Norm, the mage...is here?"

She nodded quickly as the others whipped their heads around, trying to see the magic user. "His enchantments are all over the building. We must retreat and regroup, form a plan to capture him."

The other three began to shuffle out of the booth when George said, "Wait, wait, wait; what enchantments are you talking about?"

She swallowed hard, looking impatient. "He has laid some sort of spell over all of the fixtures in the restroom; they are operating themselves. It is magic of a most unholy nature!"

George paused and looked at Calor for several beats. "So you are telling me the toilets flush themselves?"

She nodded emphatically. "Yes, it is most disturbing. And all one needs to do is to place one's hands near the sink, and it turns itself on."

Petros, Procella, and Tonare began to mutter to each other with comments of incredulity, while George squeezed the bridge of his nose. "There is nothing wrong; Norm is nowhere nearby."

Calor was taken aback. "You mean this tavern is purposefully enchanted?"

"No!" George nearly shouted then lowered his voice. "No, it's just technology. There are sensors in the bathroom fixtures that make them operate automatically when someone wants to use them. It's more sanitary and saves water."

Procella said, "Really? That is fascinating. I must see this for myself!"

They shuffled out of the booth and collectively headed to the restrooms, leaving the hapless George seated at the table, his face once again buried in his hands. It was a position he found himself in more and more often.

After nearly five minutes, the Draconauts returned to the table and an exasperated George. He tried to hide his frustration when he asked, "Are you all quite finished?"

They nodded enthusiastically as Petros answered, "Yes, your technology is amazing. Our counterparts in the mirror also took some time to explain how all of these devices work."

George sat up. "You talked to the others in your reflections?" Petros nodded, and George squeaked, "Did anyone see you?"

Petros placed his hands on his hips. "George, what do you think we are? Of course we were subtle; we would never talk to our reflections in the mirror when there are other people around."

George couldn't help but chuckle at the ridiculousness of the statement and reply, "Okay, okay. So are we ready to eat?" George explained how to go to the counter and order food, and he gave each of them money to pay for the items. He then said, "We should probably limit our choices to the chicken fingers, hamburgers, or hot dogs."

Tonare wrinkled his nose. "Chickens do not have fingers."

George explained, "No, they're called that because they are vaguely shaped like human fingers. It is really chicken breast."

Tonare nodded. "Ah, I will have the pork then."

George was confused. "They, um, don't serve pork."

Calor joined the exchange. "You said ham."

George shook his head. "No, no, a hamburger, not ham. It's made of beef."

Procella was confused. "Then why not call it beef?"

George began speaking in his all-too-familiar flustered voice. "Huh? Because I think it's named after where it was invented. Some place in Germany."

Calor added, "And it seems gruesome to serve canine to humans."

"The hot dogs?" George asked. "No, it's usually beef byproducts formed into a sausage shape and served in bread."

Tonare turned to Calor. "None of this sounds appealing."

Calor answered out of the corner of her mouth, "It is no wonder they are so plump."

George shouted, "Hey!" A couple of customers looked at them, and he quieted down. "Can you just please order? None of it will kill you, and we need to get you back to the house. I gotta get the car back home soon, so let's get on with this."

Calor, Tonare, and Procella each took turns approaching the counter, ordering their meal, and returning to the table. Calor and Tonare each came back with a hamburger, French fries, and soda, while Procella tried the chicken fingers and iced tea. It took George a few moments to orient her to the idea of a dipping sauce while Petros made his journey to the front of the store.

He approached the counter, and a voice said, "Well, hi, there, handsome."

A woman in her late forties and wearing a Dairy Queen uniform stood at the cash register. Her brown hair was pulled up in a bun under her cap, and her slender frame seemed to contradict the stereotype of those who work in the fast food industry. Elaine Stevenson was George's boss and the manager of the restaurant. She was well acquainted with Jason, who had visited George at work many times, and she had even made use of Jason's knowledge of computers.

Petros looked around confused for a few moments before he realized the woman was addressing him. "Oh…um…greetings. I would like to place an order."

Elaine looked at him oddly but smiled. "Very formal today, eh?"

Petros was confused. "I am sorry? I was just contemplating the meal I wish to consume."

"You were contemplating, huh?" she teased. "Okay, then, what meal would you like to consume, Mr. Smart Guy?"

He was thrown off by the compliment but guessed the correct thing to do would be to return it. "Uh…thank you. You seem exceptionally intelligent as well." He felt his face start to blush again.

She looked at him sideways. "You all right there, Jace?"

Petros shook his head. "I have been working a great deal of late. Forgive me if I seem out of sorts."

Mrs. Stevenson shrugged. "We're all entitled to an off day now and then. By the way, I never got to thank you for the job you did on our desktop. Seems good as new, and the kids are tickled to be back online."

Petros's eyes went wide. He had no idea what any of that meant. "Oh! Well, I am pleased that the task was successfully accomplished." He winced inside; even he knew that sounded bad. He could tell sweat was forming on his forehead.

She shook her head at his odd speech. "So what can I get for you today?"

Petros decided to improvise. "I am having difficulty deciding between the shaped chicken breast or the sausage-like meat byproducts."

Elaine looked disappointed. "Look, kiddo, I know the food isn't the best quality, but you've never made fun of it to my face before."

Worry crossed over Petros's face. "No, no disrespect was meant. I was trying to make conversation and solicit your recommendation for my meal." His heart started to beat rapidly. Petros could actually feel his breathing quicken.

She took a step back and placed her hands on her hips. "What is wrong with you today, Jason? It's you, but I feel like I am talking to a stranger."

"I...am sorry. I do not—" The palms of his hands were cold and clammy. He couldn't understand what was happening to him.

Seeing Petros struggle from the dining room, George hurried to his side. "You feeling better, Jace? You're still looking a little flushed."

Petros said, "No, George, I am fine. I was...I am trying...I am very sorry, but I need to be out in the air." He slapped his hands on the counter and then rapidly walked out of the Dairy Queen and started down Highway 2 toward the Hewes homestead.

George turned to Elaine. "He just got over the flu. Probably dehydrated."

Elaine pointed at George. "You better catch him then, huh? A boy shouldn't be walking around feeling like that."

"Will do," he said and rejoined the other Draconauts. "We gotta go. Petros just bolted, and we have to keep up with him."

Calor and Tonare were in midchew, and Procella said, "But I still have fingers of chicken remaining. I am enjoying the dipping sauce."

George gave them a look, and they reluctantly rose from their chairs, Tonare carrying his burger and unfinished fries with him. They piled into the car and slowly started down Highway 2, keeping an eye out for Petros. It wasn't long before they caught up with the boy, who looked at them over his shoulder. He saw the car and then veered off the road toward the buildings and parking lots off of the highway.

"He's heading toward Trafton Park," George stated as he began to look for a parking space. He pulled into the lot of the Phillips County Museum, which was next door to the Great Plains Dinosaur Museum, and had the other Draconauts follow him to the treeline on the bank of the Milk River. As they walked past the Dinosaur Museum, Julia was standing on the front porch, looking to the trees with a very concerned look.

"Hi, Julia!" George shouted, his voice cracking as he addressed her. He scolded himself inside.

Julia said, "I just saw Jason walk by. He didn't even answer when I called to him, but I'm sure he heard me. Is he okay?"

George thought fast. "Yeah, he ran into Stan. You know how it is with him."

Julia nodded. "All right. Just make sure he's okay."

George waved. "Working on it now."

As they came around the corner of the building, they saw Julia's large and oddly colored horse hitched up on the side. It turned and saw the group and then began to get very agitated, stomping its hooves, throwing its head back, and whinnying.

Calor commented, "Impressive-looking horse—very large, like one of the war horses from our time."

Procella added, "Yes, but the coloring is quite unusual. It is familiar, but I cannot quite place it."

George was focused on finding Petros. "We need to move...he's fast. He's probably somewhere in the trees." They searched for quite some time, following the river as it bent around the perimeter of Trafton Park. It was a slow time of the year for the park; no one was using the baseball diamond, and only two campers were parked in the lots designated for RV-style vehicles. After a half hour, they finally found Petros sitting on the river bank at a sharp turn of the river's path, where it stops running north and turns southwest. The Draconaut was quiet but sweating from his hike through the fairly thick treeline.

Procella spoke first. "Cousin, we are concerned for you."

He took a deep breath. "I do not know what happened to me at the dining establishment." He described what he felt Jason's body doing.

George replied, "Petros, I think you were just anxious. You know, Mrs. Stevenson was kind of putting you on the spot, and you had an emotional reaction. It's pretty normal."

"Anxiety?" Petros asked.

George shrugged. "Yeah, it happens to me all the—"

Petros cut him off and rose to his feet. "*Anxiety?*"

They were all taken aback at his reaction as Procella tried to respond, "Cousin, you—"

Petros cut her off as well. "Dragons do not feel anxiety! Do you understand? I am Petros, Stone dragon of the line of Earth Dragons! Born of the very substance of the world, strong as a hundred oxen! My breath will turn an entire army to stone! My scales will stop the sharpest of swords, and my wings will bear me aloft to the farthest corners of the land. I…do not…feel…anxious!" He was breathing heavily, and his eyes were open wide.

No one spoke for several moments. George sheepishly said, "You…uh…are kind of…you know…anxious right now."

Petros's shoulders slumped, and he flopped back down to the ground. "This is maddening. This body is reacting to so many things in the environment, and not only do I not have any control over it, but I do not even know what they mean. My face becomes hot and turns red when I am embarrassed; my heart palpates rapidly and my skin exudes water when I feel anxious. What else do these bodies do?"

George tried to sound reassuring. "Dude, it's all part of being human."

Petros shouted, "I am not human! Do you not understand?" He pulled the scale hanging around his neck from under his shirt and gripped it tightly. "This! This is all I have left! This is the only evidence that now exists proving I am actually—"

There was an explosion of intense light, and Jason's entire body was engulfed in the brilliance. The others staggered backward at the unexpected release of energy as they shielded their eyes from the intensity. The blast of light grew in size, and then, as quickly as it came, it faded away. Sitting in the place of Jason's body was the form of a large dragon sitting back on its haunches. Its scales were gray with brown stripes, and its massive wings were folded back against its body. Without question, this was the body of Petros the dragon.

The dragon held his forelegs to the side of his body, examining them and then looking over his entire form as well. He opened his mouth, and in Petros's deep and regal voice he said, "Whoa! No…stinkin'…way!"

The others were dumbfounded as they examined the dragon and marveled at his sudden reappearance. George came around in front of the huge body and saw an all-too-familiar smile come over the dragon's face.

Chapter 19

"Holy cow!" George exclaimed profoundly.

Jason, now in the body of Petros the dragon, looked himself over and responded, "I know, right? It's gotta be another effect of the spell; it made us switch bodies."

The other three Draconauts made their way in front of Jason. They gaped at him, exchanged glances with each other, and then began fumbling around their necks for the scales they wore.

Jason held up a claw. "Whoa, whoa, whoa, hold it, hold it." He lowered his head. "We get four dragons here in the park, we're bound to be seen. I gotta figure out how to change back."

Procella nodded. "He has a point. If we do transform, we are at great risk of being seen."

George agreed. "Right, just grab the scale around your neck and change back, Jace."

Jason looked down at his neck. "Ummm, yeah." He started patting his claws all around his long neck.

They all startled when a voice came from beyond the treeline. "'Ey! Who's back there?"

George looked panicked. "Jace, just grab the scale and transform back."

Jason gritted his long, sharp teeth. "My neck is covered with scales, George. Which one do I grab?"

George said, "The one connected to the leather cord!"

Jason growled, "There is no leather cord, genius! I'm all scales! What do I do?"

The voice shouted, "You a bunch a' kids back there? Whaddaya up to, no good?"

George exclaimed, "Do something!"

Jason shot him a look. "I'm open to suggestions, George."

Procella hissed, "Stop bickering; someone is coming!"

Jason and George each pointed at each other and said simultaneously, "He started it!"

The leaves on the trees began to rustle, and a large man wearing a New York Giants t-shirt emerged. He was quite overweight, and his face was unshaven. A hat with the same football team logo covered his dark, curly, unwashed hair, and the knees of his sweatpants were wet with water and mud. In a heavy Brooklyn accent, he said, "You kids are makin' all kinds a' racket. I'm tryin' to be on vacation here!"

Procella held her hand out subtly to ease the others as she addressed the man. "Our deepest apologies, kind sir. We were simply playing a sporting event and became overly emotional from enjoyment. We will endeavor to remain quieter."

The man said, "Who talks like that? Where're you fr...whoa! Lookit the size a' that boulder!"

George turned to see a very large dragon-sized boulder on the ground behind him, right where Jason had been sitting. George was completely taken aback at its sudden appearance, but the other three looked completely level-headed.

Tonare said, "Has it not been there all this time?"

The man said, "Lookit, smart guy. Me and my family've come here every year for five years, and we ain't never seen that rock before. Whaddaya think; it just grew up outta the ground?"

Procella answered, "No, sir, of course not. That would be very ridiculous to attempt to convince you of that."

The man pointed at Procella. "You, you talk like a whack-a-doo, but you show respect; I like you. I'm tryin' to start a fire for my family and relax and all, so jus' keep it down, got it?"

Calor's face lit up. "Perhaps I may assist you? I am, after all, a Fi—"

Procella interrupted. "You are what, *Tiffany*?"

Calor corrected herself. "A fiiiine starter of fires."

He regarded her carefully. "What, you like a Girl Scout or somethin'?

Calor looked at George, who nodded as subtly as he could. She answered, "Yes, I am exactly that."

The vacationer shrugged his shoulders. "Eh, I don't care if you're with Smokey the Bear; if you can get my fire goin', you're okay in my book. Come wit' me."

She looked back at the group, her eyes asking for help. George said, "We'll meet you at the car, Tiff." Calor scowled as she followed the man into the trees.

They waited a few moments before turning to the very large boulder. The surface of the rock began to quiver then amazingly morphed into two great wings. From underneath, Petros's long neck and head peeked out. "Is it clear?" Jason asked.

George answered, "Yeah, how did you do that?"

Jason was about to answer when Procella spoke over him. "Simple camouflage. We all can do it under the right conditions. I am amazed that you mastered the skill so quickly, Little Knight."

Jason shrugged. "I didn't know what I was doing. The guy was coming, and I just tried to be as small as possible."

George said, "Well, let's hope you can be small enough to get back to the farm without anyone seeing you 'cause I got a half hour before I have to have the car back home, so we need to get moving."

Jason nodded. "I can get back from here. You guys go, and I'll meet you in the barn, okay?"

They nodded and disappeared into the treeline, leaving Jason the dragon to figure out how to get his new and massive body back to the homestead.

***

Calor and the man from Brooklyn walked toward his camper. She could see the large bus-sized vehicle in the distance. Calor had never seen a camper before, but based on its sheer size, she gathered her gruff guide might have a fair-sized treasure back at his castle. He asked, "So you're a Girl Scout, huh?"

She nodded reluctantly. "Yes, sir, that is what they say."

He shook his head. "Nah, you call me Vic, okay. None o' this 'sir,' not that I don't appreciate it. You kids talk funny out here, but I like how you respect yer elders an' all that."

"Very well, Vic. That is your vehicle up there?"

He beamed as he answered, "That baby is all mine; paid for it in cash, mind you. I don't trust none o' these banks lately. You save yer money, and you pay for things in cash."

"What is your occupation that enables you to purchase such a fine carriage?"

"Meh, nuttin' much. I work on Wall Street."

The camper was the size of a tour bus, white with blue and red stripes running the length of the vehicle. It featured two pop-out sections, which disturbed the symmetry of the camper's shape when it was parked but increased the already vast space on the inside. Ten feet from the front door was an ersatz fire pit with several large logs leaning against each other, forming a neat wooden teepee. Underneath were many small sticks and twigs in a less neat pile.

"See?" Vic said. "I got the kindling and all that, but it won't start."

Calor examined the sticks. "All of your wood is far too wet; all it will do is smolder."

Vic nodded. "Yeah, the kids got it from next to the river. I figured as much; that's why I sent 'em into town to buy some dry stuff. 'Ey, can I get you a soda or something?"

Calor nodded as she examined the firewood. Vic disappeared inside, and she reflected how she could set this entire camp area ablaze if she were in her true form. She closed her eyes and laid her hand over the scale under her shirt, thinking how she could transform as Jason did. This was neither the time nor the place, but as she felt the scale suspended around her neck, she couldn't help but think about being a Heat dragon again. She swore she could actually feel the heat radiating from the object and smiled at the thought. In her mind, she smelled the all-too-familiar smoke of many fires she had created in her lifetime. She took a deep, cleansing breath and exhaled joyfully at the memory. The vision was so real it was almost palpable.

"Yo! How did you do that?"

Calor's eyes snapped open to see her vision of smoke was real, for the wood before her was now a blazing yet cozy campfire. Vic was standing in the doorway of his palace on wheels, holding a can of soda in each hand and looking wide-eyed at Calor. "I thought you said the wood was too wet to light?"

Calor couldn't understand what she was looking at. She had done nothing to actually start the fire, yet there it was before her. Were she still in her dragon form, she could have easily set the wood ablaze, as well as the grass around it, Vic's camper, and probably the majority of the campground. But all she had done was imagine the wood igniting and held her hand over her...

Her scale.

**

Jason crossed the Milk River with a single stride and pushed his way through the trees on the opposite bank. There were no people or developments on that side of the river, and Jason thought it would be the best place to take off and fly back to the farm. He hadn't, however, counted on his now-huge body needing to squeeze through the trees. He really didn't realize how strong Petros was until he accidentally snapped two trees at the base of their trunks as he tried to push by. It was almost effortless to do so, and he knew that he was going to need to be careful as he figured out how to live life as a dragon. However, he had to admit to himself that it was pretty cool.

He came to a clearing and looked around him before he spread his wings. He could see much greater distances with such a long neck, and Jason realized just then how much more keen a dragon's vision was. Colors were brighter, things at great distances were still in focus, and there was something else he couldn't put his finger on. He finally figured it out when the colors of objects in the direct sunlight actually seemed to glow slightly as opposed to objects in the shade. He thought to himself, *I'm seeing temperatures. I can see in the infrared spectrum. Awesome!*

It also took Jason a few moments to figure out how to spread his wings. There were joints and muscles there that were completely foreign to a human, and learning how to use a new set of limbs took some focus. But he eventually learned how to flex the new muscle groups and was soon flapping his wings in unison and kicking up quite a cloud of dust doing so. He clenched his teeth, and with the massive beat of the wings, he leapt into the air.

And fell right back down on his head.

***

Calor caught herself quickly and stammered, "I, umm, yes. I did say that, but my training as a scout of girls included setting fires even to sodden wood."

"Naw," Vic said as he pointed at her. "You jus' said the wood was too wet. What kinda game you playin' at?"

"Sir Vic," she remembered his favor for those who showed respect, "I would not try to deceive you. I simply remembered a technique I acquired in some of my more advanced training. There is no deception taking place." She tried to change the subject. "Is that beverage for me?"

He looked at the can in his hand. "Oh, yeah, here y'go." He handed it to her then shrugged. "Well, I gotta hand it to ya; you did a good job. Tanks."

She stood up and gave a micro curtsey. "The pleasure is mine. I am sure my friends are waiting for me. By your leave?"

Vic was still studying the fire. "Wha? Oh, yeah, sure, sure." He waved her off with his hand, and Calor at first walked casually, but as she got farther, she bolted into the trees, found a few sticks, and arranged them on the ground in a small pile. She knelt in front of them and tried to clear her mind. Calor recalled the image of fire and smoke in her mind, placed her hand on the scale, and focused on the idea of starting a fire. She pushed her mind hard into the image, focusing her resolve on the small pile of sticks. She began to see spots in her eyes as she strained to will a fire into existence and then opened her eyes. A small orange salamander crawled over one of the pieces of kindling, but that was the closest to fire she saw in front of her. Calor slouched in discouragement, rose to her feet, and shuffled off to find George, Procella, and Tonare.

***

Jason lay still for a moment, his humiliation the only wound he felt from the fall. Clenching his jaw, he pushed himself back up and growled, "Let's try that again." His wings stretched out and began to flap, and he started trotting across the clearing, taking little mini-leaps as he beat the wings wildly. The wind created by the flapping stirred up all forms of dirt and debris, but Jason ran and hopped, beating his new set of limbs and trying with every ounce of his gigantic, dragon being to take flight. He finally decided to run at a full-out sprint. When he reached his top speed, he beat the wings with everything he had and leaped high into the air once again. And thumped back down to the earth again as well.

For several moments, Jason lay there, stewing in the disgrace of his failure. "I'm a complete klutz when I'm a human, but you would think that, as a dragon, I'd acquire a little grace. But, nooo; I may be the first fully grown dragon that doesn't know how to fly."

He pushed himself to his feet again and began walking in circles. "I did the flapping, I took a running start, I jumped as high as I could, and now I'm walking in circles while I'm talking to myself. At least some things don't change." He gave one last-ditch attempt at flapping his wings as hard as he could but to no avail. He was grounded.

"At least I have my breath weapon." He inhaled deeply, and his massive chest expanded at the influx of air. His cheeks puffed out when he realized he couldn't inhale anymore, and then he opened his mouth wide and exhaled as hard as he could. The grass on the ground blew backward as he expelled the air from his voluminous lungs, but air and only air left his gaping maw. His face went expressionless at realizing the irony of the situation then his countenance turned downcast as he said to himself. "Just walk home, Hewes. Just walk home." He pointed himself toward the farm and began plodding across the verdant fields of Phillips County.

***

George, Procella, and Tonare were waiting in the parking lot when Calor dejectedly rounded the corner of the Dinosaur Museum. Seeing her downcast body language, they asked what was wrong, and she recounted not only her time with Vic but also what happened with the fire. Procella rubbed her chin. "First, Petros was able to repel the dark rider with Jason's body despite the rider's superhuman strength, and now somehow you start a fire with no tools or even touching the wood. I cannot believe this is coincidence, but I am also highly doubtful that this was an intended effect of Norm's spell."

"You think he didn't mean to do this?" George asked.

Procella shook her head in the negative. "No, and all of these odd occurrences seem centered around our scales, but as Calor recounted—"

Calor interrupted, "I focused all of my will into that scale and no discernable result."

George said, "Look, I'd love to unpack this with you all day, but I gotta get this car home. So if we could all pile in, I'll drive you back to Jason's, and I can get back before I lose car privileges for a month."

They agreed, and as they took their various places in the car, Tonare whispered to Calor, "Are you aware of what the loss of car privileges actually means?"

Calor shook her head as she answered. "No, but it sounds most unpleasant."

***

George dropped the three Draconauts off and reminded them that Jason indicated he would be waiting for them in the barn. They hurried off to the dilapidated building to find a crestfallen Jason in his dragon form. He was lying on the dirt floor, his head propped on his clawed arm and a look of complete discouragement on his massive face.

Procella regarded him curiously. "Something is vexing you?"

He nodded. "You could say that, yeah."

Calor prodded, "And do you wish to enlighten us as to the nature of your discord?"

Jason recounted his epic failure at both flight and using his breath weapon, and Procella responded, "Did you expect to have an inherent mastery of the workings of a dragon's body, Little Knight? From what I understand, human young take quite some time learning to simply crawl before they can even walk. Why do you think you would be immediately able to do things you describe?"

"I guess I didn't think of it like that. I've seen Petros and Tonare fly, and it looked so easy, I just thought, you know—"

Calor placed her hands on her hips. "How do you think whelpling dragons learn to fly or even birds for that matter? By watching the adults?"

Jason surrendered. "I get it, I get it. I just thought…look, I've never been the coordinated type. You know, gym class, sports, and all that, just not my thing. But then I end up in a body like this, and seeing what Petros can do, I guess it seemed finally like my time to be great at something physical."

Tonare approached. "Jason, of all the dragon species, the Air Dragons are most known for superiority in flight. We may be slightly smaller than the other species, but we have no equal in the air. Come, let me teach you about this body, and we will have you airborne in the blink of an eye."

They made their way from the barn back to the clearing in the forest at the edge of the Hewes farm. Tonare instructed Jason how to coordinate the flapping of his wings, how to use his legs and tail and other control surfaces to steer himself in flight, and how to look for air currents and vents to enhance his flight without needing to expend energy beating his wings. Jason listened intently and took time after each instruction to test the various parts of his new body and understand the nuances of using one's body for flight. Procella and Calor contributed various nuggets of wisdom here and there, but Tonare, the former Air Dragon, understood flight to a greater degree than any of the others.

Jason flapped his wings exactly as Tonare had instructed, but he still couldn't manage to become airborne. And with each try, the boy-in-a-dragon's-body became more and more frustrated with himself until his shoulders slumped forward in complete discouragement.

Tonare tried to reassure him. "It will take time. You need to continue trying, that is all. Here, show me how you tried to use your breath weapon."

Jason took a deep breath, opened his mouth widely, and exhaled as hard as he could. Warm, moist air billowed out of his mouth but no glowing cubes of orange. Tonare commented, "Using a breath weapon is not just about exhaling. It is a weapon, and weapons are used with purpose, with feeling behind them."

Jason looked confused. "But it is just breathing—"

Calor interrupted, "It most certainly is not, Little Knight. Whether it be Tonare's thunderclap, or Procella's force wave, or my heat, we never *just* breathe out. You never use a weapon like that without meaning to do so."

Jason sounded frustrated. "Well, I am meaning to breathe it out, but all I'm doing is forcing out air and making myself a little dizzy. I just don't get it."

Procella commented, "It will come in time, young one. Be patient."

"I even make a lousy dragon," he said in Petros's booming voice. The others didn't know how to respond, and as they searched for words, Jason dejectedly placed his claw over his chest, just at the base of his neck. He closed his eyes, and a glow began to emanate from beneath. It brightened and spread over his entire body. The light contracted to a much smaller size and eventually dissipated to leave the body of Jason Hewes standing there. He was holding the scale suspended from the leather cord around his neck. Petros said, "What has happened? How did I arrive in our forest?"

The others explained the situation, including Jason's experience in trying to master a dragon's body. Petros looked very troubled. "I am concerned that our young Jason will not wish to reappear in my body again."

Tonare said, "He was very distressed. I feel as if I have failed him."

Procella shook her head. "You did not, cousin. Jason simply needed more time to practice and become accustomed to a new body."

Calor commented, "He gives up too easily."

Petros retorted, "His giftings are his mind and his intellect, not his physical prowess. This is one of the reasons those older and larger than him have gone out of their way to deride him. It is an unfortunate human shortcoming—preying on others simply because they are different."

Tonare asked, "What can we do?"

Petros replied, "Very little, I am afraid. I will find a mirror and speak to him, but I feel that we owe it to Tiffany, Kinaari, and Marcus to let them experience the real world again, albeit in a dragon's body. I will stay as I am to guide them through the transition."

The three nodded and took steps back to be as far apart from each other as their dragon bodies were about to appear. Petros coached them to simply grasp their scales and focus on their true selves. They followed Petros's directions, and three brilliant bursts of light later, the bodies of Procella, Calor, and Tonare were in the forest, but their astounded expressions betrayed the human minds behind the draconic faces.

Petros smiled at them and said, "Welcome back, children. It would seem I have much to explain to you."

Chapter 20

The man inspected his appearance in his reflection. The mirrored interiors of the private elevator's doors allowed him to adjust his tailored suit and recheck his perfectly coiffed hair. During the brief moments of his ascent to the eightieth floor, the reality of how his life had changed in such a short period of time truly sank in. The interview process for this new job had been months long, and throughout the multiple face-to-face interviews, personality profiles, security checks, and psychological examinations, Tate Reigles questioned many times if the high-paying position was worth the effort. For a man in his early thirties, he had held more high-profile jobs than men with twenty years more experience. But his naturally savvy business practices, combined with a sharp wit and rugged good looks, netted him more than his fair share of powerful and well-paying positions.

Yet this new private weapons contactor, Alans Corporation, or AlansCo for short, seemed to rise out of nowhere in the last two years. With its new devices and vehicles that were beyond state of the art, the governments of several countries were now courting it for exclusive contracts; they wanted what AlansCo had and wanted no one else to have it. And with their meteoric rise, AlansCo was now looking for a new director of marketing and media relations, a face to show to the world and represent the company in the best possible fashion.

During the grueling screenings, Tate met Steven Alans, the chief executive officer of the company, and felt that he had ingratiated himself to the proverbial "man in charge" of AlansCo. However, it wasn't until the final stage of the interview that Tate learned there was another authority figure he had to meet. Despite his many questions, he was never able to actually discern what position this "other" held in the company, but it was nearly a month after his first day at AlansCo when he was finally scheduled to meet this "elder statesman," as Mr. Alans had described him.

Tate felt he was prepared for any work situation; he was wrong. In his orientation, the information he was presented with about AlansCo, Steven Alans, and nearly two thousand years of history changed his perspective of the world. In one month, Tate Reigles's eyes were not only opened to a world he thought only existed in novels and movies but also to how high the stakes were in this new and dangerous world. The past was intersecting with the future; mythical creatures, bizarre technologies, users of magic, and futuristic weapons of warfare were merging in ways that created a pit of dread in Tate's stomach. But he was in far too deep now; he had to embrace his new job, and his new future, or he stood to lose far more than he'd bargained for. And this was all culminating at this meeting with the individual who dwelt on the eightieth floor of a nondescript skyscraper in New York City.

The soft ping of the elevator chimed as he arrived at his destination. The doors slid open to reveal a small reception area. The walls were off-white with two black leather chairs facing each other from opposite walls, each with a small glass end table placed carefully next to it. Fresh flowers were in ornate vases on each end table, but no other furniture graced the waiting area. Opposite the elevator was a set of heavy oak double doors leading to whatever room lay beyond the waiting room. Mounted on the wall next to the doors was a small LCD display, showing the schedule of visitors for the day. Above the display was a retinal scanner. The scanner identified whoever was next on the schedule and automatically opened the doors when an ID was confirmed. There was no need for a receptionist; if you were supposed to be there, you would be let in by the devices. If not then access was denied. Tate felt it lacked any personal touch, but he had to admit it was efficient.

He stepped in front of the scanner, and the motion-activated laser blipped to life and scanned the interior of his right eye. He watched the image of his retina appear on the monitor and then green letters spelled out "CONFIRMED." The screen went completely blue then spelled:

Reigles, Tate
Welcome

There was a click of the door, and the releasing of the lock caused them to open a crack. Reigles tentatively opened one of the doors, swallowed hard, then passed through.

The office beyond the double doors was cavernous, nearly forty feet across with twelve-foot-high ceilings. The carpet was an Oriental pattern, and the walls were paneled with walnut from floor to ceiling. An ornate crystal chandelier hung from the center of the ceiling, and various sculptures, busts, and paintings lined the walls. Tate identified them as Eastern, most likely a mixture of Japanese, Chinese, and Indian. The far wall of the office was completely glass and overlooked downtown Manhattan. He surmised this piece of office real estate was prime in the city and probably cost tens of millions of dollars.

What surprised him most was the wildlife. In each corner of the room stood a beautifully carved bird's perch. They were large, made specifically to accommodate the creatures that were currently residing there, and they were watching him intently. To his left was one of the largest owls he had ever seen; its brown and black speckled feathers culminated into large tufts above its brilliant yellow eyes. As it watched him, Tate felt a shiver go down his spine. The bird's talons were huge, and he couldn't imagine what kind of prey they could catch. To his right was a huge vulture. Black and gray feathers covered the creature's tail, wings, and back and served to highlight the reddish-beige feathers over the rest of its body. Smaller, white feathers surrounded its face, with the exception of even more minute and shaded black ones running from its eyes to the base of its beak. The ring of red around the scavenger's pale yellow eyes made Tate feel as if the creature were drawing a target around him and then waiting for an opportunity to strike. He could make out similarly large birds in the opposite corners of the room, but they were too far to identify. Backlit by the sunlight streaming in the windows was a large man standing in the center of the wall of glass.

A rich, deep voice issued from the figure. "Magnificent, aren't they?"

Tate swallowed but tried to sound unfazed. "I haven't seen anything like them."

"To your right," the voice began, "is the bearded vulture or the lammergeiger. It is one of the largest of the Old World vultures; their wingspan can reach nine feet. In certain parts of the world, it is considered good fortune to have one of their shadows pass over you. To your left is Blakiston's fish owl. It is quite possibly the largest species of owl, and they are capable of catching fish that weigh even more than themselves."

The birds' eyes were transfixed on Tate as he tried to not make any sudden moves or show fear. "They are beautiful," he answered.

"You may enter; they will not harm you."

Tate took several steps into the large room and saw, at the far end of the room, a massive desk made of walnut to match the paneling on the wall. His host stood behind the desk, and as Tate approached, he gradually came into focus.

The man must have been seven feet tall and wore a finely tailored, gray Armani suit and highly polished, black leather wingtip shoes. But the most surprising thing about his host was the hooded cape he wore, attached around his shoulders and clasped by a golden falcon. The exterior of the cape and hood were gray, slightly darker than the color of the suit, but inside was a deep crimson velvet. The hood was deep and drawn up over his host's face; Tate could not make out any features. He approached his side of the desk and continued to stand.

"Let me introduce you to my other companions." The hooded figure pointed to his right. "This is Steller's sea eagle." Tate could now make out the third of the huge birds; black and gray feathers covered its head, and deep black feathers covered most of its body. Conversely, stripes of brilliant white feathers formed across its wings and covered its tail. Tate was struck by the bright yellow beak, much thicker and pronounced than that of a typical eagle. His host went on. "It is the heaviest and most powerful of all the eagles in the world. And, finally, my last companion is the Eurasian eagle owl. The most powerful of all the owl species, they actually prey on primates, and their talons can crush a monkey's skull while it still lives. It is the only owl species known to have killed a human." The owl stared at Tate with almost glowing orange eyes; its feathers speckled with brown, beige, and black.

"Do you know why I have these creatures as my companions, Mr. Reigles?" Reigles shrugged, and his host continued. "They are four of the most formidable birds of prey in the world. Birds are my passion, Mr. Reigles, as well as things that are formidable and powerful."

Tate nodded. "I can appreciate what they represent."

"Well said, for they represent me, and if you appreciate that then you have a respect for me as well."

Tate worked up his courage. "Sir, knowing that I have nothing but the utmost respect for you, I hope you will understand both the humility and candor of the next question I have to ask."

The figure nodded. "And that question is?"

"Who…are you, sir?"

The huge man walked to the sea eagle and stroked the feathers on its head. "I am the founder of this organization, Mr. Reigles. Yes, I realize that in the American interpretation of a corporation, a single owner is not usually the typical business model, but there is no organization in the world like AlansCo."

Tate was confused. "But…Steven Alans—"

The hooded figure continued. "Is just a display piece. Something one presents to the public to convey a certain image. I liked his name. It fit in my plans, which is a segue to discuss the outcomes of our most recent venture."

Tate knew exactly what he was talking about. "The failure of the drones, yes. I would like the record to show that I did warn the dispatchers that although their strength had been appropriately developed, they still lacked the programming on technique, specifically hand-to-hand combat."

"A situation that—"

Tate finished the sentence. "…is being remedied as we speak, sir."

"Still, I find it disturbing that two of our drones were defeated by a small group of children."

Tate nodded. "Agreed. It would seem that since they are modeled after humans, they have many of the same frailties as humans. Unfortunately, since we have termination protocols built in, we have no way of analyzing their remains to ascertain what exactly happened to them."

"I *know* what happened to them, Mr. Reigles." The imposing figure's voice took on a tone of agitation. "It is the involvement of those filthy wyrm!"

"Sir, if I may, your previous campaigns eliminated the creatures native to Asia and the Orient. It is only the European species that survived, and they were scattered across thousands of miles of the planet. Statistically speaking, they won't even be able to organize enough to pose a problem in this day and age. We should be able to systematically remove them from the playing field one by one."

"Mr. Reigles," the hooded man began, "you are attempting to inject your twenty-plus years of wisdom into a war that has waged for nearly a millennium. The wyrm..." He paused and rotated the stress out of his neck, "...dragons are much more resourceful than you would think. And these species from the West have always been the most problematic. They are organized, powerful, intelligent, nigh invulnerable; I despise them, but I respect them."

Tate nodded. "We are very close to finding the artifact. Once it is in our possession—"

"Once it is in our possession, my technomancers still have a great deal of work to do. The artifact will prove indispensable in the extinction of all dragonkind, but there is much work to be done after we find it. This war is far from over, Mr. Reigles."

He nodded. "On a positive note, the military contracts have been approved by all levels in Washington, and we are ready to go public with the new models."

"No, we are not."

Reigles was confused. "Sir?"

"All technology, Mr. Reigles, *all* technology first goes through the technomancers. I do not care about deploying these new tools in the theaters of human warfare. They need to be ready to wage *my* war, and in order to wage my war, these weapons need more than science can provide." Tate could hear the figure inhale deeply. "You have much to learn. Your handlers did not brief you properly before you were sent to me. It is a mistake I will tolerate only once. You are to leave now and not return until you understand why we are creating these new weapons and what ancient order they and the drones will be instrumental in reviving."

Tate's heart was pounding in his chest. Had his life just been threatened? He was unsure what to do. He gave a respectful bow to the large figure and said, "By your leave then."

The hooded head gave the most subtle of nods, and Tate Reigles turned and walked to the office door. The eyes of the bearded vulture and fish owl were locked on him as he approached the double doors. Their feathers ruffled, and Tate thought they were about to attack, but the latch on the door clicked open of its own accord, and Tate walked right through, not breaking his stride. He pushed it shut behind him and walked straight to the elevator. The doors opened with one click of the button, and soon he was whisking back down to his office on the fifteenth floor. He heart felt as if it were going to explode out of his chest, and he was sweating profusely under his suit. However, Tate was able to make it to his office before his fear overwhelmed him and he vomited into the garbage can.

Chapter 21

Kinaari, now in the body of the Wave dragon Procella, looked down at her clawed forelegs, "H…how long are we going to be like this?" her voice broke as she asked.

Petros answered, "Unfortunately, I do not know. It will take some time to adjust."

Tiffany examined Calor's body closely. She somehow managed to make her dragon voice growl as she did her human voice. "I could get very used to this."

Marcus looked confused. "So we're not in the mirror place anymore, right? This is real life?" Petros nodded in the affirmative, and Marcus said, "I don't know how to be a dragon, man! I'm a football player, not some, you know, mythical thing."

Petros said, "I understand, children. Believe me, adjusting to a new body is a task you are never prepared for. But I can help you, if you will let me."

Tiffany unfolded the massive wings of Calor. It was the first time she noticed how different they were than Petros's. Where the Stone dragon's wings resembled those traditionally depicted in drawings of dragons, the interior of hers were comprised of many asymmetrical, smaller membranes that came to uneven points. "They look like tongues of fire," she commented.

Petros nodded. "One of the derivations of the Fire Dragon's moniker."

Marcus looked himself up and down. "What's with my wings? They're connected all the way to my tail." He was taken aback at his own statement. "Oh, man, I have a tail."

Petros smirked. "Your wings are what make Air Dragons, well, Air Dragons. Wings such as yours make you one of the most agile dragons that exist."

Tiffany interjected, "Wait! We can fly, can't we?"

Petros reluctantly answered, "Well, yes, you can. But it is not as easy as it seems; young Jason has not yet achieved flight after many attempts." His voice trailed off as he watched Marcus flexing and contracting the various muscles of his body and carefully noted how the wings responded in turn. He flapped them once and produced a great gust of wind. He was intrigued at the result and began to rhythmically beat his wings. As the movements kicked up a great amount of the detritus on the forest floor, he actually felt his forelimbs rise off the ground. Marcus stopped and let his front legs drop back down to the ground. They all watched as he inspected the entire length of his wings one more time, and then he turned to them.

His mouth turned up in a playful smirk.

Marcus burst into a bounding run, coordinating wing beats with his running, and before he reached the end of the clearing, he was airborne and soaring over the treetops. Petros, Kinaari, and Tiffany watched in amazement as Marcus's flight started off erratically but quickly evened out as he gracefully banked to and fro around the glade of trees. Sheer delight washed over his face as he reveled in the feeling of flight. He quickly discovered he could flex and bend the two horns protruding from the back of his head; they could flatten against his body to enhance his aerodynamics.

Below, in the clearing, Petros exclaimed, "Scales and claws!"

Tiffany asked, "Have you ever seen anyone take to flight that quickly?"

Petros shook his head. "Not in my lifetime."

The exhilaration of flight finally overcame him, and Marcus found himself laughing almost uncontrollably. He performed loop-de-loops, barrel rolls, and tried to see how many maneuvers he could pull off. Finally, he pulled up and soared high, and at the apex of his flight, he took a deep breath. "Being a dragon is awesome! Wa-hoooo!"

KRA-KA-KOOM!

A peal of thunder exploded from within his lungs and issued out of his mouth. The noise took him by surprise and threw him off balance as he plummeted back to the earth. He fought to regain control over his flight as he tried to understand what had just happened, but Marcus knew he needed to get safely back on the ground first. The rushing wind helped to straighten his body into a power dive and help him regain control. Marcus then reopened his wings, caught the air, and slowed his descent. He was to get his rear legs back underneath his body. A few flaps later, he was back in control and was soon on the ground with Calor, Tiffany, and Petros.

Petros was smiling ear to ear and said, "I see you have discovered your breath weapon."

Marcus's eyes went wide. "The thunder was my breath weapon?"

Tiffany rolled her eyes. "Yes, pretty weird for a *Thunder* dragon, huh?"

Marcus glared at her. "You don't breathe thunder, freak. It's a sound."

Petros interjected, "A breath weapon is not always something tangible. We call them 'breath weapons' simply because they issue forth from our mouths. So, yes, Marcus, the thunderclap is the weapon of the Thunder dragon. I am amazed at how you discovered it so quickly but, even more so, how quickly you took to flight."

Marcus shrugged his scaled shoulders. "I dunno. Once I figured out how to move them, it seemed pretty easy."

Tiffany sat back on her haunches and folded her forelegs over her chest. "Hmmph! He's a jock; of course it was easy."

Marcus shot her a look. "Jealous much?"

Tiffany didn't know how to answer. "Well...you just...you're just throwing it in my face!"

Marcus yelled, "Hey, I'm not gonna apologize for being naturally coordinated. Just because you can't do something that I can doesn't mean I shouldn't do it just so you don't feel bad!"

"Stop it!" Kinaari suddenly shouted. Her dragon lungs amplified her voice and made the other two jump. "I can't take you two fighting! I'm so stressed out by all this; now you two are—"

Tiffany interrupted, "Oh, boy, here comes the drama queen."

Marcus threw his forelegs up. "Why do you gotta be like that, Tiff? She didn't do nothin' to you, and now you're startin' with her."

Tiffany raged, "Because here we are, in these amazing bodies, finally powerful enough to do something important, and she's whining that she won't be able to fit into her clothes or do her makeup. There're more serious things in this life than making the cheerleading squad!"

Kinaari buried her face in her claws and started to sob. Marcus scolded, "Now look at what you did; she's crying."

Petros casually walked into the center of the three arguing dragons and stared at them reproachfully. They recognized the look on his face and gave him their full attention. He asked, "Are you all quite finished?"

Tiffany casually looked her claws. "If they're done being crybabies and show-offs, I'm ready."

Marcus spat, "Okay, that's it! You need to shut your mouth, or someone's gonna have to shut it for you!"

Tiffany shouted back, "Hey, maybe you should pick on someone your own size. Oh, wait, I *am* your size, football boy. If fact, I'm bigger than you now, so bring it!"

"Enough!" Petros shouted. "It is bad enough that we have to adjust to life in these new bodies without watching the three of you sully the noble heritage of dragons with your petty squabbling and emotional fragility. Tiffany, your jealously is unbecoming and, frankly, ugly. Marcus, your vainglorious display of physical prowess was unnecessary. And, Kinaari, I am hundreds of years old, and I have never seen a dragon cry…until today. If you lack the ability to exist in dragon form then I suggest you touch those scales around your necks and return to human form. Then we can make some real progress on correcting this situation. It is what your friend Jason did, so at least one of you has some sense."

Marcus looked concerned. "Wait, what do you mean it is what Hewes did?"

Petros explained Jason's difficulty adjusting to his dragon body and his subsequent discouragement. He went on: "But he had the wherewithal to realize when it was too much for him. You three are embarrassments to the race of dragonkind."

Marcus held up his front feet in surrender. "Whoa, that's pretty harsh, Petros. You're talkin' to us like we're a—" Marcus's voice trailed off. Kinaari and Tiffany hung their heads, knowing how Marcus was going to finish the sentence.

Petros folded his arms. "Finish your statement."

A deep sigh came from within Marcus's chest. "Like we're a bunch of kids."

Petros's expression softened. "Youth! You so wish to be treated as adults and yet still want to act with the recklessness of childhood. The existence of my entire species is teetering on the brink, young ones. Failure is not an option for me. I need you all to grow up a little more, right here and right now."

Kinaari wiped her front leg across her snout and sniffled. "We understand. We're sorry."

Petros implored, "My friends, you have such amazing strengths. Why do you not use them to our advantage instead of setting them at odds with each other?"

Tiffany said, "We don't know how."

Petros walked to her and beckoned her to lower her head to him. He laid his hand on the side of her snout. "You have an inner strength and passion, young one. Your spirit is fierce; it will take you through many a hardship. Teach the others how to do similarly." He turned and walked to Marcus. "Your ability to adapt is unparalleled to any I have seen. You are a protector; you watch out for those close to you. Watch out for the others and help them adjust; teach them about their new selves." Marcus gave him a resolute nod as Petros walked to Kinaari. "You wear your emotions for all to see, yet your inner grace and beauty attract others to your cause. They will listen to what you say; learn the wisdom of choosing the right words."

The three dragons exchanged apologetic glances, and then Kinaari asked, "What about Jason? How can we help him?"

Petros nodded. "Let me handle our Little Knight. But first things first: we need to get you off the ground and flying."

Marcus took time with Tiffany and explained how he became airborne. Tiffany had many of the same coordination problems that Jason had experienced, but her resolve got her through the initial discouragement. After half an hour, she was making some real progress and was well on her way to self-sustained flight. They needed to move beyond their familiar glade of trees to get open space and practice take-offs and landings. Fortunately, there wasn't much in Montana between this small glade of trees and the Canadian border, so the risk of being seen was minimal.

Petros went with Kinaari to show her how to use the unique shape of Procella's wings for flight. She was a Water Dragon, and her wings were shaped more like the fins of a flying fish than the typical articulated, bat-shaped dragon wings. He explained to her that she would be the least maneuverable in the air, but in the water she was a force to be reckoned with. Kinaari actually took to flight quickly; she was quite the athlete herself and possessed a natural dexterity, similar to Marcus.

Within an hour, the sun was starting its descent toward the horizon, and Petros stood with the three dragons in an open and secluded expanse of the Montana countryside. They were two miles north of the Hewes homestead and felt free to really stretch their wings.

"Fly," Petros encouraged. "Experience the thrill of soaring over all the land. But in this era, you are still considered fictional creatures, so be mindful of yourselves. Do not be seen."

They all nodded in understanding, and then Marcus said, "Hey, I've got an idea."

"What's that?" Tiffany asked.

He reached out and slapped her shoulder haunch with his front leg. "Tag! You're it!" He took a running start and leapt into the air, putting as much distance between himself and the group as quickly as he could.

A wry smile came over Tiffany's face. "Oooooh, no, you didn't!" She took off into the air as well after the Thunder dragon, her huge wings kicking up clouds of loose dirt in her wake.

"Wait for me!" Kinaari giggled joyfully and followed her two friends into the Montana sky.

Petros watched them climb, turn west, and then disappear into some low stratocumulus clouds. He turned toward the farm and started the hike back, saying to himself, "I need to find a mirror and have a chat with our Little Knight."

Marcus weaved in and out of the clouds, purposely allowing the girls to see him briefly before disappearing into the billows. Tag at two thousand feet was something he never imagined, but he was loving every minute of it.

Below, Tiffany tried to draw a bead on the agile dragon but his disappear/reappear tactics made the game all the more challenging. From behind, she could hear Kinaari shout, "Hey, you can tag me, too, you know! I'm right here!"

Tiffany looked back. "Nah, you're too easy of a target. The football player is going down!" She thought for a moment and then remembered the mention that her breath weapon was pure heat. An idea sprang to mind, and she inhaled deeply and then exhaled as hard as she could. Nothing came out of her mouth.

Just then, Marcus dipped back out of the clouds and shouted, "C'mon, slowpokes! I feel like I'm scrimmaging with the middle school team!"

Tiffany felt frustration mix with anger, and she wanted nothing but to beat Marcus at his own game. An odd sensation went through her chest, a tingling mixed with warmth and pressure. If felt as if something needed to get out. Inhaling deeply again, she focused on the feeling, opened her mouth, and pushed with everything she had.

A cone of shimmering air issued forth, like the heat rising from blacktop baking in the noon-day sun. The cone hit the cloud and instantly began to vaporize the water droplets and ice crystals that made up the fluffy formation of white. She kept pushing the heat out and disintegrated more of the cloud until she exposed her blue, winged friend. The heat washed over Marcus, and he almost instantly felt his scales sizzle and wing membranes blister.

"Heyyyyowww!" he bellowed as he simultaneously lost his concentration and began to fall back to the earth. Tiffany folded her wings back and matched the speed of Marcus's fall. She got close enough to slap him on the tail and then pulled back up.

"Ha! Who's 'it' now, tough guy?" she taunted. With powerful beats of her wings, Tiffany poured on the speed and took off away from the tumbling Marcus. He tucked his body and regained control of his flight.

"Oh, so that's the way it is, huh?" he playfully shouted after her and shot after the Heat dragon.

"Hey, I'm not 'it'! Someone can tag me!" Kinaari shouted, flapping her wings furiously, but she could not outmaneuver the other two.

Marcus pursued Tiffany for all he was worth. She might not have been as agile as he, but she was stronger, and her wings were bigger. As he began to close the distance, Tiffany looked back at him and unleashed another cone of intense heat. He barely avoided the breath weapon but still felt the sweltering temperature against his underbelly.

He muttered, "So we're gonna play that way." Inhaling, he opened his mouth and unleashed a deafening thunderclap. The sound hit Tiffany, but she instinctively covered her ear cavities to protect them from the powerful noise. However, the thunder did more than overload her eardrums; it disrupted her inner ear as well, and the world began to spin as a wave of vertigo overcame her. Her flight slowed, and her path was disrupted, and Marcus seized on the opportunity to rapidly close on her. He slapped the back of her head with his tail as he whizzed past her.

Tiffany shook the dizziness out of her head as she regained control. "Oh, you are soooo dead!" she shouted and laughed at the same time. The two began to corkscrew around each other as they raced forward, dodging claw swipes, tail slaps, and wing buffets as they tried to not let the other touch them. The occasional cone of heat shot out or thunderclap sounded as the epic game of tag waged high above the Montana countryside.

Kinaari struggled to keep up and was feeling frustrated at being left out. She finally got close enough and shouted, "C'mon, you two, slow down! I want to play too! Do you hear me?" She inhaled deeply and shouted, "Stop!" But as she yelled, she felt something burst out of her mouth as a wave of pure force blasted into the twilight sky and toward her two friends. The shockwave slammed into Marcus and Tiffany like a battering ram, casting them hither and yon, one on an arcing trajectory into the clouds and the other flailing toward the earth. Kinaari couldn't recall hearing the shockwave. It was more of a feeling inside her chest; a deep thump vibrated through her when she used her breath weapon. She helplessly watched her friends thrashing head over tails as they tried to regain control of themselves. She held her front claws over her mouth, her eyes wide with panic.

Much to her relief, the two recovered and swooped back around to rendezvous with her. They circled her, and Marcus exclaimed, "Kinaari, did you do that?"

"I'm sorry!" she blurted through the claws over her mouth. "I didn't mean—"

Marcus smiled. "Girl, you got the breath weapon thing down! I felt like I got tackled by an NFL pro. That was some serious stuff."

Tiffany nodded in approval. "That was something else, prom queen. Nice job."

Kinaari lowered her front claws. "Really? I didn't hurt you?"

Marcus said, "You knocked me silly, but it's all good. I was wondering when you were gonna toughen up and go all dragon on us."

Kinaari's expression softened as she realized that her friends were not only unharmed but that she had impressed them as well. "I didn't think I was going to make a very good dragon." She felt tears coming to her eyes.

Marcus interjected, "Okay, you gotta stop with the crying, right?"

Tiffany acknowledged, "There's no crying in dragon-hood."

Kinaari nodded and wiped her eyes, and she looked down toward the earth. Her eye ridges furrowed as she asked, "Umm, where are we?"

Tiffany and Marcus both looked down. They had never comprehended how much open space their state was comprised of until they saw it from above. The sun was setting, and the earth below looked dark with just occasional clusters of city lights scattered here and there. They could make out the peaks of the mountains to the west and could see Canada to the north while the greens and browns of the many farms and fields faded to deep myrtle and sepia tones. The clouds took on more brilliant shades of orange and red as the sun descended to the western horizon. The three friends simply took in the wonder of the world. "I've never been in a plane before," Marcus commented. "This is something else."

Tiffany nodded. "Me neither. Makes you feel kind of small."

Kinaari said, "I've flown to India with my parents, but, still, everything looks so peaceful from up here. You tend to forget about the stuff that's on your mind."

A few more contemplative beats went by before Tiffany proclaimed, "Hey! We're dragons! We can fly! What are we doing watching the world go by?"

Marcus reflected her enthusiasm. "Then lead on, Miss Heat Dragon."

She looked to the setting sun. "Go west, young man. We still have some sunlight left."

The three pointed themselves toward the mountains and joyfully took wing, riding the air currents toward the twilight on the horizon.

***

Petros walked up the stairs to the bathroom near Jason's bedroom. He flipped on the light and stood before the mirror. A very dour Jason stared back at him.

"Tonare and the others told me what happened," Petros stated.

Jason frowned. "Yeah, well, I don't want to talk about it."

Petros looked irritated. "I am not going anywhere until you talk to me."

Jason shrugged. "I guess you're gonna be standing there a while."

Petros tucked the corner of his mouth in thought. "If memory serves, your father is due home tomorrow or the day after. Unless you want me to explain to him that his son is actually the consciousness of an eight-hundred-year-old dragon residing in a teenage body, I suggest you cease your sulking and talk to me about what happened and what we are going to do about it."

Jason looked surprised. "You're blackmailing me?"

Petros replied, "I am motivating you."

"You're playing dirty."

"And you are just not playing at all."

Jason said, "What if I don't like the game?"

Petros looked as sympathetic as he could. "This game is mandatory. Refusing to play is not an option."

Jason smirked. "Sounds like a dumb game."

Petros didn't change his expression. "The game of life does not always make sense."

Jason paused for what seemed like an excruciatingly long time. "Okay, I'll talk."

***

"Chief, I've got something very odd here."

The chief master sergeant looked up from studying the duty logs on her clipboard. "What is it, Airman?"

Airman Tom Flagston studied the computer screen on his station in the air control tower on Malmstrom Air Force Base outside of Great Falls, Montana. A look of concern was on his face as he set radar images side by side with network communication from airports around the state. He answered, "I'm not sure, ma'am. A couple of small fields east of here have reported three very erratic blips on their radar. They have no transponder signals and don't respond to any communications."

Chief Kathleen Rodriguez walked to the station and looked at the display. She rubbed her brow as she studied the telemetry. "That's peculiar. Do we have a visual from anyone?"

Flagston shook his head. "No, ma'am. No one has eyes on them. They are just all over the place up there, and there isn't a lot of traffic this time of night, so I can't get a visual."

The lines on Rodriguez's face deepened as her unease intensified. She was in her late thirties, and the stress of having achieved her military rank before forty only created more of the proverbial "laugh lines" around her eyes. She even began to color her jet black hair, for the infiltration of the gray intruders had begun far too prematurely. "Are they within our outer markers yet?"

Flagston nodded. "Crossed over two minutes ago."

Rodriguez straightened up and took a deep breath, exhaling slowly as she tried to formulate a plan. "You ever see aircraft fly like that before, Airman Flagston?"

He shook his head. "No, ma'am. Never seen anything manmade fly that irregularly before. First they were tracking in tight circles, then they seemed to be circling each other, and at one point they looked like they were just hovering there."

Malmstrom Air Force Base was the home to the 40th Helicopter Squadron of the US Air Force. It consisted of a group of UH-1H Huey Iroquois, not the most state-of-the-art helicopters but more than enough to provide a military presence in its sparsely populated part of the country. Real action did not come often to Malmstrom, but the men and women stationed there were certainly prepared to respond.

Rodriguez said, "Scramble four choppers, Airman. Make sure they have loaded mini-guns and proper air-to-air ordinance. I don't know what these things are, but I certainly want to be prepared if they are hostile."

Chapter 22

Petros sat on the edge of the laminate counter in the upstairs bathroom, looking at Jason through the mirror. Jason had just recounted his difficulties mastering Petros's body, and the dragon/boy was now regarding him with compassion.

"Little Knight, you have been in my body for a very short period of time. You cannot pass judgment upon yourself simply because you were unable to fly or use my breath weapon immediately."

Jason hung his head but nodded in agreement. "I know, I know. I just wanted to be good at something, you know? Naturally good...not something I had to practice over and over until I couldn't stand it. And don't say 'good things only come from hard work' or anything like that because I've heard it all before."

"If you have heard it all before," Petros said, "then why do you not take the lesson to heart?"

"Because I'm an uncoordinated wimp in real life, and I can't stand the thought of being an uncoordinated dragon as well."

Petros nodded. "I am not an uncoordinated wimp, whatever that is."

Jason managed a smirk. "No, you're not. But you've been a dragon for, like, a bazillion years, and you—" Jason stopped midsentence, realizing what he said.

Petros prompted, "Finish that statement."

Jason took a deep breath. "And you've had a lot of practice."

Petros shook his head with a grin. "I just finished lecturing your friends on the pitfalls of youth, one of the larger ones being a profound lack of patience. Skills that require diligent practice cannot happen instantaneously. Yes, there are those more naturally gifted than others, but that is more the exception than the norm."

"Then why does it seem like everyone around me fits into that 'naturally gifted' category?"

Petros shrugged. "Perhaps the problem does not lie with everyone else."

Jason rolled his eyes. "Oh, great, I've heard this one before. You're gonna tell me I don't apply myself."

"No," Petros corrected. "I was going to observe that you may suffer from chronic laziness and give up far too easily."

Jason was taken aback. "Ouch."

Petros said, "The truth about oneself can be painful. That does not make it any less the truth."

Jason smiled. "I didn't realize dragons were so good at dispensing advice."

"I am surprised myself. We usually order weak, lesser beings like humans to do our bidding at the threat of their very lives. This is uncharted territory for me."

Jason paused in shock. "You're, um, kidding, right?"

Petros nodded. "Of course," he said but then obliquely added, "mostly. But it would seem we have bigger issues we need to address."

Jason was still processing "mostly" when he responded, "Yeah, Dad's coming home soon, and we need to figure out what to do about our little magic whammy combo thing here."

Petros agreed. "Yes, but that identifies yet another problem."

Jason asked, "Which is?"

"In finding a solution to our current predicament, I see no choice but to return to Billings and find the mage. He will be the only one that can undo this spell. I do not see the cowardly simp wanting to return to Malta, so we will need to go to him."

Jason shook his head. "So not only do we need to get everyone back home, on time, and show you dragons how to live with our human families, but we then need to get everyone back down to Billings to try and reverse the gigantic mess we're in?"

Petros added, "Not to mention further addressing the mystery of the dark riders, understanding how we all came to be living in two thousand and eleven, and integrating the rest of dragonkind into modern society."

Jason's eyes went wide. "Plus, I have to go back to work the day after tomorrow. See? Just a few very minor details we need to iron out." He lowered his head in despair. "I have a headache."

Petros nodded and rubbed the matching pain in his forehead. "Yes, I know."

Tiffany, Kinaari, and Marcus soared blissfully over the twilight-covered countryside. They flew in silence and soaked in the feeling of unaided flight. Their minds worked to capture every feeling: the wind flowing over their snouts, the rushing sounds of the rapidly moving air, even the subtle vibrations of their wing membranes holding them aloft on the currents and vents rising from the cooling earth. They had maneuvered themselves into a "V" formation, with Tiffany taking the point and the others to either side of her.

Kinaari finally spoke after several minutes. "We should head back soon."

Marcus nodded, but Tiffany countered, "Or not."

Marcus looked confused. "Umm, what?"

Tiffany kept her gazed fixed on the west. "I could just keep flying. What's gonna stop me? Can't find any reason to turn back."

Marcus and Kinaari exchanged confused looks. Kinaari asked, "What is it, Tiff?"

She finally turned her neck back to look at the Water Dragon. "You both have reasons to go back, and I won't stop you. Me? Can't really see much back in Jordan that's worth going back to." She refixed her gaze on the horizon.

Kinaari asked, "But your family will miss you, right?"

Tiffany paused. "They'll probably notice my absence, but that isn't the same as missing someone."

A rumble came from the sky up ahead, and Marcus spoke up. "Tiff, look, I don't know what's going on in your head right now, but there's a storm approaching. We should turn and—" Marcus cut himself off as he looked into the distance, straining his eyes to see as far as he could.

Tiffany responded, "If you're afraid of a little thunder then feel free to turn around, Mr. Thunder Dragon."

Marcus shook his head. "That's not thunder."

They all listened against the rushing of the wind. The rumble they had heard was a constant, rhythmic, and pulsating sound, not intermittent like peals of thunder. Kinaari asked, "What is that?"

Concern washed over Marcus's face. "Trouble."

Four UH-1H Hueys thundered over the farmlands below. They kept in a diamond formation as they approached the three radar blips ahead. The pilot of the lead chopper spoke into the microphone attached to his flight helmet: "Malmstrom, we are approaching the targets. We should have visuals in two minutes."

The control tower responded, "Acknowledged, Iroquois One. Proceed with caution; advise upon immediate sight acquisition."

The pilot said, "Roger that, Tower. Iroquois Two, Three, and Four, maintain formation; targets are maintaining their present course and speed but are not making any hostile actions. Gunners, stay ready but do not engage unless ordered."

Four "rogers" came back from the gunners of the choppers.

The pilot of Iroquois Two spoke into his radio: "Squad Leader, do we have any working theories on what these things are?"

Iroquois One answered, "Negative, Iroquois Two. But based on the observed flight paths, it doesn't seem that—" The pilot trailed off.

Iroquois Three buzzed in. "Squad Leader, you got cut off. Repeat last statement."

The squad leader wondered how to answer. "I never finished, Iroquois Three. Previous flight paths are not possible by any mechanical thing that matches the size of the targets."

There was a pause over the com-link. Iroquois Four was the first to break the silence. "Are you suggesting this is an unknown technology, Squad Leader, like a UFO?"

"No," replied the pilot of Iroquois One. "I am suggesting that they may be biological," He didn't let them respond as he went on. "Eyes on the sky, squad. We should have visual any moment."

Tiffany shot a look at Marcus as she realized the noise was getting closer. "What is it then?" she asked, a slight intonation of panic in her voice.

Marcus looked toward the sound. "Helicopters. More than one of them, and they are heading our—" Realization came over his face. "Dang! We should have been paying more attention; I think we're near Malmstrom Air Force Base!"

Kinaari screeched, "Air force?"

Tiffany covered her eyes with her claw. "Great, now we've drawn the attention of the military. Didn't Petros tell us to *not* be seen? This is pretty much the opposite of *not* being seen."

"Hey!" Marcus shouted. "You're the one leading the way!"

Kinaari barked, "Stop it! Fighting won't help! It's dark; maybe they won't see us."

Just then, four spotlights shone from the helicopters and bathed them in their powerful white light.

Tiffany droned, "You were saying?"

"I'm not seeing anything," the pilot of Iroquois Two spoke into his headset. "Maybe they are in the clouds."

Iroquois One buzzed back, "Radar says they are right there. Everyone, hit the area with your spotlights."

The million-lumen spotlights attached to the landing skids of the Hueys blazed to life and quickly found three very unusually shaped targets flying above them. Iroquois Three blared over the headsets, "What in God's name are those?"

The control tower at Malmstrom joined the conversation. "Report, squadron, report! Iroquois One, what do you see?"

The pilot of Iroquois One could not believe what he was about to say. "Tower…Chief…we have three very large, flying…I don't know…creatures."

Chief Rodriguez paused. "Iroquois One, please verify. Did you say," she swallowed hard, "'creatures'?"

Iroquois One nodded. "Copy that, Tower. They're, I don't know, dinosaurs maybe?"

Iroquois Two interrupted, losing his composure. "They're not dinosaurs! They're dragons, man! We're looking at dragons! Look at 'em; they're talking to each other!"

Iroquois One shouted, "Cut the chatter, Iroquois Two! Dragons are not real. I don't know what…Tower, Tower! They are turning around and breaking formation! They're scattering!"

Chief Rodriguez shouted back, "Pursue, Iroquois; you have the 'go' to pursue! We need to know what these things are!"

Marcus shouted, "We gotta turn around and get back to the farm! Maybe if we spread out, they won't be able to follow."

Tiffany surged forward with a powerful beat of her wings, while Marcus headed toward the clouds, and Kinaari dove to a path closer to the earth. In response, the choppers broke rank as well; two continued on after Tiffany while the other two split off and headed after Kinaari and Marcus.

Iroquois One shouted, "Iroquois Two and Three, head high and low after the others. Iroquois Four, you're with me; we're keeping after the big one!"

Tiffany was accelerating with all her might when she craned her neck around and noticed the two choppers following. "Great," she growled to herself. "I'm bigger than everyone for only a day, and they're already ganging up on me." She banked hard and began to corkscrew her flight pattern in ever-widening circles, trying to confuse the pilots as to her true destination. But they held their spotlights on her body and predicted the pattern of her flight as they adjusted to keep her locked in their sights. "I gotta take out those lights," she said to herself, and she began to devise a plan to douse the intense illumination.

Marcus climbed high until he was skimming the bottom of the clouds. He knew he couldn't just disappear into a cloud bank; his pursuer would probably give up and join one of the other Hueys and pursue Kinaari or Tiffany. He had to think fast. He didn't want to risk injuring any of the pilots; they were simply doing their jobs, and they had just stumbled upon mythical beasts come to life. It wasn't a matter they were going to simply let drop. But then he had a brainstorm.

Petros told them how Jason camouflaged his dragon body by the river bank, and Marcus wondered if this was something all dragons could do. He was an Air Dragon, and he was most definitely in his element, so he began to focus on the clouds sweeping above him and thought how much he needed to hide.

The pilot of Iroquois Two had just said into his headset, "It looks like it is maintaining a steady path again." He noticed the colors of the dragon begin to shimmer as it began to become translucent. And within a few moments, the creature disappeared altogether.

"What the—" the pilot sputtered into his headset.

The tower buzzed back, "Sit-rep, Iroquois Two. What is the problem?"

He shook his helmeted head. "Tower, it just disappeared."

"It flew into the clouds?"

"No," the pilot answered. "It didn't change its trajectory. Its colors waved and shimmered then it just disappeared."

Marcus could tell by the flailing searchlight beam that his camouflage had worked and he needed to only slow down and wait just a few moments. They would completely lose him, and then he could go help his friends.

Kinaari dove back toward the earth while Iroquois Three stayed on her tail. She leveled off about twenty feet above the ground and began to bob and weave over and around the Montana topography. She hugged the crests of hills and slalomed her way in between the taller trees as she fought to escape her pursuers. Iroquois Three's pilot was exceptionally well trained; she was able to keep up with the turquoise dragon as she used the countryside as an obstacle course.

The trees and hills gave way to a small lake, and Kinaari immediately had an idea. Not wasting a second, she pointed herself at the water and splashed below the surface. Her eyes immediately adjusted to the murk of the nighttime waters as if she had an underwater equivalent of night vision, and she immediately noticed she did not need to hold her breath. Gills on her neck, just below the base of her head, took over, and Kinaari was breathing underwater. It was a sensation like she had never felt, but her body instinctively knew how to use the extra organs, and oxygen was coursing through her bloodstream as it was removed from the water. She smiled and began to swim toward the opposite shore. Kinaari cut through the water like a torpedo, and she quickly realized why she was a Water Dragon. From the fin-like wings to the gills on her neck to the structure of the membranes at the tip of her tail, it was immediately apparent that her body was built for the water. She glided through the depths as easily as Tonare's body flew through the air, and she felt complete exhilaration.

Above, Iroquois Three frantically waved its searchlight over the surface of the lake. "It went underwater, Tower, and hasn't come up yet. I think we may have lost it."

Back in the tower, Chief Rodriguez frowned. "Continue searching for a few more ticks, Three, and then go assist Iroquois Two. At least he lost his target in the clouds."

Tiffany had a sudden brainstorm, and she purposefully slowed her flight and let the choppers get closer. Then, without warning, she tucked her head and executed a half-somersault, inverting herself. She opened her wings fully and caught the wind. The resistance to the air caused a braking effect, and she slowed almost instantly, allowing the helicopters to pass on either side of her head. She puckered her mouth and blew the most focused jet of pure heat she could at the spotlight of one of the passing vehicles. The metal of the light glowed with heat almost instantly, and the glass shattered as the bulb in the housing exploded. The superheated metal actually distorted in shape as it began to melt, and the spotlight was rendered inoperable. But Tiffany did not account for the speed of the passing choppers. The helicopter shot by her, and she was unable to stop her breath weapon soon enough. The jet of superheated air passed the spotlight and washed over the landing skid closest to her. That metal instantly heated as well and began to droop under its own weight. It was too late when she realized her mistake, and the chopper was badly damaged. She pointed herself downward and tried to put distance between her and the war vehicles but realized she had miscalculated on another detail. Her maneuver had destroyed one spotlight, but now the choppers were between her and the direction she wanted to go.

The pilot of Iroquois Four shouted into his headset, "We've been attacked; I repeat, the creature attacked us and melted our starboard landing skid!"

"Melted?" the tower buzzed back. "What sort of weapon was it?"

The pilot shook his head. "Unknown, but it reduced the metal to slag in just under a second!"

Iroquois One chimed in, "We need a course of action, Tower!"

Chief Rodriguez chewed her lip as she thought. She shook her head in regret as she answered, "We have no choice. You have permission to return fire; repeat, you have the 'go' to return fire."

Tiffany hovered, watching for the Hueys to respond. They came about, and as their side doors slid open, she could see gunners taking their place behind very large weapons. She rumbled to herself, "Oh, I do *not* see this ending well."

High above, Marcus watched the interchange take place between Tiffany and her two pursuers. He had just put enough distance between himself and his chopper, but now he knew he was going to need to help Tiffany. "Aw, maaaan!" he lamented as he lost his concentration and his camouflage failed. Marcus was visible again, and a tight backflip later he was speeding back toward his Heat dragon friend.

Iroquois Two shouted, "There! Target reacquired! Re-engaging! Do I have permission to open fire if needed, Tower?"

"Permission granted," Rodriquez answered gravely.

Clouds gathered above them. There was a rumble of thunder and then a flash of lightning.

The high whine of the Huey's mini-gun stabbed into the night as a torrent of bullets and tracer rounds lanced at Tiffany. She instinctively threw a claw up over her eyes, and the rounds impacted her scales…and bounced off. The multitude of bullets careened off into the night air, and Tiffany could feel the tiny slugs of lead as only weak taps against her armored hide. The gunner swept the hail of bullets up the side of her body and began attacking her wing. As the bullets struck the wing membranes, most of the skin held, but the occasional round punctured the flesh, which made her wince in pain. She needed to get out of the way and escape; she had started this fight inadvertently and now she had to end it without anyone getting injured.

Marcus shot away from the clouds to the aid of Tiffany and saw that both choppers were now spraying her with gunfire.

"Oh, man, oh, man, oh, man! I gotta do something!" he said. He thought for a moment then said, "This should just disorient them, not hurt them, right? I mean they're enclosed in a cockpit and probably wearing earmuffs or headphones or something. Should just shake 'em up." He inhaled and then let loose a thunderclap toward the direction of the helicopters. Both of the vehicles wavered immediately following the sonic attack.

Then mayhem erupted.

Iroquois One and Four were completely unprepared for Marcus's breath weapon. The magically re-enforced sound penetrated the cockpits and headsets, simultaneously shattering the eardrums of the pilots and gunners and inducing a vertigo that brought them to the brink of vomiting. Iroquois One's pilot was screaming into his headset, "Aaagh! Some kind of sonic weapon! They blew out our ears! Everything is spinning…I can't hear, Tower, I can't hear!"

The Iroquois Four pilot was less composed. "Ggaaaaah! My ears! I'm gonna puke! I'm going down…mayday, mayday!"

Iroquois Two witnessed the event and was shouting, "Oh, man, Tower, he hit 'em both! One and Four are out of control! It was some kind of sound weapon. I think they're gonna go down; repeat, I think we're gonna lose Iroquois One and Four!"

Chief Rodriguez heard the insanity and shouted to Airman Flagston, "Scramble two F-Eighteens now! I want those fast-movers in the air and those things brought down five minutes ago!"

Tiffany saw Marcus's attack and shouted at him as he approached, "What did you do?"

Marcus nearly shrieked back, "I wasn't trying to hurt them! C'mon, we've gotta keep them from crashing!" He shot toward one of the choppers, barrel-rolling around it while it spun wildly out of control and then grasped the underside of its tail with all four of his legs. He began to beat his wings and twist the muscles of his body to stop the chopper's wild spin. He never realized the strength of the lift the rotors were throwing; he fought with nearly everything he had to stop the spin and get some semblance of control over the flying machine.

Tiffany attempted to come about with the second chopper and execute the same maneuver as Marcus. She was still, however, inexperienced with her new draconic body. In coming around the side of the vehicle, she flew too close, and the rotors smashed into her side. Tiffany shouted in pain and two of the four rotors broke off and spun wildly into the night air. Her eyes widened in panic, and she grabbed the helicopter with her legs and began beating her wings with all of her strength. At first, she felt no difference, but after several seconds she felt the momentum begin to slow. Tiffany didn't let up and fought with every ounce of her strength to lower the Huey softly and prevent everyone from losing their lives.

Iroquois Two's pilot shouted into his headset, "Tower! You're not gonna believe this! Iroquois Four just blew out its rotor on one of the things, but now it looks like two of 'em are trying to keep One and Four from crashing."

Chief Rodriguez couldn't believe what she was hearing. She was flooded with indecision for a moment. Were these things friendly? Was this all some kind of mistake? She considered altering her course of action when she remembered her training: make a decision and stick with it to its logical conclusion. She answered, "Can you get a bead on them, Iroquois Two?"

The pilot was taken aback. "Umm, no, ma'am. Not without hitting One and Four."

Rodriquez closed her eyes and winced as she followed up, "When you get a clear shot, take it, Iroquois Two. Iroquois Three, leave the third one in the water. Get up there and help the rest of your squad."

Two F-18 fighters took to the runways of Malmstrom Air Force Base. Long-range, radar-guided air-to-air missiles were securely attached to their wings. They waited for the clearance to take off.

Thunder rumbled. Lightning flashed. Clouds gathered.

Marcus couldn't stabilize the careening Huey. He was built for speed and agility; his wings were not strong enough to lift a helicopter nearly his size. Tiffany, being bigger and with a greater wingspan, fought hard to slow her chopper's descent but would be able to land it safely. Marcus shouted, "I...I can't control it! It's gonna crash!"

Tiffany strained back, "Take out the rotors! At least it'll stop fighting you!"

"I can't!" he yelled but then had a brainstorm. He reached into the cabin with his tail and found the gunner curled on the floor, screaming at the pain of his shattered eardrums. He cupped the finned tip of his tail around the soldier and scooped him right out of the cabin and, with a short toss, caught him with his rear foot. Marcus searched wildly for Tiffany, but she was too far to the ground in lowering her chopper to provide him with any aid. He knew he had to get the pilot out as well. He dug his claws into the rear of the flailing vehicle to try to solidify his grip. However, the body of the chopper was structurally weak at the point where he hung on, and the sickening sound of tearing metal pierced the cacophony of sounds swirling around him as the tail of the Huey tore completely free of its body. Marcus watched the front half of the chopper fly uncontrollably into the night sky as he gripped the tail section. All he could do was scream, "Noooooo!"

Just then the turquoise form of Kinaari, having quickly swum the length of the small lake to evade her pursuers, shot past him after the cabin of the Huey. She managed to catch one of the landing skids so she could use her other claw to tear away the windshield and wrest the disoriented pilot, and the seat to which he was buckled, out with one smooth motion.

Holding the pilot safely in her front claw, Kinaari muttered to herself, "Can't let the rest of that thing crash into some house below." She inhaled deeply and focused then let a massive shockwave burst out of her mouth. The force slammed into the rest of the Huey, pulverizing the front half of the chopper into a cloud of tiny metal pieces and shards. If anything was on the ground to be hit, the damage would be far less severe.

Iroquois Two rendezvoused with Iroquois Three as the pilot of Two said, "Tower, you're not gonna believe this," and he explained the events that had just transpired.

Chief Rodriguez listened to the account. "Iroquois Two, are you implying they destroyed or incapacitated our helicopters and then tried to save the pilots?"

Two's pilot answered, "Ma'am, I'm implying this may have been a mistake, and their intentions are peaceful."

Rodriguez responded, "Intentions? Pilot, are you suggesting there is an intelligence at work here? That those…creatures may be sentient?"

"Ma'am, I just witnessed them not only saving four human beings from certain death but actually cooperating to do so."

She gritted her teeth. "Iroquois Two, I have two F-Eighteens converging on your position. If you can confirm that these are sentient, intelligent creatures with peaceful intentions, I will order the fast-movers home. Can you confirm that, Pilot?"

Iroquois Two grimaced. "No, ma'am. I cannot confirm that with certainty."

"Then yours and Iroquois Three's orders are to return to base and let the fast-movers bring this incident to a close."

The pilot was furious. He knew in his heart of hearts that the creatures were not hostile, but he was not prepared to stake his military career on it. He saw the storm clouds gathering. "Malmstrom, Iroquois Two and Three are on their way home. A rescue party will need to be dispatched for the crews of Iroquois One and Four. I am transmitting their coordinates now."

Rodriguez came back over the headset. "Copy that, Iroquois Two. Prepping Iroquois Five and Six for rescue operations."

Marcus, Kinaari, and Tiffany carefully set their cargo down on the earth then rapidly took to the skies to get back to the farm. They had noticed the clouds over their heads gathering.

"Weird weather," Marcus commented.

Tiffany nodded. "Yeah, it just came out of nowhere." She cocked her head. "Do you hear somethi—" She was unable to finish her sentence as two F-18 Hornets rocketed by them, the roar of their engines making them reflexively cover their ear sockets. The jets immediately banked right and began to come around for another pass.

Kinaari yelled, "They're sending fighter jets after us now?"

Marcus had an odd peace as he watched the fighters looping around to face them again. "This is it. We really screwed up. We can't outrun them, and each of 'em has, what, four radar-guided missiles? We're bulletproof, but I'm not sure we can take an air-to-air missile and fly away. I'm not gonna shoot 'em down; I can't have that on my conscience. If they blow us outta the sky then that'll be that. Our mistake. We deal with the consequences."

Tiffany agreed, "Yeah, I'm not fighting any more soldiers or taking the risk of killing anyone." She began to flap her wings and hovered in place. She held her forelegs straight up as if she were raising her hands in surrender. "Maybe this will help. Maybe they won't fire. I doubt it, but I'm not destroying anything else tonight."

The other two imitated Tiffany's position and simply waited for what was to happen next. To their surprise, a bolt of lightning arced out of the sky between the two fighters. Their flight paths wavered at the close call, but as they stabilized, two more bolts lanced from the clouds right in front of each jet. Each was forced to veer off from its trajectory and dodge yet a third bolt aimed at each of them. The three Draconauts watched in amazement as the weather had somehow developed a mind of its own and was now protecting them. The F-18s tried to recover, but this time the lightning actually grazed the fuselage of each airplane, sending them flying off at random trajectories as the pilots fought to regain control of their war planes.

The three looked to each other for reactions, when a large, dark shape descended from the clouds. It took position in front of them, beating its V-shaped wings to hover in place. This was an Air Dragon but one larger than any of the three of them. A harness was fastened around its chest, securing a saddle to the back of the massive beast. They could make out a rider in the saddle, its body completely covered by some sort of makeshift armor. In its hand was a long, wickedly curved, lance-type weapon. The Storm dragon eyed them furiously as it spoke.

"If thou wishes to live though the evening, thou willst follow me and keep thy mouths silent!"

Chapter 23

Petros stood on the front porch of the Hewes homestead, looking toward the western sky. The faintest hint of purple was still visible at the horizon; the rest of the sky was filled with the blackness of night. Stars peeked out from behind the clouds drifting by overhead, their usual white transformed into the deepest of gray by the absence of the sun.

Petros kept his arms folded tightly around his torso, shielding him from the chill of the night air. He would never tell Jason, but he despised feeling this vulnerable. His own body could fly a thousand feet above the earth in a chilling winter's wind without the slightest shiver or bask in the blazing sun of the hottest desert without the need to worry of sunstroke. But this human body was so fragile, so delicate; he could not fathom what it would be like to spend a lifetime in this form.

In his hand, he held a small mirror. They had found it in a trunk containing items that once belonged to Jason's mother and older brother, a trove of keepsakes his father had saved and tried to hide from Jason. Jason's heart ached every time he thought of this trunk. It served to remind him that, after the years since the accident, there was a part of the analytical mind of his father that refused to let go of the memory of Danielle Hewes or his other son, William. But it was in this trunk that Petros found the hand mirror, a reflective plate surrounded by a white frame and mounted on a handle. The dragon knew whom it belonged to, realized its consequent importance, and handled it as cautiously as he could.

He held it at arm's length until he could see his entire face, and then the reflection's expression changed. "Any sign of them?" Jason asked.

Petros shook his head. "No, I am becoming concerned."

"It's late, isn't it? I have no idea of the time."

Petros nodded. "Yes. But I have other news; your father…what is the term? Oh, yes, 'texted' me back. He will not return until the evening of tomorrow."

Jason nodded. "That buys us some more time."

"It does. Come, then, tell me more about working at this museum of yours since I will be needing to complete these tasks on the morrow. We should utilize this time wisely. You can further instruct me in the appropriate conduct of your workplace."

"Okay. You're going to need to become familiar with the finer points of using a mop."

***

Tiffany, Marcus, and Kinaari soared over the countryside, following the massive Storm dragon. It led them to the Bears Paw Mountains, a small range nearly halfway between Malta and Great Plains. The great dragon circled majestically over the peaks and then quickly dove toward a small lake nestled among the mountains. The other three eyed each other reluctantly then followed the Air Dragon in its rapid descent.

Within moments, it was clear that the Storm dragon was not going to swerve up or even stop once it reached the lake's surface. Tiffany and Marcus gave each other nervous looks, but Kinaari smiled and took the point position behind the Storm dragon as the black waters rushed up to fill their field of vision. The surface of the lake shattered at the impact of the creatures, sending water splashing thirty feet into the night sky. The other three dragons followed into the inky depths, and within a second the small lake swallowed the four majestic creatures, leaving only concentric circles of dark water rushing toward the deserted banks.

Kinaari's eyes immediately adjusted to the blackness, and she saw the Storm dragon navigating ahead of them. She could see the rider on the dragon's back; somehow, it was unaffected by being underwater. Kinaari swore that, despite being completely submerged, the Storm dragon's passenger was surrounded by a layer of air contoured perfectly around his or her body. Marcus and Tiffany could barely see, but they were able to follow their Water Dragon friend. The lakes in this part of the state were carved out by ancient glaciers, and some were exceptionally deep. The Storm dragon led them down at least two hundred feet before it leveled its descent and headed to what appeared to be an underwater cave.

The four swam into the tunnel and followed the path for several hundred feet and finally turned upward again as they resurfaced in what appeared to be a different lake. Three of the dragons inhaled sharply as they emerged from the water, and Marcus, Tiffany, and Kinaari immediately saw they had emerged inside one of the Bears Paw Mountains. A massive cavern enclosed the lake while soft orange patches of light filtered down from the stalactites above. Tiffany whispered as they swam to the edge of the lake, "Must be a bioluminescent fungus or something; I've read about it in science class."

The Storm dragon lead them to the shore of the small lake, and they climbed out onto an expanse of rocky cave floor that went on for nearly five hundred feet before meeting the cavern's wall. Stalagmites grew nearly twenty feet high as they reached for their inverted twins hanging from the dome far above. Despite the vastness of the cavern, its stark emptiness is what truly filled the expanse. Nothing lived there; there was nothing on the cold stone floor or anything living in the water. The huge grotto was barren, save for the four dragons now drip-drying at the edge of the murky lake.

Kinaari, Marcus, and Tiffany finally had an opportunity to view details of the Storm dragon in all of its glory. The beast was easily another dragon's head taller than Tiffany and half a tail longer. Being one of the species of Air Dragons, it had wings with the "V" configuration similar to Marcus's, although the pinions and membranes didn't extend all of the way down the length of its tail. The creature was covered with dark blue scales, save for a faint yellow stripe that ran the length of its body on both sides. Spines and membranes ran the length of its back, up the neck and right to the top of its head, ending in a large horn that extended over the dragon's snout. Two more horns curved downward from both sides of its jaws and then extended forward, coming to a point nearly flush with its chin. When one was looking straight on at the dragon's face, the three horns formed an unusual tripod of boney ornamentation around its head. Vibrant blue eyes carefully regarded them from beneath pronounced and severe brows.

The rider, still completely dry, hopped off of the back of the Storm dragon. The drop to the floor was at least nine feet, but the rider landed solidly and without faltering. The three Draconauts could now see that its armor was not medieval plate like they had assumed it was but was crafted from more modern materials. A dark blue motorcycle helmet covered the head and was adorned with a bright yellow decal of a dragon. The armor was some sort of flexible material, not metallic at all. Marcus guessed it was probably Kevlar or a similar bulletproof composite. The shoulders were a similar blue to the helmet, and the rest of the jacket and pants were gray. A bright yellow lightning bolt pattern separated the two colors. Two darker blue nylon straps wrapped around the chest with a similar vertical strap going over the left shoulder, and a military-style belt adorned the rider's waist. Blue boots armored with black shin guards completed the dragon-rider's tactical appearance.

The figure wore a large sword secured to its back by what could only be a magnetic housing, for it was suspended with no need for a sheath or any type of enclosure. What the dragon-teens previously thought was a lance was now revealed as a much more unusual weapon—another type of sword but with wickedly curved blades attached to either side of the handle. The rider walked to the nearest stalagmite with the dual-bladed sword in hand and, with only a minimal effort, jammed it into the stone, leaving it embedded in the dark rock. Kinaari could have sworn she saw small wisps of smoke waft up from the wound the blade had carved into the stone.

The Storm dragon spun to face the other three. "Thou art the most irresponsible of all dragon-kin that I have encountered in my many years!" it shouted. "Thy insufferable actions tonight mayest prove to be the undoing of our entire kind! That thou wouldst think freely soaring amongst the clouds in a world like this wouldst be acceptable to—"

The rider spoke, its voice electronically modified by the helmet it wore. "Nymbus, please—"

"Nay!" Nymbus shouted back. "Do not restrain my wrath! Our agreement be-est that thou handlest all affairs involving humankind, and I will address any behavior pertaining to dragons."

Tiffany spoke up. "Hey! We didn't know we were going to cause any trouble; we were just getting in some practice that we really—"

She was cut off as Nymbus took several steps toward her. He purposefully slammed each foot down, shaking rocks and stones on the floor as he approached Tiffany. He came nearly snout to snout with her. "How it is that thou feelst compelled to fly haphazardly through the skies knowing full well that the science..." Nymbus whipped his head toward his rider. "What name doest it bear again?"

The rider answered, "Radar."

Nymbus faced Tiffany again. "That the science of radar fully possesses the capability of tracking you through the firmament?"

Tiffany did not back down. "First, I know all about radar, and it didn't cross my mind that we could be tracked by it. Second, what is with the speech? Who uses Old English or says 'firmament' anymore?"

A look of disbelief came over Nymbus's face. "Thou mockest me after thy monumental errors this evening?"

Tiffany answered, "You're the one up in my face, sparky. How about you take a few steps back."

Wham!

Nymbus's foreleg slammed into Tiffany's head, knocking her off balance as she stumbled into one of the stalagmites several feet away. She tripped on the base of the rock formation, falling into it and snapping it off midway up. She fought to regain her balance as Nymbus imperiously watched her struggle.

Marcus shouted, "Oh, no, you didn't!" as he threw himself at the Storm dragon. His arc took him directly toward Nymbus, but Nymbus took a deft step to the side and brought his gigantic wing up in a sweeping motion. The appendage stuck the much-smaller Marcus and sent him flailing off on another vector. He crashed hard into the cavern floor and bowled over two more, smaller stalagmites before coming to a stop.

Taking a couple of steps toward the melee, Kinaari implored, "Look, we don't need to fight about—" She was cut off as Nymbus's tail whipped out and wrapped around her neck. Her voice was choked to silence as he dragged her by the base of her skull and threw Kinaari into the still-struggling Tiffany. They collided with a sickening thud, and both collapsed unceremoniously to the ground.

Marcus flipped himself back to his feet and charged toward Nymbus, snarling with rage. But Marcus still fought as if he were not only a human but one of the biggest guys on the football field. Nymbus was not only much larger than he but knew how to fight like a dragon. As Marcus barreled toward the Storm dragon, Nymbus reared up on his hind legs and, when Marcus was close enough, brought his full weight down on Marcus's shoulder haunches, simultaneously crushing him into the floor and immobilizing him. The stone floor of the cavern cracked at Marcus's impact.

The interior of the cavern shook as Tiffany recovered and roared an ear-splitting dragon roar, hurling herself into battle with Nymbus. Her body slammed into his as he did not realize she had recovered so quickly. Her momentum freed Marcus as the two huge dragons tumbled across the cave, pulverizing stalagmites as they rolled in physical combat. But Nymbus's superior fighting skills still prevailed, and Tiffany found herself pressed on the ground with Nymbus standing completely on her back. He pushed off her spine and leapt from her back, driving the wind from her lungs with the powerful jump.

The rider casually strolled from behind the rubble and approached the humiliated Tiffany. "You're not going to win this, you know."

Tiffany snarled, "Watch me!" She pushed herself up and growled as she prepared to re-enter the fray.

Kinaari shouted, "Tiffany, stop! This is really dumb!"

Marcus was finally recovering as he roared, "Take 'im out, Tiff!"

The rider yelled, "Nymbus, this is ridiculous! End this!"

Nymbus nodded and inhaled deeply. Bright white points of light began to glow at the tips of his three horns. Arcs of electricity crackled from the points and merged in front of Nymbus's mouth. He opened his maw wide and unleashed his breath weapon; a massive bolt of lightning blazed forward and struck the wide-eyed Tiffany. She arched her back in a silent scream as the devastating power flowed through her body, and the cavern was now ablaze with the brilliant white light of the bolt of electricity. Nymbus held the coruscating energy on the hapless Heat Dragon for another second before he snapped his mouth shut, and everything stopped.

Silence hung in the air for several moments as the eyes of all present readjusted to the soft glow of the bioluminescent fungus. The quiet moans of the stunned Tiffany broke the silence as steam rose from the crumpled heap of her body on the floor. Unable to find words, Marcus and Kinaari rushed to her side as the smell of ozone wafting from the fallen Heat dragon began to permeate the cavern.

The rider stepped into the space between the dragons, its head shaking back and forth. "I didn't want it to come to this, but you have been behaving far too recklessly. This kind of free access in the twenty-first century is simply not permissible. The risks are too high."

Marcus whipped his head around. "What, so you just go around frying anyone and everyone who steps out of your boundaries? We don't even know you, man, and you're trying to kill us!"

Nymbus held his head high. "I desire-est not to kill any of you, young one. However, thy collective impertinence compelled that a lesson was needed."

Tiffany was now stirring, struggling to push herself to her feet. She said, "So you throw lightning bolts instead of just explaining the stakes to us?"

Nymbus narrowed his eyes. "Thy insults, Kin of the Fire, indicated thou were in no state of mind to listen to reason."

Tiffany's muscles were still spasming beneath her scales. "I was bantering. It's how we talk."

The rider's body straightened up with curiosity. "No, it's not how you talk. In fact, no dragons talk like you. For example, you're using contractions. Dragons don't use contractions; they think it is sloppy speech."

Kinaari tried to explain. "We're...we are, umm, trying to speak like the humans to better understand them."

The rider was approaching Kinaari. "No, dragons don't conform. They're superior to humans, and they know it. Why would they ever lower themselves to act like human beings?" It turned to Nymbus, who looked equally suspicious, then back to the three. "What's going on here?"

Kinaari thought fast. "You know, we have the same question for you! Who are you, riding a giant dragon like Nymbus here over the Montana countryside? You two seem to know each other well enough that it's obvious you have been together for a long time, so how is that possible? And as you have just said, dragons are superior to humans, so why would he just let you ride him like he was some overgrown horse or whatever? So you tell me: what is going on here?"

Kinaari wished she could see through the darkened visor of the rider's helmet; she was dying to know what the figure was thinking and had no facial expressions to read. After several uncomfortable moments of silence, the rider finally spoke. "Your point is made. I believe we are all on the same side here; so we'll tell you our story, and then you'll tell us yours. Deal?"

Kinaari looked back to Marcus and Tiffany. Tiffany's expression was still pained as she tried to recover from being struck by lightning, but they both nodded their approval to Kinaari. She turned to the rider. "Deal."

They gathered in a circle with the mysterious rider seated in front of Nymbus. A pile of rocks had been assembled in the middle of their circle, and Tiffany used her breath weapon on them until they were glowing a bright orange-yellow and throwing off a gentle heat to keep their human host warm in the dank, cold expanse of the cavern.

"Thank you," the rider said. "I usually handle the temperature here, but the warmth is a pleasant change." Tiffany acknowledged the appreciation with a bow of her head, and the human went on. "I wish I had more details for you than I do. I am the latest of a long line of humans preserving an ancient alliance between humans and dragons. Many of the records detailing the original need for this alliance were destroyed, and as the stories have been passed by mouth through the centuries, many particulars have been lost. Nevertheless, we are called the Order of the Scale, and we seek peaceful coexistence between human and dragonkind.

"There was a great war seven hundred years ago or so. The dragons were fighting a dreadful enemy that hated them with a seething passion. For the most part, humans took a backseat in the conflict, sometimes acting as if they were blissfully unaware that a war was taking place. But there was a faction of people that finally realized this enemy, whoever he was, would most likely set his sights on humankind if he were to defeat the dragons, or at least on the humans who weren't content to be under some crazed, megalomaniacal ruler. So the Order of the Scale was formed, and people actually started helping the dragons in the war.

"From what we could piece together, the order was able to help turn the tide, until this enemy found some kind of weapon, one that could kill even the largest of the dragons with a single blow. It must have been powerful magic. Somehow, they found a way to pass the enchantment along to other weaponry, creating an arsenal of weapons that could slice through a dragon's scales like a sword through flesh. Nothing was as potent at the original weapon, but it was enough to make the two sides nearly even."

The rider paused and took a deep sigh. "Still, the dragons and their allies from the order slowly gained more and more ground, although their losses were terrible. They had, for all intents and purposes, beaten back their enemy but at a loss of nearly eighty percent of their population. The rumors were that the entire species of dragonkind was lost in the war. The sightings of dragons became fewer and farther between, but the alliance still pressed forward, and they nearly won. But then, just as a final victory was imminent, everything just stopped."

Marcus was the first to ask, "What do you mean 'just stopped?' The war? What?"

The helmeted head shook. "I wish I knew. Yes, the war stopped, but so did the records, the reports…everything. It was like both sides just stopped fighting, and no one spoke of it again. In fact, no one even saw any dragons after that, except for a small remnant of the order."

It was now Tiffany's turn to ask, "What do you mean by a small remnant?"

"It would seem that as a measure to preserve the line of dragons in the event the great enemy was successful, the order took two of every kind of remaining species of dragon and fled the area. As soon as they were far enough from the fighting to feel safe, they split up, further fractioning the birthlines of dragons, but spreading them so far out over the globe that it would be nearly impossible to track them down and eliminate them. And there they remained in hiding; simply surviving through the centuries, never knowing the outcome of the war or the fate of the proud race of dragons."

Kinaari turned to Nymbus. "So that must make you over seven hundred years old?"

Nymbus shook his head. "It wouldst seem the case, but my birth did not occur until many centuries after the Great Fracturing."

Marcus turned up his nostrils. "The what?"

The rider answered, "The period in which the order scattered the dragons around the globe. It sounds more tragic with a dramatic name like that." Nymbus smiled at the comment.

Tiffany asked, "So did all of the other dragons in the war die? I mean how did they all just disappear?"

The figure shrugged. "I dunno. For all this time, we assumed they died in combat. But now that you three are here…it changes all of the theories. You clearly aren't 'order' dragons, so you either hatched in this modern era or you are survivors of the war. We want to try to contact members of the order across the world, but communication will be slow. We have sworn off electronic communication because our anonymity could be easily compromised. For seven hundred years we have been using more primitive, and much more subtle, forms of communication."

Nymbus spoke. "And now comes the time when thou must answereth questions for us. My companion has relayed to you all that we are able."

The rider nodded. "Right, like my first question: were you hatched in the modern era, or are you survivors of the war?"

"Ummm…" Kinaari began as she looked to the others for support, but they had none to offer. Kinaari continued, "I wish I could tell you."

The rider was taken aback. "The deal was we answer your questions and you answer ours."

"I know, I know," Kinaari said. "It's like this; if we could answer that, we would, but we don't know the answers."

Nymbus looked annoyed. "What form of double-talk is this? Thou doest not know how thou came to be?"

Kinaari hung her head. "No, it's because," she took a deep breath, "it's because we're not dragons."

Nymbus and his rider looked back and forth to each other, and Kinaari said, "I think you need to meet the real Wave dragon here."

She took several steps back, laid her claw over a spot on the base of her neck, and closed her eyes. Light began to emanate from beneath, and then blazing light burst all around her. All present had to shield their eyes from the radiance, and then the light slowly began to collapse in on itself and congealed into the shape of a human girl. The light faded, and the body of Kinaari stood in the place of the Wave dragon. Her eyes were closed, and she gripped the dragon scale tightly in one hand as it was still attached around her neck on the leather cord.

Procella opened her human eyes, slowly taking in the cavern, Marcus, and Tiffany then finally Nymbus and his rider. She inhaled sharply and said, "It would seem a great many things have happened since I was last conscious." Taking a few steps closer to Nymbus, she said, "You must be the Storm dragon that Petros has told us about."

He nodded. "I am Nymbus. But I admit I am quite befuddled as to who, or what, thou art."

She answered, "Cousin, I do not blame you for your confusion. It is a befuddling situation the children and I find ourselves in."

Nymbus's rider approached Procella, stopping only a few feet short of her. The covered face of the figure appeared to examine Procella from head to toe as it said, "You look…familiar."

Procella took a step back. "You, however, do not. I find it hard to believe that we have met."

The rider paused then answered, "Hard to believe, indeed. You mentioned a 'Petros'; sounds like a dragon name."

She nodded. "Another cousin, a Stone dragon. I believe you all have met in the skies on the way to a settlement called Billings."

The rider turned to Nymbus, who regarded the expressionless helmet curiously. The dragon said, "It wouldst seem thou hast quite the tale to relate to us."

Procella, with the help of Marcus and Tiffany, brought Nymbus and his armored companion up to speed on Petros, their arrival in Montana, Norm's failed spell, and their side of the encounter with the US Air Force. By the end of the account, Procella was beginning to shiver as the heat from the rocks finally cooled to the temperature of the air.

She smiled. "I am not accustomed to being cold."

Tiffany still fought her urges to be sarcastic and somewhat petty with Procella, for all she saw was Kinaari's body: the beautiful, charming, cheerleader type that she despised. Having gotten to know Kinaari in this wonderful and bizarre situation they were in, she knew the girl really wasn't the stereotype that Tiffany had labeled her, but she still had to fight back minor pangs of jealousy. She responded, "Procella, let me heat up the rocks again."

The Draconaut shook her head. "No, I will revert to my dragon form. I am guessing our absence is not going without notice back at the farm."

The rider sat up straight at the reference, but none present noticed its reaction. Marcus said, "Oh, man, that's right! Petros is gonna kill us; we said we weren't gonna get in any trouble."

Procella walked to a clear portion of the cave floor. "I would advise you to ask Kinaari to return to her human form when you try to explain what happened. I will be able to reason with Petros more than you human children will." She gripped the scale around her neck and closed her eyes. The light burst forth again, and when it abated, Procella's dragon form containing Kinaari's consciousness was occupying the space.

Kinaari looked around. "That is just so weird. I don't know if I'll ever get used to that."

They exchanged good-byes and approached the lake that led back to the outside world. Tiffany asked, "How do we get in touch with you if anything happens or changes? We can't just pretend you're not out here."

Nymbus looked to his companion and then back to the dragons. "We are monitoring thy situation now. If thou needest our help, we will be there."

The three stared at them for a beat. Marcus said, "That's not mysterious or anything," and they walked into the lake and disappeared below the dark surface.

Nymbus and the rider watched them submerge and then walked toward the back of the cavern before the rider sat on one of the broken stalagmites. It removed the helmet, exposing its blond hair and fair skin. "You know as well as I do that we've seen that girl before."

Nymbus nodded. "Aye, but thou needest to perfect thy abilities to hide thy reactions. Thou definitely aroused the suspicions of the Wave dragon in the girl's body."

"That's only because if that girl is who I think she is then I have a pretty good idea of whose teenage body now has the mind of a Stone dragon."

Nymbus looked surprised. "Wouldst thou care to elaborate?"

The human shook its head. "I need to be sure before I say anything. So in order to unravel this, you need to get me home so I can get a few hours of sleep before tomorrow. This is getting messier and messier. I'm not sure how we are going to gain control of this situation."

Chapter 24

Eleven o'clock ticked by on the old clock in the Hewes kitchen, and light from the overhead fixture spilled through the large window looking out onto the wraparound porch. Petros paced back and forth on the painted wood deck, the Chuck Taylor sneakers he wore making his footfalls nearly silent. Crammed onto the porch swing were Tonare, Calor, and Procella, and they watched their Stone dragon cousin pace deep in thought. Only twenty minutes earlier, their dragon bodies controlled by the consciousness of teenagers returned to the homestead and explained everything that had happened to Petros.

After the teens explained, Petros asked, as calmly as he could, to speak to his dragon cousins. The three quickly concluded that Petros was nearly exploding with anger, so they placed their claws over the bases of their necks with no argument. A trio of flashing lights later, the three dragons stood in their human bodies. Soon, Tonare was seated on the small porch swing between the two girls. They watched, wide-eyed, as Petros struggled to find words.

The dragon didn't know how to react. He knew he had taken a chance letting them go off on their own, and now events had been set in motion that he had no idea how to control. The military was aware of them, a secret society centuries old knew of their magically created predicament, and they all needed to return to their respective families before suspicions were aroused. He found himself rubbing his hand through his hair and was soon walking in circles as he thought.

Calor leaned over to Tonare. "Why do I feel like we are about to be lectured?"

Tonare shrugged. "I did nothing wrong. It was your body leading the way to the encounter with the military."

Calor glared at him. "I had nothing to do with that! It was not my idea to let the children go flying off into the night! If I recall the story correctly, you were the one whose breath weapon attacked the soldiers. You started the entire conflict."

Tonare shoved her with his shoulder. "If you had not been flying without any care as to where you were going then we would have never approached the military encampment!"

Procella chimed in, "How can you be laying the blame on the other? Our consciousnesses were not even present. We bear no responsibility for—"

Pertos finally shouted, "Enough!" He examined them, his eyes wide with frustration. "Enough! This is pointless! We are—" He looked down at his teenage body, his young hands extending toward the swing. He dropped his head and ran a hand through his hair. "We are the adults. We are responsible; we granted them permission to fly off on their own."

Procella regarded him. "Petros, are you suggesting we maintain consciousness the vast majority of the time? We cannot keep the children trapped in some magical netherworld. They—"

Petros interrupted again, "No, I am not suggesting that; that would be the definition of cruel." He sighed deeply and flopped down on one of the steps leading to the lawn below. "Are any of you parents?"

They looked back and forth at each other and shook their heads in the negative. He smiled, "Neither am I. I have never raised young; I have no idea what to do with them. But now that we are in this…predicament, I feel responsible for Jason and the others as well."

Procella stood up from the swing and sat down next to Petros, her body tucked snugly against his. The night air was getting colder, and Petros smiled as he commented. "I can feel the warmth of your body. I find it…comforting."

Procella smiled back. "Humans thrive on physical contact. Their sense of touch is much more heightened than ours."

Petros heard Tonare and Calor approaching them. He smiled and looked up at the two. "What are we to do, cousins? I am without any viable suggestions."

Calor crouched down. "We improvise. As in any battle with an unpredictable enemy, you modify your tactics as the situations arise."

Petros asked, "Who is our enemy?"

Calor rested her hand on his shoulder. Her touch provided additional comfort. "A most cunning foe: the situation itself. We cannot outthink it, we cannot subdue it, and we most certainly cannot overpower it. We can only react to it and hope for the best."

Procella nodded her agreement. "These children need to return to their parents. That is the most pressing matter right now. They are confused and frightened, and their parents will soon be missing them. They need familiar surroundings."

Petros countered, "But that truly means you all will have to live with their families as them."

Tonare said, "As you stated before, cousin, we are the adults now. We are responsible. We need to do what is necessary for their sakes."

Petros glanced up at his cousin. "A wise statement coming from one so young, Tonare."

He shrugged. "Perhaps it is time for me, too, to do some growing up."

Petros stood and gave Tonare a hearty clap on his broad shoulders. "Come, we must go to a mirror and discuss the plan with the children. We will most definitely need their input."

After the four Draconauts had a long conversation in the bathroom mirror with their reflections, a plan was put in place. It was just past midnight, and Petros stood on the front porch at the top of the steps leading down to the lawn. Procella, Tonare, and Calor stood on the lawn facing him.

"So we are agreed; the children will fly back to their hometowns, revert back to their human forms, then you will become oriented with the workings of their families so as not to arouse suspicions."

Calor folded her arms. "I am still not in favor of altering our speech patterns and using these ridiculous contractions. It sounds so clumsy."

Petros responded, "It is…iiit'sss how they speak."

She snorted, "See? Even you cannot do it!"

Procella interjected, "It will…I mean it'll require some adjustment, but it is necessary."

Tonare added, "Yes, we must... I mean we'mst practice." He smiled broadly at his accomplishment.

Petros wrinkled his nostrils. "'*We'mst*'?"

Tonare nodded. "Yes, a contraction of 'we must.' It is not that difficult."

The others nodded in agreement as Petros went on. "But, remember, once you are in their home villages, you must...pardon me, *you'mst* do as they instruct. Blending in is crucial; as the children have instructed us, their families know them best and will be suspicious of anything out of the ordinary."

Procella said, "We understand."

Petros walked down the stairs and laid his hands on their shoulders. With a worried expression, he said, "Good luck."

They each took several steps back and grasped the scales around their necks. Each shut his or her eyes tightly and concentrated, and three bursts of light came and went, replacing their human forms with three dragons. Petros said, "Fly well, young ones. Do not stop until you reach your villages. I have instructed my kin to follow your instructions, but please take advantage of their wisdom. It will serve to guide you until we all meet again in Billings."

Kinaari asked worriedly, "Do you really think we will be able to find Norm there?"

Petros answered, "We have to. It is our only hope to undoing this conundrum."

Kinaari and Tiffany exchanged nervous glances and then walked farther into the fields. They were airborne in moments and quickly disappeared into the night sky. Marcus was still with Petros. "Look, man, you and Hewes gonna be okay? It's great that you're all concerned about us and all that, but you're in it just as deep as we are. You got a job to go to and bullies and stuff. I'm just as worried about you."

Petros smiled gratefully. "You are a responsible young man, good Marcus. Your concern is much appreciated. I will...pardon me, I'll adjust just as the rest of you will."

Marcus was curious. "What's with the contractions?"

Petros said, "Dragons do not use them."

Marcus said, "You'd better start. Sounds really weird when you don't."

He nodded. "We are aware; we're trying."

Marcus turned to find space to take flight but turned back to Petros one last time. "Good luck."

Petros responded, "To you as well." He watched Marcus take to the sky and remained gazing at the stars for several minutes. He could feel his heart slow as he stared into the peaceful expanse of the night sky. He wondered if it was a domain he would ever be able to experience again, soaring on the majestic wings of an Earth Dragon. Heaving a heavy sigh, he walked back into the house and up the stairs to try to sleep.

***

In the midmorning sun, Petros stood next to Bob. He wore one of Jason's flannel shirts, Jason's helmet was pulled down over his head, and the backpack was slung over his shoulder. In his hand, he gripped the small hand mirror tightly, and, with Jason's face looking back at him, Petros stared at the Vespa.

"Well?" Jason asked. "Are you gonna get on? You have to actually be sitting on the thing to ride it."

Petros scowled. "Do not rush me, or perhaps you are prepared to fly us into your town?"

Jason's face dropped. "Touché."

"I am not accustomed to placing myself on self-propelled devices and hurtling to and fro to different destinations."

"It's a Vespa, Petros, not a sports car. You wait too much longer, and we're gonna be late for work."

Petros lamented, "Could we not have gotten up earlier to walk?"

"Walk? Petros, by the time you would get into town, you'd be too tired to actually do any work."

Petros looked into the mirror reproachfully. "That is because your lifestyle is one of laziness, and your body is not optimally honed."

Jason rolled his eyes. "Yeah, yeah, yeah, tell me something I haven't heard. Look, we gotta get going, so get on the scooter, okay? Just ride around the driveway a few times to get the hang of it before you head into town. It's pretty much a straight shot from here to the museum, so it should be a piece of cake."

"Very well," Petros said reluctantly. "But there is no promising what will happen to your soul if I die in this current state." He reached over his shoulder and slid the mirror into the backpack then slowly straddled the two-wheeled machine and gently pushed the kickstand back with his foot. He took a moment to feel the weight and balance of the vehicle then pushed the starter, and a little puff of smoke blew out of the back. He listened to the engine settle into a steady buzz before Petros said to himself, "As Jason said, twist the handle that provides locomotion slowly..." He began to twist the accelerator. "...and we are on our waaAAAYYYIEEE!"

Bob had a few new dents, and Jason's helmet had a few new scuffs before Petros was speeding down Highway 2 into Malta. Petros watched with fascination as the countryside scrolled by him; he was unused to traveling at ground level, and it offered him a new perspective, and appreciation, for the beauty of the planet. The change in pitch of a chorus of cicadas as they passed by, the sound of Bob's tires on the pavement, the smells of the old fields and cow pastures all served to show Petros a world of sensation and detail that a dragon never took time to appreciate. He couldn't help but smile and take it all in during the twenty-minute commute to the museum.

The building was just as Jason has described: a fairly nondescript bluish gray with a peaked roof. The sign in front caught his eye easily, and he knew just where to turn to pull in and park Bob. As Petros dismounted and approached the front door, he felt his heart beating quickly in his chest. After battling a Storm dragon, befriending a teenager, and searching an unfamiliar continent for more of his kind, he felt this was his first true test of integrating into the twenty-first century. He knew this is what he and Jason had wanted all along, but neither of them dreamed this would be the format of the situation. He took one last cleansing breath and pushed the door open.

Jason had spent so much time preparing Petros by showing him pictures of the building and helping him draw maps that the dragon found nothing he saw unfamiliar. From the fossils and displays to the banners hanging from the ceilings, even to the location of the janitor's closet, Petros found relief at the surprising familiarity. He even knew right where to go to drop off his backpack and begin work. First, though, he needed to get to the restroom so he could have one last briefing with Jason's reflection.

"Hiya, handsome," came a voice to his side.

He turned to see a lovely twenty-year-old woman in a red flannel shirt behind a counter. He thought to himself, *This must be Julia* as he answered, "Good morning. A very pleasant day, do you…don't you think?" He tried not to wince; even he knew that sounded awkward.

She smiled. "Why, yes, I do, Mister Early-Morning Pleasantries. I see we had plenty of Mountain Dew for breakfast."

He didn't know what that meant. "It would very well seem so, yes," he improvised.

She looked askance as him. "You sleep okay, Jace? You seem distant."

He nodded. "My sleep was refreshing, yes. I am…I'mmm slightly distracted, that is all."

She asked, "Your dad's coming back into town today, right?" Petros nodded in acknowledgement as she went on. "He'll probably stop by here and see you before he heads home. That'll be nice."

A fearful realization washed over Petros; if this was the case, he had no idea what Jason's father looked like. A son not recognizing his father would be the epitome of suspicion. His heart began to pound in his chest. "If you will excuse me, Julia, I must use the room of resting." He hurried to the bathroom, quickly entered, and locked the door behind him. He saw the mirror mounted on the wall and began to express his concerns to Jason.

"Did you really call it the 'room of resting'?" Jason whispered back through the mirror.

Petros hissed, "Is that really your primary concern right now?"

"Relax, will ya? You're gonna blow it before the day even gets started. There is a picture of me and my dad on my phone, so it's no big deal. But you need to bring it down a few dozen notches if you're gonna get by today, all right? You can do this."

Petros inhaled deeply. "Yes, I must relax."

Jason watched as Petros calmed himself. "Good, that's good. Now get back out there, champ, and mop me some floors."

Petros looked at Jason and blinked. "You are correct, you know. Julia is quite lovely; perhaps I should take this opportunity to confess my...I mean your undying love for her."

Jason's face went white. "You wouldn't dare."

Petros smiled. "I will if you refer to me as 'champ' again." He turned and exited the bathroom, prepared to begin his janitorial duties.

Thanks to Jason's extensive instructions, Petros easily found the janitor's closet, readied the mop and bucket, and began to his duties around the museum. He would stop occasionally to look around and take in the details of the museum, absorbing the information in the exhibits and actually enjoying the world from a human point of view. There was something about his cleaning duties that felt fulfilling, and despite fatigue caused by his exertions, Petros experienced an odd sense of satisfaction and accomplishment when he completed one task and was able to go on to another. He found himself stopping in the bathroom between jobs and checking in with Jason, updating him on his progress, and inquiring if he was completing the tasks appropriately. Jason acknowledged that he was but also gave Petros a scolding; the amount of trips he was making to the bathroom was going to arouse suspicion. Petros hastily exited but five minutes later was approached by Julia.

"You feeling okay, Jace?"

Petros answered, "Yes, all is well. Why do you...d'you ask?"

"'Cause you keep going in the bathroom. You have a stomach bug or something?"

He looked genuinely confused. "I have an insect in my stomach?"

Julia responded, equally befuddled, "What? No, I mean are you throwing up or, you know, the other thing?"

"I'm unaware of the other thing."

Julia rolled her eyes. "Look, Susan is noticing all of the bathroom breaks, and I don't want you to get in trouble. If you're sick or something—"

Julia was interrupted by Susan Elwick's voice shouting from the office, "Jason! I need to speak with you...now!"

Julia gave Petros a resigned look. "You had better go see her—and good luck."

Petros swallowed hard and walked into Susan's office. It was a small, windowless room with an old metal desk pushed up against the far wall. Papers were scattered across her desk in no particular order, and a coffee-stained mug with the logo of the Dinosaur Trail sat on the corner. She barely lifted her head from her paperwork as he entered. "Have a seat," she said and pointed to the metal folding chair on the other side of the desk. Petros sat cautiously.

"What's with all of the trips to the bathroom?" she asked.

"I, uh, am feeling ill." He thought quickly. "You know, the other thing."

She looked over her glasses at him then back to her paperwork. "Is your father back in town yet?"

He shook his head. "I believe his return is imminent—definitely today."

"Imminent?" she asked. "Sounds ominous. Anyway, you need to spend less time in the can and more time getting ready for the group."

Petros regarded her curiously. "Group?"

She smiled. "Yeah, we have a birthday party coming in today. You need to spend the rest of your day after lunch in the outfit. Oh..." Her smile turned slightly sinister. "...did I forget to tell you? Hmm, must've slipped my mind. Get to work and finish the cleaning then start setting up for the party."

Petros slowly walked out of the office, his eyes wide at the assignment. Jason had not prepared him for this. If he went into the bathroom to discuss it with Jason, Susan would become furious, so he had no clue what to do. He couldn't help but wonder what this ominous "outfit" was.

Julia saw the look on his face and rushed up to him. "What? What happened?" Petros explained, and a look of compassion came over Julia's face. "Oh, right," she said. "Yeah, I know how you hate wearing that thing, but it helps keep us in business. Look, take a quick break and go for a walk, and I'll start getting some of the party stuff out. But come back quick, okay? Five minutes."

Petros nodded in agreement and purposely strolled outside, but as soon as the door shut behind him, he sprinted straight to Bob and hopped on the seat. Quickly adjusting the rearview mirror until he could see his face, he shouted, "Jason!"

Jason looked back at him through the small circle of glass. "What? What is it, and why are we talking through Bob's mirror?" Petros inhaled deeply and explained the situation in one long, panicked breath. Jason listened intently, his eyes widening to match the look on Petros's face. When he was done, all Jason could say was, "Oooohh, we are so messed up."

Petros gritted his teeth. "That does not help, Little Knight."

"Doesn't."

Petros scowled. "What?"

"Doesn't…that doesn't help. Make sure you use contractions."

"Contractions are the least of my concern at this present moment!"

Jason shook his head. "Right, right, sorry. Okay, listen carefully; there's no time to really explain this well, so here are the basics. Julia is usually willing to help if you tell her you're drawing a blank on games with the kids in the group, so use that. With a little bit of luck, we'll get through this, and I won't get fired."

Humiliation. Petros could not process how a majestic Stone dragon such as himself could be subject to his current circumstances. Fifteen children between the ages of six and eight were marching around a table decorated with dinosaur favors, paper plates, napkins, plastic utensils, and juice boxes. Julia was leading them in their march as they all sang the museum's original song, "The T-Rex Trot," at the top of their lungs. His face peered through the mouth of a large, foam latex Tyrannosaurus Rex costume, which encapsulated his entire body. It was bright orange with neon green stripes going from the back of the head to the tip of the tail, and a large polka-dotted bowtie and white collar circled around the base of the neck. Each time a child passed him in their march around the table, they gave the costume's stomach three rubs, as the lyrics of the song instructed them to do. All Petros did was stare blankly ahead and attempted to summon some source of inner peace that would prevent him from running screaming from the building.

Unfortunately, each time Julia passed him as the group marched around the table, she noticed his blank and stoic expression and tried to engage him a few words at a time.

"What's the matter…" The circle went around the table. "…with you? You…" The circle went around the table. "…look like you're…" The circle went around the table. "…being tortured." The circle went around the table. "Look happy!"

On that last pass by, Julia grabbed his hand and pulled him forcefully into the circular march with the children. Petros nearly tripped at the sudden tug; the huge foam dinosaur feet that covered his own were the equivalent of walking with pillows tied around his sneakers. But he recovered his balance and plodded around the table with the gleeful children as the most ungenuine of smiles crept up the corners of his mouth and contorted his face into a grimace.

At that moment, the door of the museum opened, and George Jaworski entered. He knew that Jason was scheduled to be back at the museum today and also knew that Jason was not currently the consciousness in charge of Jason's body. George felt the need to make a stop by on his lunch break to see how Petros was faring in Jason's janitorial duties. His jaw went slack at the sight of Petros in the dinosaur costume marching with a group of children around the table. George saw Petros's head turn toward him, a look of despair across the Draconaut's face. George could see him mouth "help me" as Julia gave him a sharp tug and whipped his head away from George.

"Oh, dear Lord" was all George could manage to say at the sight. But George started as a hand slapped down on his shoulder, and he turned to see Timothy Hewes standing behind him, a big smile on his face as he watched the birthday party festivities. George was so focused on the events unfolding in front of him that he didn't notice Mr. Hewes come through the door behind him.

"So," Mr. Hewes began, "how's our Jason the dinosaur doing today, eh, George?"

George's eyes went wide with panic as he slowly lifted a hand and gave Mr. Hewes a less-than-enthusiastic thumbs up. Five seconds before, George questioned how this situation could get any worse. Now, he had an answer. He turned away from Mr. Hewes and whispered to himself, "Oh, dear Lord."

Chapter 25

George could feel Mr. Hewes's hand resting on his shoulder as they both watched a dinosaur-suited Jason being pulled along by Julia. Thoughts raced in and out of George's mind as he tried to prepare some sort of excuse or defense should Petros blow his cover. But he half-resigned himself to the idea that they were most likely doomed; there was no conceivable way Petros was going to be able to bluff his way through a children's birthday party.

Mr. Hewes said, "You have to hand it to our boy, eh, George? How many guys your age would willingly dress up like that just to entertain a group of children? As ridiculous as it looks, it makes me proud."

George swallowed hard. "It certainly stirs something in your gut, that's for sure."

Petros suffered through the remainder of the song, and then the children took their seats around the table. Julia stood next to Petros as she said, "Okay, kiddos, you know what we do after 'The T-Rex Trot,' don't you?"

As if it were rehearsed, they all shouted, "CAAAKE!"

"That's right!" Julia answered. "Hey, T-Rex Toby, isn't it about time we had some cake?" She turned to Petros for an answer. When he didn't respond, she said louder, "Right, T-Rex Toby?" On "Toby," she elbowed him sharply in the ribs.

Petros shouted at the sudden pain, "Zounds, female!"

The children burst in to laughter as Julia glared at him. "Shouldn't you go get the cake?" She tried to sound animated through her gritted teeth.

Petros finally took his cue. "Ah, yes. I shall…I will go get this…uh, *the* cake. Yes."

Petros plodded to the back room and squeezed through the door, where he found the brightly colored cake on a small, wheeled cart. He grasped the handle and awkwardly backed through the door, pulling the cart into the party area. George watched, his hand over his mouth trying to hide his terror, as the Draconaut clumsily maneuvered around the museum in the bright orange costume, occasionally sweeping objects off benches and tables with his foam tail as he finally got the cake back to the party table. The children applauded as the confectionary arrived. Julia lit the candles and then turned to Petros. "Okay, T-Rex Toby. Why don't you lead us in 'Happy Birthday'?"

Petros looked confused as he turned to Julia. "Umm, what?"

She tried not to look furious. "The 'Happy Birthday' song, Toby. Can you start it, please?" She growled the "please." Petros knew it was a demand, not a request.

He looked across the room to George, who tried his best to mouth the first syllable of the word "happy." Petros saw the clue, inhaled, and said, "Haaa..." and, to his surprise, all the children chimed in with the familiar song. A surprised grin came over the Draconaut's face, pleased that he actually was able to direct the song. Petros's chest swelled with pride.

During the remaining twenty minutes of the party, Petros underwent an unexpected transformation. His face became more animated. His look of fear turned to one of joy. The children swarmed around him, and he welcomed them, placing his foam latex-covered arms around them as he actually held conversations with the little ones. They giggled at his more formal, dragon way of talking, and he became slightly self-deprecating as he joked with them as to why he "talked so funny."

As the party dispersed, the small attendees ran up to him for good-bye hugs, and he willingly returned the affectionate gestures. His face beamed with each child's embrace, and, as they left, he missed their presence. Julia approached him. "Well, Jace, I was getting ready to give you what for, but you pulled it together at the end. The kids really enjoyed T-Rex Toby today. What was with you earlier?"

Petros searched for the words. "It has been some time since I was required to wear this costume. I was unaccustomed to it. I simply needed to, um, get used to it."

Julia shook her head. "I don't know; you seem really off today. Definitely not your usual self. Look, your dad and George are here, so go get outta that thing and give your dad a hug."

Definitely not your usual self. The words circulated through Petros's mind, and he pulled the giant orange T-Rex head off of his own and went into the back room. George quickly followed behind him and slammed the door shut.

"What was that?" George exclaimed.

"I am unsure of the nature of your question, Squire George," he responded, and he began to remove the bright orange body.

"Your first day at work in Jason's body, and you decide to do a birthday party? Seriously, Petros, are you trying to expose yourself on day one?"

Petros replied, "I was given no alternative, George! The Susan woman directed me to do so, and from what Jason has instructed me, I am obliged to follow her directions at the risk of putting Jason's livelihood in jeopardy."

George threw his hands up and spun around in frustration. "I know, I know! We just could've blown the whole thing right there, you know?"

Petros shrugged. "I thought I was doing remarkably well at the end of the festivities. The children seemed quite taken with me."

George was taken aback. "What?"

"They seemed to enjoy my interpretation of the character, and…I enjoyed interacting with them. It was quite heartwarming."

"Well, before you start signing up for babysitting lessons at the high school, can we stay on task and get planning this latest trip to Billings? I'm supposed to talk with Procella, Tonare, and Calor tonight, so I can get their status and hopefully get a date on the calendar. Hurry up and finish getting that thing off then come on out and say hi to Jason's dad. And remember to call him 'Dad,' not 'Father' or anything formal like that. Okay?"

"Very well."

George shook his head. "No! *Okay?*

Petros thought for a moment. "Ah, yes, ahem…okay."

George shook his head and squeezed the bridge of his nose as he left the back room.

Petros tentatively emerged from the back room with Jason's backpack slung over his shoulder. He knew that, at the conclusion of the party, his shift was over, and he slowly walked over to the stranger that was Jason's dad. This was the person that Jason was supposed to be the most familiar with, so Petros knew he had to put on a convincing performance. He saw the kind-faced man smiling widely at him as he approached and felt some of the tension leave his body. He drew a breath to speak, but Mr. Hewes simply embraced him and held him in a hug for several moments. Petros was unsure what to do and could see George over Timothy Hewes's shoulder. The expression on George's face indicated he was at the same loss as Petros.

Timothy held Petros at arm's length. "I see they made you wear the outfit again."

Petros smirked. "Yes, it was rather unexpected."

Mr. Hewes clapped him on the shoulder. "You're quite the trooper."

Petros did not know how to respond. "Uh, thank you?" He saw George nodding in agreement. "Yes, thank you, Fath…Dad."

He said, "I've got to meet with Susan briefly, and then we need to be in on a conference call, but how about I call in some Chinese tonight, and we watch a movie?" Petros looked to George, whose face lit up. Mr. Hewes saw George. "Hey, Georgie, why don't you come too? Call your parents, and you can stay the night if you want."

George replied, "That'll be great, Mr. Hewes. I'll ask them."

Mr. Hewes nodded at them both with a smile and walked off toward the office. Petros muttered from the corner of his mouth, "You humans and your infernal colloquialisms are going to be my undoing. Why am I a 'trooper,' and what are these Chinese things he is calling in?"

George smiled. "I'll explain later. I have to get back to work, but I'll see you later at your place…I mean Jason's place. This is all so confusing."

Petros watched George leave the museum and inhaled deeply, trying to calm his nerves, before getting ready to leave for the day.

Much to Petros's relief, the rest of the day went without any further incidents, and he was able to get back to the Hewes homestead before Mr. Hewes or George arrived. He spent quite some time debriefing the day in the mirror with Jason, who congratulated him on surviving his first day at work. George arrived at the house before Jason's dad and joined Petros in the bathroom so he could spend some time catching up with his friend. George and Jason both expressed relief that they were finally able to speak with each other face to face, and Jason and Petros took the time to catch George up on the encounter with the military and the revelations from the Storm dragon, Nymbus, and his mysterious companion. George shook his head and responded, "Just when you thought this couldn't get any more bizarre."

Their conversation came to a rapid close when Mr. Hewes returned home with Chinese food under one arm and his aged, leather satchel under the other. Within ten minutes, dinner was on the table, and Petros was regarding his chicken with snow peas suspiciously while trying to deduce what chopsticks were for. George saw Petros about to impale the chicken with a chopstick, when he knew he needed to cover.

"Hey, Jace, could you grab me a fork? Guess I'm not in the mood for chopsticks today."

Petros replied, "Ah, yes. I will do that for you. That is a good idea." He got up and walked over to the kitchen drawers, where, after opening two in error, he finally found the correct drawer containing the eating utensils. Successfully taking George's cue, Petros returned to the table with the forks and gave a thankful nod as he sat to start his dinner.

The conversation around the table was light, as Mr. Hewes talked about his most recent trip, and Petros tried as best he could to listen intently and follow along. George simply gave the obligatory yesses and nos as one would expect of a typical teenager as he shoveled his lo mein into his mouth. Jason's dad looked up. "Something's different about you, Jace. You seem more focused and attentive. Are you finally taking my advice and going to bed at a reasonable hour?"

Petros paused midchew and searched for an answer. "Yes. I have…I've finally taken your advice, Dad, and made the ende…effort to get more sleep on a nightly basis."

Timothy sat up. "You see? Right there, I would have expected a 'guess so' or a noncommittal nod, but that was a thought-out answer. I even thought you were going to say 'endeavor' for a moment."

Petros and George exchanged oblique glances as George said, "Uh, yeah, Jace. It's like you're just so used to being on your own that you need to say more than usual, kinda like you miss talking to people." George was subtly nodding as he spoke, hoping Petros would pick up on the cue.

Petros answered, "Well, yes, there is truth in that. Having conversation is plea…nice, and I simply have the desire to talk. Your absence is felt, and I am simply compensating for it."

George crinkled his nose at the last answer as Mr. Hewes said, "I like this side of you. Hopefully you'll show it off more."

The rest of dinner went by uneventfully, and Petros was learning to relax as he spoke to Jason's dad. George gave him a crash course on washing the dishes, and, after the chore was complete, the two found themselves sitting on the couch in front of the television as George flipped through the plethora of channels.

"What do we do now?" Petros asked.

George shrugged as he channel-surfed. "We hang out."

"Excuse me?"

George smiled. "We relax, enjoy the evening, you know, hang out."

Petros was confused. "But…but there is so much to do, to plan. How can you let all of this unused time go to waste?"

George shrugged again. "I'm a teenager; it's my job."

Petros stood up. "I shall not sit idly by! We have tasks to do, and I shall be about them, though you are content to behave like a sluggard!"

George kept his gaze on the flat panel. "Great. What are you going to work on first?"

Petros drew his breath in sharply, about to reply with an equally sharp retort, but then paused and thought. His expression softened until he flopped back down on the couch and answered, "I have no idea."

"Then have no idea here on the couch and hang out with me." George became more attentive to the television screen as he said, "Hey, check this out." He adjusted the volume as the news story came on.

"...and, once again, AlansCo has entered the competitive field of military contracting as they announce a major technological breakthrough. Here is Tate Reigles, their spokesperson." The story cut to a handsome blond man behind a podium as the sound bite picked up in midsentence.

"...and we are pleased that our scientists and researchers have taken a major step forward that will change the way our brave men and women protect our country from the skies. Large aircraft and gunships are expensive and easy targets. Unmanned drones are less than effective in combat situations. The United States needs a new technology, one that maintains the superiority of manned flight yet is streamlined enough to present minimized risk. At AlansCo, we believe we have accomplished just this very thing. For years, our team has been working tirelessly to find and harness the power of the graviton, the elusive particle responsible for carrying the force of gravity. And now, not only have we done so, but we have fully realized the power of what we call graviton-based technology, or GBT. GBT has allowed us to create small, manned vehicles capable of carrying significant ordinance with both ground- and air-based applications. These vehicles have minimal radar signatures and are nearly impossible to target with current radar based technologies, and they are ready to go into mass production for use by all four branches of the military.

"So please turn your attention to the display behind me as I introduce you to the AlansCo AX-Seventeen Pegasus, the AX-Twenty-Nine Griffon, and the AX-Forty-One Hippogriff—"

"Boooooring!" George blurted out as he changed the channel again. "Sorry, I thought it was going to be something cool."

Petros shook his head. "It is of no concern to me. I did not know of what the flaxen-haired man was speaking, so you may continue."

"Eh, there's nothing to watch anyway. Maybe we should stream a movie?"

Petros's face lit up. "Oh, yes, that would be an outstanding idea. I am highly in favor of streaming movies."

"Great," George replied. "Wait, where is Jason's laptop?"

Petros thought. "I believe it is still in the barn."

"Okay, hang on. I'll go get it."

As George was leaving the room, Timothy made his way in and sat down on the sofa next to Jason. Petros showed the man a pleasant smile as he sat down.

"How was it while I was gone, son?"

Petros searched for an answer. "Uneventful, Dad. I managed on my own."

He nodded. "You always do. Look, I'm sorry the job takes me away so much, you know—"

Petros interrupted, "Dad, I am...I'm aware of the demands of your voca...your job. I know my patience is often in short supply, but I very much appreciate the efforts you make to support our family."

Timothy looked surprised. "That...that is a very mature point of view, Jason. I'm not sure I've ever heard you put it that way."

Petros paused. "I have had a change of mind, so to speak."

Timothy admired his son for a few moments. "Well, don't grow up too fast on me, okay?"

Petros smiled and nodded. "I will do my best."

At that moment, they heard George call from the kitchen, "Hey, Jace, c'mere!"

Petros said, "By your leave" and stood up to go to the kitchen. George had a distressed look on his face as Petros entered. "What is troubling you?"

George said, "There's a dragon in your barn."

Petros's face dropped. "That is not amusing."

"It's not meant to be a joke. There's a dragon in your barn. A familiar dragon." And without further discussion, they hurried out of the kitchen door.

In the living room, Timothy began flipping channels on the television and went back to the news channel. The blond man was still on and was now standing next to a black motorcycle of no identifiable model. Standing behind him was a rider, dressed completely in black with its face hidden by a black motorcycle helmet. The blond man rested his hand on the motorcycle. "So, yes, this is the AX-Seventeen Pegasus, just like you saw on the video. Our operator here will now give you a live demonstration of the GBT at work and its flight capabilities."

The sun was on its way toward the western horizon as Petros and George opened one of the barn doors and squeezed inside. Seated on the floor with an indignant look on her face was Tiffany in the body of Calor, the Heat dragon.

Petros was incredulous. "What are you still doing here? The understanding was that you were to return to your family of origin so as not to arouse suspicion."

Tiffany snorted, "Yeah, well, I don't have a family of origin."

Petros was confused and looked to George for understanding. George took a couple of steps toward her. "Tiff, look, I don't know what you've been through and all, but—"

She spat back, "That's right, Mr. DQ, you don't know! So don't get all compassionate on me and try to appeal to my conscience or whatever. You have parents; you have a house and a family. I make the choices I make for my sanity, which I really question nowadays, so just back off!"

Petros walked up to Tiffany and sat on an old milking stool. "Please explain. I truly do not understand."

Tiffany took a deep breath. "Not all human parents are as kind and loving as Jason's or George's, okay? And when they aren't kind or loving, sometimes the government comes in and takes the kids away and gives them to other adults that are supposed to be kind and loving. But that doesn't always work out so hot either. So I'm taking control now. I'm a dragon; I can do what I want, including not going back to the hole they call an apartment in Jordan. I've got the power; I can take care of myself now."

Petros tried to respond, "Tiffany, I—"

"No! Don't use your ancient dragon wisdom on me, Petros. I'm beyond wisdom now. I've made up my mind. If you want to go all dragon on me and fight me for it, fine. But I swear I'll turn this place to ash before you make me go back into the system."

Petros's face turned serious at her defiance. He was not one accustomed to being threatened, so he stepped into the remaining clear half of the barn and grasped the scale hanging around his neck. The transformative light burst forth, and Jason stood in Petros's place. The barn had become a very cramped place with two dragons now occupying its space. George tried very hard to find a corner where he could stay out of the way.

Tiffany glared at Jason. "So this is how it's going to go down?"

Jason was completely confused. "How what's going to go down? Why is Tiffany still here? What's going on?"

George stepped between them. "Petros wants you to use his body to force Tiffany to go back home against her will." George went on to explain Tiffany's presence and her reluctance to leave. Tiffany never stopped scowling at Jason the entire time.

Jason looked incredulous. "Wait, Petros wants us to fight it out? That's not like him."

George countered, "She, umm, kinda challenged him."

Jason responded, "She what?"

Tiffany sneered, "I told him I would turn this place to ash before you made me go back."

Jason shot a look at her. "Really? You threatened to destroy my home? This is all me and my dad have left, and you know that. Why would you say that?"

After an uncomfortable silence, her expression softened. "Sorry, I didn't mean it. If you won't let me stay here, fine. I'll find my way on my own. But I'm not going back to Jordan, and I'm not turning human until you all get that."

"Whoa, wait," Jason began. "Tiff, that's not fair to Calor. She doesn't—"

"I already discussed it with her," Tiffany interrupted.

"Huh?"

"The mirror thing works when we're in dragon form too. I found a pond, and we discussed all of this in our reflection in the water. She understands my situation and agreed to let me stay this way until everyone is in agreement. So I'm prepared to even set off on my own if needed, but, as of right now, I'm independent."

Jason thought for several moments and looked to George for answers, but he only held up his hands in surrender. He finally said, "You know what? We hid Petros in here, so we can do the same for you, but you need to agree to be as discreet and careful as Petros was."

She nodded. "I can do that."

"Great, this will actually make things a little easier as we plan to go back to Billings."

"How are you going to explain this to Petros?"

Jason thought for a moment. "Not sure, but I'll figure it out. I'll take care of it, though."

As the two Draconauts continued to speak for some time, a figure clad in black motorcycle gear and helmet listened intently at the barn door. Silently, it padded around the back of the barn to a flat black motorcycle of no particular make or model. The figure mounted the cycle, and, with a kick to the ground, the machine hovered above the earth several inches. The front and rear tires each split in half along the circumference and then splayed outward until the halves were parallel with the earth. Then, without a sound, the machine and its rider sailed into the night sky.

Chapter 26

The next morning, George sat on the porch swing of the Hewes home as Mr. Hewes and Petros finished getting ready for their trip into town. Petros had another shift to work at the museum, and Mr. Hewes needed to finish some paperwork there and run some errands around town. Feeling he had enough to occupy himself during Jason's six-hour shift, Mr. Hewes offered Petros a ride into town and then back home again. Seeing the opportunity to avoid riding Bob to and fro for a second day, Petros readily accepted.

"You sure you're okay waiting for your parents out here, George?" Mr. Hewes asked. "You're more than welcome to wait inside."

"Nah," George answered. "They'll be here any minute. I'm good."

"I could've dropped you off at your house."

"They've got something to do over in Dodson, so they'll just pick me up on the way. I have the day off, so it's not like I have anything to do."

Mr. Hewes shrugged. "Suit yourself. But you know where the spare key is if you change your mind." He began to head down the porch and then snapped his fingers. "Forgot to pack my laptop. Be right back."

The two boys watched him go back in the house, and then Petros whispered, "I am still very uncomfortable with this plan. Letting Tiffany stay in the barn will be a monumental error. I do not understand why she cannot return to her place of origin."

George quickly checked to see if Mr. Hewes was still occupied before he answered, "We discussed this last night, Petros. You don't understand her situation. Jason and I will handle it. That's why I'm staying here for a while to talk with her, okay? Just...trust us. We got it."

"Very well, but—" Petros saw Jason's dad approaching the door again and said, "I'll call you later on the cell phone. Does this sound like a plan?"

George cringed inside. "Yeah, it sounds like a plan. You guys have a good day."

Mr. Hewes gave George a casual wave as they hurried down the stairs, took their places in the old pickup, and sped away with a friendly honk.

George watched them drive off before he made his way to the barn. He checked for any random onlookers one more time and then opened the doors and entered. Tiffany was still in her dragon form and had fallen asleep curled up on the hay-covered wooden floor. One of her eyes popped opened. "Is everyone gone?"

He nodded. "Yep, they all left a few minutes ago."

"Good," she commented as she stood up and stretched her massive body. She tried to unfold and flex her wings, but they crashed into the rafters, sending layers of dust down on George. "Oops, sorry," she apologized.

George looked annoyed as he rubbed the dust out of his hair and brushed it off of his shoulders. "First day with the new wings, huh?"

She smiled sheepishly and sat down on her haunches. "Sorry about last night. I should have said something to you guys."

"Tiff, look, I know we barely know each other, but if there is something we can do to help—"

She shook her head. "Hey, I appreciate it and all, but there are just some things you gotta figure out on your own. I've been thinking of running away for a few months now; I've even looked into becoming an emancipated minor."

"Is it that bad? Your foster parents, I mean."

She sighed before she answered, stirring up more dust with her much-greater lung capacity. "No...not really. I can tell they care, but they get so caught up in museum stuff. It was their life before I came along. I guess they can't have kids, so they went through the system and took all the foster parent classes, but they're more focused on their jobs. And Jordan is so small...I just can't take it anymore."

George paused before he asked his next question. "What about your real parents?"

She looked at him askance. "Mmm, still too sensitive of a topic, Georgie."

He held up his hands. "No, no, don't worry; you don't need to answer."

"Not that I don't appreciate the effort." She smiled.

George nodded. "Where are you really from then?"

"Bozeman," she answered. "You know, the 'big city.'" She attempted to make air quotations with her dragon claws.

"Ah, now I can see why Jordan would drive you crazy."

She held her forelegs out. "But now look at me. I can fly, I can breathe heat that will melt metal in seconds, my skin is bulletproof; this girl can survive on her own now. I don't need help; heck, I can just go right off of the map. No one's gonna look for me for any length of time; it's *my* life now."

"Yeah, but you have to share your life with someone else. What is the 'other you' going to say to all this?"

She glared at him. "You really don't believe me that I talked this over with Calor."

George shrugged. "Tiff, come on; you weren't exactly truthful about the whole going-home-but-hiding-in-the-barn thing."

She paused, her face expressionless. She placed her claw over the base of her neck, and her body was engulfed in light. The brightness faded, and the slight, darkly clad body of Tiffany stood in the dragon's place. Calor looked around the barn, and a look of slight disgust came over her. "Ah, yes, the barn. How charming." She looked to George, "I see our covert strategy was exposed. How long did it take for you to figure it out?"

"We found Tiffany here last night."

She examined her body. "Does this girl always wear black?"

George smiled. "Seems so; I guess it's her way."

"Hmph," Calor huffed. "I will not pretend to understand the nuances of human parentage, but I find it unacceptable that the girl's parents relinquished their given duties to raising her."

George looked surprised. "She told you what happened?" Calor only nodded as George continued, "Well? What was it?"

This time, Calor shook her head. "I have taken an oath of secrecy. I do not betray oaths."

He folded his arms in frustration. "Figures."

She rubbed her hand over her stomach. "This body hungers. Does she never feed it?"

"I don't know. I guess that's why she is in such good shape...I mean why she's so slim." He blushed at his slip of the tongue.

"I must eat before I collapse. How long have I been away?"

"Not sure, probably a few days. Are you aware of the passage of time when you're, you know, someone else?" They began walking back toward the house.

Calor answered, "Not at all. Last I recall I was standing on Jason's porch. There was a flash of light, and then I was discussing plans with Tiffany in our reflection in the pond. There was then another flash of light, and I am here now."

George commented, "Wow, freaky."

Calor scowled. "I have no idea what that means."

The two walked up the porch steps as George knelt down to one of the floorboards. He wiggled it and it lifted up from the rest of the planks. He reached in and found the spare key to the kitchen, and, within moments, they were inside and George was pouring cereal and milk for Calor.

She looked around the kitchen. "Is there any of the bubbling yellow drink that Jason has?"

"Mountain Dew? You sure you should have some after last time?"

"I will consume it in moderation. Please, Squire George, the situation I am in is very stressful, and anything enjoyable would be a welcome diversion."

George saw the look in her eyes, and his heart melted. Tiffany had an attractiveness all her own. Kinaari was the glamorous type, but it wasn't until then that George saw a dark, mysterious beauty in Tiffany that caught his eye. He felt his throat tighten and tried hard not to let his voice crack. "Yeah, there's some in the fridge. I'll get it."

Calor was soon eating Cheerios and drinking Mountain Dew, and George was on Jason's laptop, surfing the Internet. He stole sideways glances at Calor, trying to not make it obvious he was watching her. But she was engrossed in her meal and had no idea George was admiring her. He tried to break the silence. "So, that wing symbol thing on the scary motorcycle dude's uniform…you sure you don't recognize it?" She shook her head in the negative, her cheeks full of food. He went on, "Yeah, I'm not coming up with anything in the image searches. Maybe I'm not describing it right. Lemme try something."

Using the touch pad and an art program, George rudimentarily sketched out the symbol and then let the search engine try to match it, but it yielded no results. George's shoulders slumped in frustration. Calor saw George's body language and slid her chair over to his until they were shoulder to shoulder. George felt his cheeks flushing. She looked at the symbol he drew and said, "The symbol was surrounded by a circle with a single line bisecting it. You did not include that detail in your sketch."

"Oh, I forgot that part," he replied as he went to alter the picture.

She commented as she continued eating, "Your cheeks appear red and have an elevated temperature, consistent with the blushing response. Are you embarrassed about something?"

He cleared his throat as he re-entered the search strings. "No, umm, you're just a little, you know, close."

"Ah, my proximity is undesired. I will return to—"

George interrupted, "No! I mean, ahem, no. It's fine. I'm just not, you know, used to it."

"Odd. Bodily contact is an important method of conveying emotion to humans, is it not?"

George craned his neck to relieve his tension. "You could say that, yes."

Calor took another spoonful and spoke with her mouth full. "You humans are very perplexing."

George was relieved when the computer chimed, glad for the excuse to change the subject. He said, "Whoa, I found something."

Calor leaned even closer to George as she read the screen. "What did you find?"

George's voice cracked slightly. "Yeah, it seems like this symbol is pretty old, like thirteenth or fourteenth century old. I'm looking for a name but don't see one. Looks like the first mention is around the time of the crusades. The knights and their armies were trying to retake the Holy Land—"

Calor interrupted, "Holy Land?"

George explained, "Right, modern-day Israel, other side of the world, in the Middle East. Anyway, two knights get holed up in a city called Lod and fortified themselves in a collapsed temple, but then they stumble across a tomb."

"Tomb? Who was enshrined there?"

George looked more carefully then shook his head. "It doesn't say. Whoever was in it was dead for almost a millennium, but they do find some sort of weapon. No other details than it was tipped with a cross. So it says they examine the weapon, but…whoa."

"What is it?"

"Wow, this is getting weird. It says a figure seemed to approach them out of nowhere, like it was waiting for them inside the tomb. The figure was wearing a long cloak with a hood drawn over its head, completely obscuring its face. It offered them use of the weapon, which would grant them immeasurable power to rid the world of a great evil. All they had to do was abandon their current allegiances and follow him…or her or whatever this thing was."

"What happened from there?"

"Hmm," George scanned the website. "Looks like one of the knights accepted the hooded guy's offer, but the other one sensed evil coming from Hoodie and pledged to fight against whatever plans they put into place."

Calor sat back in her chair. "Does it say what this 'great evil' is that the weapon is supposed to destroy?"

George began to scroll through the screen faster. "Umm, I don't see…wait, here we go. Oh." He sat up and looked at Calor. "Dragons. The weapon was supposed to be the bane of dragons."

Dread came over Calor's face as she stood up. Unconsciously, she placed her hand over the scale hanging around her neck. "I have no memory of this. There is a...a shadow, a fog...in the back of my mind."

George was completely fascinated and kept scanning the document. "Ah, I get it now. They formed a new crusade, one to eliminate all dragons, so they took this weapon and adopted this symbol as their coat of arms. I don't see what they called themselves. Ah, wait, here we go; they called themselves the Wyrmkil."

At the mention of the name, Calor staggered. George finally noticed her and her look of disorientation. "No. Stop. We don't use that word. We...I am suffocating—" She was breathing heavily as her disorientation turned to distress. George began to sweat as the temperature in the kitchen began to rise. A small thermometer hung by the door, and George could actually see the red liquid inside climbing in the small glass tube. In mere moments, it rose past eighty-five and quickly headed to ninety.

"Calor, what's going on? You okay?" he asked as he wiped the sweat from his brow. A small temperature alarm window popped up on the laptop, warning it was overheating, and it began to shut itself down. The thermometer rose to 110 degrees and was quickly heading to top out at 120. He said, "What are you doing? You need to get outside."

He barely finished the sentence as she was bursting out of the door and running down the steps to the lawn. George followed and saw her stooped over, one hand resting on her knee but the other still firmly over the scale around her neck. She was taking heavy, deep breaths. Every time she exhaled, George saw the grass in front of her blacken, shrivel, and smoke. His eyes went wide with alarm, but he tried to help. "Calor, tell me what is going on! What is it? Is it the article about the Wyrmkil?"

She whipped around to face him, her eyes wild. She bellowed, "Do not use that word!" As she shouted at him, the air temperature of a furnace blasted from her mouth. He fell backward from the pure heat, and, as Calor watched him fall, she covered her mouth with her hands in disbelief at what she had done. The surrounding air immediately began to cool, and George instinctively began to examine himself for injuries. Several small, smoldering holes peppered the front of his t-shirt, and he quickly slapped at them to put them out. His hands ran over his face, and his skin smarted with pain, as if he was sunburned. He also felt a distinct thinning of his eyebrows, and most of his eyelashes were gone.

George was incredulous. "Wha, what was that?"

Calor stammered, "Geor...Squire George...I—"

"What are you doing to me? You burned off my eyebrows, you gave me sunburn; Calor, you used your breath weapon on me! How did you do that? What did I say?"

She tried to answer. "The word 'wyrm'...it is an insult to my kind. It is demeaning, a term of contempt. I—"

George interrupted, "Well, how the heck was I supposed to know that?"

Calor answered, "No, George, there is no way you could, but the story, the name of the group...something happened to me. My mind started to swirl as if something was trying to push into my consciousness but couldn't. Then, hearing that word, I became angry and lashed out."

"But you used your breath weapon on me. How could that have happened? Wait, you had your hand over that scale the whole time. What if...here, try breathing out your heat but keep your hands at your side. Let the scale hang loosely."

Calor let her arms hang at her side as she took a deep breath and exhaled strongly but with no effect. George said, "Now put your hand over your scale and press it against your body. But breathe gently, nothing too big." She pushed the scale into the skin of her chest and immediately felt a warmth spread from the scale into her chest, and it seemed to permeate to the depth of her being. She took a deep breath again and exhaled forcefully. The space in front of her shimmered with the sudden introduction of heat as the superheated air shot forward in a cone-like shape and ignited a large strip of the grass almost instantly. Calor quickly shut her mouth in surprise and looked wide-eyed at George.

"Gah!" he shouted and hurried to get the garden hose connected to the spigot on the outside of the house. He doused the burning lawn with water until there was only mud and blackened grass in the decimated strip on the Hewes yard. George watched the water soak into soil and realized he was breathing heavily from the anxiety-producing turn of events. He tried to look away from the scorched earth, but his eyes remained fixed on the soggy grass before him as he took several moments to calm his breathing. Finally, George slowly lifted his scorched face, contorted in a deep scowl, and locked his eyes with those of Calor.

She shifted her eyes back and forth uncomfortably, trying not to meet George's accusatory gaze. "So, this was an…unanticipated turn of events, would you not say?"

"You set the lawn on fire!" he exploded. "My eyebrows look like burned fuzz, my eyelashes are almost gone, and my face looks like I've been suntanning in a microwave oven! You're not even supposed to be here! How am I gonna explain this to Mr. Hewes or my mom? Oh, man, my mom…she's not gonna let me out of the house for a week if I can't come up with a reason for this! Look at me, Calor; you don't get like this from one overnight stay at your best friend's house!"

She placed her hands on her hips. "Well, if you had been more careful as to when and where you directed me to experiment with my breath weapon then this unfortunate incident would not have occurred, would it?"

George glared at her then dropped the hose and stormed into the house without a word. Calor watched him go in and waited several moments before she followed him. As she walked up the porch steps, she muttered to herself, "Feh, humans take no responsibility for their actions."

Chapter 27

"So what did you do to cover the scorched earth?"

George stood in one of the corners at the back of the dinosaur museum with Petros, having recounted the events that transpired in the morning. George's skin was still pink from his encounter with Calor's heat breath, but he had brushed the dried and scorched eyebrows and eyelashes off of his face. Once he got to a mirror, he was relieved that it didn't look as bad as he thought, and he invented the excuse for his parents that there was a mishap with one of the ovens at work, and he received a face full of oven-hot air. It was partially true, but George knew it was partially a lie as well. He always thought the truth was the best option. But when it comes to hiding mythological creatures, covering up stories of secret societies a millennium old, and not telling about mysterious, super-strong motorcycle riders, his previous beliefs about falsehoods needed to be re-evaluated. His world—the world—had changed, and he didn't know what to do about it.

He answered Petros, "I used the lawn mower, trimmed down some of the taller grasses around the yard, and then sprinkled the clippings over the bare patch. It'll only last a day or two, so you may need to repeat the process until the grass starts growing back."

Petros nodded. "I do not know what a lawn mower is."

George sighed. "Of course you don't."

"I am even more intrigued about our ability to access our breath weapons while in these human bodies. You are sure it all centers around our scales?"

George nodded. "Pretty sure. She just pressed it up against her chest but didn't fully grasp it like you do when you transform back to a dragon."

Petros's hand went to the scale tucked under his shirt and gently applied pressure. "I feel nothing."

George pursed his lips. "She was emotional about the information I found on the net. She was thinking of herself as a dragon. I bet that's it, you know, the emotional component; it wasn't just about the physical touch."

Petros kept his hand over the scale and closed his eyes. His mind began to recall battles he had been in, times when he was soaring over the countryside and turning his foes to stone with a mighty blast of his magical breath. As the images solidified in his mind, he felt a warmth spread from the scale and into his chest. An irresistible urge came over him to inhale deeply as he felt the sensation intensify to his lungs. He was about to exhale when he felt his shoulder being forcefully shaken. His eyes snapped open, and the feeling dissipated.

George had a grip on his shoulder. He hissed through gritted teeth, "Hey! Not here, man. You're gonna give the whole thing away."

Petros nodded in the affirmative, but a residual tingle was still in his chest. "We need to tell the others."

"Yeah," George replied. "I've got a Skype session set up tonight. You need to be on it too. You have all of the directions I wrote out for you on how to do that, right?" Petros nodded as George went on. "Okay. Has Jason's dad said anything about when he's going out of town next?"

Petros answered, "He made a reference to such today, but there were no specifics."

George nodded in understanding. "Hey, do you ever miss having Jason around, you know, talking to him in person?"

Petros was somewhat taken aback by the question and thought for several moments before answering, "I have not given that much thought until this moment, but there is a part of me that does miss his presence. I would assume that, since you are inquiring, you would also answer in the affirmative?"

George sighed. "It's nothing personal. It's just that he's my best friend, and you're cool and all, but it's not the same."

Petros smiled sympathetically and rested a hand on George's shoulder. "There is no offense. I understand. I look like your good friend, but I am not him. With the way things stand, finding opportunities for you to spend time with him are few and far between. When you do get to speak, it is either through a mirror or staring into the face of a dragon."

The teen took a deep breath and let out a cleansing sigh. "Yeah, it's pretty much just like that."

"Keep your spirits up, Squire George; we will return to Billings soon and undo this unfortunate situation."

George returned home, and Petros finished his work day at the museum. The Draconaut was rapidly catching on to Jason's job, and by the end of the second day he was even receiving compliments from Susan herself. She said, "Hmm. I don't know what has gotten into you, Jason, but you're not leaving me anything to get on your case about. Good job."

He found himself able to engage in small talk with Jason's father on the way home and even managed two spontaneous contractions. He further surprised Timothy when he expressed interest in watching him make meat loaf, saying to the adult Hewes, "I am fascinated by the preparation of food. It would seem there is quite a skill level necessary to master it."

Timothy smiled. "Well, I wouldn't call myself a 'master,' but I do make a pretty darn good meat loaf. Go wash your hands, and we'll get started."

When dinner was finished, Petros went to Jason's room to begin the Skype session with George and the other three Draconauts. He found the written instructions exactly where George left them and logged onto the video chat service. George was late, and, as Petros waited, he saw his own image on the laptop's monitor, displayed via the webcam. As he reflected on the current state of his life, the image on the laptop spoke. "Okay, this is getting weirder and weirder."

Petros was initially startled but then asked, "Little Knight?"

Jason's face nodded. "Yep, it would seem that the mirror talking thing extends to webcams and laptops as well."

Petros scrunched up his nose. "How is this possible? This is far different from a mirror."

"Hey, you're the one from magical times, so you tell me. I have no idea what's going on, but I'm getting so used to all this bizarre stuff that it's not even surprising me anymore."

George finally joined the call, and his image blinked to life in a new window on the monitor. He said, "Oh, Petros, you made it. Good."

Jason said, "Nope. Right face, wrong consciousness."

"Jason?" George questioned.

He nodded. "Yessir. Seems the mirror thing extends to laptops and webcams."

Petros asked, "So how will I be a part of this conversation?"

"No idea." Jason shrugged.

George asked, "No idea what?"

Jason replied, "I was talking to Petros."

Petros sat up straight. "He cannot hear me?"

"Seems like I can't hear him," George said.

Jason smiled. "He just said that."

George asked, "Who just said what?"

"I did," Petros answered.

Jason stated, "He can't hear you."

George asked, "Who can't hear me?"

"No, I was talking to Petros," Jason replied.

George raised an eyebrow. "Petros can't hear me?"

Jason answered, "No, you can't...okay, everyone stop. My head is swimming; George, Petros can see and hear me, I can hear us both, but you can't hear Petros. Since I can hear you and Petros, I'm going to have to tell you what he is saying. Petros, you're probably not going to be able to talk to anyone but me on this call. I have a feeling it's gonna be the same for Kinaari and Marcus. Hey, what's the story with Tiffany?"

George answered, "I already told her Petros or I would fill her in on what was discussed. She's still out in the barn."

The Skype conversation went exactly as Jason had predicted; Jason, George, Kinaari, and Marcus were all able to communicate with each other in the magically altered cyberspace, while Petros, Procella, and Tonare all sat in their human forms in front of the computers and passed their comments through their digital images. The teens were overjoyed at the opportunity to speak with each other again, and, in their opinions, the conversation ended much too soon. But the sun was setting, and they didn't want to raise parental suspicion over Skype calls going late into the night. So they each reluctantly signed off, and Petros was left alone in Jason's room again with nothing but his thoughts.

The last streaks of red and orange were just visible at the edge of the horizon as Petros stepped off the front porch to get some fresh air and update Tiffany on the Skype conversation. As he began to walk toward the barn, a voice came to him from the corner of the house. "So it would seem we finally get the opportunity to meet."

Petros jumped at the voice and whipped his head around to find the source. Leaning against one of the support posts for the porch and roof was a figure clad in blue and gray padded armor and a similarly colored motorcycle helmet. A bright yellow dragon decal adorned the helmet that completely hid the figure's features, and a long, bladed weapon was affixed to its back. He opened his mouth to speak, but the mysterious rider of Nymbus cut him off. "Don't pretend to not know who I am or that I don't know what you are. I'm sure your other dragon/human friends told you all about me."

Petros thought about trying to keep up his ruse but saw no point in it. "Yes, they updated me on their encounter. How did you find out who I was?"

The figure shrugged. "You don't get to do what I do without developing some degree of investigative skills and deductive reasoning."

Petros made an exaggerated effort to look around the rider. "You seem to be missing a rather large dragon." Petros did his best to channel some of Jason's sarcasm.

"And you seem to be missing a rather large dragon's body, but we both knew that, didn't we?"

Petros narrowed his eyes. "You have me at a distinct disadvantage, and your presence here is unwanted. If you expose us to Jason's father—"

The rider interrupted, "Relax. Subtlety is also one of my strong points. I was able to track you down without coming to your notice."

"You wear the vestments of a warrior, but you speak with the voice of one of these teenagers. You are quite the conundrum, dragon rider."

"I make an effort to be such; keeps you on your toes."

Petros paused for a moment, trying to read the body language of the dragon rider and see through the black visor of its helmet but to no avail. "Why are you here?"

"I felt it was necessary. Your other three friends told me about you, but I wanted to lay eyes on you myself. Can't have an unaccounted-for dragon/human hybrid—"

Petros interrupted, "Draconaut."

The rider cocked its head. "What?"

"We call ourselves Draconauts. We find ourselves explorers of a territory never before encountered."

"Yeah, I hear you on that. I'm not sure if I've ever heard of a spell effecting humans, or especially dragons, quite in this way before. But I gotta admit, the name is, well…"

Petros said, "Goofy?"

The rider held up its hands. "Well, yeah."

Petros replied, "Yes, the children used the same word, but we are fond of it. I have a hard time believing you are simply here to, as you say, 'lay eyes on me.'" He thought for a moment then decided to risk a question. He narrowed his eyes. "Is this about the Wyrmkil?"

The figure paused and looked uncharacteristically flustered. "How do you know about that?"

Petros knew his bluff had worked. "You don't get to do what I do without developing some degree of investigative skills and deductive reasoning," he quoted back. In his mind, he saw the figure smiling.

"Touché," it said. "So you know, then, that forces are at work, dark forces that are seeking to reignite a centuries-old war."

"Yes. But my knowledge of the situation ends there."

"Oh." The rider sounded disappointed. "We were hoping you knew more. Nymbus was hatched after the Great Fracturing, but you and your friends seem to be some kind of refugees from the war."

Petros nodded. "It would seem so, but what caused our memories to be erased and what moved us across an ocean to reside in this country remain shrouded in mystery."

"I see," the armored figure said. "You know, Nymbus and I, we aren't your enemies."

Petros looked skeptical. "Our encounter over the plains of Montana weeks ago would seem to suggest otherwise. And the lightning bolt Nymbus threw at Tiffany was not taken as a gesture of good will."

"Yeah, we kind of regret—"

Petros interrupted. "This Order of the Scale, does it always put those of such youth, human and dragon alike, on the field of battle? Your behaviors betray your inexperience. Power must be tempered with responsibility and patience, qualities that come with maturity."

The rider paused before responding, "I...I was still in training when my mentor was injured. We were the only members of the order in the United States. I hear rumors of another member in the northern territories of Canada, but we have had no contact in my lifetime."

"And what of the Storm dragon?"

"My f...my mentor was Nymbus's third partner. I'm his fourth; that makes him maybe a couple of hundred years old."

Petros added, "Just a young adult in the life cycle of my kind."

The helmeted head nodded in agreement. "Slightly older than the Air Dragon you have on your side but not by much."

"You bear the weight of much responsibility on your shoulders, young rider."

"You don't know the half of it." There was a long silence before the rider spoke again. "But I want to tell you we are here to help. I know you need to return to Billings to find the mage, and I offer Nymbus and myself to help wherever we can, but you need to be aware that we think your movements are being tracked. So you need to be cautious as you proceed with your plans."

Petros was about to respond when he heard Timothy Hewes call for him from inside the house. He shouted back, "I will…I'll be right there!" But as he turned his head back to address the rider, it was gone. He stared at the spot where it had been standing and raked his fingers through his hair. He shook his head at the turn of events and re-entered the house, lost in thought.

Chapter 28

The hot summer days turned into hot summer weeks as Jason, Petros, and the rest of the Draconauts waited for their opportunity to engage in the Norm-finding trek to Billings. Jason had commented that he couldn't remember the last time his dad went so long between out-of-town trips required for his job. There were a select few day trips here and there but none that would have provided the opportunity for Jason and Tiffany to take wing to the large city to the south and, hopefully, sever their magical link with the dragons. George expressed concerns that Marcus and Kinaari would be able to get away from their homes when Mr. Hewes finally left town again, but they both assured George it would not be an issue. The whole scheme was dependent on Jason's father.

Jason, Kinaari, and Marcus were enjoying being able to speak to each other through their laptops and the Internet. It felt almost normal for them to communicate in this fashion, and they found themselves bonding during these Skype sessions; they were becoming genuine friends. Jason and Marcus learned about Kinaari's very "proper" upbringing and that her parents were as concerned about her outer appearance as they were her inner character. Kinaari said she valued the discipline but often felt very stifled and was concerned that her little brother would soon feel the same pressure as she did.

Jason and Kinaari learned that Marcus's family was huge, not just in his home but all over the state. His father's grandparents had initially settled in Montana, and two generations later there were Weltons all over the state working in all different kinds of jobs. From executives in Butte to farmers in Havre to professors in the university system, Marcus's relatives had become a fixture in Montana and were proud of it.

Tiffany was the holdout from the Skype sessions. She kept everyone at a proverbial arm's length, and the teens suspected whatever secrets she kept about her life were to blame for her self-imposed exclusion. Still, she had found a confidant in Calor, and, per the advice of Marcus, that would do for the time being.

The first few days of August flew by before Timothy Hewes announced that he needed to travel to the Badlands of South Dakota for a week. Petros tried his best to feign the disappointment that Jason often expressed when his father left town, but he was truly filled with a sense of relief that their magically created conundrum was entering its final stages. As had become their standard lines of communication, Petros passed the message to George, who updated Tonare and Procella via email. During the weeks they were waiting for Mr. Hewes to leave, all the dragons, with the exception of Calor, were becoming quite proficient in using the Internet. But Procella progressed even further. Unbeknownst to George, she established her own email address, developed a Facebook page, and even created her own separate profile on Kinaari's laptop, complete with a password. On several occasions, she had found herself exploring the Internet late into the night and often woke up in the early hours of the morning having fallen asleep on the computer's keyboard and run the laptop's battery to zero percent.

Upon their receipt of George's news, emails, text messages, and instant chats began flying back and forth. It wasn't long before a day and time were set, a meeting place was identified, and a rudimentary script was developed for what they were going to say to the wizard. Petros went out to the barn and updated Tiffany on the situation. She was in her dragon form and lying on the floor of the barn, looking indifferently at Petros.

Petros was slightly annoyed by her look. "Am I boring you?"

"No," she rumbled. "But you have forgotten a major problem."

He eyed her suspiciously. "And that would be?"

She sighed heavily and pushed herself up to her elbows. "So you're saying that we will all fly down to Billings in our dragon forms under the cover of darkness and rendezvous in the Rims like you did before?"

"Yes," Petros stated. "That is the plan."

Tiffany paused. "You really don't see it, do you?"

He glowered at her. "You are beginning to enrage me, girl. What am I missing?"

She smirked. "I want to talk to Jason."

"I do not see why you cannot—" Petros saw the look of determination on her face and slumped his shoulders. "Very well." He stepped back while Tiffany made as much room as she could for a second dragon in the old barn. A burst of light later, Jason was crouched in the now very crowded space.

"Hey," he greeted her. "What's going on?"

"Did they tell you this plan of theirs?"

He nodded. "Yeah, I helped come up with it."

"Really?" she said, placing her claws on what would have been her hips. "*You* came up with the idea of all of us flying to Billings."

He turned his head away, now looking at her askance. "Well, yeah. It's a good plan; we'll get there quickly."

"And did anyone bother to raise the point that you can't fly yet, genius?"

"I…was gonna practice," he muttered.

She leveled her stare at him. "You were going to practice."

His eyes darted back and forth as he searched for an answer. "Yeah, you know, I was gonna get out and get the whole flying thing down before the trip. It'll be fine."

"Jason, why don't you just let me fly Petros down to—"

"No," he interrupted.

She went on. "It'll be the easiest thing. That way—"

"No!" The strength of his voice made the wall boards vibrate.

There was silence for a moment as they tried to stare each other down. Tiffany finally asked, "Why are you being so stubborn about this?"

"Ha! That's the pot calling the kettle black. Why are you trying to make me look like an idiot?"

She wrinkled her snout. "Huh? I'm not trying to make you look like anything."

"Oh, now that you're all big and bad and can fly and use your breath weapon and all, you're gonna turn out like everyone else; you pick on the weaker ones just to make yourself look better. If it isn't bad enough that I'm the only one that can't fly, now you want to humiliate me more by making Petros ride on you and reminding everyone of how Jason Hewes is such a lousy teen…I mean dragon."

His slip of the tongue was enough to enlighten Tiffany. Her voice softened. "Jace, I'm not trying to do any of that. We need to get down to Billings in the easiest and most efficient—"

"Yeah, yeah, yeah," he interrupted, turning his head away from her. "Whatever. I get the message."

"Fine!" This time her voice shook the walls. "We're gonna do this your way…you know, the hard way. Let's go!"

His head whipped around, a shocked look on his face. "What? Go where?"

Her look was steely in its determination. "To practice."

Tiffany led as they snuck out of the barn, through the field, past the glade of trees, and ending in a large, unpopulated expanse. The Canadian border was the only thing north of their location, and a whole lot of nothing was in between. Here, they would not be seen or heard.

When they assured themselves the coast was clear, Tiffany turned to Jason. "So let's do this, dragon boy. Show me how you are going to practice flying."

Jason stammered, "I…can't while you're watching."

She rolled her eyes. "Oh, please, give me a break. Get a running start and flap your wings. That's all there is to it."

"It's not that easy," he growled.

"Sure it is. If two girls like Kinaari and me can learn to fly then you sure can."

"Hey, I never said that."

"But I bet you thought it, didn't you?"

He was looking nervous. "That's not fair. Don't lay all of that on me."

Tiffany interrupted, her tone becoming more confrontational. "Well, of course you won't say it, Jace. But you have to be thinking it, right? You're telling me that it doesn't irk you in the least that you're the only one who hasn't figured out how to fly or use his breath weapon."

"Well, yeah, it bothers me." Jason felt a burning in his great chest. His talons dug into the ground.

"It 'bothers you'? Oh, come on, Jace, that's a weenie answer."

His voice dropped as he snarled, "Don't call me that."

Tiffany noticed the change in his voice. She saw his talons gripping the earth and small veins of light rising into his legs. "Hey, I gotta call it like I see it. This whole not trying to learn how to be a dragon, it's kind of a weenie thing."

"I said don't call me that!"

Tiffany started at the exclamation and saw Jason raising himself to his full height. The teenage slump of the shoulders and neck was gone, and the proud, majestic stance of a dragon was now present. She smirked on the inside; her ploy was working. "Why? How does it make you feel?"

"Angry!" he bellowed. His eye slits grew until his irises appeared completely black. The veins of light were halfway up his legs, and he bared his teeth at the Heat dragon. He was looking very alarming, even to Tiffany.

"Oh, really?" she shouted back at him. "Then what are you going to do about it?"

Jason unleashed an ear-splitting dragon roar as his chest rapidly expanded and he pointed his serpentine neck at Tiffany. She barely jumped out of the way as a torrent of glowing orange cubes burst forth from the gaping maw of the Stone dragon. His wings beat furiously as his breath weapon bathed a wide swath of the earth in its energies. His front legs rose off the ground as the leathery wings assaulted the air until gravity itself seemed to give way to the rage of the Earth Dragon. Jason poured years of repressed frustration into the magical attack as grass, soil, weeds, small trees, and any insects or rodents caught in the blast transformed into stone. The ferocity of the breath weapon finally relented, and Jason opened his eyes, having realized they had been shut the entire time. He raised his neck and unclenched his talons; before him a cone of earth two hundred feet long and fifty feet wide at its base was now transformed into the hardest granite. His pupils returned to their normal size, and the veins of light in his legs faded.

"Whoa!" he exclaimed, wide eyed.

Tiffany quietly stole up next to him. "Thus endeth the lesson," she said coyly.

By the time they returned to the barn, Jason was still trying to figure things out. "Yeah, you all told me that before. I needed to *want* to use my breath weapon. But those times I did; I really wanted to see what it would do."

"No, you're not getting it," she replied as she shook her head. "You didn't want to use it then, like you would for an attack or defense or something. You were just curious, but there was no need there. I just wanted to get you angry so you would lash out in frustration to make you want to break something in a fit of rage. Haven't you ever wanted to do that?"

"Well, yeah, but if I break something, I have to fix it. I don't like having to fix things."

"See?" she said, frustrated. "That is the other problem. You're kind of lazy, Jace, and you give up way too easily. If you want something like this, you have to work at it."

"I work," he replied defensively.

She looked over her snout at him. "That isn't what I mean, and you know it."

"Look, I know how things are; you try something and end up looking stupid in front of everyone, and then you never hear the end of it."

Tiffany furrowed her eye ridges. "Is that what you think of us?"

He rolled his eyes. "No, but—"

"No 'buts,'" she interrupted. "Don't lump the people who really care about you in the same category as this Stan guy. We want to see you succeed, and I don't care how many tries it takes, so the self-pity ends here. Pick yourself up and dust yourself off. There is way more at stake here then your insecurities, and we have to get past them for this plan to work. Got it?"

"Got it." He smiled. "Thanks, Tiff. Look, it's almost supper time. Petros better get back inside."

The day finally arrived for Mr. Hewes's departure, and Petros walked with him out to the truck. He opened the passenger-side door and deposited his leather duffel bag on the worn, vinyl bench seat. He then turned to Petros. "You sure you're going to be all right?"

Petros nodded. "Yes, I don't anticipate anything eventful occurring while you are away."

Mr. Hewes put his arm around Jason's shoulders and walked him to the driver's seat. He was smiling and shaking his head. "I don't know what has gotten into you these past few weeks, son, but you are different. I can't put my finger on it, but something has changed."

Petros searched for an excuse. "I believe I have finally taken the advice to 'grow up' a little. Isn't that what you wanted?"

Timothy sat in the truck and pulled the door closed. He spoke through the open window. "Sometimes. But don't grow up too fast; you only get to be a kid once."

"I will consider that," he replied.

Mr. Hewes turned to back the truck out of the driveway but then turned back to Petros. "And don't think I haven't noticed that you are struggling with contractions. Maybe you need a speech therapist or something."

Petros had no idea what he was talking about. "Perhaps that would be prudent."

Mr. Hewes smiled at that last statement as he backed the truck onto Highway 2 and motored off to the airport. Petros breathed a heavy sigh and walked straight to the barn. He opened the doors and found Tiffany examining the saddle Jason had jury-rigged for his first flight with Petros.

"Do you believe it will still work?" he asked.

She shrugged her shoulders. "It shouldn't be a problem."

"I will contact Squire George," he replied as he took the smart phone out of his pocket.

Tiffany teased, "Awww, look at you making phone calls all by yourself." She sighed deeply. "My little dragon-boy-guy is growing up." She placed her claws over her heart and fluttered her eyelids.

Petros leveled a stare at her. "What is it Jason says? Oh, yes. 'You are hysterical; you should go on tour.'" He waited a few moments for George to answer then said into the phone, "Yes, it is me. We are ready."

The door to the massive and opulent office on the eightieth floor swung open for Tate Reigles as he stepped onto the plush maroon carpet. The lammergeiger and the fish owl gazed at him, their intense stare making Mr. Reigles's stomach sink. He swallowed hard and looked across the room to the cloaked figure standing before the windows, gazing out over the concrete jungle of Manhattan. He swore the figure hadn't moved since his last visit to the office weeks ago.

The figure spoke. "I would assume by your presence here that you now understand my goals in this age and how the wyrm fit into them?"

"I do, sir." He fought to not let his voice crack.

"My lord."

He frowned. "I'm sorry? I missed that."

The hooded head turned slightly toward him. "You will address me as 'my lord,' or you may find yourself relieved of the need to address anyone ever again."

Reigles could feel the bitter bile rising in his throat. "I understand, my lord."

"Very good. You have news?"

He fought to compose himself. "Yes. Our listening post says they are about to move."

There was a pause. "Excellent. Will the human whelps be with the wyrm?"

"They are working together, so it would be a logical conclusion."

"The male wyrm are to be slain and the females brought to the designated coordinates. The children are collateral; what happens to them is of no consequence to me."

"Understood, my lord." Reigles was repulsed at the thought. He was not hired to see children murdered.

The figure went on. "It is time to lay our trap. Have our clean-up technologies standing by. We will offer our services with the most haste and free of charge. No local government will refuse millions of dollars of free services."

Chapter 29

They flew under the cover of the early-morning hours and chose to rendezvous at the same place in the Rims that Jason and Petros landed in their previous visit to the large city. Dawn was just creeping over the horizon as Tiffany, the last to arrive, touched down. She and Petros had rigged the saddle to fit her, and he was tightly secured to the ersatz seat. Petros had not bargained on how weary he would feel waking up at two o'clock in the morning, and by the time Tiffany had landed, he was asleep and slumped over; the rigged bungee cords and leather belts had kept him from falling to his doom. But the jostling about of Tiffany's landing roused him back to coherence.

Petros rubbed the sleep out of his eyes, and Kinaari commented, "He looked so peaceful asleep like that."

Marcus smirked a toothy grin. "See? Bein' human isn't all it's cracked up to be, is it?"

Petros smiled. "Your need for daily sleep is an inconvenience, but being human has benefits as well." He paused and looked at the Thunder and Wave dragons. "It is good to see you, my friends."

Marcus nodded. "You too, buddy." He turned to Tiffany. "You holding up okay, Tiff?"

"I'm fine," she answered. "It's, umm, good seeing you in person again. Well, not in *person*, but you know what I mean."

Kinaari put a claw on Tiffany's shoulder. "We missed you too."

Tiffany was glad she could not blush and quickly changed the topic. "Okay, we'd better get to this. It's gonna be a long day."

Three flashes of light later, the four Draconauts were hiking their way out of the Rims and into the city, heading for the designated McDonald's on Grand Avenue to clean up, eat some breakfast, and lay out their plans to get to Norm's shop. The hike to the fast-food restaurant took nearly an hour, and they were all perspiring and covered with a fine layer of grime from the dust they kicked up from the journey. They all took a turn in the restroom to wash off their faces and arms and change into the extra clothes they brought.

Soon, they were seated at a booth, refreshed and eating various McMuffins. A flat-panel television on the wall was tuned to the local news, and they were huddled around Jason's smart phone studying the preprogrammed map of Billings.

"So if we take this mode of conveyance," Petros pointed out, "it should get us to within a few streets of the mage's place of business. It will only be a short walk from there."

Procella nodded. "Yes, we will only need to deposit one dollar's worth of coin to ride the coach as well. It is very economical."

"I know so very little of the plan," Calor growled. "I know my agreement with the girl was to let her stay in my dragon form, but now it would seem the cost is my lack of tactical knowledge on this mission."

"You speak as if we are going to war." Procella smiled.

"We are confronting the mage again, this time in decidedly more inferior human bodies. Of course I regard it as war."

Petros noticed that Tonare's attention was drawn to the television. "Cousin, I think your attention would be more wisely given to the plan before us."

Tonare shook his head. "I think your attention would be more wisely given to the information being displayed on this television. This 'mission' may be over before it even starts."

They all turned to face the flat screen, where a young, well-groomed man wore a windbreaker sporting the logo of the local news station. He was holding a large black microphone also bearing the logo of the television channel. "...I'm not sure we've ever seen anything like this in Billings before. To bring those of you up to date if you just tuned in, early this morning, carbon monoxide detectors within a large section of downtown Billings simultaneously began to sound their alarms. Oddly enough, the alarms are not resetting properly, so city officials and emergency response personnel are at a loss to explain the phenomena. Detectors brought into the area by the fire department are also indicating lethal levels of the dangerous gas. The entire area has been evacuated and cordoned off as a safety precaution. Needless to say, city personnel are overwhelmed by the situation and are struggling to not only figure out the source of the contamination but to put a stop to it. But in a surprising development, the Alans Corporation, recently recognized for state-of-the-art defense equipment, has offered their personnel and advanced detection technologies to the city for no cost. Their employees and clean-up crews are currently on the scene trying to resolve this extremely bizarre and dangerous situation."

Calor huffed, "What significance does this bear for us? These humans are weak and paranoid. Come, let us proceed with—"

"The significance is," Procella interrupted as she held up the map on the smart phone, "that Norm's place of business is in the middle of the restricted area. We will be prevented from going there."

Petros raked his fingers through his hair. "There is a second problem as well." The three looked at him for an answer as he pointed back to the television. Behind the cameraman and the barricade blocking the street, a black cargo van was parked next to Transwestern Plaza, where the First Interstate Center was located. Next to the van were black motorcycles whose riders, clad completely in black, dismounted the nondescript vehicles and entered the van. Petros asked, "I know I need not inquire, but does anyone recognize those figures?"

Their countenances dropped as they simultaneously sat back in their seats. Calor said, "There are sinister machinations at work here, more than just our current conundrum."

Procella added, "This Alans Corporation, the black riders, the Wyrmkil…they are all linked."

Petros nodded thoughtfully. "And I do not see their presence here on this very same day we chose to enter the city as a coincidence."

"How could they have been aware? We have been so careful," Procella replied.

He shrugged his shoulders. "I do not know. They know where Jason lives, but as far as any of us can determine, they did not see any of us in dragon form. The only ones outside of the individuals around this table that know anything are George, Norm the mage, and Nymbus and his mysterious rider."

Carol sneered, "I knew the mage would betray us."

"We know nothing of this Order of the Scale," Procella countered. "Perhaps it is all a ruse. Nymbus has attacked each and every one of us. Perhaps that is his true nature."

Tonare slammed his hand on the table. "Enough! We can mew on about this until these bodies reach adulthood, but it does not change the fact that we still need to get to Norm's shop. I say we proceed anyway and let these dark riders try to stop us. We have access to our dragon abilities, my cousins; we are not without a means to defend ourselves! Norm has much to answer for, and it is time for a reckoning."

They all exchanged glances as Petros smiled at his Air Dragon cousin. "Then let us be on with it."

They managed to navigate the MET bus schedule and get themselves on the correct route that would have taken them right into the cordoned-off area. However, as expected, the driver took a detour at the barricades, and Procella indicated they wanted to be dropped off at a corner just down the street from where traffic was being diverted.

The barricade began by the Billings Clinic, one of the main medical facilities in the city. Patients were being diverted to many of the other medical providers in the city, but the system was quickly becoming overtaxed. The four Draconauts watched city officials conferring just beyond the saw horses blocking the streets, scrambling to find a solution to the crisis.

Procella was the first to speak. "The structure is for the sick and infirm. Many will not receive healing on this day."

Calor pursed her lips. "I am sure it is inconvenient for the humans, but it is not a concern of ours."

Petros turned to Calor. "I find it surprising that after this length of time you have spent as a human that your compassion for them is so minimal."

"I am in agreement with her," Tonare added. "We cannot afford to invest too much compassion into these lesser beings. Once we have reacquired our true forms, we can debate over those who are worthy of our compassion."

"Still," Procella said toward Calor, "I find it disturbing that, for a Heat dragon, your heart can be so cold."

Petros held up the smart phone. "This is a discussion for another time. The map indicates the mage's place of business is several blocks ahead. We must find a way into the restricted zone."

They proceeded down the street to the boundary. Two police cars blocked any further progress as one of the officers said, "Keep on moving, kids. I can't let you through."

Petros began to sniffle and cough deeply. Procella picked up on his cue and said to the officers, "But my friend is ill. We were entering the healing house to find one practiced in medicine."

Calor and Tonare began to nod emphatically as Tonare added, "Oh, yes, my friend has been ill for quite some time. We are concerned and alarmed."

The officers exchanged suspicious looks. "You kids aren't from around here, are you?"

Calor rolled her eyes. "You have no idea."

"Look," the second officer said, "I can't allow anyone into the building until we figure out where all of the carbon monoxide is coming from. There is a walk-in several block west; that is the best I can offer. You want us to arrange for you to get a ride there?"

Procella was about to answer when she saw two of the dark riders come around the corner of the clinic. The riders raised their heads and then began to walk toward them. She replied, "That is a most generous offer, but we will find our way. Thank you, good sirs." The other three spotted the figures in black at the same time, and all began to walk quickly to the west, following the edges of the barricade and trying to put enough buildings, cars, and trees between them and the two riders until they were out of sight.

They walked for nearly forty-five minutes, following the edges of the restricted area west then south until their feet began to ache from the pace they maintained.

"We need to rest," Calor finally spoke up. "My heart is as vast at the great deserts of the East, but this body is fairly weak."

Tonare smiled. "I am still capable of maintaining this march. It is good to be the largest and strongest for once."

Petros answered, "We stay together. We will sit and rest."

The four sat down on a curb and stared at the buildings across from them. Calor dabbed the sweat on her upper lip with her sleeve, while Petros rubbed his cheek against his shoulder and mopped the beads of perspiration coming from his sideburns. Tonare turned his head sideways as he looked at the building across the street. "What is a 'doll museum'?"

Procella glanced at the building sideways. "I have no idea." She was about to close and rub her eyes when she paused and looked at the building again. "Are the rest of you making the same observation that I am?"

The Legacy Doll Museum sat on an awkward junction where three streets met. Directly behind the museum was the cordoned-off area. Calor surveyed their position then replied, "If we could get through that building, we would be one step closer to our destination."

Petros nodded. "Yes, but how do we get in? All of the places of business are shut down."

"Come with me," Calor said as she rose back to her feet.

The Draconauts strolled across the street as casually as they could and stopped in front of the doll museum. It was a quaint building with white and lavender signs above the windows and doors. It was friendly for a building, a place that invited young girls and their mothers to see the toys of yesteryear.

Calor positioned herself in front of the door and looked inside. It was dark, but she could see a myriad of small doll eyes staring back at her. She commented to herself, "That is unsettling, even for a dragon. We need to look for a lull in street traffic and pedestrians before I can act."

They nodded and began to watch the cars and people going by, hoping for a break when they wouldn't be seen. It was a few minutes before there was a sufficient gap in both car and foot traffic, but it was enough time for Calor to do her work. A small poster for a local stage production was taped to the front door, and Calor lifted the poster up, pressed her scale against her chest, puckered her lips, and blew a very focused stream of pure heat at the window. The glass quickly glowed and melted away, forming a hole she could reach through. She deftly reached through, unlocked the deadbolt to the doll museum door, and then covered the hole with the poster. The others checked one last time that they weren't being watched and then slipped into the building.

Shelves of wide-eyed dolls gazed at them as they quietly closed the door and crouched low to the floor, careful not to be seen through the windows. They could not help but survey the room; the intense lifeless stare of the hundreds of glass eyes made them feel very tentative. But Petros said, "Come, we must press on. Hopefully there is a rear entrance, and we can get into the restricted zone."

They shuffled across the floor in their crouched positions as they made their way around the counter and into the back room. There, the four were able to stand at their full height and quickly found the emergency exit but paused at the presence of the alarmed crash bar that latched and unlatched the door—but not without sounding a very loud and very attention-drawing claxon.

"These humans are quite paranoid," Tonare commented. "They have locks and alarms everywhere."

Procella commented, "It is not unlike our kind and our penchant for accumulating and guarding treasure."

"True," Tonare acknowledged. "Now that I reflect upon it, I find it quite odd that I have not felt the desire for treasure since we awoke in this twenty-first century."

Petros interrupted, "I have noticed the same, but that is a topic for later discussion. I believe I can disable the alarm." He pressed his scale against his chest and breathed a cone of orange cubes on the crash bar, bathing it in the magic of his breath weapon. The red and orange decals on the bar quickly drained of their color, and then the entire mechanism turned into gray stone. Petros pressed the scale tighter against his skin and shut his eyes, concentrating on the earth beneath the store. He felt power flow into his body as he channeled the surge into his free arm. He slowly raised the arm above his head, allowing the power from the earth to focus in his fist. All at once, his eyes snapped open, and he slammed his fist down onto the petrified crash bar, shattering the stone that now comprised it and reducing it to rubble.

The other three Draconauts stepped back in surprise as Procella said, "Impressive! Is your hand harmed?"

Petros opened and closed his fist several times, examining it. "No," he commented. "It would appear the magic that augmented my strength also offered protection from harm."

"Yes, yes, enough self-admiration," Tonare said impatiently. "We must press on."

He slowly pushed the emergency exit open just enough so he could peer into the street beyond. Several doors up was the barricade blocking all traffic and pedestrians from access to their section of the city. A police car sat behind the large saw horses, and an officer in the driver's seat was occupied by the cruiser's laptop. Tonare crouched low, the others followed suit, and they made a quick dash to a van parked on the street and hid behind it. Looking in the opposite direction down the street, they saw several vehicles in the distance but all too far to present a threat. The four quickly ran to the building across the street and hid behind it, escaping the view of the police officer.

And so went their duck-and-run tactics for several blocks, often narrowly escaping detection from the local authorities or the black-clad representatives of AlansCo. Along the way, they not only saw many of the unmarked, flat-black motorcycles they had seen back in Malta but two other, more unusual vehicles as well. The first resembled a four-wheel all-terrain vehicle that many used for both sport and utility. However, the rear wheels had been replaced with a three-sided tread, vaguely similar to that of a tank. These odd ATVs were flat black as the motorcycles were and had no identifying marks. But the most curious were the three-wheeled vehicles. Where the rear resembled the back of a motorcycle, the front wheel was replaced by an axle with a tire attached to each end. Handlebars steered the front two wheels, and the rider was protected with an aerodynamic windshield, which was shaped just like that of the black motorcycles. And like its two- and four-wheeled cousins, this three-wheeled oddity was the same nondescript flat black.

The Draconauts stole their way through the deserted city blocks for more than an hour before the smart phone's GPS indicated they were close to their final destination. Petros said, "We are close, cousins. Our moment is nearly at hand."

Procella asked, "What reason do we have to believe that Norm will actually be in his shop?"

"What are you speaking of?" Calor asked.

"I am saying that if this entire section of this city has been evacuated, would not the mage have been cleared out as well?" They exchanged nervous glances for a few moments before Procella hissed, "Are we saying that no one has thought of this possibility?"

Petros shook his head. "It does not matter. Even if the mage is not there, we will make our way into his store and wait for him. With our dragon abilities, this should not be difficult. Agreed?"

"Agreed," Calor sneered, angry at the error in the plan. "Our minds are becoming dull; I fear we have been human too long. We must get back into our own bodies."

They finally reached the corner that turned down the street of Norm's Random Stuff. They paused one last time to confirm they were on the correct course, when they heard a voice from several doors behind them shout, "Hey, you! This area is restricted! What are you doing here?" They turned to see a local police officer flanked by two black riders coming toward them.

"Go!" Petros shouted as they sprinted to their final destination. In a few short heartbeats, they experienced a tremendous fear of being caught mixed with an elation of successfully navigating the city and reaching the end of their quest. They were finally going to have the answers they sought: Why did the spell go wrong? What exactly had Norm done to them? And, most importantly, how was he going to reverse it?

They skidded to a stop in front of the store, and, in an instant, confusion and dread replaced their earlier feelings. In the front window of the store, a sign read:

After ten years, I have been forced to close
Norm's Random Stuff permanently.
Thank you for your years of patronage.

Tonare stammered, "Wha…what does this mean?"
Calor growled, "It means we will never be dragons again."

Chapter 30

Petros was completely stunned.

He stood at the front door, staring at the sign, realizing that in an instant all of their hopes for their restoration were shattered. One simple poster, one brief declaration of a former shop owner, was enough destroy the aspirations of four of the most magnificent and powerful beings the world had ever known. For Petros, the future had just ceased to exist.

He came back to reality, finding Tonare pulling at his arm while Calor and Procella were beginning to run down the street. Tonare was urging, "Come, Petros, we must move! Now!"

Petros turned his head to see a police officer and three black-clad riders many doors down the street breaking into a run. Tonare couldn't wait any longer; he hauled Petros off his feet, slung him over his broad shoulder, and began to sprint after the two girls. The jostling of the linebacker's body jarred Petros to his full senses as he shouted, "I can run; put me down!"

Without breaking stride, Tonare lifted him into the air and scolded back, "Then run!" Petros hit the ground and nearly stumbled, but Tonare supported him as he came up to speed, and in seconds they were right behind Calor and Procella.

Within moments, they were at the end of the street and breathing hard from being pursued. Calor turned left, and the others followed as they continued to flee from the sinister riders. They skidded to a stop at the next intersection but could hear the officer shouting at them from the previous corner. Calor turned left again, and the others followed. They were on the other side of the city block, and the street before them was narrow and long with no shelter in sight. "Run!" Tonare shouted as, despite their gasping for breath, they all broke into a full sprint once again.

Without warning, Procella shouted, "Wait, stop!" and their feet slapped at the pavement in their deceleration. "Look" was all she could manage as she pointed at a plain, gray metal door. The small placard on it read:

Shipping/Receiving
Norm's Random Stuff

"It is a back door," Petros stated as he laid his hand over his scale, raised up his foot, and, with a powerful thrust, kicked the door open. They practically fell into the building as Petros slammed the door closed again but realized he had shattered the lock and latch. The door couldn't be secured.

They were in a short, dark hallway, and ahead they could see the empty interior of Norm's abandoned shop. To their left was another plain door marked "office." They opened the door and found two metal filing cabinets and an old desk. Without a word, Tonare grabbed one of the filing cabinets and began to drag it into the hallway and barricade the back door. "Get the other," he grunted as Procella and Petros responded and managed to manhandle the second piece of office furniture into place next to the first.

The only sounds in the store were lungs gasping for breath as they recovered from their flight. All four were using their sleeves to wipe the sweat from their foreheads as Petros finally caught his breath enough to talk. "Do you think we have evaded them?"

Procella swallowed hard and shook her head. "Uncertain."

There was another pause as they caught their breath. Calor snarled, "This did not go according to plan." The other three leveled a glare at her, and then, as if on cue, they all burst into laughter. It went on for several moments before Petros was able to speak again through his laughs. "It most certainly did not."

They composed themselves, and Tonare slumped down to the floor. "What are we doing to do, cousins?"

Petros replied, "I do not know. One would think that as creatures hundreds of years old, we would be able to formulate a solution. However, I am at a complete loss for ideas."

"We should look around this establishment," Procella suggested. "Perhaps Norm left behind some evidence as to where he has fled."

Tonare stood up, and they proceeded to spread themselves around the abandoned store. Calor and Tonare walked to the empty showroom, while Procella entered the office. Petros began to quietly open the drawers of the file cabinets barricading the back door. In a matter of minutes, Procella called out, "Petros, come here."

He quickly entered the office. "You found information?"

"No," she answered, "but I did find this item." She was seated at the old metal desk and had opened one of the large bottom drawers. In it, she has found a black nylon belt pack that seemed to be filled with items. Procella unzipped it and withdrew a pack of sidewalk chalk, a chalk eraser, a pair of swimming goggles, a ballpoint pen decorated with a pharmaceutical logo, and an Incredible Hulk wristwatch. She looked at Petros. "What do these items do? What significance do they possess?"

"I truly have no idea," he answered, shaking his head. Petros heard Calor call to him from the showroom, and he quickly left the office as Procella was picking up the goggles and examining them closely.

As he entered the main shopping area, he could see Calor and Tonare looking up toward the ceiling. Very concerned looks were on both of their faces as he asked, "What have you found?"

Calor gestured at the space on the wall just below the ceiling. Although Norm had cleared out the vast majority of his stock on the shelves, he had left behind several old posters and wall hangings, those presumably without value. Old wooden shields were also left hanging at the tops of the walls, each painted differently with its own unique "crest." One bore a black castle on a yellow field, and a second displayed a yellow lion chasing a deer on a blue field. But the third shield, the one with a red bat-like wing surrounded by a circle with a line through it, was the source of their concern.

"The Wyrmkil," Petros muttered. "Norm has betrayed us. His intention was never to help us."

Calor's face was filled with rage. Her hand was pressed against her scale as she sneered, "If I ever find that mage…" As she spoke, waves of heat issued forth from her mouth.

Tonare put his huge hand on her shoulder. "Calm yourself, cousin, or you will burn this building down around us." She reluctantly lowered her hand to her side, and the temperature around them quickly began to cool.

Procella entered the room, holding the belt pack, wearing the swim goggles, and looking quite ridiculous. She quickly looked at the shields and said, "Oh. Well, that answers some questions now, does it not?"

Petros replied, "And yet raises even more questions. For example, one would be, 'What in the name of the Great Scale are you wearing?'"

Her head spun around to them as she squinted to focus through the goggles. "Yes, it would seem these items are not just random bric-a-brack. They are enchanted."

Calor leveled a disbelieving stare at her. "Enchanted? That? You cannot be serious."

"Oh, I am completely serious," she replied. "And the glow around your body only proves my point."

"Glow?" Calor looked at her arms and chest. "I am not glowing. What folly is this?"

Procella removed the goggles and handed them to her Heat dragon cousin, but Tonare intercepted them and quickly put them on his own face. "Zounds!" he exclaimed. "We are all surrounded by a rather brilliant aura! There are several other faint points of light on many of these bare shelves but nothing as bright as the four of us." He took them off and handed them to an annoyed Calor. "What do they do?" he asked.

"I am not completely sure," she began, "but I surmise they reveal if something is enchanted or been put under a spell. The other items I found with it also glowed when I viewed them through the lenses."

Calor removed the goggles and handed them to Petros as she asked, "So why do the empty shelves have faint points of light?"

"My guess is that Norm had other items in the shop that may have had minor enchantments on them. This is most likely why he had the goggles to begin with, so he could identify items he acquired as being magical or not. I would guess he kept most, but the objects of no use to him were most likely sold."

Petros nodded in agreement. "And if those objects sat on the shelves, they probably left behind a faint residual charge. But you are saying the other items in the bag were magical as well?"

She nodded. "Yes, all of them."

He raked his fingers through his hair. "That is slightly concerning."

Procella continued nodding. "Yes, I have the same concern."

Tonare and Calor exchanged confused glances. "What? What is so concerning?" Tonare asked.

Petros drew in a worried breath. "These lenses, the writing implement, and especially the time keeper—all are fairly modern items, and, to this point, I did not think they could sustain an enchantment."

"I do not understand," Calor said.

Procella responded, "Back in our era, it was rumored among the magic-using community that a small faction of mages and wizards were experimenting with putting enchantments on machines, on technology. However, magic users from many races—humans, elves, dragonkind, and so on—did not believe that objects made up of multiple parts could be made to sustain magical charges. The interaction of the eldritch energies among so many different moving pieces could not be properly stabilized...or so they thought. Still, these technomancers continued to operate in secret, despite the greater magical community condemning such practices. Most of their experiments ended disastrously, but rumors floated about that, every so often, they were successful, and machines, both powerful and terrible, were wrought."

Petros continued, "The very fact that we have three modern, technological items that have a stable and functional enchantment means that the practice of technomancy has not only survived the centuries but has proven successful in this twenty-first century."

Calor looked unimpressed. "So Norm has made a magical pen. Feh, hardly an accomplishment by any mage's standards."

"Perhaps for just a pen," Petros stated, "but what if there are others, those much more skilled and knowledgeable in this treacherous art of technomancy? What if one of those flying machines, those helicopters, that you battled in the sky could be enchanted? Those machines were formidable on their own. Imagine someone magically enhancing a war machine such as that. An entirely new era of weaponry and warfare could begin."

"A new era of death and destruction as well," added Procella.

"Do you think that is what the Wyrmkil are doing?" Tonare asked, a look of concern on his face.

"Unknown," Procella replied. "It could be just Norm dabbling in the art, not knowing the ramifications. After all, he does not seem to operate within any sort of organized magical community. But, still, we cannot be certain."

They had been brooding over their discovery for several moments when Petros noticed a door leading to a small lavatory behind the store's counter. He walked into the room and flipped on the light. It was a room barely big enough for one, and it had not seen a mop, spray bottle of bleach, or toilet brush for quite some time. Petros, however, was only focused on the small mirror above the sink. His reflection blinked back at him and then took on a life of its own.

Jason said, "Oh, hey." He looked around. "Where are you?"

Petros answered soberly, "There is much to tell you."

He spent several minutes updating Jason and answering his questions before Jason finally concluded, "This is really bad."

"You have a talent for understatement," Petros replied.

Jason stammered, "You…you gotta get out of there. If they catch you—"

"'They' who, Little Knight? We have a foe here that we know nothing of, with motives we cannot determine, using means and methods we cannot even identify. I do not know whom to run from or in which direction to escape. They somehow knew of our plans to come here, and they orchestrated a scheme that affected the greater part of an entire city. How do we combat that? What are we even battling?"

"Petros, I don't know, okay? I have no idea what is going on. And I'm trapped in this mirror and can't do anything to help."

Before Petros could answer, he heard Calor shout, "You had best rejoin us, Petros; the situation has taken a turn for the worse!"

"Go!" Jason shouted as Petros switched off the light and joined the others. They looked into the back hallway toward the barricaded door and heard someone shouting from the other side, "Here! This door is dented. Looks like someone busted it in."

Calor sneered, "Finally! A foe to combat!"

Procella glared at her. "We are in no condition to combat the authorities of this city or the riders in black."

"I grow weary of running. We have our breath weapons; let me turn them to ash!"

"You will turn no one to ash, Calor," Petros countered. "We need to get back to Malta. It is our only logical choice."

The file cabinets holding the door shut began to move as the individuals on the other side began to force their way in. Tonare turned to the front door for escape, but his stomach sank as he saw four of the riders waiting on the sidewalk just outside. "It would appear we are trapped," he said as he pointed toward the new development.

Procella's gaze became steely. "No, we are not."

Calor countered, "You just said we are in no condition to fight."

Her hand pressed her scale against her chest as she responded, "That does not mean we cannot escape with a dramatic flair. Get behind me and cover your ears."

They followed her directions as Procella focused on her scale and felt a pressure mount in her chest. The back door began to push open against the cabinets as a black-gloved hand reached in to feel what was blocking their entrance. She lowered her head and shut her eyes, the power building inside her. The back door opened more as a black-clothed figure began to shove its way through the gap. Petros saw the development and nervously called, "Procellaaaaa…"

Procella's head snapped up, and her eyes opened. They glowed with the deep blue of the ocean, and her hand firmly pressed the scale into her skin. She raised her other hand in a gesture at the front of the store, opened her mouth, and said, "Be gone." The shockwave of her breath weapon exploded outward, blowing every shelf, display stand, and end cap toward the front of the raggedy store. The wave continued on as every inch of glass, wood, brick, and mortar that made up the façade of Norm's Random Stuff blew into the street, throwing the four black riders clearly across the road and half-burying them in debris. The other three ducked behind Procella and were left untouched despite the ferocity of her breath weapon.

She grabbed Calor and Petros by the arms, kicked Tonare hard in the leg, and said, "Come, we must flee!" Not wasting time, they ran into the street and quickly got their bearings as they searched for an escape route.

Petros spoke rapidly. "There is no time to argue; we must split up and confuse them. Procella just bought us several moments, and we must take advantage. We know what to do: rendezvous in Malta. Get there quickly and safely, understood?" They all nodded in agreement as he went on. "Tonare, you are with me. We will head west. Procella, take Calor and flee to the north. They are behind us and to the east, so these paths will lead us from them."

"Understood," Procella acknowledged. "And stay safe."

Petros smirked. "I have never understood anything more clearly. Now, run!"

With that, they ran in their separate directions, hoping to find a way out of the city.

Chapter 31

Calor and Procella sprinted northward up the abandoned 27th Street as they fled from the pursuing authorities and made for the boundary of the restricted zone. The riders Procella had blasted into the building across from Norm's shop were not showing any signs of recovery. However, those that were breaking through the back door of the store had made their way past the file cabinet barricade, out the devastated façade of the establishment, and were calling for reinforcements to begin their pursuit of the now-divided group of Draconauts.

They made it a few blocks before Calor began to huff, "This body is in no shape for this exertion. I cannot go much further."

Procella, in the more athletic body of Kinaari, replied, "They will be mounting their vehicles soon; we need to find cover, or we will be overtaken." Up ahead was a Kentucky Fried Chicken whose doors were closed and windows darkened due to the health scare. Procella pointed to the restaurant and said, "There…go around the back of the structure." They sprinted faster to get off of the street as quickly as they could and bolted behind the white and red building. A large, metal, windowless door provided a second entrance, and they shook the handle as soon as they were upon it.

Calor sneered, "It is locked."

Procella looked around, trying to find a way in. "Of course it is locked; it is a place of business. They do not wish miscreants to loot their wares."

Calor spat back, "How do you suggest we get in then? You are a Water Dragon; you are supposedly the smartest of us all. Tell me your plan!"

Procella glared at her. "Your sarcasm is unwelcome at the present moment, as is your temper. Now is the time for level thinking, not brashness."

"Neither of us have the strength of an Earth Dragon, so we cannot break the door down. Perhaps we can reason with it, correct?"

Procella threw her a sideways glare. "No, but we can reason an alternative to strength." She took a step back and placed her hand over her scale. As Procella closed her eyes, she began to concentrate on slowing her heart and focusing the strength she felt building in her chest. Slowly, she opened her eyes and gracefully knelt down in front of the locked handle. She moved her face to within six inches of the lock and, ever so gently, whispered an unintelligible word. A small, focused shockwave impacted the lock, and with a metallic pop, the mechanism broke free from the door and fell to the floor inside the KFC. Procella grasped the handle, thumbed the latch, and quietly opened the back door.

"See?" she finally said. "Reason and planning triumph again." With that, she entered the building.

Calor smoldered as she muttered under her breath, "Cursed Water Dragons…think they are so smart." She followed Procella and pushed the door closed behind her.

***

Petros and Tonare set the First Interstate Center, the tallest building in all of Montana, in their sights and ran as fast as they could toward it. Tonare easily outpaced Petros in Marcus's tall, muscular body and found himself having to frequently slow down to allow Petros to catch up. The third time he turned to see how Petros was faring, he saw a small group of police and black riders come around a corner and break out into a run after them.

"What do we do?" Tonare asked.

Petros huffed, "We try to flee."

"No," Tonare said defiantly. "They will overtake us, and we will be captured. I do not relish that possibility."

"Then what do we do?"

Tonare replied, "We fight back."

"Tonare, I—"

"Petros, I grow weary of running. If we show them we are a threat, perhaps they will stop pursuing us. We have access to our natural abilities; we need to show them that we are not to be trifled with."

To Tonare's surprise, Petros began to slow and came to a stop. He was breathing heavily but replied to his Air Dragon cousin, "You are right. I grow weary of being pursued as well." He half turned to see their pursuers. "Let them come, and let them know that the Draconauts fight back."

***

"It smells good in here."

Calor inhaled the scent of eleven herbs and spices as they tentatively walked through the darkened kitchen of the Kentucky Fried Chicken restaurant. For the most part, the kitchen and its stations were well cleaned, but a few boxes of frozen food had been left on the counters as the early arriving prep staff were forced to evacuate the establishment.

Procella nodded. "I do like the fried chicken. There is something to be said for some of the food these humans consume."

"It must be nutritious as well," Calor added, "based on the vast amounts of it that are eaten."

They quietly stole through the kitchen and then ducked low as they came around the counter to the dining area. The large number of windows threatened to betray their presence if they did not take precautions, so they stayed low to the tiled floor as they tried to observe their pursuers on the streets.

The activity was quickly increasing as police officers ran by and black-leather-clad riders were seen mounting their unusual vehicles. Police were chatting through their radios, but the black riders did not appear concerned with coordinating their efforts. Occasionally, a person wearing khakis and an AlansCo-emblazoned polo shirt stepped into view and appeared to inspect the feature-concealing helmets on the riders' heads. These inspectors went to each rider in view and performed the same checks before a slap on the top of the helmet sent the rider functioning independently again.

"What are they doing?" Calor asked.

Procella shook her head concernedly. "Unknown. These riders are an enigma."

Calor paused then looked to her cousin. "Where is that eyewear you found at Norm's?"

Procella had fastened the belt pack around her waist. She unzipped the pouch, removed the swim goggles, and handed them to Calor. Calor pulled them over her eyes and gazed out the window.

"This is alarming; the riders are glowing."

"What?" Procella replied with surprise in her voice. "The riders are magical?"

Calor shrugged. "Either that or the uniforms they wear are. It would also appear their vehicles are enchanted as well, based on the brilliant glow I see through these lenses." She pulled the goggles off with one hand and handed them to Procella, who seized them and quickly put them on. A few moments after she surveyed the streets outside, she removed them and sat cross-legged on the floor.

"This is growing more and more sinister. A large, modern organization that is supposedly helping with a local crisis dispatches magically enhanced personnel and equipment to intervene with the problem. In addition, they wear the logo of a secret society devoted to destroying dragons."

Calor interrupted, "And they have attacked us at Jason's home."

There was a long pause before Procella spoke again. "Secret societies, modern corporations, technomancy…how can this all be related?"

Calor shook her head. "I cannot fathom how. You are the smart one, remember?" Procella smirked as Calor went on. "We need to get out of this city. I fear that if the riders somehow knew we were coming here then this is all a giant ruse designed to capture us."

Procella processed Calor's last thought. "That…that is a staggering thought."

Calor nodded. "We need to get out of here."

***

The two dragon/boys stood defiantly as they were approached by a group of Billings police officers and riders in black leather. Petros stood several steps behind Tonare, and they both had their hands placed firmly over their dragon scales. Several officers had their hands resting on the handles of their pistols, hesitant to draw them, but each of the riders had their tasers trained on the Draconauts.

An officer spoke, trying to sound calm. "All right, you two, I don't know why you are here or what you did to that store back there, but I want you to put your hands on your heads and kneel down. I don't want anyone to get hurt."

Neither Petros nor Tonare responded, but Tonare could be seen expanding his chest as if he were inhaling deeply. The officer said, "Come on, boys. Let's just work together. No need for this to get violent."

Tonare opened his mouth, and Petros ducked down and covered his ears as tightly as he could. Tonare mouthed the word "no," but what issued from his mouth was an ear-splitting peal of thunder. Windows on the building to either side of them shattered at the deafening sound, and the officers all went to their knees, their hands covering their ears as they howled in pain. The black riders were not affected as the officers were, but they still staggered back at the onslaught of sound.

Petros quickly jumped in front of Tonare as veins of light could be seen flowing from the ground and into his legs. The riders triggered their tasers, but Tonare's breath weapon had affected several of them as the charged probes were launched in several directions. Some still stayed true with their aim, but Petros had prepared for that contingency as well. The small, metallic barbs impacted him, but his skin had been hardened to the strength of stone, causing the electrical weapons to bounce off in random directions. Petros and Tonare both charged the disoriented riders, and Tonare threw all of his weight into one, hitting it with a sickening crunch. His momentum carried them both to the ground, but he continued to summon his draconic power through his scale. Being the most agile of the dragon species, Tonare somersaulted in the air and flipped himself back to his feet. Without breaking stride, he barreled into a second rider and took that one down as well.

Meanwhile, Petros channeled his strength and ran to the rider closest to him, delivering a savage uppercut to the figure's head. He heard the plastic of the helmet crack with the impact, and the rider flew fifteen feet backward from the force of the punch. Petros grabbed the next by the collar of his jacket and tossed him like a baseball across the street and into a parked car, shattering the window of the vehicle and leaving a large dent in the rear door.

All of the riders were down, and the police officers were still trying to get their bearings. Petros and Tonare looked at each other, smiled, and Petros asked, "Now we run?"

Tonare nodded, and they began sprinting to the west again.

***

Procella and Calor crouched low as they slowly opened the back door to the restaurant again and peered through the crack until they were confident they were not being observed. They quickly exited the building and began to work their way north, this time trying to squeeze behind the rows of buildings on 27th Street in order to stay out of sight instead of directly following the wide street as they had previously. Unfortunately, the going was slow as they dodged between cars in parking lots, crossed the avenues perpendicular to 27th Street, and even made their way through residential yards.

After fighting their way through a row of hedges, Calor growled, "It will be dark before we reach the border of the restricted zone. We should have stayed on the main street."

"And risk being apprehended?" Procella countered. "Taking our time will prove much more beneficial."

They both paused and heard a faint peal of thunder, but as they looked up, the partly sunny skies betrayed that the sound was not weather-related. "Tonare," Calor commented.

Procella nodded. "It is not a good omen that he has been forced to use his breath weapon. We can only hope that they have not been caught."

Trying to shut the thought from her mind, she pushed Procella forward. "Come, let us continue."

They eventually crossed 9th Avenue and found themselves in front of the Dehler Park baseball stadium, home of the Billings Mustangs. They snuck along the perimeter of the building until they could see 27th Street again and spotted the barricades at the edge of the restricted zone. It was only two blocks past the stadium, and they felt a glimmer of hope that they were almost in the clear.

Calor, the more saavy and strategic of the two, had taken the lead and turned to her cousin. "I say we sprint for the border. We just keep on running until we are past. The constables will not realize we are coming until we are too close to stop, and they will not train their weapons upon us."

Procella was looking past her, back down 27th Street, as she said, "A sound plan...except for that." She pointed down the street and saw an officer with two riders. They had clearly spotted the girls, and the officer was speaking into his radio. "He is summoning reinforcements."

Calor surveyed their surroundings, looking for options. "Into the coliseum behind us; we need shelter and time to think."

The area in front of Dehler Park consisted of nine squares of red brick paving leading up to the main gates. It was very open and welcoming, which was the exact opposite of what Calor and Procella were seeking. They arrived at the locked gates, and after Calor gave them a rattle, she placed her hand over her scale and began to summon her breath weapon. Procella looked behind them and saw that several more officers had gathered, as well as at least fifteen riders, many of whom were on their black two- or three-wheeled vehicles. "Hurry, cousin," she prompted as Calor trained her breath weapon on one section of the gate. The metal quickly began to glow red then yellow, and pieces began to break away and fall to the pavement. "Bring the whole thing down; this is no time for subtlety." Calor nodded and exhaled harder. Entire sections of the gate gave way, and the air around it shimmered with the extreme heat. Soon, an opening was wide enough for a person to pass through, and the Draconauts bounded past the glowing metal and sprinted into the stadium.

"Just go straight across!" Procella shouted. "There must be an opening on the other side." They broke into a full run and darted across the expanse of the baseball field, but as they reached second base, an amplified voice shouted, "Halt!"

They froze in their tracks when the voice came again. "Turn around slowly!" They obeyed and saw seven police officers and twenty riders, six on motorcycles and five on three-wheeled cruisers. They slowly closed the distance between themselves and the girls as the officer holding the bullhorn spoke again. "I don't know what you did back there, but you are obviously armed. Put your hands on your heads and lie down on the ground!"

Calor muttered, "Do what you must."

Procella calmly replied, "Do what he said. It will protect you."

Calor nodded and followed the officer's directions. "You, too, glamour girl!" he shouted at Procella. As she slowly began to raise her hands above her head, she shut her eyes and focused on her chest. She could feel the scale resting against her skin and concentrated on the feeling. *Why must we press the scale against us?* she thought to herself as she began to feel the magic flow from the scale into her body. The pressure of her breath weapon began to build inside her as she smiled with the realization of what she had discovered. Sweat began to collect on her brow as the magical energies built deeper and stronger. She felt the pain of the mounting power but reveled at the thought of what she was about to do.

"On the ground...now!" shouted the officer.

Her eyes opened. They were glowing a brilliant deep blue. The officer froze in his tracks at the sight.

Procella smirked, opened her mouth, and spoke.

"No."

All of the energy of her breath weapon was released at the sound of the word. The turf on the field itself cracked and blew forward under the force of the pressure wave. The officers and riders had nowhere to run as the invisible force slammed into them and cast them away as easily as the wind blows the dust from the sidewalk. Even the bulkier vehicles could not stand against the onslaught as they, too, were thrown into the bleachers, and their polymer chasses dented and buckled under the pressure.

The shockwave dissipated, and the officers were left on the ground, groaning from the assault. The black riders were still as Procella smiled at her handiwork. But then, one by one, the magical riders began to stir and try to stand. Her eyes widened with surprise as she bent down, grabbed Calor, and shouted, "We must flee!"

***

Petros and Tonare sprinted three more blocks before they could see reinforcements arriving at the scene they left behind. Vehicles, as well as additional personnel, were gathering at the scene of the fight and preparing to give chase. A look of concern came over Petros's face.

"They will overtake us if I continue on with you. You will make the barrier if you run on your own."

Tonare whipped his head around to Petros. "There is not any option of leaving you behind. We flee together; we will fight our way through if we have to."

"They will overwhelm us with numbers," Petros responded. They found themselves next to the First Interstate Center, and Petros examined the tall building. "I will find adequate shelter in that building. I can easily force my way in and bide my time until they move on with their pursuit."

Tonare shook his head emphatically, almost desperately. "No. Petros, we need to stay together. I will not abandon you!"

"Cousin, you must. Get past the barricade and rendezvous with the others. I can do this; please do not make an issue of this."

The struggle was evident on Tonare's face, but he finally relented. He pointed his large finger at Petros. "You do everything you must to stay hidden. I will be exceedingly cross with you if you are captured and tortured."

Petros smiled. "If I am captured and tortured, I will be the first to admit that you were correct. Agreed?"

Tonare smiled back and then turned for the barricade and began running. Petros quickly sized up the tall building before him and then ran to the plaza surrounding the structure.

Chapter 32

Tonare sprinted for all he was worth toward the edge of the
barricade. Ahead, he saw two police officers, their backs to him,
standing shoulder to shoulder and listening to the broadcast
coming over the radio. Tonare's mind went to the worst; the
officers were receiving a warning about the confrontations with
Petros and himself, and, as soon as they turned around, they would
see him. He knew he needed to move faster but was running as fast
as his human legs would carry him. He entertained the thought of
converting to his dragon form but realized that would probably be
the worst thing he could do. Then a second thought entered his
head.

Air Dragons are the most agile of the dragons and also the
fastest. I wonder…

He pressed his scale against his chest and felt a surge of
strength in his legs. He found himself able to run harder and faster,
and the world around him actually seemed to slow as his speed
increased. Soon, he was running double and then triple the speed
of a typical human, and the distance between him and the police
officers was rapidly shrinking. He was almost upon them as they
finally turned, but Tonare was moving too fast for them to react.
He ran between them and caught each with one of his shoulders.
The high-speed impact did not hurt them but sent them spinning
out of control and slamming into their respective cars, parked to
either side. Without looking back, Tonare ran for several more
blocks past the barricades before he realized he was safe and
finally slowed down.

***

Procella had Calor by the arm as she pulled her to her feet
and ran across the infield into one of the dugouts at the edge of the
baseline. Inside the bullpen was a door leading to the team locker
room, and, after making short work of the lock, the two Draconauts
were inside looking for an escape route. The walls of the room

were lined with wooden partitions labeled with the names and jersey numbers of the Billings Mustangs, and their uniforms and various other pieces of baseball equipment were neatly stored on the shelves and wall pegs in each of the dressing areas. The only detail that concerned the two girls was the glowing letters of the sign at the opposite end of the large room spelling "exit."

They quickly covered the distance to the door, but before they could push through, muffled voices were heard on the other side: "Four of you stay here. It's an emergency exit, but they could try to get out this way." They turned back toward the door to the dugout but could hear commotion on the other side.

"We are trapped," Procella said.

Calor pointed to a small office to the side of the locker room. "There," she signaled as they ran to the door. To their good fortune, it was unlocked, and they quickly ducked inside, shut the blinds to the windows looking out on the large team room, locked the door, and sat as quietly as they could.

The locker room quickly filled with officers and riders as they searched for Procella and Calor. They started as they heard the doorknob to the little office rattle and heard a voice say, "This is locked, but they could be in there. Go find a key."

Calor and Procella exchanged nervous glances. Calor crawled over to the door, placed her hand on her scale, and, through puckered lips, exhaled a thin stream of super heated air. The lock inside the doorknob began to glow, and the entire mechanism fused into one solid piece of metal. She returned to Procella's side. "That should buy us some time when they locate the key."

Procella whispered back, "Yes, but now we are trapped in here."

Calor leaned her head against the wall. "One crisis at a time, cousin, one crisis at a time."

***

The First Interstate Center, the tallest building in Montana, also had a smaller, two-story annex attached to the larger tower of the bank. The façade of this smaller office structure was predominately glass, and much of the interior could be seen from the street. As Petros quickly ran around this portion of the building, he knew none of those rooms would be a viable hiding place for any length of time. He needed to find a door, force his way inside, and then locate a suitable place where he could not be found.

Petros finally came across a double door that was, inevitably, locked and trained his breath weapon on the glass. He turned the entire pane to rock and, with a kick enhanced by his dragon strength, destroyed the sheet of stone and granted himself access to the tower. He found himself in a large lobby adorned with a massive reception desk that bore the name and logo of the bank in shining gold letters. The lobby was deserted, as was every other building in the restricted zone, and Petros vaulted himself over the large desk and headed deeper into the hallways of the opulent banking center.

The interior halls were surprisingly dark to Petros, despite the sunny weather outside and the preponderance of windows on the outer walls of the building. With all of the lights turned out, the sunlight spilling through the interior windows of the various offices was not sufficient to maneuver through the halls. Petros was missing the superior vision of his dragon eyes. But it was only a few minutes before he made out an elevator sign leading to the upper floors of the tower. His goal was to find an abandoned closet or forgotten supply room and simply hide there until they believed he had eluded them and was on the run again.

He thought the plan was a good one until he turned the corner to the elevators and beams of light hit his eyes. He froze in his tracks and held his hands out in front of him, trying to shield his face from the source of the light. A voice stated, "Okay, stop where you are, kid. We saw you coming in here, so we have your way back out blocked. Just put your hands up and lie down on the floor. I've got eight officers and ten of these AlansCo folks here, so you're not going anywhere. Give yourself a break and do what I say."

For a brief moment, Petros actually considered complying. The local constabulary would have no idea of what he really was and wouldn't let the black riders take him. Being locked in a holding cell might be the safest place for him. But he knew he couldn't do that to Jason or his father; Jason was far too young to have a reputation with the law. Out of the corner of his eye, he saw a door labeled "stairs" next to him. At first, he feigned a motion to get down on the floor as the officer had suggested but quickly bolted through the door and turned his breath weapon on the lock as soon as he had pushed it closed, turning the locking mechanisms into one solid piece of rock. The stairwell wound up the multiple floors that made up the First Interstate Center but also led down several stories into the sub-basements of the building foundation. Looking down, he saw beams from flashlights waving unsteadily below; somehow, his pursuers had found a lower entrance and were climbing the stairs to him. Hearing the police pounding on the other side of the door he'd just come through, he knew it wouldn't be long before they shattered the stone of the petrified lock.

"Very well, up it is," he muttered to himself, and he began a sprint up the stairs and into the tower.

***

Calor looked to Procella. "I do not know how we are going to escape."

They could hear the police rattling the lock on the other side of the door. Procella said, "It is hard to believe our adventure will end here."

"You sound as if you are surrendering."

"I do not see any other option. We are trapped in a room to which the authorities will gain access sooner or later. In these close quarters, our breath weapons will be lethal to the humans, and I do not think that is a line we should cross."

Calor nodded. "Agreed, but with great reluctance. I do not wish to be captured."

"You have no argument from me on that point." They could hear the one officer scolding the other at being unable to unlock the door and demanding he give the other the key. As Procella smiled at the confusion they had created, a thought came to her. She began to fumble at the belt pack as she said, "Do you remember how the mage came to us in the forest when he cast the spell?"

Calor shrugged. "Yes, some form of magic portal."

She asked, "What color was the light?"

Calor thought for a moment. "It was red; it looked like he just drew it in thin…" Her voice trailed off as a look of comprehension spread over her. "Find the drawing implements, quickly!"

Procella unzipped the pack and withdrew the box of sidewalk chalk. She opened the tuck lid and found three large sticks, one blue, one green, and one red. She held the swimming goggles over her eyes and said, "Yes, they are magical."

"How do we work them?" Calor asked.

Procella stood up, turned to the wall farthest from the door, and drew the outline of a doorway on the wall with the red chalk. The red line clung to the wall but did nothing.

Calor slumped. "Well, we can add defacing property to our list of crimes."

"I was hopeful that would work."

Calor agreed. "Perhaps we are unable to use the magic. Perhaps only the mage could."

Procella shook her head. "I do not see him as being that thorough."

"Where were we going to go, had you been able to create a portal?"

"I did not even think of that; I was just looking to escape."

Calor leveled a glare at her. "How did you expect that to work if you had no destination in mind?"

Procella paused for a moment and stared at the chalk, wondering if it was that simple. "Where would we go?"

"The safest place," Calor thought. "The barn…Jason's barn."

Despite the pounding on the office door and the shouting on the other side, Procella closed her eyes and focused on the chalk in her hand. She conjured a vivid image of the Hewes barn in her mind, remembering the creaky wooden floor, the scent of the hay bales, the way the dust tickled the inside of her nose and brought her to the verge of a sneeze. Calor watched her cousin as a warm, crimson light began to emanate from the chalk; Procella opened her eyes and took in the same sight. She cautiously turned back to the wall and retraced the red line she had drawn moments ago. This time, the line glowed as she slowly redrew the doorway on the wall. When she had finished, the wall inside the glowing lines began to ripple like a pond on a breezy day. The effect grew more intense until another image began to replace that of the wavering wall: the inside of the Hewes family barn. Within seconds, a clear image of the old structure could be seen through the magic portal, and the smells of baled hay and decades-old wood wafted out to their noses.

The two cautiously stepped to the edge of the portal. Procella motioned to Calor. "After you." The Draconaut swallowed hard and then stepped through the magic doorway and right into the Hewes barn. She turned to Procella and said, "It is safe." Procella followed her through, and, for several moments, they simply stood shoulder to shoulder in the Hewes barn.

"I had visions of it being more dramatic than that," Calor commented.

Procella smiled, but they both whirled around to see the office door caving in as two black riders repeatedly rammed their shoulders into it.

Calor said, "I would assume that as long as the portal is open, they could follow us through."

Procella started rummaging through the belt pack again. "There was some other item in here that he used to close the portal."

Calor watched the two riders, who were almost completely into the office. Her voice sounded more strained. "I suggest you hurry because they are almost upon us."

Procella finally retrieved the chalk eraser as one rider finally stepped into the office and began to reach for them through the doorway. Procella dove forward and swept the eraser in a wide arc along the right side of the glowing rectangle. There was a small cloud of red dust, and the gateway ceased to exist. The only remaining evidence was the severed hand of the rider that reached for them now lying on the barn floor. It had been removed halfway up the forearm, but to the surprise of the two girls, there was no blood or any other grisly material coming from the displaced limb. Instead, they watched the glove slowly collapse as an ashen gray dust poured out of the opening. Eventually, the ash itself began to dissolve and disappear into the very air, leaving only a flat, empty, black leather glove on the wooden floor.

Calor picked up the glove and examined it carefully as she held it between her thumb and index finger. She then looked around the barn and walked to the doors. Procella followed, and they carefully pushed the doors open, taking in the sight of the Hewes homestead in northeast Montana. Calor turned to Procella. "Well, that was not as bad as I thought it would be."

***

Petros's legs screamed for relief after seven flights of stairs, but he knew he had to push through the pain and continue his ascent. The pursuing officers had stopped at the ground floor to try to open the door for the other officers and black riders, but they directed them to keep up the pursuit. Petros tried to not let his speed falter, but he knew he was getting tired and had to find a way to further distract his pursuers.

At the tenth floor, he summoned his dragon strength through his scale and kicked in the door leading back into the offices of the tower but then turned and continued his ascent up the stairs. He slowed his speed and yanked off Jason's Chuck Taylor shoes so he could climb more silently. He was at the fourteenth floor when he could tell the group behind him had stopped at the tenth floor to see if Petros had re-entered the building. When he was sure his ruse had worked, Petros began climbing as quickly as

he could once again to further extend his lead but only made it two
more floors when he heard shouting below, telling him the decoy
had not worked, and the police had continued their pursuit.

He continued up the stairway, his legs feeling as if more
and more weights were being tied to them with every step he took.
Petros's stomach sank as he realized the error of his plan; any floor
he chose to hide in would inevitably be a trap. The police and
black riders were far too numerous for him to evade, and they were
far too clever to fall for any other attempts at subterfuge. His
options faded from few to none as he reached to door leading to
the roof. It was locked, but he quickly bypassed the obstacle with a
blow from his magically enhanced strength. He stepped out onto
the windy surface of the tower's roof and pushed the door shut
behind him. He leaned against it and looked for a place to hide.
Multiple air-conditioning units were interspersed over the surface,
and he darted to one and crouched behind it as he tried to slow his
breathing. He chided himself; his plan was foolish, and now his
options were exhausted.

He thought furiously as the door burst open and a veritable
multitude of police and black-clad Wyrmkil operatives slowly
spread out onto the gravel-covered roof. The police rested their
hands on the handles of their holstered weapons, but the riders
freely carried their tasers in the open, searching for their target.
One last option, one desperate option, flashed into Petros's mind. It
would only work if he stayed out of range of the tasers.

He shouted, "I am here, and I am unarmed!"

His pursuers all froze. An officer shouted, "Then show
yourself and keep your hands in the air!"

Petros's legs screamed at him as he slowly pushed himself
back to his feet. "I have nothing to harm you with," he stated with
his hands high above his head. He saw the riders fanning out as
they sought to surround him. "Tell them to stop," he shouted,
"or…or I will leap to my death!"

The officer's eyes went wide as he held up a hand signaling
everyone to stop their advance. "Kid, look, you've been a real pain
in a lot of people's butts today, but I don't want this to end with

you turning into street pizza. Let's just all dial it down a few notches and talk this out."

Not knowing what "street pizza" or "dialing a few notches" meant, Petros responded, "We need to allow reason to prevail; I do not wish to jump."

The officer looked perplexed but went on. "Come on out from behind there, and we'll go back downstairs, all right?"

Petros shook his head and took a step toward the edge of the roof. "No. I wish to go free. You must guarantee me safe passage out of the city."

"That's not gonna happen, kid. We have to take you in custody and call your parents. You caused a lot of people a lot of trouble, not to mention the damage you and your friends did to several buildings around the city. For Pete's sake, kid, you assaulted police officers; that's a serious crime."

His stomach sank. It never crossed his mind before, but he realized the police were innocent in all of this. "I...I am truly sorry. Is anyone seriously damaged?"

The officer looked confused. "No. Your concern is noted but way too late to do any good. You have to come with us."

Petros quickly realized this had all gone too far. He and the others had acted far too recklessly. Property damage, innocents injured...none of this was intended. He knew there was only one way for this to end.

He took two more steps backward. The officer saw and shouted, "Kid! No...it'll all work out. Come with us!"

"I am truly sorry," Petros responded and summoned every last ounce of strength remaining in his legs. He sprinted toward the edge of the roof and, with one final push, hurled himself over the edge.

Chapter 33

Captain Kevin Weyman of the Billings Police Department stood impatiently inside the barricade of the restricted area of the city. Officers swarmed around him as they compared city maps and communicated vital information about the unprecedented situation that engulfed such a large portion of their city. Weyman paced back and forth, his face red and temper fuming as he waited. Finally, an officer carrying a laptop approached him and set it down on the hood of one of the city cruisers.

"I finally have him. He insisted on video chat," the flustered officer said.

Weyman swore under his breath then stepped in front of the laptop. Tate Reigles's image filled the screen as Weyman shouted, "What have you gotten us into here, Reigles? We said we'd help you with your operation; you said it would be no more than an hour disruption! Now I've got the façades of entire buildings exploding, teenagers throwing our people around like they're softballs, and kids just disappearing into thin air!"

Reigles's face showed no emotion. "Yes, well, these events were completely unforeseen. But not to worry; everything is under control."

Weyman could no longer contain himself. "Under control? This is like something right out of a comic book, Reigles! These kids look like they have...I don't know, super powers, for Pete's sake! One of 'em just said one word, *one word*, and threw a dozen of our men and their vehicles around like they were nothing! And now I have over two dozen men chasing some skinny punk up the stairwell of the First Interstate Center! What is going on here?"

Tate Reigles's face finally showed concern. "Yes, well, no one had predicted any of this."

Weyman was about to chew him out some more when another officer approached. "Sir, I—"

Weymen whirled to the officer. "What is it?"

The officer swallowed hard. "The youth...he just jumped off the roof."

***

For a brief moment, Petros was flying again, and he basked in the feeling. There was nothing between him and the earth below; the wind blew in his face, and the sound of the wind rushed in his ears. He remembered, even for a fraction of a second, what it was like to be a dragon; it had been a very long time since he had felt that way.

He closed his eyes, and his hand went to the scale around his neck. Petros gripped it tightly as he focused his will into the object. Brilliant white light engulfed his body and grew in size until it faded again, and the form of a mighty stone dragon was in its place. Jason's eyes were closed as he began to talk. "Okay, what have you gotten us into nowwOOOOOAHHAAA!" He opened his eyes and saw he was in midair, and the ground was quickly rushing toward him. "OHMANOHMANOHMANOHMAN!" he bellowed as his wings opened on instinct, and he began flapping madly. His body continued to plummet to the pavement below as he flapped for all he was worth. Panic turned to fear as he wondered if even a dragon would die from a fall at this height. But in his alarm, some instinct he never knew he had began to manifest. His wings began to work together, coordinated, in rhythm. To his surprise, they extended simultaneously and caught the air. His body righted, and his fall slowed and finally stopped as Jason began to ride the winds and actually soar away from the tower. A wide smile came over his face when he realized what was happening. He beat his wings once then a second time. His speed increased; he controlled the direction of his flight. Tears began to flow from his dragon eyes as he shouted, "I...I'm flying. Lookit me...I'm flying!"

Jason quickly realized he was over the downtown area of Billings, and although he didn't know why, he knew he was exposed and had to get out of town. He banked hard and began to head for the Rims and hopefully get on the correct vector back to Malta. He said to himself, "Jeez, Petros, not exactly the best time to give me a do-or-die lesson in flying." He shook his head. "Man, even as a dragon I still talk to myself. At least I'm not walking in circles. Hey, I'm not walking at all; I'm flying!"

An odd sound behind him brought his head around as he saw over a dozen small black shapes rising from the city and taking flight behind him. Some were the black motorcycles of the Wyrmkil riders, their wheels split in two along their circumference and splayed out as they sped through the skies. The three-wheeled vehicles had taken to the air as well, the front wheels having rotated to face downward and the third, rear wheel now facing backward. Finally, the treaded ATVs soared through the skies with their front wheels and rear treads tucked underneath the machines' frames. Helmeted, black-clad riders piloted each of the flying devices and were in hot pursuit of the dragon.

"What the…" Jason said aloud as he began to beat his wings harder, accelerating and putting more space between him and the mysterious vehicles. But the motorcycles proved to be the quickest of the three as they darted through the air and rapidly came alongside Jason as he tried to flee. The riders pointed much larger versions of their tasers at Jason and pulled the trigger, launching a small black cartridge that somehow stuck to his armored hide. A massive current was released into his body by the cartridges, but, to Jason, they felt like a minor skin irritation. As he tried to shake the devices off of his body, each rider pointed an automatic weapon at him and unleashed a hail of armor-piercing rounds. The bullets bounced off of his scales, but he grimaced in pain as they impacted the membranes of his wings and passed straight through the more fragile flesh.

"Ooooh, no, you don't," he growled as he banked to one side and, on the beat of his wing, battered three of the riders with the huge appendage. Two were thrown off of the vehicles and fell to the earth below, and one spun out of control and fell far behind. With two powerful flaps, he pulled ahead of the two riders on his other side and batted them out of the sky with a brutal swipe of his tail.

Jason smirked and muttered to himself, "It's kinda cool being a dragon." But the smile left his face when he felt a blistering pain above his left flank. He banked hard to the right as he saw a burst of green energy lance by under his wing. He turned his head to see the three-wheeled vehicles spitting the emerald bursts of power from their headlight area. His eyes went wide at the unusual attacks, and he began to zigzag his flight pattern in attempts to dodge this new threat. Jason was able to avoid many of the green bursts, but several still impacted his armored hide, each sending a pain-filled wave through his entire form.

Jason tried to think of what to do and quickly formulated a strategy. All at once, he turned his wings sideways and brought his body to a vertical position. His wings caught the air and slowed him instantly, catching his pursuers off guard and causing them to rocket by him. As they passed, Jason deftly grabbed one of them in each of his front claws and violently cast them to either side. He was surprised that he was actually able to accomplish such a feat but theorized that his dragon reflexes must be much better than those of his human body. He poured on the speed again and caught up to the rest of the riders. He balled up one claw into a fist and shattered one vehicle with a brutal punch. Another went careening out of control with a tail swipe, while the last he actually caught in his jaws and bit cleanly in half. He watched the rider and the front half of the three-wheeler plummet to the ground as he spat the second half after it.

He was reveling in his handiwork when a brutal force slammed into the side of his head and sent him spinning out of control. He tumbled head over tail and fell toward the ground. He saw the last of the Rimrocks pass below as he tumbled wildly and finally slammed into the Montana countryside. As he flipped head over tail, some dragon instinct took over, and he pushed forward with his forelegs, down with his wings, and immediately righted himself. Jason dug his talons into the earth as he brought himself skidding to a stop.

He marveled at his agility as he said, "Cool" and then quickly turned his attention to the rest of the riders chasing him. Several of the four-wheeled vehicles barreled down at him as one released a burst of red energy, which struck him cleanly in the chest and knocked him off balance with its pure force. "Great," Jason muttered as two more of the crimson energy spheres lanced his way. He knew the power they carried as he deftly dodged the attacks and watched as the vehicles pulled back up and began to come around for another run.

Anger began to well up in Jason's chest; he was getting tired of this fight. The vehicles completed their final arc before they began another attack, and Jason sneered, "Not this time!" Some unknown part of his mind told him to dig his claws into the earth and, with his very essence, reach down to the core of the planet for strength. Bright veins of light flowed up his legs, across his chest, and into his wings, where they made the membranes appear to glow. A look of conviction washed over his face as he felt the power permeate his body. He turned his attention back to the black riders as they unleashed their powered weapons at him again. One of the energy bursts hit the ground next to him, leaving a small crater, but a second took a trajectory toward Jason's chest. He swept one of his wings at the red force and batted it into the fields around him. Another was about to hit his head, but he swatted it with his other wing and sent it back toward one of the flying vehicles. The energy slammed into the machine, shattering it and sending the rider flailing through the Montana sky.

Jason felt invincible. The power of the earth cascaded through his body, and it seemed as if nothing could harm him. Two more Wyrmkil vehicles streaked toward him, and, with a mighty roar, Jason unleashed a torrent of glowing orange cubes. His breath weapon fully engulfed the two targets, and their momentum carried them past Jason and slammed them into the ground, having been transformed into solid stone. As he sought out his last targets, his vision began to blur, and a buzzing washed into the back of his skull. His concentration rapidly broke, and the light flowed back from his body and into the soil in which his claws were tightly clenched. The strength left his body, and he felt his legs quiver from the sudden weakness that replaced it. He began to panic at the feeling and then remembered what had happed to Petros those many weeks ago when he did the same thing: a depleted, weakened dragon that could barely fly. Three more flying riders remained, and the combined red bursts from their vehicles sent Jason sprawling. He was down, and he didn't know if he had the strength to get back up.

Jason craned his neck around and saw the riders landing. Their wheels and treads slid back out from under the bodies of the ATVs and took the correct positions at the sides as they touched down in the field. He could see the three black riders dismount and draw large guns from the backs of their mechanical mounts, each gun fitted with a very wicked-looking blade under the barrel. He feared this was the end; he didn't know how much more his dragon body could take. He tried to muster the strength for a burst of his breath weapon but only ended up coughing random sparks of dull orange. The riders took a position on his left flank and aimed their weapons at his head. He lowered his neck to the ground, closed his eyes, and waited for the end. Jason saw a large shadow pass over him, a portent of his impending doom.

To his surprise, he heard a small thud, as if something landed nearby. He opened one eye and saw a fourth figure standing behind the three Wyrmkil riders. It was shorter then them, clad in blue and gray padded armor with lightning bolt accents across the chest. The figure wore a motorcycle helmet adorned with a yellow dragon's head, and the visor completely obscured its face. In the figure's right hand was a double-bladed weapon taller than the armored figure itself, and it spun the blades deftly over its head and cut one of the riders down with a single swipe. The remaining two black figures turned to face this new arrival, but it crouched and spun on one foot, kicking out with the other and sweeping the legs of a second rider out from under it. The black figure fell clumsily to the grass as Nymbus's agile rider cartwheeled back to its feet and swept its weapon up, cutting off the barrel of the third rider's weapon. The member of the Order of the Scale twirled its dual-bladed spear above its head again and, with a swift cut, removed the third rider's head from its shoulders. Gray ash cascaded from the wounds of the fallen Wyrmkil as both of the fallen riders' leather uniforms collapsed into emptiness.

The order warrior wasted no time in turning its attention to the second rider as it began to lumber back to its feet. An upsweeping cut took the black rider's legs out from under it, and a final downward stab pinned the figure to the ground; gray ash poured out and blew away on the breeze. The warrior paused for a moment to survey its surroundings and, confirming it was safe, turned to Jason. "That was a foolish thing to do; tap the power of the earth when you have multiple targets."

Jason was trying not to be dumbfounded at the arrival of the warrior and spoke as dragon-like as he could. "I…felt I had no other option."

The figure yanked its dual spear out of the ground. "You don't need to pretend with me. I know you're a kid inside there. I've spoken to Petros before."

Jason couldn't hide his surprise. "I…how?"

"It's my job to know these things. Get up slowly; that power channeling thing you do is potent as all get-out, but it comes with a cost. You can't summon up that much raw energy without weakening yourself afterward. Even a dragon's body can't handle that kind of power for long."

Jason nodded. "I wish he would have told me that."

"He who?"

"Petros. I watched him use it when he fought…" His voice trailed off.

"When he fought Nymbus and me. You can say it; I was there."

Jason smiled. "How did you know to be here, in Billings, today? I mean no one contacted you."

"Like I said before, it's my job to know these things."

"That's really getting annoying," Jason grumbled.

"I know," the figure answered. "But you're tough; you can take it."

Jason inhaled deeply and pushed himself to his feet. "You say that as if you know me."

"Sounds that way, doesn't it?" it replied.

He shook his head. "Look, I get the whole motorcycle-helmet, mysterious-figure thing. But it isn't exactly fair that you know all about me, and I know nothing about you."

The warrior was lifting one of the weapons of the fallen Wyrmkil to examine it. "Well, get used to disappointment."

Jason furrowed his eye ridges. "Yeah, yeah, yeah, I saw *The Princess Bride* too. You can kick butt, and you watch cool movies. Way to make a guy feel inadequate."

The figure whirled to face him. "Says the teenager in the body of a mythological creature."

Jason inhaled, preparing to give a sharp retort, but instead acknowledged, "Touché."

He watched the armored figure walk over to the three ATVs parked on the field. It examined them closely before gesturing to Jason. "Come check this out."

Jason wearily stepped over to the vehicles and asked, "What am I looking at?"

"They are linked to their riders, probably more of this technomancy we have been suspecting. The drones turn to ash, and now look at their rides." She pointed to the engine of one ATV. Jason could see that spots of rust had formed and grew at a visible rate. Similar corrosions were appearing all over the machine and spreading rapidly. "They will be nothing but piles of rust in minutes."

"What do you mean by 'drones'?" Jason asked.

Without looking away from the decaying vehicles, the warrior responded, "The riders...they aren't human. Some sort of automaton. They walk like humans, move like humans, and have some human weaknesses, but there is nothing alive about them. That's why I had no problem slicing them into puppy chow back there."

"How do you know all of this?" he asked, throwing up his forelegs in frustration. "And don't tell me it's your 'job'!"

The figure shrugged its armored shoulders. "Then I don't have an answer for you. As part of the Order of the Scale, I have to know as much as it takes to protect dragonkind. The order made a pact centuries ago with the dragons, and the more I know, the better I can do my part to fulfill the oath."

A shadow crossed over both of them again as Nymbus swooped down out of the clouds and landed deftly next to his rider. He looked Jason up and down. "I have not seen thee since our battle all those many a week ago. It hast been at least a fortnight, has it not?"

Jason shrugged. "Yeah, about that, except—"

Nymbus cut him off. "Except there was a different consciousness in thy mind, was there not?" Jason nodded, and the Storm dragon continued. "Thou hast summoned the power of the earth to thine aid again. Art thou able to fly back to the farm after such an exertion?"

Jason paused. "I would feel embarrassed not to try."

Nymbus nodded. "A noble response. We will accompany you and bear thee up should thou falter."

Nymbus and Jason walked away from the ATVs as the order warrior watched their final collapse. Jason took advantage of being alone with Nymbus. "Can I ask you a question?"

The mighty Storm dragon nodded. "Aye."

He gestured back with his head. "Who is he?"

Nymbus looked askance at Jason. "He who?"

"The guy in the armor, your rider. He seems all official and all that, and he can definitely swing that Darth Maul-style blade of his. But he talks like he's close to my age. It's really weird."

Nymbus paused. "Thou assumes a great many things, Draconaut."

"What, you mean he's older than he sounds?"

The dragon smirked with another dramatic pause. "Mayhaps."

"Jeepers, you Oder of the Scale folks must have to take lessons in being all dark and mysterious. I can't figure you two out."

"Alas, it is the way I prefer things, young one."

"Well, it's frustrating," Jason stated as the rider rejoined them.

"Aww, look at you two bonding. It's a very special dragon moment, this fall on the Hallmark Channel," the rider teased.

Jason looked at Nymbus. "See what I mean."

Nymbus glowered at his rider. "Yes, well, the term 'frustrating' oft applies to this one, I must say."

Jason wished he could see the rider's reaction, but all it did was climb into the saddle on Nymbus's back. "Let's get to the sky. There's nothing left to see here, and it will be dark by the time we get near Malta. Don't want anyone getting lost on their way back." With that, the two dragons took to the skies, Nymbus without any effort and Jason showing signs of fatigue from the battle with the Wyrmkil.

Chapter 34

"You just flew back? That was it?"

Jason heard Tiffany grumble the question in their odd dimension-within-a-mirror. Petros, Tonare, Procella, and Calor all sat in the actual Hewes upstairs bathroom and positioned themselves in front of the mirror. As had happened since the spell was cast in the forest those many weeks ago, their reflections came to life and then could converse with the young humans with which they shared a body. The four teenagers, trapped in a mirror reality, and the four dragons, trapped in human bodies, were finally able to speak face to face.

"Well, yeah." Jason shrugged. "You know, we said stuff here and there. It was loud from the wind and all, and I was tried, so it was hard to talk. Mainly, we just flew."

Tiffany narrowed her eyes. "You just spent hours with a Storm dragon and this Order of the Scale person, and you didn't say anything, didn't talk to them or find out more about who they are or where they come from?" Jason looked for support from Marcus, who gave him a "you're on your own" look. Jason just shook his head in the negative. Tiffany rolled her eyes and folded her arms. "You are such a guy!"

It was the morning after the fateful trip into Billings. Calor and Procella had arrived early the previous day at the farm via the magic portal, and Jason had returned toward dusk. Nymbus and his rider veered off and bid him a farewell as they approached the county limits, and Jason continued on to the glade of trees, where he landed, reverted back to his human form, and then let Petros walk back to the house. It wasn't until nearly midnight that Tonare made his entrance into the homestead. He had gotten lost trying to get out of the city and took until nightfall to make his way back to the Rims, turn back to his dragon form, and let Marcus fly back to Malta.

They paused in their conversation as they heard the porch door fly open and foot falls run toward the staircase. George flew up the stairs and took in the sight of the four of them crowded in the bathroom, talking to their reflections. He blurted, "So what happened? Did you find Norm? Did he fix everything?"

From the other side of the mirrored glass, Jason answered, "George, we're still talking to ourselves in the mirror. How do you think it went?"

"Oh." He paused. "Right, umm, sorry. What happened?"

Procella took the time to recount the events, and George was slack-jawed by the end of the story. He stammered, "It…it was all over the news. They said it was some kind of gang forming and trying to disrupt the crisis going on downtown but that everyone was apprehended. You guys are the gang?"

Tiffany shrugged. "Yep, that's us. We're pretty scary-looking, aren't we? The beauty queen here looks like she can take out two or three policemen with one high heel, doesn't she?"

Kinaari folded her arms in anger. "Hey! That was unnecessary!"

They started to bicker as a chime sounded on George's phone. He casually looked at it, and his face immediately sunk. Petros saw his change in demeanor and asked, "Squire George, what is it?"

George swallowed hard. "Umm, it's one of my RSS news feeds." He started to read, "'To complicate the matters of the odd and somewhat violent string of events that took place in downtown Billings yesterday, eyewitnesses report seeing what is described as a large, winged creature leaping from the top of the First Interstate Center and flying beyond the city limits, eventually disappearing into the Rimrocks. Officials are not substantiating any of the claims, but one witness said it looked like a prehistoric pterodactyl, while yet another even more outrageously claimed it was a dragon. No one knows the truth or how this staggering report even relates to the incident that occurred downtown, but investigations will continue to look for anything that may link these two stories together.'"

They paused in silence after George finished reading. Jason finally said, "Oops."

Everyone turned to scowl at him as George scolded, "'Oops'? That's the best you have?"

"What do you want me to say, George? I know why Petros went all dragon in the middle of the city. It was the best choice: get captured, turn into street pizza, or risk being seen. We went with risk being seen."

Petros whispered to Tonare, "What is this 'street pizza'? It is the second time I have heard it mentioned."

Tonare shrugged and whispered back, "It must be some sort of dark magic since one transforms into it under adverse circumstances."

Marcus stepped in. "No sense gettin' all worked up about it, Georgie. It's done; you can't fix it. Just deal with it and move on."

Kinaari added, "You worry way too much, George. It's not good for your aura."

Tiffany rolled her eyes at the last statement and said matter-of-factly, "There's no way they are going to trace us up here. Jason disappeared into the Rims, and that was it. We'll be fine."

All but George nodded in agreement and sat in thought for several moments. Jason broke the silence again. "So what are we going to do now?"

"Breakfast?" Marcus asked sheepishly.

"No," Jason chided, "I don't mean right this second. I mean what are we going to do? We're stuck this way, we don't have a Norm or any other mage, you all have to get back home, and we're being pursued by an ancient order of dragon haters who want nothing but our impending doom."

"Thanks for that last picker-upper there," Tiffany grumbled.

"And school starts in a couple of weeks," Kinaari added.

Calor picked up her head. "School? Education? No one told us about that. I cannot be confined to a building with hordes of children for hours on end."

Tiffany glared back at her own face. "You are one of those children now, Calor."

Calor's shoulders slumped in frustration as Procella spoke. "We do the only thing we can do: adapt. We have no other choice, correct?"

"Nope," Jason answered, shaking his head. "We need to face it; this is the new normal. No mage to turn us back…nothing. We have to get used to living each other's lives: work, school, family, everything."

They were silent for several moments before Petros stated, "Come, three of you have long journeys ahead. George will still keep us connected, but the elder Hewes will be returning home soon, and, as difficult as it may be, we have to maintain the ruse that all is well. We have a great deal to learn."

***

Dusk was creeping over the wide skies of Montana as the four Draconauts and George stood at the treeline in their now-familiar small glade to the north of the Hewes property. The high clouds were taking on fiery shades as the sun began to complete its westward descent. A cool breeze kept the temperatures in the midsixties, and the five simply stood in silence as their hair flowed and faces cooled with the wind. The air carried a palpable bite of the soon-arriving autumn, a reflection of the changes that had happened in recent months.

Tonare was the first to step away. He faced them and stated, "It is time. My journey is longest, and I may have stretched the patience of Marcus's parents. They are remarkable for humans, you know. They have many children, and all are polite, respectful, and behaved."

Petros smiled and laid his hand on his cousin's tall shoulder. "Fly well. Be safe. We will be in contact."

Tonare gave a reassuring nod and grasped the scale around his neck. The familiar burst of light followed, and Marcus in his Thunder dragon form stood before them. "Not sure I'll ever get used to that. You all gonna be good? This could get weird, especially with those Wyrmkil lookin' for us. Make sure you let me know if anyone needs help, 'kay? I can get away from the family pretty easily."

Petros smiled. "You are valiant, good Marcus—brave of the heart and level of the head. Please use that to teach young Tonare responsibility. He needs lessons of life to ground him."

"And you keep an eye on Jason, got it?" With that, Marcus deftly took to the air, and they watched as he soared into the clouds.

Calor stepped out next. "I believe I should be the next to take my leave."

"Have you discussed with Tiffany where you will go?" Procella asked.

She nodded. "Yes, but she still swears me to secrecy."

Petros frowned. "I do not like this, Calor. You only exacerbate her dysfunction."

Calor held up her hands. "Petros, you need to trust me. The fire that burns within her is formidable, but that which fuels the fire is unstable. I must help her balance her past with her present."

George shook his head. "I don't like it."

"As is true to your nature," Procella countered, "but I have grown to see the wisdom and experience our Heat dragon cousin possesses. I think we should let her handle the situation as she sees fit."

Petros gave a resigned look as Calor stepped back and transformed to her dragon form. Tiffany asked, "Did she explain everything to you?"

"Yes and no. I have concern for your wellbeing, young one."

She smiled. "I'm a dragon now, and probably for the first time in a long time I'm happy with who I am. Calor will keep me on the straight and narrow so don't worry." Before anyone could respond, she took to the air and flew off toward the setting sun.

Procella smirked. "Caring for the girl is tempering her nature. Calor is thinking and acting with thought and purpose…very usual for any Fire Dragon."

Petros sighed deeply. "I do not know if that is by chance or design, but, yes, I cannot ignore the change I see in her."

"My time, unfortunately, has come as well. Kinaari's family will grow suspicious soon. They are very protective of her."

Petros said, "You have been a voice of reason in all of this chaos, Procella. The deep wisdom of the Water Dragons lives strongly in you."

Procella approached Petros and George and gave them each a soft kiss on the cheek. Petros looked confused, but George's eyes went wide, and he held his hand over his cheek. Procella asked, "A human sign of affection, is it not?"

George nodded enthusiastically as his face flushed. Procella transformed to her Water Dragon body, and Kinaari looked oddly at the speechless George. "George, what's wrong? You look like you've just seen a ghost."

Petros chuckled. "Far from it, Kinaari. It would seem George is not accustomed to certain kinds of human interactions."

"Well, I'm not sure what that means, but I guess you two have it all under control. I've gotta get going; my parents are going to have kittens if I'm not home on time."

Petros nodded. "Fly well, Kinaari. Take advantage of the wisdom of your counterpart."

"I will." She smiled as she took a running start and leapt into the air. With a few beats of her wings, she was soaring over the Montana countryside on her way home.

George's voice cracked as he tried to shout, "Bye, Kinaari!" but he blushed even more deeply at the sound. "Dang it! I can't even talk to a girl when she is in the body of a dragon."

Petros laughed out loud, and he put one arm around George's shoulder and began to lead him back to the house. "Come, Squire George. Put aside your embarrassment and teach me about this thing called 'high school.' I believe this may indeed be the greatest challenge of my life."

***

A gurney flanked by four EMTs was wheeled out of the immense and opulent office at the top of the AlansCo tower. The shape lying on the wheeled table was encased in a large black bag zippered closed from one end to the other. The jackets of the EMTs bore the logo of AlansCo.

An impeccably dressed woman gracefully shut the office door as the seven-foot-tall hooded figure stepped away from the windows at the far end of the room. The woman wore a form-fitting, navy blue business suit, and her raven black hair was done up in a tight and perfect bun. She took the glasses from the top of her head and neatly rested them on the bridge of her nose as she looked down at the tablet computer she cradled on her forearm.

She confidently spoke to the hooded figure. "How should we handle the follow-up with Mr. Reigles's family?"

The figure walked over to the sea eagle and gently stroked the feathers on the bird's head. It lowered its beak and welcomed the affection of its master. "How would I even need to concern myself with a detail like that, Ms. Moore?"

Veronica Moore nodded. "Very well. The autopsy will reveal a congenital heart defect that was undiagnosed in a man as young and healthy as Mr. Reigles. Steve Alans will send a personalized letter and make a donation to the family double the amount of his company life insurance policy."

"Fifty percent. Do not be so generous."

She didn't blink at the correction. "Very well, fifty percent." She tapped the screen of the tablet as she made the adjustments.

"Are you up to the task of replacing that failure, Ms. Moore? I will not announce you to the public until I am sure you will not act with the reticence our Mr. Reigles did."

She looked at him without emotion. "My lord, Mr. Reigles wore his heart on his sleeve. This is business; you tell me what to do, and I do it. No questions asked. You have obviously been…governing far longer than anyone I am aware of, and therefore that depth of knowledge and experience leaves little to question."

She could see the hood nodding. "A most wise answer. Tell me where we stand on the location of the artifact."

"Progress has been made in this area. We have located the artifact, but extracting it from its resting place is proving most difficult, both from a practical and political point of view."

"Why do we not just wrest it from where it lays?"

She looked over her glasses at him. "Is this another test, my lord? You know as well as I do the political implications of such as act. Governments will be set at odds, and our entire operation could be compromised."

A brief chuckle came from beneath the hood. "Very good, Ms. Moore. How long before the artifact is secure?"

She tapped the tablet a few more times. "I would estimate another month to go through the proper channels, file the appropriate paperwork, and distribute the bribes. I have already coordinated with our, shall I say, specialists, and they will begin their work as soon as the item is in hand."

"And what of the wyrm and these children that possess their abilities?"

She gave a nonchalant shrug of her shoulders. "Sadly, Mr. Reigles did not research this thoroughly. I cannot continue work that was not started in the first place. The answer seems to lie with the mage, who, at the present time, remains missing. Mr. Reigles acted too quickly to secure the wizard and summarily frightened him into hiding. Our agents are working on the problem now."

The figure inhaled sharply and rose to his full height. "You know that is an answer that does not please me."

No emotion showed on her face. "I am sorry you are displeased, my lord, but the truth is the truth. Would you prefer that I lie to you, only to have you discover the truth at a later time and incur your wrath all the more?"

There was a long pause. "Carry on, Ms. Moore. I will summon you at a later time." She nodded in acknowledgement and left the room without a word.

The imposing figure put a finger under the beak of the sea eagle and lifted its head to meet his eyes. "Yes, she will do just fine."

***

Nymbus and his rider sat in their subterranean cavern under one of the Bears Paw Mountains. The rider's helmet was sitting on a rock as she tied her blond hair on top of her head again. "That helmet makes this impossible. How am I supposed to be a vanguard for all dragonkind and manage my split ends at the same time?"

Nymbus shook his massive head. "I fail to understand thy humor."

She shrugged. "We've been at this for a few years. You should know me by now."

"I bore thy predecessor for decades; him I knew well."

Her mood instantly soured. "Yeah, well, that didn't work out too well for either of us, did it?"

Nymbus gave a conciliatory bow. "My apologies."

"It's nothing," she said, waving him off.

The water of the connecting lake began to stir and bubble, and Nymbus came to attention as his rider put her helmet back on and said, "Showtime."

Two large horns were the first to break the surface and were quickly followed by the tan, scaled, draconic head they were attached to. The body of a grown Heat dragon emerged from the depths and stood on the shore of the grotto. Nymbus and the rider approached the dragon as the rider said, "I didn't think you were going to follow through with this."

Tiffany answered, "Why not? I've got nowhere else to go."

"You have a family, right?"

She shrugged her dragon shoulders. "Not really. Not a real family."

Nymbus looked over his snout at her. "And thou art prepared to commit to this endeavor?"

She nodded. "One hundred percent. Teach me how to be part of the order."

* * *

Petros lay in Jason's bed, deep in sleep. His eyes darted back and forth beneath his eyelids as dreams filled his subconscious.

Images of dragons soaring through the air filled his mind's eye as breath weapons both powerful and terrible blasted through the skies. He was witnessing an epic battle as other winged creatures, none of which he could identify, lanced to and fro amid the battling dragons. Feathers mixed with flying scales, and blood whirled about in the chaos as Petros strained to make out any meaningful detail.

Soon, nothing but the death cries of dragons could be heard as his kin began to fall from the skies, some torn limb from limb. But the cries began to fade as a new sound arose. A deep, sinister laugh began to drown out the cries of dying dragons and eventually all other sound. The laugh echoed through Petros's head as, in his dream, he began to scream, "Enough! Enough! Enough!" From the darkness, a hooded face rushed up and swallowed him whole.

He awoke with a start as sweat dripped down his face and back. He was breathing deeply and rapidly, and his heart pounded with fear. He swallowed hard and uttered one word:

"Karura."

The End

Jason, Petros and their friends will return in

Jason and the Draconauts:
The Council of Ancients

About the Author

Paul Smith lives in upstate New York with his wife and two sons, where he works with emotionally disturbed and mentally ill children. He earned a master's degree in social sciences from Binghamton University in 1999.

A lifelong love of science fiction, fantasy, and superhero stories influences Paul's writing. His most recent work was a popular weekly online series that generated over 20,000 views. *Jason and the Draconauts* is his first novel.

CPSIA information can be obtained at www.ICGtesting.com
Printed in the USA
LVOW10s1607100214

373093LV00018B/1207/P